Unexpected weddings!

WEDDING
Vows
WITH THIS RING

CARA COLTER
BARBARA HANNAY
FIONA McARTHUR

WEDDING
—Vows—
COLLECTION

WEDDING
Vows
JUST MARRIED

April 2015

WEDDING
Vows
WITH THIS RING

May 2015

WEDDING
Vows
SAY I DO

June 2015

WEDDING
Vows
I THEE WED

July 2015

WEDDING
Vows
WITH THIS RING

CARA COLTER
BARBARA HANNAY
FIONA McARTHUR

MILLS &
BOON

Published in Great Britain 2015
by Mills & Boon, an imprint of Harlequin (UK) Limited,
Eton House, 18-24 Paradise Road, Richmond, Surrey, TW9 1SR

WEDDING VOWS: WITH THIS RING © 2015 Harlequin Books S.A.

Rescued in a Wedding Dress © 2010 Cara Colter
Bridesmaid Says, 'I Do!' © 2011 Barbara Hannay
The Doctor's Surprise Bride © 2006 Fiona McArthur

ISBN: 978-0-263-25373-3

011-0515

Harlequin (UK) Limited's policy is to use papers that are natural, renewable and recyclable products and made from wood grown in sustainable forests.The logging and manufacturing processes conform to the legal environmental regulations of the country of origin.

Printed and bound in Spain
by CPI, Barcelona

RESCUED IN A
WEDDING DRESS
CARA COLTER

Cara Colter lives in British Columbia with her partner, Rob, and eleven horses. She has three grown children and a grandson. She is a recent recipient of an *RT Book Reviews* Career Achievement Award in the Love and Laughter category. Cara loves to hear from readers and you can contact her or learn more about her through her website: www.cara-colter.com.

CHAPTER ONE

MOLLY MICHAELS stared at the contents of the large rectangular box that had been set haphazardly on top of the clutter on her desk. The box contained a wedding gown.

Over the weekend donations that were intended for one of the three New York City secondhand clothing shops that were owned and operated by Second Chances Charity Inc—and that provided the funding for their community programs—often ended up here, stacked outside the doorstep of their main office.

It did seem like a cruel irony, though, that this donation would end up on *her* desk.

"Sworn off love," Molly told herself, firmly, and shut the box. "Allergic to amour. Lessons learned. Doors closed."

She turned and hung up her coat in the closet of her tiny office, then returned to her desk. She snuck the box lid open, just a crack, then opened it just a little more. The dress was a confection. It looked like it had been spun out of dreams and silk.

"Pained by passion," Molly reminded herself, but even as she did, her hand stole into the box, and her fingers touched the delicate delight of the gloriously rich fabric.

What would it hurt to *look?* It could even be a good exercise for her. Her relationship with Chuck, her broken engagement, was six months in the past. The dress was probably ridiculous. Looking at it, and feeling *nothing,* better yet *judging* it, would be a good test of the new her.

Molly Michaels was one hundred percent career woman now, absolutely dedicated to her work here as the project manager at Second Chances. It was her job to select, implement and maintain the programs the charity funded that helped people in some of New York's most challenged neighborhoods.

"Love my career. Totally satisfied," she muttered. "Completely fulfilled!"

She slipped the pure white dress out of the box, felt the sensuous slide of the fabric across her palms as she shook it out.

The dress *was* ridiculous. And the total embodiment of romance. Ethereal as a puff of smoke, soft as a whisper, the layers and layers of ruffles glittered with hundreds of hand-sewn pearls and tiny silk flowers. The designer label attested to the fact that someone had spent a fortune on it.

And the fact it had shown up here was a reminder that all those romantic dreams had a treacherous tendency to go sideways. Who sent their dress, their most poignant reminder of their special day, to a charity that specialized in secondhand sales, if things had gone well?

So, it wasn't just *her* who had been burned by love. *Au contraire!* It was the way of the world.

Still, despite her efforts to talk sense to herself, there was no denying the little twist of wistfulness in her tummy as Molly looked at the dress, *felt* all a dress like that could stand for. *Love. Souls joined. Laughter shared. Long conversations. Lonely no more.*

Molly was disappointed in herself for entertaining the hopelessly naive thoughts, even briefly. She wanted to kill that renegade longing that stirred in her. The logical way to do that would be to put the dress back in the box, and have the receptionist, Tish, send it off to the best of Second Chances stores, Wow and Then, on the Upper West Side. That store specialized in high-end gently used fashions. Everything with a designer label in it ended up there.

But, sadly, Molly had never been logical. Sadly, she had not missed the fact the dress was *exactly* her size.

On impulse, she decided the best way to face her shattered dreams head-on would be to put on the dress. She would face the bride she was never going to be in the mirror. She would regain her power over those ever so foolish and hopelessly old-fashioned dreams of *ever after.*

How could she, of all people, believe such nonsense? Why was it that the constant squabbling of her parents, the eventual dissolution of her family, her mother remarrying *often,* had not prepared Molly for real life? No, rather than making her put aside her belief in love, her dreams of a family, her disappointment-filled childhood had instead made her *yearn* for those things.

That yearning had been drastic enough to make her ignore every warning sign Chuck had given her. And there had been plenty of them! Not at first, of course. At first, it had been all delight and devotion. But then, Molly had caught her intended in increasingly frequent insults: little white lies, lateness, dates not kept.

She had forgiven him, allowing herself to believe that a loving heart overlooked the small slights, the in-considerations, the occasional surliness, the lack of enthusiasm for the things she liked to do. She had managed to minimize the fact that the engagement ring had been embarrassingly tiny, and efforts to address setting a date had been rebuffed.

In other words, Molly had been so engrossed in her fantasy about love, had been so focused on a day and a dress just like this one, that she had excused and tolerated and dismissed behavior that, in retrospect, had been humiliatingly unacceptable.

Now she was anxious to prove to herself that a dress like this one had no power over her at all. None! Her days of being a hopeless dreamer, of being naive, of being romantic to the point of being pathetic, were over.

Over and done. Molly Michaels was a new woman, one who could put on a dress like this and *scoff* at the beliefs it represented. *Round-faced babies, a bassinet beside the bed, seaside holidays, chasing children through the sand, cuddling around a roaring fire with him, the dream man, beside you singing songs and toasting marshmallows.*

"Dream man is right," she scolded herself. "Because that's where such a man exists. In dreams."

The dress proved harder to get on than Molly could have imagined, which should have made her give it up. Instead, it made her more determined, which formed an unfortunate parallel to her past relationship.

The harder it had been with Chuck, the more she had tried to make it work.

That desperate-for-love woman was being left behind her, and putting on this dress was going to be one more step in helping her do it!

But first she got tangled in the sewn-in lining, and

spent a few helpless moments lost in the voluminous sea of white fabric. When her head finally popped out the correct opening, her hair was caught hard in one of the pearls that encrusted the neckline. After she had got free of that, fate made one more last-ditch effort to get her to stop this nonsense. The back of the dress was not designed to be done up single-handedly.

Still, having come this far, with much determination and contortion, Molly somehow managed to get every single fastener closed, though it felt as if she had pulled the muscle in her left shoulder in the process.

Now she took a deep breath, girded her cynical loins, and turned slowly to look at herself in the full-length mirror hung on the back of her office door.

She closed her eyes. *Goodbye, romantic fool.* Then she took a deep breath and opened them.

Molly felt her attempt at cynicism dissolve with all the resistance of instant coffee granules meeting hot water. In fact everything dissolved: the clutter around her, the files that needed to be dealt with, the colorful sounds of the East Village awaking outside her open transom window, something called out harshly in Polish or Ukrainian, the sound of a delivery truck stopped nearby, a horn honking.

Molly stared at herself in the mirror. She had fully expected to see her romantic *fantasy* debunked. It would just be her, too tall, too skinny, redheaded and pale-faced Molly Michaels, in a fancy dress. Not changed by it. Certainly not *completed* by it.

Instead, a princess looked solemnly back at her. Her red hair, pulled out of its very professional upsweep by the entrapment inside the dress and the brief fray with the pearl, was stirred up, hissing with static, fiery and free. Her pale skin looked not washed out as she had thought it would against the sea of white but flawless, like porcelain. And her eyes shimmered green as Irish fields in springtime.

The cut of the dress had seemed virginal before she put it on. Now she could see the neckline was sinful and the rich fabric was designed to cling to every curve, making her look sensuous, red-hot and somehow *ready*.

"This is not the lesson I was hoping for," she told herself, the stern tone doing nothing to help her drag her eyes away from the vision in the mirror. She ordered herself to take off the dress, in that same easily ignored stern tone. Instead, she did an experimental pose, and then another.

"I would have made a beautiful bride!" she cried mournfully.

Annoyed with herself, and with her weakness— eager to get away from all the feelings of loss for dreams not fulfilled that this dress was stirring up in her—she reached back to undo the fastener that held the zipper shut. It was stuck fast.

And much as she did not like what she had just discovered about herself—romantic notions apparently hopelessly engrained in her character—she could not bring herself to damage the dress in order to get it off.

Molly tried to pull it over her head without the benefit of the zipper, but it was too tight to slip off and when she lowered it again, all she had accomplished was her hair caught hard in the seed pearls that encrusted the neckline of the dress again.

It was as if the dress—and her romantic notions— were letting her know their hold on her was not going to be so easily dismissed!

Her phone rang; the two distinct beeps of Vivian Saint Pierre, known to one and all as Miss Viv, beloved founder of Second Chances. Miss Viv and Molly were always the first two into the office in the morning.

Instead of answering the phone, Molly headed out of her own office and down the hall to her boss's office to be rescued.

From myself, she acknowledged wryly.

Miss Viv would look at this latest predicament Molly had gotten herself into, know instantly *why* Molly had been compelled to put on the dress and then as she was undoing the zip she would say something wise and comforting about Molly's shattered romantic hopes.

Miss Viv had never liked Chuck Howard, Molly's fiancé. When Molly had arrived at work that day six months ago with her ring finger empty, Miss Viv had nodded approvingly and said, "You're well rid of that ne'er-do-well."

And that was even before Molly had admitted that her bank account was as empty as her ring finger!

That was exactly the kind of pragmatic attention Molly needed when a dress like this one was trying to undo all the lessons she was determined to take from her broken engagement!

With any luck, by the end of the day her getting stuck in the dress would be nothing more than an office joke.

Determined to carry off the lighthearted laugh at herself, she burst through the door of Miss Viv's office after a single knock, the wedding march humming across her lips.

But a look at Miss Viv, sitting behind her desk, stopped Molly in her tracks. The hum died midnote.

Miss Viv did not look entertained by the theatrical entrance. She looked horrified.

And when her gaze slid away from where Molly stood in the doorway to where a chair was nearly hidden behind the open door, Molly's breath caught and she slowly turned her head.

Despite the earliness of the hour, Miss Viv was not alone!

A man sat in the chair behind the door, the only available space for visitors in Miss Viv's hopelessly disorganized office.

No, not just a man. The kind of man that every woman dreamed of walking down the aisle toward.

The man sitting in Miss Viv's office was not just handsome, he was breathtaking. In a glance, Molly saw neat hair as rich as dark chocolate, firm lips, a strong chin with the faintest hint of a cleft, a nose saved from perfection—but made unreasonably more attractive— by the slight crook of an old break and a thin scar running across the bridge of it.

The aura of confidence, of *success,* was underscored by how exquisitely he was dressed. He was in a suit of coal-gray, obviously custom tailored. He had on an ivory shirt, a silk tie also in shades of gray. The ensemble would have been totally conservative had it not been for how it all matched the gray shades of his eyes. The cut of the clothes emphasized rather than hid the pure power of his build.

The power was underscored in the lines of his face.

And especially in the light in his eyes. The surprise that widened them did not cover the fact he radiated a kind of self-certainty, a cool confidence, that despite the veneer of civilization he wore so well, reminded Molly of a gunslinger.

In fact, that was the color of those eyes, *exactly,* gunmetal-gray, something in them watchful, *waiting.* She shivered with awareness. Despite the custom suit, the Berluti shoes, the Rolex that glinted at his wrist, he was the kind of man who sat with his back to the wall, always facing the door.

The man radiated power and the set of his shoulders telegraphed the fact that, unlike Chuck, this man was pure strength. The word *excuse* would not appear in his vocabulary.

No, Molly could tell by the fire in his eyes that if the ship was going down, or the building was on fire—if the town needed saving and he had just ridden in on his horse—he was the one you would follow, he was the one you would rely on to save you.

An aggravating conclusion since she was so newly committed to relying on herself, her career and her co-workers to save her from a disastrous life of unremitting loneliness. The little featherless budgie she had at home—the latest in a long list of loving strays that had populated her life—also helped.

The little *swish* of attraction she felt for the stranger made her current situation even more annoying. It didn't matter how much he looked like the perfect person to cast in the center of a romantic fantasy! She had given up on such twaddle! She was well on her way to becoming one of those women perfectly comfortable sitting at an outdoor café, alone, sipping a fine glass of wine and reading a book. Not even slipping a look at the male passers-by!

Of course, this handsome devil appearing without warning in her boss's office on a Monday morning was a test, just like the dress. It was a test of her commitment to the new and independent Molly Michaels, a test of her ability to separate her imaginings from reality.

Look at her deciding he was the one you would follow in a catastrophe when she knew absolutely nothing about him except that he had an exceedingly handsome face. Molly reminded herself, extra sternly, that all the catastrophes in her life had been of her own making. Besides, with the kind of image he portrayed— all easy self-assurance and leashed sexuality—probably more than one woman had built fantasies of hope and forever around him. He was of an age where if he wanted to be taken he would be. And if his ring finger— and the expression on his face as he looked at the dress—was any indication, he was not!

"Sorry," Molly said to Miss Viv, "I thought you were alone." She gave a quick, curt nod of acknowledgment to the stranger, making sure to strip any remaining *hopeless dreamer* from herself before she met his eyes.

"But, Molly, when I rang your office, I wanted you to come, and you must have wanted something?" Miss Viv asked her before she made her escape.

Usually imaginative, Molly drew a blank for explaining away her attire and she could think of not a single reason to be here except the truth.

"The zip is stuck, but I can manage. Really. Excuse me." She was trying to slide back out the door when his eyes narrowed on her.

"Is your hair caught in the dress?"

His voice was at least as sensual as the silk where the dress caressed her naked skin.

Molly could feel her cheeks turning a shade of red that was probably going to put her hair to shame.

"A little," she said proudly. "It's nothing. Excuse

me." She tried to lift her chin, to prove how *nothing* it was, but her hair was caught hard enough that she could not, and she also could not prevent a little wince of pain as the movement caused the stuck hair to yank at her tender scalp.

"That looks painful," he said quietly, getting to his feet with that casual grace one associated with athletes, the kind of ease of movement that disguised how swift they really were. But he was swift, because he was standing in front of her before she could gather her wits and make good her escape.

The smart thing to do would be to step back as he took that final step toward her. But she was astounded to find herself rooted to the spot, paralyzed, helpless to move away from him.

The world went very still. It seemed as if all the busy activity on the street outside ceased, the noises faded, the background and Miss Viv melted into a fuzzy kaleidoscope as the stranger leaned in close to her.

With the ease born of supreme confidence in himself—as if he performed this kind of rescue on a daily basis—he lifted the pressure of the dress up off her shoulder with one hand, and with the other, he carefully unwound her hair from the pearls they were caught in.

Given that outlaw remoteness in his eyes, he was unbelievably gentle, his fingers unhurried in her hair.

Molly's awareness of him was nothing less than shocking, his nearness tingling along her skin, his touch melting parts of her that she had hoped were turned to ice permanently.

The moment took way too long. And not nearly long enough. His concentration was complete, the intensity of his steely-gray gaze as he dealt with her tangled hair, his unsettling nearness, the graze of his fingers along her neck, stealing her breath.

At least Molly didn't feel as if she was breathing, but then she realized she must, indeed, be pulling air in and out, because she could smell him.

His scent was wonderful, bitingly masculine, good aftershave, expensive soap, freshly pressed linen.

Molly gazed helplessly into his face, unwillingly marveling at the chiseled perfection of his features, the intrigue of the faint crook in his nose, the white line of that scar, the brilliance of his eyes. He, however, was pure focus, as if the only task that mattered to him was freeing her hair from the remaining pearl that held it captive.

Apparently he was not marveling at the circumstances that had brought his hands to her hair and the soft place on her neck just below her ear, apparently he was not swamped by their scents mingling nor was he fighting a deep awareness that a move of a mere half inch would bring them together, full frontal contact, the swell of her breast pressing into the hard line of his chest…

The dress, suddenly freed, fell back onto her shoulder. He actually smiled then, the faintest quirk of a gorgeous mouth, and she felt herself floundering in the depths of stormy sea eyes, the chill gray suddenly illuminated by the sun.

"Did you say the zipper was stuck as well?" he asked.

Oh, God. Had she said that? She could not prolong this encounter! It was much more of a test of the new confidently-sitting-at-the-café-alone her than she was ready for!

But mutely, caught in a spell, she turned her back to him and stood stock-still, waiting. She shivered at the thought of a wedding night, what this moment meant, and at the same time that unwanted thought seeped warmly into her brain, he touched her.

She felt the slight brush of his hand, again, on delicate skin, this time at the back of her neck. Her senses were so intensely engaged that she heard the faint pop of the hook parting from the eye. She registered the feel of his hand, felt astounded by the hard, unyielding texture of his skin.

He looked like he was pure business, a banker maybe, a wealthy benefactor, but there was nothing soft about his hand that suggested a life behind a desk, his tools a phone and a computer. For some reason it occurred to her that hands like that belonged to people who handled ropes…range riders, mountain climbers. Pirates. Ah, yes, pirates with all that mysterious charm.

He dispensed with the hook at the top of the zipper in a split second, a man who had dispensed with such delicate items many times? And then he paused, apparently realizing the height of the zipper would make it nearly impossible for her to manage the rest by herself— she hoped he would not consider how much determination it had taken her to get it up in the first place—and then slid the zipper down a sensuous inch or two.

With that same altered sense of alertness Molly could feel cool air on that small area of her newly exposed naked back, and then, though she did not glance back, she could feel heat. His gaze? Her own jumbled thoughts?

Molly fought the chicken in her that just wanted to bolt out the open door. Instead, she turned and faced him.

"There you go," he said mildly, rocking back on his heels. The heat must have come from her own badly rattled thoughts, because his eyes were cool, something veiled in their intriguing silver depths.

"Thank you," she said, struggling to keep her voice deliberately controlled to match the look in his eyes. "I'm sorry to interrupt."

"No, no, Molly," Miss Viv said, and it was a mark of the intensity of her encounter with him that Molly was actually jarred by the fact Miss Viv was still in the room. "I called your office to invite you to meet Mr. Whitford. I'm going on an unscheduled holiday, and Mr. Whitford is taking the helm."

Molly felt the shock of Miss Viv's announcement ripple down a spine that had already been thoroughly shocked this morning. But even as she dealt with the shock, part of her mused with annoying dreaminess, *helm. Pirate. I knew it.*

"Houston Whitford, Molly Michaels," Miss Viv said. The introduction seemed ridiculously formal considering the rather astounding sense of intimacy Molly had just felt under his touch.

Still, now she felt duty-bound to extend her hand, and be touched again, even as she was digesting the fact *he* was in charge. How could that be? Molly was always in charge when Miss Viv was away!

And Miss Viv was going on a holiday, but hadn't told anyone? Second Chances was a family and far better than Molly's family of origin at providing a place that was safe, and supportive, and rarely unpredictable.

"There are going to be a few changes," Miss Viv said, cheerfully, as if Molly's nice safe world was in no way being threatened. "And no one is more qualified to make them than Mr. Whitford. I expect Second Chances is going to blossom, absolutely go to the next level, under his leadership. I'm thrilled to pass the reins to him."

But Molly felt the threat of her whole world shifting.

Miss Viv was stepping down? The feeling only intensified when Houston Whitford's hand—warm, strong,
cool—touched her skin again. His hand enveloped her
hand and despite the pure professionalism of his shake,
the hardness of his grip told her something, as did the
glittering silver light in his eyes.

He was not the usual kind of person who worked an
ill-paying job at a charity. His suit said something his
hands did not: that he was used to a world of higher
finances, higher-power, higher-tech.

The only thing that was higher at Second Chances
was the satisfaction, the feeling of changing the world
for the better.

The cost of his suit probably added up to their oper-
ating budget for a month! He didn't fit the cozy, casual
and rather shabby atmosphere of the Second Chances
office at all.

She felt the unmistakable tingle of pure danger all
along her spine. There was something about Houston
Whitford that was not adding up. Change followed a
man like that as surely as pounding rain followed the
thunderstorm.

Molly, her father had said, on the eve of leaving their
family home forever, *there is going to be a change.*

And she had been allergic to that very thing ever since!
She wanted her world to be safe and unchanging and that
view had intensified after she had flirted with a major life
change in the form of Chuck. Since then Second Chances
had become more her safe haven than ever.

"What kind of changes?" she asked Miss Viv now,
failing to keep a certain trepidation from entering her
voice.

"Mr. Whitford will be happy to brief you, um, after

you've changed into something more appropriate," Miss Viv said, and then glanced at her watch. "Oh, my! I do have a plane to catch. I'm going to a spa in Arizona, my dear."

"You're going to a spa in Arizona, and you didn't tell anyone?" It seemed unimaginable. That kind of vacation usually should have entailed at least a swimsuit shopping excursion together!

"The opportunity came up rather suddenly," Miss Viv said, unapologetically thrilled. "A bolt from the blue, an unexpected gift from an old friend."

Molly tried to feel delighted for her. No one deserved a wonderful surprise more than her boss.

"For how long?" she asked.

But the shameful truth was Molly did not feel delighted at her boss's good fortune. *Sudden change.* Molly hated that kind more than the regular variety.

"Two weeks," Miss Viv said with a sigh of anticipated delight.

Two weeks? Molly wanted to shout. *That was ridiculous. People went to spas for a few hours, maybe a few days, never two weeks!*

"But when you come back, everything will be back to normal?" Molly pressed.

Miss Viv laughed. "Oh, sweetie," she said. "What is normal? A setting on a clothes dryer as far as I'm concerned."

Molly stared at her boss. What was normal? Not something to be joked about! It was what Molly had never had. She'd never had a normal family. Her engagement had certainly not been normal. It felt as if she had spent a good deal of her life searching for it, and coming up short. Even her pets were never normal.

Molly's life had been populated with the needy kind of animal that no one else wanted. A dog with three legs, a cat with no meow. Her current resident was a bald budgie, his scrawny body devoid of feathers.

"I've been thinking of retiring," Miss Viv shocked Molly further by saying. "So, who knows? After the two weeks is up, we'll just play it by ear."

Molly wanted to protest that she didn't like playing it by ear. She liked plans and schedules, calendars that were marked for months in advance.

If Miss Viv retired, would Houston Whitford be in charge forever?

She could not think of a way of asking that did not show her dread at the prospect!

Besides, there is no *forever,* Molly reminded herself. That was precisely why she had put on this dress. To debunk *forever* myths.

She particularly did not want to entertain *that* word anywhere near the vicinity of him, a man whose faintest touch could make a woman's vows of self-reliance disintegrate like foundations crumbling at the first tremor of the coming quake.

CHAPTER TWO

THE bride flounced out of the room, and unbidden, words crowded into Houston's brain.

And then they lived happily ever after.

He scoffed at himself, and the words. Yes, it was true that a dress like that, filled out by a girl like Molly Michaels, represented a fairy tale.

But the fact she was stuck in it, the zipper stubborn, her hair wound painfully around the pearls, represented more the reality: relationships of the romantic variety were sticky, complicated, *entrapping*.

Besides, a man didn't come from the place Houston Whitford had come from and believe in fairy tales. He believed in his own strength, his own ability to survive. He saw the cynicism with which he had regarded that dress as a *gift*.

In fact, the unexpected appearance of one of the Second Chances employees in full wedding regalia only confirmed what several weeks of research had already told him.

Second Chances reminded Houston, painfully, of an old-style family operated bookstore. Everyone was drawn to the warmth of it, it was always crowded and full of laughter and discussion, but when it came time to actually buy a book it could not compete with the online giants, streamlined, efficient, economical. Just how Houston liked his businesses, running like well-oiled machines. No brides, no ancient, adorable little old ladies at the helm.

He fought an urge to press the scar over the old break on the bridge of his nose. It ached unbearably lately. Had it ached ever since, in a rare moment of weakness, he had agreed to help out here? This wasn't his kind of job. He dealt in reality, in cold, hard fact. Where did a poorly run charity, with brides in the hallways and octogenarians behind the desks, fit into his world?

"And that was our Molly," Miss Viv said brightly. "Isn't she lovely?"

"Lovely," Houston managed. He recalled part two of his mission here.

Miss Viv had confessed to him she was thinking of retiring. She loved Molly and considered her her natural successor. But she was a little worried. She wanted his opinion on whether Molly was too soft-hearted for the job.

"Is she getting ready for her wedding?" On the basis of their very brief encounter, Molly Michaels seemed the kind of woman that a man who was not cynical and jaded like him—a man who believed in fairy tales, love ever after, family—would snatch up.

He didn't even like the direction of those thoughts. The wedding dress should only be viewed in the context of the job he had to do here. What was Miss Michaels doing getting ready for her wedding at work? How did that reflect on a future for her in management?

The job he hadn't wanted was getting less attractive by the second. A demand of complete professionalism was high on his list of fixes for the ailing companies he put back on the track to success.

"She's not getting ready for her wedding," Miss Viv said with a sympathetic sigh. "The exact opposite, I'm afraid. Her engagement broke off before they even set a date. A blessing, though the poor child did not see it that way at the time. She's not been herself since it happened."

At this point, with anyone else, he would make it clear, right now, he didn't want to know a single thing about Molly Michaels's personal life. But this job was different than any he'd ever taken on before. And this was Miss Viv.

Everybody was a *poor child* to her. His need to analyze, to have answers to puzzles, surprised him by not filing this poor child information under strictly personal, none of his business, nothing to do with the job at hand. Instead, he allowed the question to form in his mind. *If a man believed in the fairy tale enough to ask someone like Molly Michaels to be his wife, why would he then be fool enough to let her get away?*

Because the truth was *lovely* was an unfortunate understatement, and would have been even before he had made the mistake of making the bridal vision somehow *real* by touching the heated silk of Molly's skin, the coiled copper of her hair.

Molly's eyes, the set of her sensuous mouth and the corkscrewing hair, not to mention the curves of a slender figure, had not really said *lovely* to him. Despite the fairy tale of the dress the word that had come to mind first was *sexy*.

Was that what had made him get up from his chair? Not really to rescue her from her obvious discomfort, but to see what was true about her? Sexy? Or innocent?

He was no Boy Scout, after all, not given to good deeds, which was another reason he should not be here at Second Chances.

Still, was his need to know that about Molly Michaels personal or professional? He had a feeling at Second Chances those lines had always been allowed to blur. *Note to self,* he thought wryly, *no more rescuing of damsels in distress.*

Though, really that was why he was here, even if Miss Viv was obviously way too old to qualify as a damsel.

Houston Whitford was CEO of Precision Solutions, a company that specialized in rescuing ailing businesses, generally large corporations, from the brink of disaster. His position used all of his strengths, amongst which he counted a formidable ability to not be swayed be emotion.

He was driven, ambitious and on occasion, unapologetically ruthless, and he could see that was a terrible fit with Second Chances. He didn't really even *like* charities, cynically feeling that for one person to receive the charity of another was usually as humiliating for the person in need as it was satisfying for the one who could give.

But the woman who sat in front of him was a reminder that no man had himself alone to thank for his circumstances.

Houston Whitford was here, at Second Chances, because he owed a debt.

And he was here for the same reason he suspected most men blamed when they found themselves in untenable situations.

His mother, Beebee, had suggested he help out. So, it had already been personal, some line blurred, even before the bride had showed up.

Beebee was Houston's foster mother, but it was a distinction he rarely made. She had been there when his real mother—as always—had not. Beebee had been the first person he had ever felt genuinely cared about him and what happened to him. He owed his life as it was to her *charity,* and he knew it.

Miss Viv was Beebee's oldest friend, part of that remarkable group of women who had circled around a tough boy from a terrible neighborhood and seen something in him—*believed in something in him*—that no one had ever seen or believed in before.

You didn't say *sorry, too busy* in the face of that kind of a debt.

It had started a month ago, when he'd hosted a surprise birthday celebration for Beebee. The catered high tea had been held at his newly acquired "Gold Coast" condominium with its coveted Fifth Avenue address, facing Central Park.

Beebee and "the girls" had been all sparkle then, oohing over the white-gloved doorman, the luxury of the lobby, the elevators, the hallways. Inside the sleek interior of his eleven-million-dollar apartment, no detail had gone unremarked, from tiger wood hardwood to walnut moldings to the spectacular views.

But as the party had progressed, Miss Viv had brought up Second Chances, the charity she headed, and that all "the girls" supported. She confessed it was having troubles, financial and otherwise, that baffled her.

"Oh, Houston will help, won't you, dear?" his foster mom had said.

And all eyes had been on him, and in a blink he wasn't a successful entrepreneur who had proven himself over and over again, but that young ruffian, *poor child,* rescued from mean streets and a meaner life, desperately trying to live up to their expectation that he was really a good person under that tough exterior.

But after that initial weakness that had made him say yes, he'd laid down the law. If they wanted his help, they would have to accept the fact he was doing it his way: no interfering from them, no bringing him home-baked goodies to try to sway him into keeping things the very same way that had gotten the charity into trouble in the first place and *especially* no references to his past.

Of course, they hadn't understood that.

"But why ever not? We're all so proud of you, Houston!"

But Beebee and her friends weren't just proud of him because of who he was now. No, they were the ones who held in their memories that measuring stick of who he had once been…a troubled fourteen-year-old kid from the tenements of Clinton, a neighborhood that had once been called Hell's Kitchen.

They saw it as something to be admired that he had overcome his circumstances—his father being sent to prison, his mother abandoning him—but he just saw it as something left behind him.

Beebee and Miss Viv dispensed charity as easily as they breathed, but as well-meaning as they were, they had no idea how shaming that part of his life, when he had been so needy and so vulnerable, was to him. He did not excuse himself because he had only been fourteen.

He still felt, sometimes, that he was their *poor child,* an object of pity that they had rescued and nursed back to wellness like a near-drowned kitten.

Was he insecure about his past? No, he didn't think so. But it was over and it was done. He'd always had an ability to place his life in neat compartments; his need for order did not allow for overlapping.

But suddenly, he thought of that letter that had arrived at his home last week, a cheap envelope and a prison postmark lying on a solid mahogany desk surely a sign that a man could not always keep his worlds from overlapping.

Houston had told no one about the arrival of that letter, not even the only other person who knew his complete history, Beebee.

Was that part of why he was sending her away with Miss Viv? Not just because he knew they could probably not resist sharing the titillating details of his past with anyone who would listen, including all the employees here at Second Chances, but because he didn't want to talk to Beebee about that letter? The thought of that letter, plus being here at Second Chances, made him feel what Houston Whitford hated feeling the most: *vulnerable,* as if that most precious of commodities, *control,* was slipping away from him.

And there was something about this place—the nature of charity, Miss Viv and his history, Molly, sweetly sensual in virginal white—that made him feel, not as if his guard was being let down, but that his bastions were being stormed.

He was a proud man. That pride had carried him through times when all else had failed. He didn't want Miss Viv's personal information about him undermining his authority to rescue her charity, changing the way people he had to deal with looked at him.

And when people found out his story, it did change the way they looked at him.

He could tell, for instance, Molly Michaels would

fall solidly in the soft-hearted category. She'd love an opportunity to treat him like a kitten who had nearly drowned! And he wasn't having it.

"Let's discuss Molly Michaels for a minute," he said carefully. "I'd like to have a little talk with her about—"

"Don't be hard on her!" Miss Viv cried. "Try not to judge Molly for the outfit. She was just being playful. It was actually good to see that side of her again," Miss Viv said.

Playful. He liked playful. In the bedroom.

In the office? Not so much.

"Please don't hurt her feelings," Miss Viv warned him.

Hurt her feelings? What did feelings have to do with running an organization, with expecting the best from it, with demanding excellence?

He did give in to the little impulse, then, to press the ridge of the scar along his nose.

Miss Viv's voice lowered into her *juicy-secret* tone. "The broken engagement? She's had a heartbreak recently."

It confirmed his wisdom in sending Miss Viv away for the duration of the Second Chances business makeover. He didn't want to know this, *at all.* He pressed harder. The ache along the scar line did not diffuse.

"A cad, I'm afraid," Miss Viv said, missing his every signal that he did not want to be any part of the office stories, the gossip, the personalities.

Despite his desire to remove himself from it, Houston felt a sudden and completely unexpected pulsing of fury.

Not for the circumstances he found himself in, certainly not at Miss Viv, who could not help herself. No, Houston felt an undisciplined desire to hurt a man he did not know for breaking the heart of a woman he also did not know—save for the exquisite tenderness of her neck beneath his fingertips.

That flash of unreasonable fury, an undisciplined reaction, was gone nearly as soon as it happened, but it still served to remind him that things did not always stay in their neat compartments. He had not overcome what he had come from as completely as everyone believed.

He came from a world where violence was the default reaction.

Houston knew if he was to let down his guard, lose his legendary sense of control for a second—one second—he could become that man his father had been, his carefully constructed world blown apart by forces—fury, passion—that could rise up in a storm that he had no hope of taming.

It was the reason Houston did not even allow himself to contemplate his life in the context of fairy tales represented by a young woman in a bridal gown. There was no room for a compartment like that in the neat, tidy box that made up his life.

There was a large compartment for work, an almost equally large one for his one and only passion, the combat sport of boxing.

There were smaller compartments for his social obligations, for Beebee, for occasional and casual relationships with the rare member of the opposite sex who shared his aversion for commitment. There were some compartments that were nailed shut.

But now the past was not staying in the neat compartment system. The compartment that held Houston's father *and* his mother was being pried up, despite the nails trying to hold it firmly shut.

Houston's father had written his only son a letter

that asked nothing and expected nothing. And yet at the same time Houston was bitterly aware that how he reacted to it would prove who he really was.

After nineteen years, his father was getting out of prison.

And it felt as if all those years of Houston outdistancing his past had been a total waste of energy. Because there it was, waiting for him, right around the next bend in time.

The scar across his nose flared with sudden pain, and Houston pressed a finger into the line of the old break, aware he was entering a danger zone that the mean streets of Clinton had nothing on.

"Have a seat," Houston invited Molly several hours later, after he had personally waved goodbye to Beebee and Miss Viv at the airport.

"Thank you." She took a seat, folded her hands primly in her lap and looked at him expectantly.

It was his second encounter with her, and he was determined it was going to go differently than the first. It was helpful that Miss Viv was not there smiling at him as if he was her favorite of all charity cases.

And it was helpful that Molly Michaels was all business now, no remnant of the blushing bride she had been anywhere in sight. No, she was dressed in a conservative slack suit, her amazing hair pinned sternly up on her head.

Still, it was way too easy to remember how it had felt underneath his hands. He was not going to allow himself to contemplate the fact that even after untangling her from that dress several hours ago he was no closer to knowing her truth: was she sexy? Or innocent?

Not thoughts that were strictly *professional*. In

fact, those were exactly the kind of thoughts that made a man crazy.

"I'm sorry about the dress. You must think I'm crazy."

Damn her for using that word!

The nails holding a compartment of Houston's past shut gave an outrageous squeak. Houston remembered the senior Whitford had been made *crazy* by a beautiful woman, Houston's mother.

Who hadn't she made crazy? Beautiful, but untouchable. Both of them had loved her desperately, a fact that had only seemed to amuse her, allowed her to toy with her power over them. The truth? Houston would have robbed a bank for her, too, if he'd thought it would allow him to finally win something from her.

The memory, unwanted, of his craving for something his mother had been unable to give made him feel annoyed with himself.

"Crazy?" he said. *You can't begin to know the meaning of the word.* "Let's settle for eccentric."

She blushed, and his reaction was undisciplined, *unprofessional,* a ridiculous desire, like a juvenile boy, to find out what made her blush and then to make it happen *often.*

"So, you've been here how long?" Houston asked, even though he knew, just to get himself solidly back on the professional track.

"As an employee for several years. But I actually started here as a volunteer during high school."

Again, unprofessional thoughts tickled at him: what had she been like during high school? The popular girl? The sweet geek? *Would she have liked him?*

Houston remembered an incident from his own high school years. She probably would not have liked him, *at all.* He shook off the memory like a pesky fly. High school? That was fifteen years ago! That was the problem with things coming out of their compartments. They could become unruly, pop up unannounced, uninvited, in moments when his concentration was challenged, when his attention drifted.

Which was rarely, thank God.

Since the memories had come, though, he exercised cool discipline over them. He reminded himself that good things could come from bad. His mother's abandonment had ultimately opened the door to a different world for him; the high school "incident" had led to Beebee putting him in boxing classes "to channel his aggression."

Houston was more careful than most men with the word *love,* but he thought he could honestly say he loved the combat sport of boxing, the absolute physical challenge of it, from the grueling cardiovascular warm-up to punching the heavy bags and the speed bags, practicing the stances, the combinations, the jabs and the hooks. He occasionally sparred, but awareness of the unexpected power of fury prevented him from taking matches.

Now he wondered if a defect in character like fury could lie dormant, spring back to life when it was least expected.

No, he snapped at himself.

Yes, another voice answered when a piece of Molly's hair sprang free of the restraints she had pinned it down with, curled down the soft line of her temple.

She'd been engaged to a cad.

Tonight, he told himself sternly, he would punch straight left and right combinations into the heavy bag until his hands, despite punch mitts, ached from it. Until his whole body hurt and begged for release. For now he would focus, not on her hair or her past heartbreaks, but on the job he was here to do.

Houston realized Molly's expression had turned quizzical, wondered how much of the turmoil of that memory he had just had he had let slip over his usually well-schooled features.

Did she look faintly sympathetic? Had she seen something he didn't want her to see? Good grief, had Miss Viv managed to let something slip about him?

Whatever, he knew just how to get rid of that look on her face, the look of a woman who *lived* to make the world softer and better.

A cad could probably spot that gentle, compassion-filled face from a mile away! It would be good for her to toughen up.

"Let me be very blunt," he said, looking at the papers in front of him instead of her hair, the delicate creamy skin at her throat. "Second Chances is in a lot of trouble. I need to turn things around and I need to do it fast."

"Second Chances is in trouble?" Molly was genuinely astounded. "But how? The secondhand stores that provide the majority of our funding seem to do well."

"They do perform exceedingly well. The problem seems to be in an overextension of available funds. Your department?"

Here it was: could she make the kind of hard decisions that would be required of her if she took over the top spot in the newly revamped Second Chances?

The softness left her face, replaced with wariness. Better than softness in terms of her managerial abilities. If that was good, why did he feel so bad?

"You can't run an organization that brings in close to a million dollars a year like a mom and pop store. You can't give everyone who comes in here with their hand out and a hard luck story everything they ask for."

"I don't!" she said. "I'm very careful what I fund."

He saw her flinch from his bluntness, but at this crucial first stage there was no other way to prepare people for the changes that had to happen. Another little curl broke free of her attempt to tame her hair, and he watched it, sentenced himself to another fifteen minutes on the bag and forged on.

"Two thousand dollars to the Flatbush Boys Choir travel fund? There is no Flatbush Boys Choir."

"I know that now," she said, defensively. "I had just started here. Six of them came in. The most adorable little boys in matching sweaters. They even sang a song for me."

"Here's a check written annually to the Bristol Hall Ladies' Lunch Group. No paperwork. No report. Is there a Bristol Hall Ladies' Lunch Group? What do they do? When do they meet? Why do they get money for lunch?"

"That was grandfathered in from before I started. Miss Viv looks after it."

"So, you're project manager, except when Miss Viv takes over?"

"She is the boss," Molly said uneasily, her defensive tone a little more strident.

"Ah." He studied her for a moment, then said softly, "Look, I'm not questioning your competence."

She looked disbelieving. Understandably.

"It's just that some belt-tightening is going to have to happen. What I need from you as I do research, review files and talk to people is for you to go over your programming in detail. I need exact breakdowns on how you choose programs. I need to review your budgets, I need to analyze your monitoring systems."

She looked like she had been hit by a tank. Now would be the wrong time to remember the sweet softness of her skin under his fingertips, how damned protective he had felt when he heard about the *cad*. Now he was the cad!

"How soon can you have that to me?" he pressed.

"A week?"

A chief executive officer needed to work faster, make decisions more quickly. "You have until tomorrow morning."

She glared at him. That was good. Much easier to defend against than sweet, shocked vulnerability. The angry spark in her eyes could almost make him forget her hair, that tender place at her nape. Almost.

He plunged forward, eager to get the barriers—compromised by hands in hair—back up where they belonged. Eager to find out what he needed to know about her—professionally—so he could make a recommendation when the job here was done and move on.

"I've been sorting through paperwork for a number of weeks," he told her. "I have to tell you, after a brief look, it's quite evident to me that you're going to have to ax some of your projects. Sooner rather than later. I've short-listed a few that are on the block."

"Ax projects?" she said with disbelief. "Some of *my* projects are on the block?"

He nodded. He felt not the least like a knight riding in to rescue the business in distress. Or the damsel. He was causing distress, in fact. The feeling of being the cad intensified even though he knew in the long run this would pay off for Second Chances, guarantee their good health and success in the coming years and possibly decades if this was done right, if they had the right leader to move ahead with.

"Which ones?" She went so pale a faint dusting of freckles appeared over the bridge of her nose.

He was annoyed that his feeling of being the cad only deepened, and that she was acting as if he had asked her to choose one of her children to float down the river in a basket. He was aware of feeling the faintest twinge of a foreign emotion, which after a second or two he identified, with further annoyance, as guilt.

Houston Whitford did not feel guilty about doing his job! Satisfied, driven, take charge, in control. Of course, generally, it would be fairly safe to say he didn't *feel,* period.

He used a reasonable tone of voice, designed to convince either her or himself that of course he was not a cad! "We have to make some practical decisions for the future of this organization."

She looked unconvinced about his cad status, and the careful use of the *we* did not even begin to make her think they were a team.

She looked mutinous, then stunned, then mutinous again. Her face was an open book of emotion.

"Is it that bad?" she finally sputtered. "How can it be? Miss Viv never said a word. She didn't even seem worried when she left!"

He had actually sheltered Miss Viv from how bad things were as he had begun to slug his way through the old gal's abysmal record and bookkeeping systems. Miss Viv—and his mother, Second Chances's largest patron—trusted him to fix this. He would. Neither of them needed to know the extent he had to go to. But Molly Michaels did, since the mantle of it all could quite possibly fall on her slender shoulders.

"Yes, it's bad." He closed the fuchsia cover on one

of the project reports, the mauve one on another and put those files on the desk between them. "The Easter Egg hunt is gone. The poetry competition is out. And I'm looking at the prom dress thing, and—"

"Prom Dreams?" she gasped. "You can't! You don't know what it means to those girls."

"Have you ever known real hardship?" he asked her, his voice deliberately cold. This job was not going to be easy no matter how he did it. Hard choices had to be made. And he had to see if she was willing to make them. There was no way she was going to be suited to taking over the top job at Second Chances if she was always going to be blinded by the stars in her eyes.

But cad that he was, his gaze went to the lip that she was nibbling with distraction. He was shocked that out of the blue he wondered if one of his hard choices was not going to be whether or not to taste those luscious lips before he made his escape!

She met his eyes. Stopped nibbling. Things that should be simple, cut-and-dried, suddenly seemed complicated. He wished she wasn't looking at him as if she was remembering, too, that unguarded moment when two strangers had touched and the potential for something wild and unpredictable had arced in the air between them.

"My parents divorced when I was young," she offered, softly. "I considered that a terrible hardship. The only one I've known, but life altering."

Thank God she didn't mention the cad! He could see the pain in her eyes. Houston reminded himself, sternly, that he likely had a genetic predisposition toward allowing women to make him crazy. Because he had no business thinking of trying to change the light in her eyes. But he was thinking of it, of how soft her lips would be beneath his own.

Why would that genetic predisposition toward *crazy* be surfacing now, for God's sake? He'd been around many, many beautiful women. He'd always taken his ability to keep his emotional distance for granted, one of the few gifts from his chaotic childhood.

Don't form attachments. Don't care too deeply.

Except for his business and boxing. Both had rigid guidelines and rules that if followed, produced a predictable result. That made them safe things to care about. An occasional bruised knuckle or fat lip, a skirmish in the business world, those hazards were nothing compared to the minefields of becoming attached to people, where the results were rarely predictable.

No, he knew exactly where he was going to channel his substantial passion and energy.

He was being drawn backward, feeling shadows from his past falling over him, entirely against his will. He blamed the letter from his father and the unfortunate fact it coincided with the past weeks of going over files of people who were as desperate and as needy as his family had once been.

It was his annoyance at himself for allowing those thoughts into his business world that made his tone even sharper than it had to be, even if he was testing her ability to run a million dollar corporation.

"Have you ever been hungry?" But even as he asked it, he knew that question, too, stemmed not so much from professional interest as from a dark past he thought he had left behind.

"No," she said, "but I think I can imagine the desperation of it."

"Can you?" he said cynically.

Without warning a memory popped over the barrier of the thick, high wall he had constructed around the compartment of his childhood.

So hungry. Not a crumb of food in the house. Going into Sam's, the bakery at the corner of his street, Houston's heart beating a horrible tattoo in his chest, his mouth watering from the smells and the sights of the freshly baked bread. Looking around, it was crowded, no one paying any attention to him. Sam's back turned. Houston's hands closing around one of the still-warm loafs in a basket outside the counter, stuffing it under his thin jacket. Lifting his eyes to see Sam looking straight at him. And then Sam turning away, saying nothing, and Houston feeling the shame of the baker's pity so strongly he could not eat the bread. He brought it home to his mother, who had been indifferent to the offering, uncaring of what it had cost him.

Molly was looking at him, understandably perplexed by the question.

Stop it, he ordered himself. But another question came out anyway, clipped with unexpected anger. "Out of work?"

"I don't suppose the summer I chose to volunteer here instead of taking a paying job counts, does it?"

"The fact you could make a choice to volunteer instead of work indicates to me you have probably not known real hardship."

"That doesn't make me a bad person!" she said sharply. "Or unqualified for my job!"

"No," he said, taking a deep breath, telling himself to smarten up. "Of course it doesn't. I'm just saying your frame of reference when choosing projects may not take into account the harsh realities the people you are helping live with."

Another memory popped over that wall. His father drunk, belligerent, out of work again. Not his fault. Never his fault. His mother screaming at his father. You loser. The look on his father's face. Rage. The flying fists, the breaking glass.

Houston could feel his heart beating as rapidly as though it had just happened. Molly was watching him, silently, the dismay and anger that had been in her face fading, becoming more thoughtful.

He ordered himself, again, to stop this. It was way too personal. But, master of control that he was, he did not stop.

"Have you ever had no place to live?"

"Of course not!"

Homelessness was so far from her reality that she could not even fathom it happening to her. Not that he had any right to treat that as a character defect, just because it had once been part of his childhood reality.

The eviction notice pounded onto the door. The hopeless feeling of nowhere to go and no place to feel safe. That sense that even that place he had called home was only an illusion. A sense that would be confirmed as the lives of the Whitfords spiraled steadily downward toward disaster.

Again Molly was silent, but her eyes were huge and had darkened to a shade of green that reminded him of a cool pond on a hot day, a place that promised refuge and rest, escape from a sizzling hot pressure-cooker of a world.

Her expression went from defensive to quiet. She studied his face, her own distress gone, as if she saw something in him, focused on something in him. He didn't want her to see his secrets, and yet something in her steady gaze made him feel seen, vulnerable.

"You're dealing with desperation, and you're doling out prom dresses? Are you kidding me?"

Houston was being way too harsh. He drew a deep breath, ordered himself to apologize, to back track, but suddenly the look on her face transformed. Her expression went from that quiet thoughtfulness to something much worse. *Knowing.*

He felt as transparent as a sheet of glass.

"You've known those things, haven't you?" she guessed softly.

The truth was he would rather run through Central Park in the buff than reveal himself emotionally.

He was stunned that she had seen right through his exquisite suit, all the trappings of wealth and success, seen right through the harshness of his delivery to what lay beneath.

He was astounded that a part of him—a weak part— *wanted* to be seen. Completely.

He didn't answer her immediately. The part of him that felt as if it was clamoring to be acknowledged quieted, and he came back to his senses.

He had to apply his own rules right now, to set an example for her. Don't form attachments. Don't care too deeply. Not about people. Not about programs.

And he needed to take away that feeling he'd been *seen.* Being despised for his severity felt a whole lot safer than that look she'd just given him.

He was laying down the law. If she didn't like it, too bad. It was his job to see if she was capable of doing what needed to be done. Miss Viv wanted to hand this place over to her. There was absolutely no point doing any of this if six months later soft hearts had just run it back into the ground.

"Prom Dreams is gone," he said coolly. "It's up to you to get rid of it."

She bit her lip. She looked at her shoes. She glanced back at him, and tears were stinging her eyes.

There was no room for crying at work!

And absolutely no room for the way it made him feel: as if he wanted to fix it. For Pete's sake, he was the one who'd created it!

"I can see we are going to have a problem," he said. "You are a romantic. And I am a realist."

For a moment she studied him. For a moment he thought she would not be deflected by Prom Dreams, by his harshness, that despite it she would pursue what he had accidentally shown her.

But she didn't.

"I am not a romantic!" she protested.

"Anyone who shows up for work in a wedding gown is a romantic," he said, pleased with how well his deflection had worked. It was about her now, not about him, not about what experiences he did or didn't know.

"I didn't arrive in it," she said, embarrassed and faintly defensive, again. "It was a donation. It had been put on my desk."

"So naturally you had no alternative but to try it on."

"Exactly. I was just checking it for damage."

"Uh-huh," he said, not even trying to hide his skepticism. "Anyone who wants to buy dresses instead of feeding people is a romantic."

"It's not that black and white!"

"Everything is black and white to a realist. Rose-colored to a romantic."

"I might have been a romantic once," she said, her chin tilted proudly, "but I'm not anymore."

Ah, the cad. He shoved his hands under his desk when they insisted on forming fists.

"Good," he said, as if he were the most reasonable of men. "Then you should have no problem getting on board for the kind of pragmatic changes that need to be made around here."

He knew she was kidding herself about not being a romantic. Despite the recent heartbreak Miss Viv had told him about, it seemed that Molly had hopes and dreams written all over her. Could she tame that enough to do the job Second Chances needed her to do?

"Couldn't we look at ways to increase funding, rather than cutting programs?"

Ah, that's what he wanted to hear. Realistic ideas for dealing with problems, creative approaches to solutions, coming at challenges from different directions, experimenting with angles.

For the first time, he thought *maybe*. Maybe Molly Michaels had the potential to run the show. But he let nothing of that optimism into his voice. It was just too early to tell. Because it couldn't work if she was so attached to things that she could not let go of the ones that were dragging the organization down.

"Believe me, I'm looking at everything. That's my job. But I still want every single thing Second Chances funds to have merit, to be able to undergo the scrutiny of the people I will be approaching for funding, and to pass with flying colors."

"I think," she said, slowly, "our different styles might work together, not against each other, if we gave them a chance."

He frowned at that. He wasn't looking for a partnership. He wasn't looking to see if they could work together. He wanted to evaluate whether she could work alone. He wasn't looking for anything to complicate what needed to be done here. It already was way too complicated.

Memories. Unexpected emotion.

Annoyed with himself, he put Houston Whitford, CEO of Precision Solutions, solidly back in the driver's seat.

"What needs to be done is pretty cut-and-dried," Houston said. "I've figured it out on paper, run numbers, done my homework. A team of experts is coming in here tomorrow to implement changes. Second Chances needs computer experts, business analysts, accounting wizards. It needs an image face-lift. It needs to be run like a corporation, stream-lined, professional."

"A corporation?" she said, horrified. "This is a family!"

"And like most families, it's dysfunctional." *That* was the Houston Whitford he knew and loved.

"What a terribly cynical thing to say!"

Precisely. And every bit of that cynicism had been earned in the school of hard knocks. "If you want Walt Disney, you go to the theater or rent *Old Yeller* from the video store. I deal in reality."

"You don't think the love and support of a family is possible in the business environment?"

The brief hope he'd felt about Molly's suitability to have Miss Viv turn over the reins to her was waning.

"That would assume that the love and support of family is a reality, not a myth. Miss Michaels, there is no place for sentiment in the corporate world."

"You're missing all that is important about Second Chances!"

"Maybe, for the first time, someone is seeing exactly what *is* important about Second Chances. Survival. That would speak to the bottom line. Which at the moment is a most unbecoming shade of red."

She eyed him, and for a moment anger and that other thing—that soft *knowing*— warred in her beautiful face. He pleaded with the anger to win. Naturally, the way his day was going, it didn't.

"Let me show you *my* Second Chances before you make any decisions about the programs," she implored. "You've seen them in black and white, on paper, but there's more to it than that. I want to show you the soul of this organization."

He sighed. "The soul of it? And you're not romantic? Organizations don't have souls."

"The best ones do. Second Chances does," she said with determination. "And you need to see that."

Don't do it, he ordered himself.

But suddenly it seemed like a life where a man was offered a glimpse at soul and refused it was a bereft place, indeed. Not that he was convinced she could produce such a glimpse. Romantics had a tendency to see things that weren't there. But realists didn't. Why not give her a chance to defend her vision? Really, could there be a better way to see if she had what it took to run Second Chances?

Still, he would have to spend time with her. More time than he had expected. And he didn't want to. And yet he did.

But if he did go along with her, once he had seen she was wrong, he could move forward, guilt-free. Make his recommendations about her future leadership, begin the job of cutting what needed to be cut. Possibly he wouldn't even feel like a cad when he axed Prom Dreams.

Besides, if there was one lesson he had carried forward when he'd left his old life behind him, it was to never show fear. Or uncertainty. The mean streets fed on fear.

No, you set your shoulders and walked straight toward what you feared, unflinching, ready to battle it.

He feared the *knowing* that had flashed in her eyes, the place that had called to him like a cool, green pond to a man who had unknowingly been living on the searing hot sands of the desert. If he went there could he ever go back to where—to what—he had been before?

That was his fear and he walked toward it.

He shrugged, not an ounce of his struggle in his controlled voice. He said, "Okay. I'll give you a day to convince me."

"Two."

He leaned back in his chair, studied her, thought it was probably very unwise to push this thing by spending two days in close proximity to her. And he realized, with sudden unease, the kind of neighborhoods her projects would be in. He'd rather hoped never to return to them.

On the other hand the past he had been so certain he had left behind was reemerging, and he regarded his unease with some distaste. Houston Whitford was not a man who shirked. Not from *knowing* eyes, not from the demons in his past.

He would face the pull of her and the desire to push away his past in the very same way—head-on. He was not running away from anything. There was nothing he could not handle for two short days.

"Okay," he said again. "Two days."

Maybe it was because it felt as if he'd made a concession and was giving her false hope—maybe it was to fight the light in her face—that he added, "But Prom Dreams is already gone. And in two days all my other decisions are final."

CHAPTER THREE

MOLLY was glad to be home. Today easily qualified as one of the worst of her life.

Right up there with the day her father had announced her parents' plan to divorce, right up there with the day she had come home from work to find her message machine blinking, Chuck's voice on the other end.

"Sorry, sweetheart, moving on. A great opportunity in Costa Rica."

Not even the courtesy of a face-to-face breakup. Of course, if he'd taken the time to do that, he might have jeopardized his chances of getting away with the contents, meager as they had been, of her bank account.

A note had arrived, postmarked from Costa Rica, promising to pay her back, and also telling her not to totally blame him. *Sweetheart, you're a pushover. Don't let the next guy get away with pushing you around.* To prove she was not a pushover, she had taken the note directly to the police and it had been added to her complaint against Chuck.

A kindly desk sergeant had told her not to hold her breath about them ever finding him or him ever sending a check. And he'd been right. So far, no checks, but the advice had probably been worth it, even if so far, there had been no *next* guy.

Besides, the emptied bank account had really been a small price to pay to be rid of Chuck, she thought, and then felt startled. It was the first time she had seen his defection in that light.

Was it Houston, with his hard-headed pragmatism, that was making her see things differently? Surely not! For all that he was a powerful presence, there was no way she could be evaluating Chuck through his eyes!

And finding the former coming up so lacking.

Perhaps change in general forced one to evaluate one's life in a different light?

For instance, she was suddenly glad she had never given in to Chuck's pressure to move in with her, that she had clung to her traditional values, that it was marriage or nothing.

She had actually allowed Chuck access to her bank account to take the sting out of that decision, one she'd been unusually firm about even in the face of Chuck's irritation.

Because of that decision today she could feel grateful that her apartment remained a tiny, cozy space, all hers, no residue of Chuck here.

Usually her living room welcomed her, white slip-covers over two worn love seats that faced each other, fresh flowers in a vase on the coffee table between the sofas. The throw cushions were new to pick up the colors from her most prized possession, acquired since Chuck's defection from her life.

It was a large, expensively framed art poster of a flamboyantly colored hot air balloon rising at dawn over the golden mists of the Napa Valley.

There were two people standing at the side of the basket of the rising balloon, sharing the experience and each other at a deep level that the photographer had managed to capture. Tonight, Molly Michaels looked at it with the fresh eyes of one who had been judged, and felt defensive.

She told herself she hadn't bought it because she was a *romantic,* as a subliminal nod to all she still wanted to believe in. No, Molly had purchased the piece because it spoke to the human spirit's ability to rise above turmoil, to experience peace and beauty despite disappointments and betrayals.

And that's why she'd tried on the wedding dress, too?

The unwanted thoughts made her much loved living space feel like a frail refuge from the unexpected storm that was battering her world.

Hurricane Houston, she told herself, out loud trying for a wry careless note, but instead she found she had conjured an image of his eyes that threatened to invade even the coziness of her safe place.

Which just went to show that Houston Whitford was a man she *really* would have to defend herself against, if the mere remembering of the light in his eyes could make him have more presence here in her tiny sanctuary than Chuck had ever had.

That begged another question. If someone like Chuck—unwilling to accept responsibility for anything, including his theft of her bank account—could devastate her life so totally, how much more havoc could a more powerful man wreak on the life of the unwary?

Molly remembered the touch of Houston's hands on her neck, and shivered, remembering how hard the texture of his skin had been, a forewarning he was much tougher than the exquisite tailoring of the suit had prepared her for.

Have you ever been hungry?

What had she seen in him in that moment? Not with her eyes, really, her heart. Her heart had sensed something, known something about him that he did not want people to know.

Stop it, she ordered herself. She was only proving he was right. Hearts sensing something that the eyes could not see was romantic hogwash.

He had already axed Prom Dreams. That's what she needed to see! She was dealing with a man who was heartless!

Though she rarely drank and never during the week, she poured herself a glass of the Biale Black Chicken Zinfandel from the region depicted on the poster. She raised her glass to the rising hot air balloon.

"To dreams," she said, even though it was probably proving that Houston Whitford was right again. A romantic despite her efforts to cure herself of it. She amended her toast, lifted the wineglass to the photo again. "To hope."

With uncharacteristic uncertainty tormenting her, Molly spent the evening reviewing her projects—alternately defending each and every one, and then trying to decide which ones to take him to in the two days he had reluctantly allotted her.

And she tried desperately to think of a way to save Prom Dreams. They always had lots of donations of fine gowns, but never enough. It had to be supplemented for each girl who wanted a dress to get one. The thought of phoning the project coordinator and canceling it turned her stomach. Hearts would be broken! For months, girls looked forward to the night the Greenwich Village shop, Now and Zen, was transformed into prom dress heaven.

Could she wait? Hope for a change of heart on his part? A miracle?

If she could convince him of the merit of her other projects, would there be a chance he might develop faith in her abilities? Could she then convince him Prom Dreams had to be saved?

She was not used to having to prove herself at work! The supportive atmosphere at Second Chances had always been such that she felt respected, appreciated and approved of! None of her projects had ever come under fire, none had ever been dismissed as trivial! Of course there had been a few mistakes along the way, but no one had ever made her feel incompetent because of them! She had always been given the gift of implicit trust.

That was part of the *soul* of Second Chances. It trusted the best in everyone would come out if it was encouraged!

Could she make Houston Whitford see that soul as she had promised? Could she make him feel that sense of family he was so cynical about? Could she make him understand the importance of it in a world too cold, and too capitalistic and too focused on those precious bottom lines?

But she was suddenly very aware she did not want to think of Houston Whitford in the context of a family.

That felt as if it would be the most dangerous thing of all, as if it would confirm what her heart insisted it had glimpsed in him when he had talked about hunger and hardship.

That he was lonely. That never had a man needed a family more than he did.

Stop it, she told herself. That was exactly the kind of thinking that got her into trouble, made her a pushover as Chuck had so generously pointed out from the beaches of Costa Rica, no doubt while sipping Margaritas paid for with her money! Molly took far too long the next morning choosing her outfit, but she knew she needed to look and feel every inch a professional, on even footing, in a position to command both respect and straight answers.

She had to erase the message that the wedding dress had given. She had to be seen as a woman who knew her job, and was a capable and complete professional.

The suit Molly chose was perfect—Calvin Klein, one-inch-above-the-knee black skirt, tailored matching jacket over a sexy hot-pink camisole. But somehow it wasn't quite right, and she changed it.

"You don't have time for this," she wailed, and yet somehow *looking* calm and confident when that was the last thing she was feeling seemed more important than ever.

She ended up in a white blouse and a spring skirt—splashes of lime-green and lemon-yellow—that was decidedly flirty in its cut and movement. She undid an extra button on the blouse. Did it back up. Raced for the door.

She undid the top button again as she walk-ran the short distance to work. She was going to need every advantage she could call into play to work with that man! It seemed only fair that she should keep him as off balance as he made her.

Only as soon as she entered the office she could see they were not even playing in the same league when it came to the "off balance" department.

The Second Chances office as she had always known it was no more.

In its place was a construction zone. Sawhorses had been set up and a carpenter was measuring lengths of very expensive looking crown molding on them. One painter was putting down drop cloths, another was leaning on Tish the receptionist's desk, making her blush. An official looking man with a clipboard was peering into filing cabinets making notes. A series of blueprint drawings were out on the floor.

Molly had ordered herself to start differently today. To be a complete professional, no matter what.

Bursting into tears didn't seem to qualify!

How could he do this? He had promised to give her a chance to show him where funding was needed! How could he be tearing down the office without consulting the people who worked there? Without asking them what they needed and wanted? Why had she thought, from a momentary glimpse of something in his eyes, that he had a soft side? That she could trust him? Wasn't that the mistake she insisted on making over and over again?

Worst of all, Prom Dreams was the first of her many projects being axed for lack of funding, and Houston Whitford was in a redecorating frenzy? There were four complete strangers hard at work in the outer office, all of whom would be getting paid, and probably astronomical amounts! Molly could hear the sounds of more workers, a circular saw screaming in a back room.

Calm and control, Molly ordered herself. She curled her hands in her skirt to remind herself why she had taken such care choosing it. *To appear a total professional.*

Storming his office screaming could not possibly accomplish that. Not possibly.

Instead, she slid under an open ladder—defying the bad luck that could bring—and went through the door of her own office. Molly needed to gather her wits and hopefully to delay that temper—the unfortunate but well-deserved legacy she shared with other redheads—from progressing to a boil.

But try as she might, she could not stop the thoughts. *Office renovation? Instead of Prom Dreams?*

Houston Whitford had insinuated there was *no* money, not that he was reallocating the funds they had. She needed to gather herself, to figure out how to deal with this, how to put a stop to it before he'd spent all the money. Saving Prom Dreams was going to be the least of her problems if he kept this up. Everything would be gone!

A woman backed out of the closet, and Molly gave a startled squeak.

"Oh, so sorry to startle you. I'm the design consultant. I specialize in office space and you need storage solutions. I think we can go up, take advantage of the height of this room. And what do you think of ochre for a paint color? Iron not yellow?"

He'd told her there was no money for Prom Dreams, but there was apparently all kinds of money for things he considered a priority.

Foolish, stupid things, like construction and consultants, that could suck up a ton of money in the blink of an eye. How could complete strangers have any idea what was best for Second Chances?

Molly was suddenly so angry with herself for always believing the best of people, for always being the reasonable one, for always giving the benefit of the doubt.

Pushover, an imaginary Chuck toasted her with his Margarita.

She had to make a stand for the things she believed in. Be strong, and not so easy for people to take advantage of.

"The only colors I want to discuss are the colors of prom dresses," she told the surprised consultant.

Molly's heart was beating like a meek and mild schoolteacher about to do battle with a world-wise gunslinger. But it didn't matter to her that she was unarmed. She had her spirit! She had her backbone! She turned on her heel, and strode toward the O.K. Corral at high noon.

This had already gone too far. She didn't want another penny spent! He had called her favorite program frivolous? How dare he!

She stopped at the threshold of Miss Viv's office, where Houston Whitford had set up shop.

He looked unreasonably gorgeous this morning. Better than a man had any right to look. "Ready to go?" he asked mildly, as if he wasn't tearing her whole world apart. "I need half an hour or so, and then I'm all yours."

Don't even be sidetracked by what a man like that being *all yours* could mean, she warned the part of herself that was all too ready to veer toward the romantic!

Molly took a deep breath and said firmly, not the least sidetracked, "This high-handed hi-jacking of Second Chances money is unacceptable to me."

He cocked his head at her as if he found her interesting, maybe even faintly amusing.

"Mr. Whitford, there is no nice way to say this. Miss Viv left you in charge for a reason I cannot even fathom, but she could not have been expecting this! This is a terrible waste of the resources Miss Viv has spent her life marshalling! Construction and consultants? Are you trying to break her heart? Her spirit?"

She was quite pleased with herself, assertive, a realist, speaking a language he could understand! Well, maybe the last two lines had veered just a touch toward the romantic.

Still, Molly was making it clear to herself and to him that she wasn't *trusting* anymore.

Not that he seemed to be taking her seriously!

"From what I've seen of Miss Viv," he said, with a touch of infuriating wryness, "it would take a little more than a new paint job, a wall or two coming down, to break her spirit."

"Are you deliberately missing my point? This is *not* what Second Chances is about. We are not about slick exteriors! We are about helping people, and being of genuine service to our community."

"Pretty hard to do if you go belly-up," he pointed out mildly.

"Isn't a renovation of this magnitude going to rush us toward that end?"

He actually smiled. "Not with me in charge, it isn't."

She stared at him, unnerved by the colossal arrogance of the man, his confidence in himself, by his absolute calm in the face of her confusion, as if ripping apart people's lives was all ho-hum to him!

"There's someone in my office wanting to know if I like ochre," Molly continued dangerously. "Not the yellow ochre, the iron one. I'd rather have new prom dresses."

"I thought I made it clear the prom dress issue was closed. As for design money for the offices, I've allocated that from a separate budget."

"I don't care what kind of shell game you play with the money! It's all coming from the same pot, isn't it?"

He didn't answer her. He was not even trying to disguise the fact, now, that he found her attempts at assertiveness amusing. She tried, desperately, to make him see reason.

"Girls who are dying to have a nice dress won't get

one, but we'll have the poshest offices in the East Village! Doesn't something strike you as very wrong about that?"

But even as Molly said it, she was aware it wasn't all about the girls and their dresses. Maybe even most of it wasn't about that.

It was about turning over control. Or not turning over control. To people who had not proven themselves deserving. Especially handsome men people!

"Actually, no, it doesn't strike me as wrong. Prom dresses in the face of all this need is what's *wrong*."

Part of her said maybe her new boss was not the best place to start in standing her ground. On the other hand, maybe it was just time for her to learn to stand her ground no matter who it was with.

"This is what's wrong," she said. "How on earth can you possibly justify this extravagance? How? How can you march in here, knowing nothing about this organization, and start making these sweeping changes?"

"I've made it my business to know about the organization. The changes you're seeing today are largely cosmetic." A tiny smile touched his lips. "Sweeping is tomorrow."

"Don't mock me," she said. "You told me I could have two days to convince you what Second Chances really needs."

"I did. And I'm ready to go."

"But you're already spending all our money!"

"Second Chances hasn't begun to capitalize on the kind of money that's available to organizations like this. A charity, for all its noble purposes, is still a business. A business has to run efficiently, this kind of business has to make an impression. Every single person who walks through the front door of this office has the potential to be the person who could donate a million dollars to Second Chances. You have one chance to make a first impression, to capitalize on that opportunity. One. Trust me with this."

Molly suddenly felt like a wreck, her attempt to be assertive backfiring and leaving her feeling regretful and uncertain. Trust him?

Good grief, was there a job she was worse at than choosing whom to trust? She wished Miss Viv was here to walk her through this minefield she found herself in—that she hated finding herself in! Second Chances was supposed to be the place where she didn't feel like this: threatened, as if your whole world could be whipped out from under you in the blink of an eye.

Molly, there are going to be some changes.

"I'll be ready in half an hour," she said with all the dignity she could muster. She was very aware that it rested on her shoulders to save the essence of Second Chances. If it was left to him the family feeling would be stripped from this place as ruthlessly as Vikings stripped treasures from the monasteries they were sacking!

The consultant, thankfully, was gone from her office, and Molly sat down at her desk, aware she was shaking from her heated encounter with Houston, and determined to try to act as if it was a normal day, to regain her equilibrium. She would open her e-mail first.

Resolutely she tapped her keyboard and her computer screen came up. She was relieved to see an e-mail from Miss Viv.

Please give me direction, she whispered to the computer. *Please show me how to handle this, how to save what is most important about us. The love.*

Aware she was holding her breath, Molly clicked. No message—a paperclip indicated an attachment.

She clicked on the paperclip and a video opened. It was a grainy picture of a gorgeous hot air balloon, its colors, purple, yellow, red, green, vibrant against a flawless blue sky, rising majestically into the air. What did this have to do with Miss Viv?

The utter beauty of the picture was in such sharp contrast to the ugly reality of the changes being wrought in her life that Molly felt tears prick her eyes. She had always thought a ride in a hot air balloon would be the most incredible experience *ever.* Just last night she had toasted this very vision.

She squinted at the picture, and it came into focus. Two little old ladies were waving enthusiastically from the basket of the balloon. One of them blew a kiss.

Molly frowned, squinted hard at the grainy picture and gasped.

What was Miss Viv doing living Molly's dream? If this video was any indication, Miss Viv had complete trust in Houston Whitford being left in charge! Apparently she wasn't giving her life back here—or her Second Chances family—a single second thought.

In fact, Miss Viv was waving with enthusiasm, decidedly carefree, apparently having the time of her life. It made Molly have the disloyal thought that maybe she, Molly, had allowed Second Chances to become too much to her.

Molly's job, her career, especially in the awful months since Chuck, had become her whole life, instead of just a part of it.

What had happened to her own dreams?

"Dreams are dangerous," she reminded herself.

But that didn't stop her from envying the carefree vision Miss Viv had sent her. She wished, fervently, that they could change places!

She hit the reply button to Miss Viv's e-mail. "Call home," she wrote. "Urgent!"

CHAPTER FOUR

HOUSTON regarded the empty place where Molly had just stood, berating him, with interest. In terms of the reins of this place being handed over to her one day, it was a good thing that she was willing to stand up for issues that were important to her. She had made her points clearly, and with no ultimatums, which he appreciated.

He would be unwilling to recommend her for the head spot if she was every bit as soft as she looked. But, no, she was willing to go to battle, to stand her ground.

Unreasonable as it was that she had chosen him to stand it with! And her emotional attachment to the dress thing was a con that clearly nullified the pro of her ability to stand up.

Unreasonable as it was that the fight in her had made her just as attractive as her sweetness in that wedding dress yesterday.

Maybe more so. Fights he knew how to handle. Sweetness, that was something else.

Still, for as analytical as he was trying to be, he had to acknowledge he was just a little miffed. He had become accustomed to answering to no one, he had earned the unquestioning respect of his team and the companies he worked for.

When Precision Solutions went in, Houston Whitford's track record proved productivity went up. And revenue. Jobs were not lost as a result of his team's efforts, but gained. Companies were put on the road to health, revitalized, reenergized.

There was nothing personal about what he did: it purely played to his greatest strengths, his substantial analytical skills. Except for the satisfaction he took in being the best, there was no emotion attached to his work.

Unlike Molly Michaels, most people appreciated that. They appreciated his approach, how fast he did things, how real and remarkable the changes he brought were. When he said cut something, it was cut, no questions asked.

No arguments!

They *thanked* him for the teams of experts, the new computers and ergonomically designed offices, and carefully researched paint colors that aided higher productivity.

"Maybe she'll thank you someday," he told himself, and then laughed at the unlikelihood of that scenario, and also at himself, for somehow wanting her approval.

This would teach him to deny his instincts. He had known not to tackle the charity. He had known he was going to come up against obstacles in the casually run establishment that he would never come across in the business world.

A redheaded vixen calling him down and questioning his judgment being a case in point!

But how could he have refused this? How could he refuse Beebee—or her circle of friends—anything? He owed his life to her, and to them. In those frightening days after his father had first been arrested, and his mother had quickly defected with another man— Houston had been making the disastrous mistake of trying to mask his fear with the anger that came so much more easily in his family.

He'd already worked his way through two foster homes when suddenly there had been Beebee. He had been in a destructive mode and had thrown a rock through the window of her car, parked on a dark street.

She had caught him red-handed, stunned him by not being the least afraid of him. Instead, she had looked at him with that same terrible *knowing* in her eyes that he had glimpsed in Molly's eyes yesterday.

And she had taken a chance. Recently widowed, and recently retired as a court judge, she had been looking for something to fill the sudden emptiness of her days. He still was not quite sure what twist of fate had made that *something* him.

And a world had opened up to him that had always been closed before. A world of wealth and privilege, yes, but more, a world without aggression, without things breaking in the night, without hunger, without harsh words.

It was also a world where things were expected of him that had never been required before.

Hard work. Honesty. Decency. She had gathered her friends, her family, her circle—including Miss Viv— around him. Teaching him the tools for surviving and flourishing in a different kind of world.

Houston shook his head, trying to clear away those memories, knowing they would not help him remain detached and analytical in his current circumstances.

Houston was also aware that it was a careful balancing act he needed to do. He needed to save the charity of the women who had saved him. He needed to decipher whether Molly was worthy to take the helm, but he could not afford to alienate her in the process, even if in some way, alienating her would make him feel safer.

It was more than evident to him, after plowing his way through Miss Viv's chaotic paperwork, that Molly Michaels was practically running the whole show here. Would she do better at that if she was performing in an official capacity? Or worse? That was one of the things he needed to know, absolutely, before Miss Viv came back.

He decided delay was not the better part of valor. He didn't want to allow Molly enough time to paint herself into a corner she could not get out of.

He went down the hallway to Molly's office. A ladder blocked the door; he surprised himself, because he was not superstitious, by stepping around it, rather than under it.

She was bent over her computer, her tongue caught between her teeth, a furious expression of concentration on her face.

She hit the send button on something, spun her chair around to face him, her arms folded over her chest.

"I'm hoping," he said, "that you'll give the changes here the same kind of chance to prove their merit that I'm giving you to prove the merit of your programs."

"Except Prom Dreams," she reminded him sourly.

"Except that," he agreed with absolutely no regret. "Let's give each other a chance."

She looked like she was all done giving people chances, residue from her *cad,* and the new wound, the loss of Prom Dreams.

And yet he could see from the look on her face that

she was basically undamaged by life. Willing to believe. Wanting to trust. A *romantic* whether she wanted to believe it of herself or not.

Houston Whitford did not know if he was the person to be trusted with all that goodness, all that softness, all that compassion. He didn't know if the future of Second Chances could be trusted with it, either.

"All right," she said, but doubtfully.

"Great. Where are we going first?"

"I want to show you a garden project we've developed."

Funny, that was exactly what he wanted to see. And probably not for the reason Molly hoped, either. That land was listed as one of Second Chance's assets.

He handed her a camera. "Take lots of pictures today. I can use them for fundraising promotional brochures."

The garden project would be such a good way to show Houston what Second Chances *really* did.

As they arrived it was evident spring cleanup was going on today. About a dozen rake and shovel wielding volunteers were in the tiny lot, a haven of green sandwiched between two dilapidated old buildings. Most of the people there were old, at least retirement age. But the reality of the neighborhood was reflected in the fact many of them had children with them, grandchildren that they cared for.

"This plot used to be a terrible eyesore on this block," Molly told Houston. "Look at it now."

He only nodded, seeming distant, uncharmed by the sprouting plants, the fresh turned soil, the new bedding plants, the enthusiasm of the volunteers.

Molly shook her head, exasperated with him, and

then turned her back on him. She was greeted warmly, soon at the center of hugs.

She felt at the heart of things. Mrs. Zarkonsky would be getting her hip replacement soon. Mrs. Brant had a new grandson. Sly looks were being sent toward Mr. Smith and Mrs. Lane, a widower and a widow who were holding hands.

And then she saw Mary Bedford. She hadn't seen her since they had put the garden to bed in the fall. She'd had some bad news then about a grandson who had been serving overseas.

Molly went to her, took those frail hands in her own.

"How is your grandson?" she asked. "Riley, wasn't it?"

A tear slipped down a weathered cheek. "He didn't make it."

"Oh, Mary, I'm so sorry."

"Please don't be sorry."

"How can I not be? He was so young!"

Mary reached up and rested a weathered hand against her cheek. It reminded Molly of being with Miss Viv when she looked into those eyes that were so fierce with love.

"He may have been young," she said, "but he lived every single day to the fullest. There are people my age who cannot say that. Not even close."

"That is true," Molly said.

"And he was like you, Molly."

"Like me?" she said, startled at being compared to the young hero.

"For so many of your generation it seems to be all about *things*. Bank accounts, and stuff, telephones stuck in your ears. But for Riley, it was about being of service. About helping other people. And that's what it's about for you, too."

Molly remembered sending that message to Miss Viv this morning, pleading for direction.

And here was her answer, as if you could not send out a plea for direction like the one she had sent without an answer coming from somewhere.

Ever since the crushing end of her relationship with Chuck, Molly had questioned everything about herself, had a terrible sense that she approached life all wrong.

And now she saw that wasn't true at all. She was not going to lose what was best about herself because she'd been hurt.

And then she became aware of her new boss watching her, a cynical look on his face.

For a moment she criticized herself, was tempted to see herself through his eyes. I *am too soft,* she thought. *He sees it.* For a moment she reminded herself of her vow, since Chuck, to be something else.

But then she realized that since Chuck she *had* become something else: unsure, resentful, self-pitying, bitter, frightened.

When life took a run at you, she wondered, did it chip away at who you were, or did it solidify who you really were? Maybe that was what she had missed: it was her *choice.*

"The days of all our lives are short," Mary said, and patted her on the arm. "Don't waste any of it."

Don't waste any of it, Molly thought, being frightened instead of brave, playing it safe instead of giving it the gift of who you really were.

The sun was so warm on her uplifted face, and she could feel the softness of Mrs. Bedford's tiny, frail hand in hers. And she could also feel the hope and strength in it.

Molly could feel love.

And if she allowed what Chuck—what life—had done to her to take that from her, to make her as cynical as the man watching her, then hadn't she lost the most important thing of all?

Herself.

She was what she was. If that meant she was going to get hurt from time to time, wasn't that so much better than the alternative?

She glanced again at Houston. That was the alternative. To be so closed to these small miracles. To know the price of everything and the value of nothing.

She suddenly felt sorry for him, standing there, aloof. His clothing and his car, even the way he stood, said he was so successful.

But he was alone, in amongst all the wonder of the morning, and these people reaching out to each other in love, he was alone.

And maybe that was none of her business, and maybe she could get badly hurt trying to show him there was something else, but Molly suddenly knew she could not show him the soul of Second Chances unless she was willing to show him her own.

And it wasn't closed and guarded.

When she had put on that wedding dress yesterday for some reason she had felt more herself than she had felt in a long time.

Hope filled. A believer in goodness and dreams. Someone who trusted the future. Someone with something to give.

Love.

The word came to her again, filled her. She was not sure she wanted to be thinking of a word like that in such close proximity to a man like him, and if she had not just decided to be brave she might not have. She might have turned her back on him, and gone back to the caring that waited to encircle her.

But he needed it more than she did.

"Houston," she said, and waved him over. "Come meet Mary."

He came into the circle, reluctantly. And then Mary had her arms around his neck and was hugging him hard, and even as he tried to disentangle himself, Molly saw something flicker in his face, and smiled to herself.

She was pretty sure she had just seen his soul, too. And it wasn't nearly as hard-nosed as he wanted everyone to believe.

The sun was warm on the lot and she was given a tray of bedding plants and a small hand spade. Soon she was on her knees between Mrs. Zarkonsky and Mr. Philly. Mrs. Zarkonsky eyed Houston appreciatively and handed him a shovel. "You," she said. "Young. Strong. Work."

"Oh, no," Molly said, starting to brush off her knees and get up. "He's…" She was going to say *not dressed for it,* but then neither was she, and it hadn't stopped her.

He held up a hand before she could get to her feet, let her know that would be the day that she would have to *defend* him, and followed the old woman who soon had him shoveling dirt as if he was a farm laborer.

Molly glanced over from time to time. The jacket came off. The sleeves were rolled up. Sweat beaded on his forehead. Was it that moment of recognizing who she really was that made her feel so vulnerable watching him? That made her recognize she was weak and he was strong, she was soft and he was hard? The world yearned for balance, maybe that was why men and women yearned for each other even in the face of that yearning being a hazardous endeavor.

Houston put his back into it, all mouthwatering masculine grace and strength. Molly remembered the camera, had an excuse to focus on him.

Probably a mistake. He was gloriously and completely male as he tackled that pile of dirt.

"He looks like a nice boy," Mary said, following her gaze, but then whispered, "but a little snobby, I think."

Molly laughed. Yes, he was. Or at least that was what he wanted people to believe. That he was untouchable. That he was not a part of what they were a part of. Somewhere in there, she could see it on his face he was just a nice boy, who wanted to belong, but who was holding something back in himself.

Was she reading too much into him?

Probably, but that's who she was, and that's what she did. She rescued strays. Funny she would see that in him, the man who held himself with such confidence, but she did.

Because that's what she did. She saw the best in people. And she wasn't going to change because it had hurt her.

She was going to be stronger than that.

Molly was no more dressed for this kind of work than Houston. But she went and got a spade and began to shift the same pile of topsoil he was working on. What better way to show him *soul* than people willing to work so hard for what they wanted? The spirit of community was sprouting in the garden with as much vitality as the plants.

The spring sun shone brightly, somewhere a bird sang. What could be better than this, working side by side, to create an oasis of green in the middle of the busy city? There was magic here. It was in the sights and the sounds, in the smell of the fresh earth.

Of course, his smell was in her nostrils, too, tangy and clean. And there was something about the way a bead of sweat slipped down his temple that made her breath catch in her throat.

Romantic weakness, she warned herself, but half-heartedly. Why not just enjoy this moment, the fact it included the masculine beauty of him? Now, if only he could join in, instead of be apart. There was a look on his face that was focused but remote, as if he was immune to the magic of the day.

Oh, well, that was his problem. She was going to enjoy her day, especially with this new sense of having discovered who she was.

She gave herself over to the task at hand, placed her shovel, then jumped on it with both feet to drive it in to the dirt. It was probably because he was watching—or maybe because of the desperately unsuited shoes—that things went sideways. The shovel fell to one side, throwing her against him.

His arm closed around her in reaction. She felt the hardness of his palm tingling on the sensitive upper skin of her arm. The intoxicating scent of him intensified. He held her arm just a beat longer than he had to, and she felt the seductive and exhilarating *zing* of pure chemistry.

When he had touched her yesterday, she had felt these things, but he had looked only remote. Today, she saw something pulse through his eyes, charged, before it was quickly doused and he let go of her arm.

Was it because she had made a decision to be who

she really was that she couldn't resist playing with that *zing?* Or was it because she was powerless not to explore it, just a little?

"You're going to hurt yourself," he said with a rueful shake of his head. And then just in case she thought he had a weak place somewhere in him, that he might actually care, that he might be feeling something as intoxicatingly unprofessional as she was, he said, "Second Chances can't afford a compensation claim."

She smiled to herself, went back to shoveling.

He seemed just a little too pleased with himself.

She tossed a little dirt on his shoes.

"Hey," he warned her.

"Sorry," she said, insincerely. She tossed a little more.

He stopped, glared at her over the top of his shovel. She pretended it had been purely an accident, focused intently on her own shovel, her own dirt. He went back to work. She tossed a shovel full of dirt right on his shoes.

"Hey!" he said, extricating his feet.

"Watch where you put your feet," she said solemnly. "Second Chances can't afford to buy you new shoes."

She giggled, and shoveled, but she knew he was regarding her over the top of his shovel, and when she glanced at him, some of that remoteness had gone from his eyes, *finally,* and this time it didn't come back. He went back to work.

Plop. Dirt on his shoes.

"Would you stop it?" he said.

"Stop what?" she asked innocently.

"You have something against my shoes?"

"No, they're very nice shoes."

"I know how to make you behave," he whispered.

She laughed. This is what she had wanted. To know

if there was something in him that was playful, a place she could *reach*. "No, you don't."

He dangled it in front of her eyes.

A worm! She took a step back from him. "Houston! That's not funny!" But, darn it, in a way it was.

"What's not funny?" he said. "Throwing dirt on people's shoes?"

"I hate worms. Does our compensation package cover hysteria?"

"You would get hysterical if I, say, put this worm down your shirt?"

He sounded just a little too enthused about that. It occurred to her they were flirting with each other, cautiously stepping around that little *zing,* looking at it from different angles, exploring it.

"No," she said, but he grinned wickedly, sensing the lie.

The grin changed everything about him. Everything. He went from being too uptight and too professional to being a carefree young man, covered in dirt and sweat, real and human.

It seemed to her taking that chance on showing him who she really was was paying off somehow.

Until he did a practice lunge toward her with the worm. Because she really did hate worms!

"If I tell your girlfriend you were holding worms with your bare hands today, she may never hold your hand again."

"I don't have a girlfriend."

Ah, it was a weakness. She'd been fishing. But that's what worms were for!

He lunged at her again, the worm wiggled between his fingers. He looked devilishly happy when she squealed.

Then, as if he caught himself in the sin of having fun, he abruptly dropped the worm, went back to work.

She hesitated. It was probably a good time to follow his lead and back off. But, oh, to see him smile had changed something in her. Made her willing to take a risk. With a sigh of surrender, she tossed a shovel of dirt on his shoes. And he picked up that worm.

"I warned you," he said.

"You'd have to catch me first!"

Molly threw down her shovel and ran. He came right after her, she could hear his footfalls and his breathing. She glanced over her shoulder and saw he was chasing her, holding out the worm. She gave a little snicker, and put on a burst of speed. At one point, she was sure that horrible worm actually touched her neck, and she shrieked, heard his rumble of breathless laughter, ran harder.

She managed to put a wheelbarrow full of plants between them. She turned and faced him. "Be reasonable," she pleaded breathlessly.

"The time for reason is done," he told her sternly, but then that grin lit his face—boyish, devil-may-care, and he leaped the wheelbarrow with ease and the chase was back on.

The old people watched them indulgently as they chased through the garden. Finally the shoes betrayed her, and she went flying. She landed in a pile of soft but foul-smelling peat moss. He was immediately contrite. He dropped the worm and held out his hand—which she took with not a bit of hesitation. He pulled her to her feet with the same easy strength that he had shoveled with. Where did a man who crunched numbers get that kind of strength from? She had that feeling again, of something about him not adding up, but it was chased away by his laughter.

"You don't laugh enough," she said.

"How do you know?"

"I'm not sure. I just do. You are way too serious, aren't you?"

He held both her hands for a moment, reached out and touched a curl, brushed it back from out of her eyes.

"Maybe I am," he admitted.

Something in her felt absolutely weak with what she wanted at that moment. To make him laugh, but more, to *explore* all the reasons he didn't. To find out what, exactly, about him did not add up.

"Truce?" he said.

"Of course," she panted. She meant for all of it, their different views of Second Chances. All of it.

He reached over, snared the camera out of her pocket and took a picture of her.

"Don't," she protested. She could feel her hair falling out, she was pretty sure there was a smudge of dirt on her cheek, and probably on her derriere, too!

But naturally he didn't listen and so she stuck out her tongue at him and then struck a pose for him, and then called over some of the other gardeners. Arms over each other's shoulders, they performed an impromptu can-can for the camera before it all fell apart, everyone dissolving into laughter.

Houston smiled, but that moment of spontaneity was fading. Molly was aware that he saw that moment of playfulness differently to her. Possibly as a failing. Because he was still faintly removing himself from them. She had been welcomed into the folds of the group, he stood outside it.

Lonely, she thought. *There was something so lonely about him.* And she felt that feeling, again, of wanting to explore.

And maybe to save. Just like she saved her strays. But somehow, looking at the handsome, remote cast of his face, she knew he would hate it that she had seen anything in him that needed saving. That *needed,* period.

They got back in the car, she waved to the old people. Molly was aware she was thrilled with how the morning had gone, by its unexpected surprises, and especially how he had unexpectedly revealed something of himself.

"How are your hands?" she asked him. He held one out to her. An hour on a shovel had done nothing to that hand.

"I would have thought you would have blisters," she said.

"No, my hands are really tough."

"From?"

"I box."

"As in fight?"

He laughed. "Not really. It's more the workout I like."

So, her suspicions that he was not quite who he said were unfounded. He was a high-powered businessman who sought fitness at a high-powered level.

That showed in every beautiful, mesmerizing male inch of him!

"Wasn't that a wonderful morning?" she asked, trying to solidify the camaraderie that had blossomed so briefly between them. "I promised I would show you the soul of Second Chances and that's part of it! What a lovely sense of community, of reclaiming that lot, of bringing something beautiful to a place where there was ugliness."

She became aware he was staring straight ahead. Her feeling of deflation was immediate. "You didn't feel it?"

"Molly, it's a nice project. The warm and fuzzy feel good kind."

She heard the *but* in his voice, sensed it in the set of his shoulders. Naturally he would be immune to warm fuzzy feeling good.

"But it's my job to ask if it makes good economic sense. Second Chances owns that lot, correct?"

She nodded reluctantly. Good economic sense after the magical hour they had just spent? "It was donated to us. Years ago. Before I came on board it was just an empty lot that no one did anything with."

If she was expecting congratulations on her innovative thought she was sadly disappointed!

"Were there provisos on the donation?"

"Not that I know of."

"I'll have to do some homework."

"But why?"

"I have to ask these questions. Is that the best use of that lot? It provides a green space, about a dozen people seem to actually enjoy it. Could it be liquidated and the capital used to help more people? Could it be developed—a parking lot or a commercial building—providing a stream of income into perpetuity? Providing jobs and income for the neighborhood?"

"A parking lot?" she gasped. And then she saw *exactly* what he was doing. Distancing himself from the morning they had just shared—distancing himself from the satisfaction of hard work and the joy of laughter and the admiration of people who would love him.

Distancing himself from her. Did he know she had *seen* him? Did he suspect she had uncovered things about him he kept hidden?

He didn't like *feelings*. She should know that first-hand. Chuck had had a way of rolling his eyes when she had asked him how he was feeling that had made her stop asking!

But, naive as it might be, she was pretty sure she had just glimpsed the real Houston Whitford, something shining under those layers of defenses.

And she wasn't quite ready to let that go. It didn't have to be personal. No, she could make it a mission, for the good of Second Chances, she told herself, she would get past all those defenses.

For the good of Second Chances she was going to rescue him from his lonely world.

CHAPTER FIVE

"HEY," she said, "there's Now and Zen."

She could clearly see he was disappointed that she had not risen to the bait of him saying he was going to build a parking lot over the garden project.

"Why don't we go in?" she suggested. "You can look for some gardening shoes."

She was not going to give up on him. He was not as hard-nosed as he wanted to seem. She just knew it.

How could he spend a morning like they had just spent in the loveliness of that garden, and want to put up a parking lot? Giving up wasn't in her nature. She was finding a way to shake him up, to make him see, to make him connect! Lighten him up.

And Now and Zen was just plain fun.

"Would you like to stop and have a look?"

He shrugged, regarded her thoughtfully as if he suspected she was up to something but just wasn't quite sure what. "Why not?"

Possibly another mistake, she thought as they went in the door to the delightful dimness and clutter of Now and Zen. He'd probably be crunching the numbers on this place, too. Figuring out if its magic could be bottled and sold, or repackaged and sold, or destroyed for profit.

Stop it, she ordered herself. *Show him. Invite him into this world. He's lonely. He has to be in his uptight little world where everything has a price and nothing has value.*

She tried to remind herself there was a risk of getting hurt in performing a rescue of this nature, but it was a sacrifice she was making for Second Chances! Second Chances needed for him to be the better man that she was sure she saw in there somewhere, sure she had seen when he was putting his all into that shovel.

That was muscle, a cynical voice cautioned her, *not a sign of a better man.*

Something caught her eye. She took a deep breath, plucked the black cowboy hat from the rack and held it out to him in one last attempt to get him to come into her world, to see it all through her eyes.

"Here, try this on."

Now and Zen was not like the other stores, but funky, laid-back, a place that encouraged the bohemian.

The whole atmosphere in the store said, *Have fun!*

He looked at her, shook his head, she thought in refusal. But then he said, "If I try that on, I get to pick something for you to try on."

She felt the thrill of his surrender. So, formidable as his discipline was, she could entice him to play with her!

"That's not fair," Molly said. "You can clearly see what I want you to try on, but you're asking me for carte blanche. I mean you could pick a bikini!"

"Did you see one?" he asked with such unabashed hopefulness that she laughed. It confirmed he did have a playful side. And she fully intended to coax it to the surface, even if she had to wear a bikini to do it.

Besides, the temptation to see him in the hat—as the gunslinger—proved too great to resist, even at the risk that he might turn up a bikini!

"Okay," she said. "If you try this on, I'll try something on that you pick."

"Anything?" He grinned wickedly.

There was that grin again, without defenses, the kind of smile that could melt a heart.

And show a woman a soul.

He took the hat from her.

"Anything," she said. The word took on new meaning as he set the hat on his head. It didn't look corny, it didn't even look like he was playing dress-up. He adjusted it, pulled the brim low over his brow. His eyes were shaded, sexy, silver.

She felt her mouth go dry. *Anything.* She had known that something else lurked between that oh so confident and composed exterior. Something dangerous. Something completely untamed. Could those things coexist with the better man that she was determined to see?

Or maybe what was dangerous and untamed was in her. In every woman, somewhere. Something that made a prim schoolteacher say to an outlaw, *anything. Anywhere.*

"My turn," he said, and disappeared down the rows. While he looked she looked some more, too. And came up with a black leather vest.

He appeared at her side, a hanger in his hand.

A feather boa dangled from it, an impossible and exotic blend of colors.

"There's Baldy's missing feathers!" she exclaimed.

"Baldy?"

"My budgie. With hardly any feathers. His name is Baldy." It was small talk. Nothing more. Why did it feel as if she was opening up her personal life, her world, to him?

"What happened to his feathers?"

"Stolen to make a boa. Kidding." She flung the boa dramatically around her neck. "I don't know what happened to his feathers. He was like that when I got him. If I didn't take him…" She slid her finger dramatically over her throat.

"You saved him," he said softly, but there was suspicion in his eyes, worthy of a gunslinger, *don't even think it about me.*

No sense letting on she already was!

"It was worth it. He's truly a hilarious little character, full of personality. People would be amazed by how loving he is."

This could only happen to her: standing in the middle of a crazy store, a boa around her neck, discussing a bald budgie with a glorious man with eyes that saw something about her that it felt like no one had ever seen before.

And somehow the word *love* had slipped into the conversation.

Molly took the boa in her hand and spun the long tail of it, deliberately moving away from a moment that was somehow too intense, more real than what she was ready for.

He stood back, studied her, nodded his approval. "You could wear it to work," he decided, taking the hint that something too intense—though delightful—had just passed between them.

"Depending where I worked!"

"Hey, if you can wear a wedding gown, you can wear that."

"I think not. Second Chances is all about image now!"

"Are you saying that in a good way?"

"Don't take it as I'm backing down on Prom Dreams, but yes, I suppose I could warm to the bigger picture at the office. Don't get bigheaded about it."

"It's just the hat that's making you make comments about my head size. I know it."

She handed him the vest. "This goes with it."

"Uh-uh," he said. "No freebies. If I try on something else, I get to pick something else for you."

"You didn't bring me a bikini, so I'll try to trust you."

"I couldn't find one, but I'll keep looking."

He slipped on the vest. She drew in her breath at the picture he was forming. Rather than looking funny, he looked coolly remote, as if he was stepping back in time, a man who could handle himself in difficult circumstances, who would step toward difficulty rather than away.

He turned away from her, went searching again, came back just as she was pulling faded jeans from a hanger.

He had a huge pair of pink glass clip-on earrings.

"Those look like chandeliers. Besides, pink looks terrible with my hair."

"Ah, well, I'm not that fond of what the hat is doing to mine, either."

She handed him the jeans.

"You're asking for it, lady. That means I have one more choice, too."

"You can't do any worse than these earrings! My ears are growing by the second."

His eyes fastened on her ears. For a moment it felt as if the air went out of the room. He hadn't touched her. He hadn't even leaned closer. How could she possibly have felt the heat of his lips on the tender flesh of her earlobe?

He spun away, headed across the store for one of the

change rooms. She saw him stop and speak to Peggy for a moment, and then he disappeared into a change room.

Moments later, Peggy approached her with something. She held it out to Molly, reverently, across two arms. "He said he picks this," she said, wide-eyed, and then in a lower tone, "that man is hotter than Hades, Molly."

Peggy put her in the change room beside his. The dress fit her like a snakeskin. It dipped so low in the front V and an equally astonishing one at the back, that she had to take it off, remove her shoes and her underwear to do the dress justice. She put it back on and the lines between where she ended and the dress began were erased.

Now, that spectacular dress did her justice. It looked, not as if she was in a funky secondhand store, but ready to walk the red carpet. Molly recognized the intense over-the-top sensuality of the dress and tried to hide it by putting the feather boa back on.

It didn't work.

She peeked out of the dressing room, suddenly shy.

"All the way out," he said. He was standing there in his jeans and vest and hat, looking as dangerous as a gunslinger at high noon.

She stepped out, faked a confidence she wasn't feeling by setting a hand on the hip she cocked at him and flinging the boa over her shoulder.

His eyes widened.

She liked the look in them so much she turned around and let him see the dipping back V of the dress, that ended sinfully just short of showing her own dimples.

She glanced over her shoulder to see his reaction.

She tried to duck back into the change room, but his hand fell, with exquisite strength, on her shoulder. She froze and then turned slowly to face him.

"I do declare, miss, I thought you were a school-marm," he drawled, obviously playing with the outfit she had him in. Isn't this what she'd wanted? To get the walls down? To find the playful side of him? For them to connect?

But if his words were playful, the light in his eyes was anything but. How could he do this? How could he act as if he'd had a front row seat to her secret fantasy about him all the time? Well, she'd asked for it by handing him that hat!

"And I thought you were just an ordinary country gentleman," she cooed, playing along, *loving* this more than a woman should. "But you're not, are you?"

He cocked his head at her.

"An outlaw," she whispered. *Stealing unsuspecting hearts.*

She saw the barest of flinches when she said that, as if she had struck a nerve, as if there was something real in this little game they were playing. She was aware that he was backing away from her, not physically, but the smooth curtain coming down over his amazing eyes.

Again she had a sense, a niggle of a feeling, *there is something about this man that he does not want you to know.*

She was aware she should pay attention to that feeling.

One of the girls turned up the music that played over the store's system. It was not classical, something raunchy and offbeat, so instead of paying attention to that feeling, Molly wanted to lift her hands over her head and sway to it, invite him deeper into the game.

"Would you care to dance?" she asked, not wanting him to back away, not wanting that at all, not really caring who he was, but wanting to be who she really was, finally. Unafraid. Molly held her breath, waiting for his answer.

For a long moment—forever, while her heart stopped beating—he stood there, frozen to the spot. His struggle was clear in his eyes. He knew it wasn't professional. He knew they were crossing some line. He knew they were dancing with danger.

Then slowly, he held up his right hand in a gesture that could have been equally surrender or an invitation to put her hand there, in his.

She read it as invitation. Even though this wasn't the kind of dancing she meant, she stepped into him, slid her hand up to his. They stood there for a suspended moment, absolutely still, palm to palm. His eyes on her eyes, his breath stirring her hair. She could see his pulse beating in the hollow of his throat, she could smell his fragrance.

Then his fingers closed around hers. He rested his other hand lightly on her waist, missing the naked expanse of her back by a mere finger's width.

"The pleasure is all mine," he said. But he did not pull her closer. Instead, a stiffly formal schoolboy, ignoring the raunchy beat of the music, he danced her down the aisle of Now and Zen.

She didn't know how he managed not to hit anything in those claustrophobic aisles, because his eyes never left her face. They drank her in, as if he was memorizing her, as if he really was an outlaw, who would go away someday and could not promise he would come back.

Molly drank in the moment, savored it. The scent of him filling her nostrils, the exquisite touch of his hand on her back, the softness in his eyes as he looked down at her. She had intended to find out something about him, to nurse something about him to the surface.

Somehow her discoveries were about herself.

That she *longed* for this. To be touched. To be seen. To feel so exquisitely feminine. And cherished. To feel as if she was a mystery that someone desperately wanted to solve.

Ridiculous. They were virtually strangers. And he was her boss.

The song ended. Peggy and the other clerk applauded. His hands dropped away, and he stepped back from her. But his gaze held.

And for a moment, in his eyes, her other secret longings were revealed to Molly: babies crawling on the floor; a little boy in soccer; a young girl getting ready for prom, her father looking at her with those stern eyes, saying, *You are not wearing that.*

Molly had never had these kinds of thoughts with Chuck. She had dreamed of a wedding, yes, in detail she now saw had been excessive. A marriage? No. A vision of the future with Chuck had always eluded her.

Maybe because she had never really known what that future could feel like. Nothing in her chaotic family had given her the kind of hope she had just felt dancing down a crowded clothing aisle.

Hope for a world that tingled with liveliness, where the smallest of discoveries held the kernels of adventure, the promise that exploring another person was like exploring a strange country: exotic, full of unexpected pleasures and surprises. Beckoning. For the first time since Molly had split from Chuck she felt grateful. Not just a little bit grateful. Exceedingly.

She could have missed *this*. This single, electrifying moment of knowing.

Knowing there were things on this earth so wonderful they were beyond imagining. Knowing that there was something to this word called *love* that was more magnificent than any poem or song or piece of film had ever captured.

Love?

That word again in the space of a few minutes, not in the relatively safe context of a bald budgie this time, either.

Pull away from him, she ordered herself. He was casting a spell on her. She was forgetting she'd been hurt. She was forgetting the cynicism her childhood should have filled her with.

She was embracing the her she had glimpsed in the garden, who thought hope was a good thing.

But couldn't hope be the most dangerous thing of all?

Pull back, she ordered herself. *Molly, I mean it!* This wasn't what she had expected when she had decided to live a little more dangerously.

This was *a lot* more dangerously.

Yes, she had decided she needed to be true to herself, but this place she was going to now was a part of herself unexplored.

He was her boss, she told herself. In her eagerness to reach him, to draw him into the warmth of her world, she had crossed some line.

How did you get back to normal after something like that?

How did you go back to the office after that? How did you keep your head? How did you not be a complete pushover?

"Dior," Peggy whispered, interrupting her thoughts. "I've been saving that dress for Prom Dreams. Do you want to see the poster I'm sending out to the schools to advertise the Prom Dreams evening? It just came in."

Molly slid Houston a look. Whatever softening had happened a moment ago was gone. He was watching her, coolly waiting for her to do what she needed to do.

But she couldn't.

The mention of the probably defunct Prom Dreams should have helped Molly rally her badly sagging defenses, make her forget this nonsense about bringing him out of his lonely world, showing him the meaning of soul.

It was just too dangerous a game she was playing.

On the other hand, she could probably trust him to do what she could not! To herd things back over the line to proper, to put up the walls between them.

Outside he said to her, no doubt about who was the boss now, "Why didn't you tell her Prom Dreams has been canceled?"

He said it coolly, the remoteness back in his eyes.

She recognized this was his pattern. Show something of himself, appeal to his emotion, like at the garden, and then he would back away from it. There he had tried to hide behind the threat of a parking lot.

This time by bringing up the sore point of Prom Dreams.

He knew, just as she did, that it was safer for them to argue than to chase each other with worms, to dance down dusty aisles.

But despite the fact she knew she should balance caution with this newly awakened sense of adventure, she felt unusually brave, as if she never had to play it safe again. Of course, the formidable obstacle of his will was probably going to keep her very safe whether she wanted to be or not!

She tilted her chin at him. "Why didn't you?"

"I guess I wanted to see if you could do it."

"I can. I will if I have to. But not yet. I'm hoping for a miracle," she admitted. Because that was who she was. A girl who could look at herself in a wedding dress, even after her own dreams had been shattered, even in the face of much evidence to the contrary, a girl who could still hope for the best, hope for the miracle of love to fix everything.

And for a moment, when his guard had gone down, dancing with him, she had believed maybe she would get her miracle after all....

"A miracle," he said with a sad shake of his head. He went and opened the car door for her, and drove back to Second Chances in silence as if somehow she had disappointed him and not the other way around.

A miracle, he thought. If people could really call down such a thing, surely they would not waste that power on a prom dress. Cure world hunger. Or cancer. He was annoyed at Molly.

For not doing as he had asked her—a thinly veiled order really—and canceling Prom Dreams, at least she should have told that girl to get ready for the cancellation of it.

But more, for wheedling past his defenses. He had better things to be doing than dancing with her in a shabby store in Greenwich Village.

It was the type of experience that might make a man who knew better hope for a miracle.

But hadn't he hoped for that once?

The memory leaped over a wall that seemed to have chinks out of it that it had not had yesterday.

It was his birthday. He was about to turn fifteen. He'd been at Beebee's for months. He was living a life he could never have even dreamed for himself.

He had his own room. He had his own TV. He had his own bathroom. He had nice clothes.

And the miracle he was praying for was for his mother to call. Under that grand four-poster bed was a plain plastic bag, with everything he had owned when he came here packed in it.

Ready to go. In case his mother called. And wanted him back.

That was the miracle he had prayed for that had never come.

"I don't believe in miracles," he said to Molly, probably way more curtly than was necessary.

"That's too bad," she said sympathetically, forgiving his curtness, missing his point entirely that there was no room in the business world for dreamers. "That's really too bad.

"Why don't we call it a day?" she said brightly. "Tomorrow I'll take you to Sunshine and Lollipops, our preschool program. It's designed to assist working poor mothers, most of them single parents."

Houston Whitford contemplated that. Despite the professionalism of her delivery, he knew darn well what she was up to. She was taking down the bricks around his carefully compartmentalized world. She was *getting* to him. And she knew it. She knew it after he had chased her in the garden with that worm, danced with her.

She was having quite an impact on his legendary discipline and now she was going to try to hit him in his emotional epicenter to get her programs approved. Who could resist preschoolers, after all?

Me, he thought. She was going to try to win him over

to her point of view by going for the heart instead of the head. It was very much the romantic versus the realist.

But the truth was Houston was not the least sentimental about children. Or anything else. And yet even as he told himself that, he was aware of a feeling that he was a warrior going into battle on a completely unknown field, against a completely unknown enemy. Well, not completely. He knew what a powerful weapon her hair was on his beleaguered male senses. The touch of her skin. Now he could add dancing with her to the list of weapons in the arsenal she was so cheerfully using against him.

He rethought his plan to walk right into his fear. He might need a little time to regroup.

"Something has come up for tomorrow," he said. *It was called sanity.*

"You promised me two days," she reminded him. "I assume you are a man of honor."

More use of her arsenal. Challenging his *honor.*

"I didn't say consecutively."

She lifted an eyebrow, *knowing* the effect she was having on him, knowing she was chiseling away at his defenses.

"Friday?" he asked her.

"Friday it is."

"See you then," he said, as if he wasn't the least bit wary of what she had in store for him.

Tonight, and every other night this week, until Friday, he would hit the punching bag until the funny *yearning* that the glimpse of her world was causing in him was gone. He could force all the things he was feeling—*lonely, for one*—back into their proper compartments.

By the end of the week he would be himself again.

He'd experienced a temporary letting down of his guard, but he recognized it now as a weakness. He'd had a whole lifetime of fighting the weaknesses in himself. There was no way one day with her could change that permanently.

Sparring with Molly Michaels was just like boxing, without the bruises, of course. But as with boxing, even with day after day of practice, when it came to sparring, you could take a hair too long to resume the defensive position, and someone slipped a punch in. Rattled you. Knocked you off balance. It didn't mean you were going to lose that fight! It meant you were going to come back more aware of your defenses. More determined. Especially if the bell had rung between rounds and you had the luxury of a bit of a breather.

She wasn't going to wear him down, and he didn't care how many children she tried to use to do it.

CHAPTER SIX

HOUSTON WHITFORD congratulated himself on using his time between rounds wisely. By avoiding Molly Michaels.

And yet there really was no avoiding her. With each day at Second Chances, even as he busied himself researching, checking the new computer systems, okaying details of the renovations, there was no avoiding her influence in this place.

Molly Michaels was the sun that the moons circled around. Just as at the garden, she seemed to be the one people gravitated to with their confidences and concerns. She was warm, open and emotional.

The antithesis of what he was. But what was that they said? Opposites attract. And he could feel the pull of her even as he tried not to.

They had one very striking similarity. They both wanted their own way, and were stubborn in the pursuit of it.

Tuesday morning three letters had been waiting for him on his desk when he arrived. The recurring theme of the three letters: *Why I Want a Prom Dress.* One was on pink paper. One smelled of perfume. And he was pretty sure one was stained with tears.

Wednesday there were half a dozen.

Yesterday, twenty or so.

Today he was so terrified of the basket overflowing with those heartfelt feminine outpourings that he had bypassed his office completely! The Sunshine and Lollipops program felt as if it had to be easier to handle than those letters!

Molly was chipping away at his hardheaded jadedness without even being in the same room with him.

Today children. He didn't really have a soft spot for children, but a few days ago he would have said the same of teenage girls pleading for prom dresses!

Molly was a force to be reckoned with. Houston was fairly certain if he was going to be here for two months instead of two weeks, by the end of that time he would be laying down his cloak over mud puddles for her. He'd probably be funding Prom Dreams out of his own pocket, just as he was donating the entire office renovation, and the time and skill of his Precision Solutions team.

The trick really was not to let Molly Michaels know that her charm was managing to permeate even his closed office door! The memory of the day they had already spent together seemed to be growing more vibrant with time instead of less.

Because she was a mischievous little minx—laughter seemed to follow in her wake—and she would not hesitate to use any perceived power over him to her full advantage!

So, the trick was not to let her know. They hailed a cab when she took one look at his car and pronounced it unsuitable for the neighborhood they were going into.

As someone who had once put a rock through a judge's very upscale Cadillac, Houston should have remembered that his car, a jet black Jaguar, would be a target for the angry, the greedy and the desperate in those very poor neighborhoods.

The daycare center was a cheery spot of color on a dreary street that reminded Houston of where he'd grown up. Except for the daycare, the buildings oozed neglect and desperation. The daycare, though, had its brick front painted a cheerful yellow, a mural of sunflowers snaked up to the second floor windows.

Inside was more cheer—walls and furniture painted in bright, primary colors. They met with the staff and Houston was given an enthusiastic overview of the programs Second Chances funded.

He was impressed by the careful shepherding of the funds, but how he'd seen people react to her in the garden was repeated here.

Dealing with people was clearly her territory. He could see this aspect of Second Chances was her absolute strength. There was an attitude of love and respect toward her that even a jaundiced old businessman like him could see the value of. Money could not buy the kind of devotion that Molly inspired.

Still, aside from that, analytically, it was clear to him Molly had made a tactical error in bringing him here. He had always felt this particular program, providing care for children of working or back-to-school moms, had indisputable merit. She had nothing to prove, here.

Obviously, in her effort to show him the soul of Second Chances she was trying to find her way to his heart.

And though she made some surprising headway, the terrible truth about Houston was that other women had tried to make him feel things he had no intention of feeling, had tried to unlock the secrets of his heart.

They had not been better women than Molly, but

they had certainly been every bit as determined to make him feel something. He dated career women, female versions of himself, owned by their work, interested only in temporary diversion and companionship when it came to a relationship. Sometimes somebody wanted to change the rules partway in, thinking he should want what they had come to want: something deeper. A future. Together. Babies. Little white picket fences. Fairy tales. Forever.

Happily ever after.

He could think of very few things that were as terrifying to him. He must have made some kind of cynical sound because Molly glanced at him and smiled. There was something about that smile that made him realize she hadn't played all her cards yet.

"We're going to watch a musical presentation, and then have lunch with the children," she told him.

The children. Of course she was counting on them to bring light to his dark heart, to pave the way for older children, later, who needed prom dresses, though of course it was the *need* part that was open to question.

"Actually we could just—"

But the children were marching into the room, sending eager glances at their visitors, as excited as if they would be performing to visiting royalty.

He glared at Molly, just to let her know using the kids to try to get to him, to try to get her way, was the ultimate in cheesy. He met her gaze, and held it, to let her know that he was on to her. But before she fully got the seriousness of his stern look, several of the munchkins broke ranks and attacked her!

They flung themselves at her knees, wrapping sturdy arms around her with such force she stumbled down.

The rest of the ranks broke, like water over a dam, flowing out toward the downed Molly and around her until he couldn't even see her anymore, lost in a wriggling mass of hugs and kisses and delightful squeals of *Miss Molly!*

Was she in danger? He watched in horror as Molly's arm came up and then disappeared again under a pile of wiggling little bodies, all trying to get a hold of her, deliver messy kisses and smudgy hugs.

He debated rescuing her, but a shout of laughter—female, adult—from somewhere in there let him know somehow she was okay under all that. Delighting in it, even.

He tried to remain indifferent, but he could not help but follow the faint trail of feeling within him, trying to identify what it was.

Envious, he arrived at with surprise. Oh, not of all those children, messy little beings that they were with their dripping noses and grubby hands, but somehow envious of her spontaneity, her ability to embrace the unexpected surprise of the moment, the gifts of hugs and kisses those children were plying her with.

Her giggles came out of the pile again. And he was envious of that, too. When was the last time he had laughed like that? Let go so completely to delight. Had he ever?

Would he ever? Probably not. He had felt a tug of that feeling in the garden, and again in Now and Zen. But when had he come to see feeling good as an enemy?

Maybe that's what happened when you shut down *feeling:* good and bad were both taken from you, the mind unable to distinguish.

Finally she extricated herself and stood up, though

every one of her fingers and both her knees were claimed by small hands.

The businesswoman of this morning was erased. In her place was a woman with hair all over the place, her clothes smudged, one shoe missing, a nylon ruined.

And he had never, ever seen a woman so beautiful.

The jury was still out on whether she would make a good replacement for Miss Viv. So how could he know, he who avoided that particular entanglement the most—how could he know, so instantly, without a doubt, what a good mother Molly would make with her loving heart, and her laughter filled and spontaneous spirit?

And why did that thought squeeze his chest so hard for a moment he could not breathe?

Because of the cad who had made her suffer by letting her go, by stealing her dreams from her.

No, that was too altruistic. It wasn't about her. It was about him. He could feel something from the past looming over him, waiting to pounce.

As Molly rejoined him, Houston focused all his attention on the little messy ones trying so hard to form perfect ranks on a makeshift stage. It was painfully obvious these would be among the city's neediest children. Some were in old clothes, meticulously cared for. Others were not so well cared for. Some looked rested and eager, others looked strangely tired, dejected.

With a shiver, he knew exactly which ones lay awake with wide eyes in the night, frightened of being left alone, or of the noises coming from outside or the next rooms. He looked longingly for the exit, but Molly, alarmingly intuitive, seemed to sense his desire to run for the door.

"They've been practicing for us!" she hissed at him, and he ordered himself to brace up, to face what he feared.

But why would he fear a small bunch of enthusiastic if ragamuffin children? He seated himself reluctantly
in terribly uncomfortable tiny chairs, the cramped space
ringing with children's shouts and shrieks, laughter. At
the count of three the clamor of too enthusiastically
played percussion instruments filled the room.

Houston winced from the racket, stole a glance at
Molly and felt the horrible squeeze in his chest again.
What was that about?

She was enchanted. Clapping, singing along, calling
out encouragement. He looked at the children. Those
children were playing just for her now. She was
probably the mother each of them longed for: engaged,
fully present to them, appreciative of their enthusiasm
if not their musical talent.

And then he knew what it was about, the squeezing
in his chest.

*He remembered a little boy in ragged jeans, not the
meticulously kept kind, at a school Christmas concert.
He had been given such an important job. He was to put
the baby Jesus in the manger at the very end of the performance. He kept pulling back the curtain. Knowing his
dad would never come. But please, Mommy, please.*

*Hope turning to dust inside his heart as each moment
passed, as each song finished and she did not enter the
big crowded room. His big moment came and that little
boy, the young Houston, took that doll that represented
the baby Jesus and did not put him in the waiting crib.
Instead, he threw it with all his might at all the parents
who had come. The night was wrecked for him, he
wanted to wreck it for everybody else.*

Houston felt a cold shadow fall over him. He glanced
at Molly, still entranced. He didn't care to know what a

good mother she would be. It hurt him in some way. It made him feel as he had felt at the Christmas play that night. Like he wanted to destroy something.

Instead, he slipped his BlackBerry out of his pocket, scanned his e-mails. The Bradbury papers, nothing to do with Second Chances—all about his other life—had just been signed. It was a deal that would mean a million and a half dollars to his company. Yesterday that would have thrilled him. Filled him.

Yesterday, before he had heard her laughter emerge from under a pile of children, and instantly and without his permission started redefining everything that was important about his life.

He shook off that feeling of having glimpsed something really important—maybe the only thing that was important—he shook it off the same way he shook off a punch that rattled him nearly right off his feet. Deliberately he turned his attention to the small piece of electronics that fit in the palm of his hand.

Houston Whitford opened the next e-mail. The Chardon account was looking good, too.

Molly congratulated herself on the timing of their arrival at the daycare program. The concert had been a delight of crashing cymbals, clicking sticks, wildly jangling triangles. Now it was snack time for the members of the rhythm section, three and four year olds.

They were so irresistible! They were fighting for her hands, and she gave in, allowed herself to be tugged toward the kitchen.

She glanced back at Houston. He was trailing behind. How could he be looking at his BlackBerry? Was she failing to enchant him, failing to make him *see?*

Well, there was still time with her small army of charmers, and Molly had never seen a more delightful snack. She felt a swell of pride that Second Chances provided the funding so that these little ones could get something healthy into them at least once a day.

Healthy but fun. The snack was so messy that the two long tables were covered in plastic, and the children, about ten at each long, low table, soon had bibs fashioned out of plastic grocery bags over their clothes.

On each table were large plastic bowls containing thinly cut vegetables—red and green peppers, celery, carrots—interspersed with dips bowls mounded with salad dressing.

The children were soon creating their own snacks—plunging the veggies first into the dressing, and then rolling the coated veggie on flat trays that held layers of sunflower seeds, poppy seeds, raisins.

Though most of the children were spotlessly clean beneath those bibs and the girls all had hairdos that spoke of tender loving care, their clothes were often worn, some pairs of jeans patched many times. The shoes told the real story—worn through, frayed, broken laces tied in knots, vibrant colors long since faded.

Molly couldn't help but glance at Houston's shoes. Chuck had been a shoe aficionado. He'd shown her a pair on the Internet once that he thought might make a lovely gift from her. A Testoni Norvegese—at about fifteen hundred dollars a pop!

Was that what Houston was wearing? If not, it was certainly something in the same league. What hope did she have of convincing him of the immeasurable good in these small projects when his world was obviously so far removed from this he couldn't even comprehend it?

She had to get him out of the BlackBerry! She wished she had a little dirt to throw on those shoes, to coax the happiness out of him. She had to make him *see* what was important. This little daycare was just a microcosm of everything Second Chances did. If he could feel the love, even for a second, everything would change. Molly knew it.

"Houston, I saved you a seat," she called, patting the tiny chair beside her.

He glanced over, looked aghast, looked longingly— and not for the first time—at the exit door. And then a look came over his face—not of a man joining pre-schoolers for snack—but of a warrior striding toward battle, a gladiator into the ring.

The children became quite quiet, watching him.

If he knew his suit was in danger, he never let on. Without any hesitation at all, he pulled up the teeny chair beside Molly, hung his jacket over the back of it— not even out of range of the fingers, despite the subtle Giorgio Armani label revealed in the back of it—and plunked himself down.

The children eyed him with wide-eyed surprise, silent and shy.

Children, Molly told herself, were not charmed by the same things as adults. They did not care about his watch or his shoes, the label in the back of that jacket.

Show me who you really are.

She passed him a red pepper, a silly thing to expect to show you a person. He looked at it, looked at her, seemed to be deciding something. She was only aware of how tense he had been when she saw his shoulders shift slightly, saw the corners of his mouth relax.

Ignoring the children who were gawking at him,

Houston picked up a slice of red pepper and studied it. "What should I do with this?"

"Put stuff on it!"

He followed the instructions he could understand, until the original red pepper was not visible any longer but coated and double coated with toppings.

Finally he could delay the moment of truth no longer. But he did not bite into his own crazy creation.

Instead, he held it out, an inch from Molly's lips. "My lady," he said smoothly. "You first."

Something shivered in her. How could this be? Surrounded by squealing children, suddenly everything faded. It was a moment she'd imagined in her weaker times. Was there anything more romantic than eating from another's hand?

Somehow that simple act of sharing food was the epitome of trust and connection.

She had wanted to bring him out of himself, and instead he was turning the tables on her!

Molly leaned forward and bit into the raisin-encrusted red pepper. She had to close her eyes against the pleasure of what she tasted.

"Ambrosia," she declared, and opened her eyes to see him looking at her with understandable quizzicalness.

"My turn!" She loaded a piece of celery with every ingredient on the table.

"I hate celery," he said when she held it up to him.

"You're setting an example!" she warned him.

He cast his eyes around the table, looked momentarily rebellious, then nipped the piece of celery out of her fingers with his teeth.

Way too easy to imagine this same scenario in very different circumstances. Maybe he could, too, because his silver-shaded eyes took on a smoky look that was unmistakably sensual.

How could this be happening? Time standing still, something in her heart going crazy, in the middle of the situation least like any romantic scenario she had ever imagined, and Molly was guilty of imagining many of them!

But then that moment was gone as the children raced each other creating concoctions for their honored guests. As when his shoulders had relaxed, now Molly noticed another layer of some finally held tension leaving him as he surrendered to the children, and to the moment.

They were calling orders to him, the commands quick and thick. "Dunk it." "Roll it." "Put stuff on it! Like this!"

One of the bolder older boys got up and pressed right in beside Houston. He anchored himself—one sticky little hand right on the suit jacket hanging on the back of the chair—and leaned forward. He held out the offering—a carrot dripping with dressing and seeds—to Houston. Some of it appeared to plop onto those beautiful shoes.

Molly could see a greasy print across the shoulder lining of the jacket.

A man who owned a suit like that was not going to be impressed with its destruction, not able to see *soul* through all this!

But Houston didn't seem to care that his clothes were getting wrecked. He wasn't backing away. After his initial horror in the children, he seemed to be easing up a little. He didn't even make an attempt to move the jacket out of harm's way.

In fact he looked faintly pleased as he took the carrot that had been offered and chomped on it thoughtfully.

"Excellent," he proclaimed.

After that any remaining shyness from the children dissolved. Houston selected another carrot, globbed dressing on it and hesitated over his finishing choices.

The children yelled out suggestions, and he listened and obeyed each one until that carrot was so coated in stuff that it was no longer recognizable. He popped the whole concoction in his mouth. He closed his eyes, chewed very slowly and then sighed.

"Delicious," he exclaimed.

Molly stared at him, aware of the shift happening in her. It was different than when they had chased each other in the garden, it was different than when they had danced and she was entranced.

Beyond the sternness of his demeanor, she saw someone capable of exquisite tenderness, an amazing ability to be sensitive. Even sweet.

Molly was sure if he knew that—that she could see tender sweetness in him—he would withdraw instantly. So she looked away, but then, was compelled to look back. She felt like someone who had been drinking brackish water their entire life, and who had suddenly tasted something clear and pure instead.

The little girl beside Houston, wide-eyed and silent, held up her celery stick to him—half-chewed, sloppy with dressing and seeds—plainly an offering. He took it with grave politeness, popped it in his moth, repeated the exaggerated sigh of enjoyment.

"Thank you, princess."

Her eyes grew wider. "Me princess," she said, mulling

it over gravely. And then she smiled, her smile radiant and adoring.

Children, of course, saw through veneers so much easier than adults did!

I am allowing myself to be charmed, Molly warned herself sternly. And of course, it was even more potent because Houston was not trying to charm anyone, slipping into this role as naturally and unselfconsciously as if he'd been born to play it.

But damn it, who wouldn't be charmed, seeing that self-assured man give himself over to those children?

I could love him. Molly was stunned as the renegade thought blasted through her brain.

Stop it, she ordered herself. She was here to achieve a goal.

She wanted him to acknowledge there was the potential for joy anywhere, in any circumstance at all. Bringing that shining moment to people who had had too few of them was the soul of Second Chances. It was what they did so well.

But all of that, all her motives, were fading so quickly as she continued to *see* something about Houston Whitford that made her feel weak with longing.

He couldn't keep up with children hand-making him tidbits. In minutes he had every child in the room demanding his attention. He solemnly accepted the offerings, treated each as if it was a culinary adventure from the five-star restaurant he was dressed for.

He began to really let loose—something Molly sensed was very rare in this extremely controlled man. He began to narrate his culinary adventure, causing spasms of laughter from the children, and from her.

He did Bugs Bunny impressions. He asked for

recipes. He used words she would have to look up in the dictionary.

And then he laughed.

Just like he had laughed in the garden. It was possibly the richest sound she had ever heard, deep, genuine, true.

She thought of all the times she had convinced Chuck to do "fun" things with her, the thing she deemed an in-love couple should do that week. Roller-skating, bike riding, days on the beaches of Long Island, a skiing holiday in Vermont. Usually paid for by her of course, and falling desperately short of her expectations.

Always, she had so carefully set up the picture, trying to make herself feel some kind of magic that had been promised to her in songs, and in movies and in storybooks.

Molly had tried so hard to manufacture the exact feeling she was experiencing in this moment. She had thought if she managed this outing correctly she would show Houston Whitford the real Second Chances.

What she had not expected was to see Houston Whitford so clearly, to see how a human being could shine.

What if this was what was most real about him? What if this was him, this man who was so unexpectedly full of laughter and light around these children?

What if he was one of those rare men who were made to be daddies? Funny, playful, able to fully engage with children?

"I told you, you don't laugh enough," she whispered to him.

"Ah, Miss Molly, it's hard for me to admit you might be right." And then he smiled at her, and it seemed as if the whole world faded and it was just the two of them in this room, sharing something deep and splendid.

Molly found herself wanting to capture these

moments, to hold them, to keep them. She remembered the camera he had given her, took it out and clicked as he took a very mashed celery stick from a child.

"The best yet," she heard him say. "To die for. But I can't eat another bite. Not one."

But he took one more anyway, and then he closed his eyes, and patted his flat belly, pretending to push it out against his hand. The children howled with laughter. She took another picture, and Molly laughed, too, at his antics, but underneath her laughter was a growing awareness.

She had thought bringing Houston to her projects would show her the real Houston Whitford. And that was true.

Unfortunately, if this laughing carefree man was the real Houston, it made her new boss even more attractive, not less! It made her way too aware of the Molly that had never been put behind her after all—the Molly who yearned and longed, and ultimately *believed*.

"Will you stay for story time?"

No. Nothing that ended happily-ever-after! Please! She suddenly wanted to get him out of here. Felt as if something about her plot to win his heart was backfiring badly. She had wanted to win him over for Second Chances! Not for herself.

He was winning her heart instead of her winning his, and it had not a single thing to do with Second Chances.

"Not possible," Molly said, quickly, urgently. "Sorry."

It wasn't on the schedule to stay, thank goodness, but even before the children started begging him, it seemed every one of them tugging on some part of him to get him up off the floor, his eyes met Molly's and she knew they weren't going anywhere.

With handprints and food stains all over the pristine

white of that shirt, Houston allowed himself to be dragged to the sinks, where he obediently washed his own hands, and then one by one helped each of the children wash theirs.

After he washed "Princess's" face, the same child who had sat beside him at snack, she crooked her finger at him. He bent down, obviously thinking, as Molly did, that the tiny tot had some important secret to tell him.

Instead she kissed him noisily on his cheek.

Molly held out the camera, framed the exquisite moment. *Click.*

He straightened slowly, blushing wildly.

Click. She found herself hoping that she was an accomplished enough photographer to capture that look on his face.

"Did you turn me into a prince, little princess?" Houston asked.

The girl regarded him solemnly. "No."

But that's not how Molly felt, at all. A man she had been determined to see as a toad had turned into a prince before her eyes.

Again she realized that this excursion was not telling her as much about Houston Whitford as it was telling her about herself.

She wanted the things she had always wanted, more desperately than ever.

And that sense of desperation only grew as Molly watched as Houston, captive now, like Gulliver in the land of little people, was led over to the story area. He chose to sit on the floor, all the children crowding around him. By the time they were settled each of those children seemed to have claimed some small part of him, to touch, even if it was just the exquisitely crafted soft leather of his shoe. His "little princess" crawled into his lap, plopped her thumb in her mouth and promptly went to sleep.

Molly could not have said what one of those stories was about by the time they left a half hour later, Houston handing over the still sleeping child.

As she watched him, she was in the grip of a tenderness so acute it felt as if her throat was closing.

Molly was stunned. The thing she had been trying to avoid because she knew how badly it would weaken her—was exactly what she had been brought.

She was seeing Houston Whitford in the context of family. Watching him, she *felt* his strength, his protectiveness, his *heart*.

She had waited her whole life to feel this exquisite tenderness for another person.

It was all wrong. There was no candlelight. It smelled suspiciously like the little girl might have had an accident in her sleep.

Love was supposed to come first. And then these moments of glory.

What did it mean? That she had experienced such a moment for Houston? Did it mean love would come next? That she could fall in love with this complicated man who was her boss?

No, that was exactly what she was not doing! No more wishing, dreaming! Being held prisoner by fantasies.

No more.

But as she looked at him handing over that sleeping little girl, it felt like she was being blinded by the light in him, drawn to the power and warmth of it.

Moth to flame, Molly chastised herself ineffectively.

"Sorry she's so clingy," the daycare staff member

who relieved him of her said. "She's going through a rough time, poor mite. Her mother hasn't been around for a few days. Her granny is picking her up."

And just like that, the light she had seen in his face snapped off, replaced by something as cold as the other light had been warm.

Selfishly, Molly wanted to see only the warmth, especially once it was gone. She wanted to draw it back out of him. Would it seem just as real outside as it had in? Maybe she had just imagined it. She had to know.

She had to test herself against this fierce new challenge.

As they waited for a cab on the sidewalk, he seemed coolly remote. The electronic device was back out. She remembered this from yesterday. He came forward, and then he retreated.

"You were a hit with those kids." She tried to get him back to the man she had seen at lunch.

He snorted with self-derision, didn't look up. "Starving for male attention."

"I can see you as a wonderful daddy someday," she said.

He looked up then, gave her his full attention, a look that was withering.

"The last thing I would ever want to be is a daddy," he said.

"But why?"

"Because there is quite a bit more to it than carrot sticks and storybooks."

"Yes?"

"Like being there. Day in and day out. Putting another person first forever. Do I look like the kind of guy who puts other people first?"

"You did in there."

"Well, I'm not."

"You seem angry."

"No kidding."

"Houston, what's wrong?"

"There's a little girl in there whose mom has abandoned her. How does something like that happen? How could anybody not love her? Not want her? How could anybody who had a beautiful child like that not devote their entire life to protecting her and making her safe and happy?"

"An excellent daddy," she said softly.

"No, I wouldn't," he said, coldly angry. "Can you wait for the cab yourself? I just thought of something I need to do."

And he left, walking down the street, fearless, as though that fancy watch and those shoes didn't make him a target.

Look at the way he walked. He was no target. No victim.

She debated calling after him that she had other things on the agenda for today. But she didn't. This was his pattern. She recognized it clearly now.

He felt something. Then he tried to walk away, tried to reerect his barriers, his formidable defenses, against it.

Why? What had happened to him that made a world alone seem so preferable to one shared?

"Wait," she called. "I'll walk with you."

And he turned and watched her come toward him, waited, almost as if he was relieved that he was not going to carry some of the burden he carried alone.

CHAPTER SEVEN

HOUSTON watched Molly walking fast to catch up with him. The truth was all he wanted was an hour or so on his punching bag. Though maybe he waited, instead of continuing to walk, because the punching bag had not done him nearly the good he had hoped it would last night. Now it felt as if it was the only place to defuse his fury.

That beautiful little girl's mother didn't want her. He knew he was kidding himself that his anger was at *her* mother.

From the moment he'd heard Molly laughing from under the pile of children a powerless longing for something he was never going to have had pulled at him.

You thought you left something behind you, but you never quite left that. The longing for the love of a mother.

The love of his mother. She was dead now. He'd hired a private detective a few years back to find her. Somehow he had known she was dead. Because he'd always thought she would come back. He would have left Beebee's world in a minute if his mother had loved him and needed him.

It had been a temporary relief when the private eye had told him. Drugs. An overdose.

Death. The only reasonable explanation for a mother who had never looked back. Except, as the P.I. filled in the dates and details, it wasn't the explanation he'd been seeking after all. She'd died only a few years before he made the inquiries about her—plenty of time to check in on her son if she had wanted to.

She hadn't.

And he was powerless over that, too.

There was nothing a man of action like Houston hated so much as that word. *Powerless.*

Molly came and walked beside him. He deliberately walked fast enough to keep her a little breathless; he knew intuitively she would have a woman's desire to *talk,* to probe his wounds.

He could feel his anger dispersing as they left the edgier part of the Lower East Side and headed back to where Second Chances was in the East Village.

"This is where I live," she said as they came to a well-kept five-story brownstone. "Do you want to stop for a minute? Meet Baldy? Have a coffee?"

She obviously intended to pursue this thing. His *feelings.* He was not going to meet her bird, enter her personal space and have a coffee with her!

On the other hand, the punching bag had not been working its normal magic. He hesitated. And she read that as a yes. In the blink of an eye she was at the door with her key out.

He still had a chance to back away, but for some reason he didn't. In fact, he ordered himself to keep walking, to call after her, *Maybe some other time.* But he didn't.

Instead, feeling oddly *powerless* again, as if she might have something he was looking for, he followed her up the three flights of stairs to her apartment.

"Close it quick," she said, as he came through the door behind her. "Baldy."

And sure enough out of the darkness of the apartment a tiny missile flew at them, a piece of flesh-colored putty with naked wings. It landed on her shoulder, pecked at her ear, turned and gave him a baleful look.

"Good grief," he said, but he was already glad he had come. The bird was so ugly he was cute. The tiny being's obvious adoration for Molly lightened something in Houston's mood. "ET call home!"

Still, there was something about that bird, looking as if it, too, would protect her to the death, that tugged at a heart that had just faced one too many challenges today.

The bird rode on her shoulder as she guided him into the apartment which looked to be all of five hundred square feet of pure feminine coziness.

The bird kissed her cheek and made a whimpering noise that was near human. She absently stroked his featherless body with a tender finger. The bird preened.

"Just have a seat," she said. "I'll make coffee."

But he didn't have a seat. Instead he questioned his sanity for coming in here. He studied the framed poster of a balloon rising over the Napa Valley in California. He turned away from it. How was it her humble five hundred square feet felt like *home* in a way he had never quite managed to achieve?

It must be the fresh flowers on the coffee table between the two sofas.

"Nice flowers," he heard himself say.

"Oh, I treat myself," she called from the kitchen. "There's a vendor on the way home from work."

He went and stood in the doorway of her tiny kitchen, watched her work.

"No boyfriend buying you flowers?"

That's exactly why it had been a mistake to accept her invitation into her personal space. This was going too far. He'd chased her with a worm. And danced with her. He'd felt the exquisite plumpness of her lip on his finger when he'd fed her from his hand. Now he was in her house.

In high school, he scoffed at himself, that might count as a relationship. But for a mature man?

"Believe me," she muttered, "the boyfriend I had never bought me flowers."

"Really?" he said, and some of his dismay at that must have come through in his tone. What kind of cad wouldn't buy her flowers? He would buy her flowers if he was her boyfriend.

Now that was a dangerous side road his mind had just gone down!

Her tongue was caught between her teeth as she concentrated on putting coffee things on a tray. She pressed by him in the narrow doorway, set the tray on the coffee table by the flowers.

It all looked very cozy. He went and sat down.

She poured coffee. "He was more than my boyfriend. My fiancé."

"Ah." He took a generous gulp of coffee, burned his mouth, set it down and glared at it.

She took a tiny sip of hers. "His name was Chuck. We were supposed to get married and live happily ever after. Instead, he emptied my bank account and went to live on a beach in Costa Rica. That's what finished me for being a romantic."

Why was she telling him this? He got it very suddenly. They were going to share confidences.

"Now I see it as a good thing," she said. "It got me ready for you."

He stared.

"Hardened me," she declared. "So that I'm not a romantic anymore. So that I can handle all the changes at work."

And he wasn't aware he had stopped breathing until he started again. For a suspended moment in time, he had thought she was going to say losing her fiancé had freed her to love him. What would give him such a notion?

Still, it was very hard not to laugh at her declaration that she was *hardened*. "But there's such a thing as being too hard," she went on.

"I guess there is," he agreed warily.

"I'd like you to trust me. Tell me why the situation at the daycare with the little girl and her mother made you so angry today?"

Her perception—the feeling that she could see what he least wanted to be seen—was frightening.

What was even more frightening was the temptation that clawed at his throat. To take off all the armor, and lay it at her feet. Tell her all of it. But the words stuck.

"When I was little," she told him, still thinking it was a confidences exchange, "my mom and dad fought all the time. And I dreamed of belonging to a family where everyone loved each other."

"Ah," he said, unforthcoming.

"Do you think such a family exists?"

"Honestly? No."

"You're very cynical about families, Houston. Why?"

She wanted to know? Okay, he'd tell her. She probably wasn't going to be nearly as happy to know about him as she thought she was going to be!

"Because I grew up in one just like yours. Constant fighting. Drama. Chaos. Actually it would probably make yours look like something off a Christmas card. And it made me feel the opposite of you. Not a longing for love. An allergy to it."

"Isn't that lonely?"

He didn't answer for a long time. "Maybe," he finally said. "But not as lonely as waiting for something that never happens. That's the loneliest."

"What did you wait for that never happened?"

This was what he had come here for. For her to coax this out of him.

He was silent.

"Trust me," she said quietly.

And he could not resist her. Even though he pitted his whole strength against it, he heard himself say, his voice a low growl of remembered pain, "Once, when I was quite small, I was in a Christmas concert."

And somehow he told her all of it. And with every single word it felt like a chain that had been wrapped hard around his heart was breaking apart, link by link.

Somehow, when he was finished, she had moved from the couch across from him to the place right beside him. Her hand was in his. And she was silent for the longest time.

"But why didn't she come?" she finally asked.

"I don't know," he said. "I don't remember."

"Was it just that once that she didn't come?"

Here she was dragging more out of him.

"No, it was all the time."

"Because she couldn't care about anybody but herself," Molly said sadly. "Did you think it was about you?"

As she spoke those words Houston knew a truth he

did not want to know. Of course he had thought it was about him.

It was not his father he had never forgiven. Not entirely.

Somewhere in him, he had always thought the truth was that he was a person no one could care about. Not if tested. Not over time. If his own mother had found him unworthy of love, that was probably the truth.

It was not his mother he had not forgiven, either.

It was himself he had never forgiven. For not being worthy of love. For not being a person that his mother and father could have at least tried to hold it all together for.

Molly reached up and guided his hand to her face. It was wet with her tears. It was such a tender powerful gesture, without words.

Something in him surrendered. He allowed himself to feel something he had not felt for a very long time. At home. As if he belonged. As if finally, in this world, there was one place, one person who could accept him for what he was.

He contemplated the temptation to tell her more, not sure if a man could put things back the way they used to be after he had experienced such a thing as this.

And it felt like a weakness that he could not fight and that he was not sure if he wanted to.

Damn it, he wanted to. He could not give in to this.

But then, his hand that rested on the wetness of her cheek went, it seemed of its own volition, to the puffiness of her lip. He traced the fullness of it with his thumb, took in the wideness of her eyes, the gentle puff of her breath touching his thumb.

I'm going to kiss her, he thought, entranced. Dismayed.

He snapped back from her, dropped his hand from the full and exquisite temptation of her lips.

But she wasn't having it. When he pulled away, she stretched forward. She had clearly seen what he would have loved to have kept hidden. In every sense.

Her lips grazed his. Tender. Soft. Supple.

Sexy.

It took every ounce of his considerable discipline to pull away from her. He got to his feet, abruptly, aware if he stayed on that couch with her he was not going to be fully in control of what happened next.

"That shouldn't have happened," he said gruffly.

"Why?" she said softly.

She knew why. She knew she was crashing through his barriers faster than he could rebuild them.

"It was inappropriate. I apologize."

"I think it was me who kissed you. And I'm not apologizing."

"Molly, you have no idea what you are playing with," he told her softly, sternly.

"Maybe I do."

As if she saw him more clearly than he saw himself! Just because he had told her one thing. He didn't like it that he had told her that. That brief moment of feeling unburdened, not so damned lonely, was swiftly changing to regret.

"I have work to do," he said, hardened himself to what these moments had made him feel, turned and walked away, shutting the door firmly behind him.

But he didn't go back to Second Chances, despite his claim he had work to do. He also had no work at home, not even his laptop. He didn't even feel compelled to check his BlackBerry. Life could go on without him for one evening.

He was sitting out on his terrace, overlooking Central Park.

The terrace was as beautifully furnished as his apartment, dark rattan furniture with deep white cushions, plants flowering in a glorious abundance of color under the new warmth of the spring sun.

Houston was sipping a glass of wine, a Romanée-Conti from the Burgundy region of France. The wine was so rare and sought after it had to be purchased in boxes that contained a dozen bottles of wine, only one the coveted Romanée-Conti, the other eleven from other domains.

For as spectacular as the wine was, it occurred to him this was the kind of wine that seemed as if it would lend itself to romance.

Over the sounds of the traffic, he could hear the pleasant *clip clop* of the hooves of a horse pulling a carriage.

For the second time—unusual since Houston was not a man given to romantic thoughts—his mind turned to romance. He wondered if young lovers, or honeymooners, in New York for the first time—were riding in that carriage.

He wondered if they were full of hope and optimism, were enjoying the spring evening, snuggled under a blanket, the world looking brighter because they were seeing it through that lens of love. He resisted an impulse to go give them the remainder of that exquisite bottle of wine.

Houston realized, not happily, that he felt lonely. That the merest touch of Molly's lips had unleashed something terrifying in him.

He realized, too, that he usually kept his life crammed full enough that he could avoid feelings like that—a sudden longing to share a moment like this one with someone else.

Molly Michaels if he wanted to get specific. The truth was they had shared some moments that had forged an instant sense of bonding, of intimacy. It was hard to leave it behind. That was all. It was natural to feel this way.

But it wasn't natural for *him* to feel this way.

He realized he still had Molly's camera in his pocket, and he took it out, scanned idly through the pictures.

He stopped at the one where *Princess* was kissing his cheek.

Something had changed for him, Houston acknowledged, in that exact moment. Because at that moment, he had surprised himself. He had surprised himself by so clearly seeing—no, not just seeing, *knowing*—the need in those children. But the biggest surprise had come when he had embraced that need instead of walking—no, running—away from it.

Everything had become personal after that.

It hadn't been about helping out Beebee and Miss Viv anymore, doing his civic duty, get in, get out, goodbye.

Those kids in that daycare, wistful for the fathers and mothers they didn't have, had hurt him, reminded him of things long buried, which made the fact he'd embraced their need even more surprising to him.

They called to who he had once been, and he wondered if there was something in that self he had left behind that had value.

"I doubt it," he muttered, wanting a beer out of a bottle being a prime example. The fact that, even though he was doing nothing else tonight, he was avoiding answering the letter from his father, being another example.

Houston wished, suddenly, wearily, that he had delegated the whole Second Chances project to someone else. It was bringing things to the surface that he had been content to leave behind for a long time.

He scanned through more pictures on the camera, stopped at the one of Molly that he had taken in the garden. She was leaning on the shovel, a smudge of dirt on her cheek, her hair wild around her, her eyes laughing, the constant wariness finally, finally gone from them.

Some tension she always held around him had relaxed in that garden. The playful part that he had glimpsed the first time he had seen her—in a bridal gown at work—had come back out at the garden. And at the preschool.

People loved her. That was evident in the next picture, her in the very middle of a line of ancient grandmothers, unaware how her youth and vitality set her apart, how beautiful she looked with her head thrown back in laughter as she kicked her leg up impossibly high. And in another of her at Sunshine and Lollipops, of her laughing, unaware there was salad dressing in her hair.

Ah, well, that was the promise that had been in her eyes all along. That she could take a life that had become too damned serious and insert some fun back in it.

What would she add to an evening like this one? Would she be content to sit here, listening to spring sounds? Or would she want to be out there, part of it?

Houston thought of the taste of her lips beneath his—raindrop fresh—and felt a shiver of pure longing that he killed.

Because the bigger question was what *price* would he pay to know those things? Would it be too high?

"Ah, Houston," he said. "The question isn't whether the price you would pay would be too high. It's what price would be asked of her, and if it would be more than she was willing to pay?"

Because to satisfy his curiosity by inviting her into his life would only invite trouble. Eventually she would want things he could not give her.

Because you could not give what you did not know. What you had never known. Though he felt how disappointed Beebee would be to know that even her best efforts had not taught him the lesson she most wanted to give him. That a life well lived was rarely lived alone.

And certainly not without love.

She had really come along too late. He'd been fourteen, his life lessons already learned, his personality long since shaped.

He tossed back a wine that was meant to be savored. He did not want to even think the word *love* on the same day he had told her things he had never told another living soul.

Told her? Ha! Had it dragged out of him!

He got up abruptly, went inside, closed the French doors on the sounds of spring unfolding relentlessly all around him.

He thought of her guiding his hand to the tears slipping down her cheeks, and something happened that hadn't happened to him since he had learned his mother was dead.

A fist closed in his throat, and something stung behind his eyes.

That's what he needed to remember about love, he told himself sternly. It hurt. It hurt like hell. It could make a strong man like his father weak.

Or a strong man like him.

A man needed to approach these kinds of temptations

with a plan, with a road map of how to extricate himself from sticky situations.

And so when he saw her next, he would be coolly professional. He would take a step back from all the lines that had been crossed. He would not think of chasing her with a worm, or dancing with her, or holding her and telling her one small secret. He would not think of how it had felt to open his world just a little bit to another human being.

He steeled himself against the temptation to go those few steps down the hall to her office, just to see her, make small talk, ask about the stupid budgie.

So, when she arrived in the doorway of his office just before lunch the next day, he hardened himself to how beautiful she looked in a white linen suit, a sunshine-yellow top, her hair already doing its escape routine.

He had one more week here, and then he was never going to see her again. He could suck it up for that long.

"They finished painting my office yesterday," she said, cheerfully, as if her lips had not touched his. "The ochre isn't that bad."

"That's good." Apparently she had decided she could suck it up for that long, too. Keep it professional, talk about paint, not revisit last night. *Is that why it had taken her so long to come and see him today?*

"I was at the Suits for Success auction this morning."

As if he had asked why he hadn't seen her!

"How was it?"

"Great."

They stood on a precipice. Were they going to go deeper? Were they going to remember last night or move on?

She jumped off it.

"My bird likes you," she said, and then she smiled. "He doesn't like everybody."

Her bird liked him? Wasn't she thinking about that kiss? Had it been a sympathy kiss, then? Good grief!

"That's good." How ridiculous was it to preen slightly because her bird liked him? And didn't like just anybody? Houston fought the urge to ask her if the bird had liked Chuck, as if he could use that to judge the bird's true skill.

"I want you to know it meant a lot to me. The whole day yesterday. Letting me show you the soul of Second Chances." Her voice dropped lower. "And then showing me a bit of yours."

"I don't like pity, Molly."

"Pity?" She looked genuinely astounded, and then she laughed. "Oh, my God, Houston, I cannot think of a man who would inspire pity less than you."

And he could tell that she meant it. And that the kiss had not been about pity at all. And she was so beautiful when she laughed.

Houston knew he could not spend another day with her. She made him too vulnerable. She opened something in him that was better left closed. He could not be with her without looking at her lips and remembering.

The research portion of the job at Second Chances was done. He knew exactly what each store brought in, he knew what their staffing and overhead costs were, he'd assigned a management team to go in and help them streamline, improve their efficiency, develop marketing plans.

One week left. He could suck it up for that long if he avoided her. If he stayed in Miss Viv's newly revamped office with the door firmly shut and the Do Not Disturb sign out.

Houston Whitford had built a career on his ability to be in control.

But this week was showing him something different about himself. And that version of himself could not refuse what she was offering.

One week. There were really two ways of looking at it. He could avoid her. Or he could engage with her.

Why not give himself that?

Because it's dumb, his more reasonable self said, *like playing with fire.*

But he felt the exquisite freedom of a man who had just ripped up his plan and thrown away the map. Like he could do anything and go anywhere.

For one week.

"Do you want to go for lunch?"

Molly was beaming at him. The late morning light was playing off her hair, making the copper shimmer with flame and reminding him what it was like to play with fire, why children were drawn to sticks in campfires. Because before fire burned, it was irresistible, the temptation of what it offered wiping out any thought of consequences.

Molly didn't taste one single bite of the five-star meal she had ordered. She didn't think of Miss Viv, or Prom Dreams or what the future of Second Chances was going to look like with him as the boss.

When she left him after lunch, she felt as if she was on pins and needles waiting to see him again, *dying* to see him again. Thinking uncontrollable thoughts of how his lips had felt beneath hers.

Was he feeling it, too?

When her phone rang, and it was him, she could hear something in his voice.

"I noticed that boys' soccer team we sponsor are playing on the Great Lawn fields at Central Park tonight. That's close to home for me. I wouldn't mind going."

With me?

"With you."

There was a momentary temptation to manufacture an exciting full schedule to impress him, to play hard to get, but she had played all the games before and knew they were empty. What she wanted now was real.

"I'd love to join you," she said.

And that's how they ended up spending most of the week together. The soccer game—where she screamed until she was hoarse—led to dinner. Then he said he had been given tickets for *Phantom of the Opera* for the next evening. Though it was the longest running show in Broadway history, Molly hadn't seen it, and was thrilled to go with him.

After, she was delighted when he insisted on seeing her home. And then said, "If I promise to be a perfect gentleman, can I come in and see Baldy?"

He came in. She made coffee. Baldy decided to give him a chance. She was not sure she had ever seen anyone laugh so hard as when Baldy began to peck affectionately on Houston's ear.

Being with Houston was easy and exhilarating. She found herself sharing things with him that she had rarely told anyone. She told him about the pets that had pre-existed Baldy. She told him things from her childhood, anecdotes about the long chain of step-fathers. Finally it was he who remembered they both had to work in the morning.

He hesitated at her door. For a moment she thought he would kiss her, again, and her life as she had known it would be over because she knew they were reaching the point where neither of them was going to be able to hold back.

But clearly, though the struggle was apparent in his face, he remembered his promise to be a gentleman.

At work the next day, she appreciated his discipline. It was hard enough to separate the personal from the professional without the complication of another kiss between them.

But even without that complication her life suddenly felt as if it were lit from within.

They had gone from being combatants to being a team. They were working together, sharing a vision for Second Chances. Houston could make her laugh harder than she had ever laughed. He could take an ordinary moment and make it seem as if it had been infused with sunshine.

There was so much to be done and so little time left to do it as they moved toward the reopening of the office, the open house unveiling party set for Friday afternoon. The personal and the professional began to blend seamlessly. They worked side by side, late into the night, eating dinner together. He always walked her home when they were done.

She was beginning to see how right he had been about Second Chances, it could be so much better than she had ever dreamed possible.

And her personal life felt the same way. Life could be so much better than she had ever dreamed was possible!

It seemed like a long, long time ago, she had tried on that wedding dress, and felt all that it stood for. In this week of breathtaking changes and astounding togetherness, Molly had felt each of those things. *Souls joined. Laughter shared. Long conversations. Lonely no more.*

Was she falling in love with her boss? She had known the potential was there and now she evaluated how she was feeling.

If falling in love meant feeling gloriously alive every minute you spent together, then yes. If falling in love meant noticing a person's eyes were the exact color of silver of moonlight on water, yes. If falling in love was living for an accidental brush of a hand, yes.

If falling in love made the most ordinary things—coffee in the morning, the phone ringing and his voice being on the other end—extraordinary, then yes.

She glanced up to see him standing in her office doorway, looking at her. Something in his face made a shiver go up and down her spine.

"Tomorrow's the big day," she said, smiling at him.

But he didn't smile back.

"Molly, I need to show you something."

There was something grim about him that stopped the smile on her lips. He ushered her outside to a waiting cab, and gave the driver an address she didn't recognize.

But somehow her gut told her they were going somewhere she did not want to go.

CHAPTER EIGHT

HOUSTON knew something that Molly didn't. Their time together was ticking down. Only Houston was so aware now that the week he had given himself didn't seem like enough. He was greedy. He wanted more. A woman like her made a man feel as if he could never get enough of her. Never.

Giving himself that week had made him feel like a man who had been told he only had a week to live: on fire with life, intensely engaged, as awake as he had ever been.

But there was that shadow, too. A feeling of foreboding from knowing that thing that she didn't. Nothing good ever lasted.

He realized the thought of not seeing her was like putting away the sun, turning his world, for all its accomplishments, for all he had acquired, back into a gray and dreary space, not unlike this neighborhood they were now entering.

He was not sure when he had decided to take this chance, only that he had, and now he was committed to it, even though his spirits sank as they got closer to the place that he had called home, and that somehow, he had never left behind. This was the biggest chance of his life.

What if he let her know the truth of him? All of it?

"I want to show you something," he said to her again as the cab slowed and then stopped in front of the address he had given the driver. He helped her out of it. She was, he knew, used to tough neighborhoods. But there were certain places even the saints of Second Chances feared to go.

"This is Clinton," he said, watching her face. "They don't call it Hell's Kitchen anymore."

The cab drove away, eager to be out of this part of town.

"You've found us a new project?" she asked. She had the good sense to frown at the cab leaving.

Maybe a project so challenging even Molly would not want to take it on.

"Not exactly. This is where I grew up."

"This building?"

He scanned her face for signs of reaction. He was aware pity felt as though it would kill him. But there was no sign of pity in her face, just the dawning of something else, as if she knew better than him why he would bring her here.

Why had he? A test.

"Yes. I want to show you something else." He walked her down the street. "This didn't used to be a liquor store," he told her quietly. "It used to be a bank."

She waited, and he could tell she knew something was coming, something big. And that she wanted it to come. Maybe had waited for this. He plunged on, even while part of him wanted to back away from this.

"When I was fourteen my dad lost his job. Again. My mother was her normal sympathetic self, screaming at him he was a loser, threatening to trade up to someone with more promise."

Again, he scanned her face. If *that* look came across it, the drowned kitten look, like he needed rescuing by *her,* they were out of here.

"He took a gun, and he came down here and he held that gun to the teller's nose and he took all the money that poor frightened woman could stuff into a bag. On his way out, a man tried to stop him. My father shot him. Thankfully he didn't kill him.

"He went to jail. Within a week my mother had traded up as promised. I never saw her again."

"But what happened to you?" Molly whispered.

"I became the kind of bitter man who doesn't trust anyone or anything."

"Houston, that's not true," she said firmly. "That's not even close to true."

He remembered the first day he had met her, when he had talked about being hungry and out of work and not having a place to live, had talked about it generically but her eyes had still been on his face, *knowing.*

"What is true then?" he asked her roughly. What if she *really* knew? He was aware of holding his breath, as if he had waited his whole life to find out.

Her eyes were the clearest shade of green he had ever seen as she gazed at him. A small smile touched her lips, and she took a step toward him, placed her hand on his chest, her palm flat, the strength of her *knowing* radiating from her touch.

"This is true," she whispered. "Your heart."

And the strangest thing was that he believed her. That somewhere in him, safe from the chaos, his heart had beat true and strong.

Whole.

Waiting.

"Did you think this would change how I feel about you?" she asked softly.

It was a major distraction. How *did* she feel about him?

"I always knew there was something about you that made you stronger than most people," she said.

He suddenly knew why he was here. He was asking her, *are you willing to take a chance on me?* And it was only fair that she knew the whole story before she made that decision. Still, he made one last ditch effort to convince her she might be making a mistake.

"There's nothing romantic about growing up like this, Molly. Maybe it makes you strong. Or maybe just hard. I have scars that might never heal."

"Like the one on your nose?"

"That's the one that shows."

"I think love can heal anything," she said quietly, and somehow it felt as if she had just told him how she felt about him, after all.

Something felt tight in his chest. She was the one who believed in miracles. And standing here at the heart of Clinton, seeing the look in her eyes, it occurred to him that maybe he did, too.

"There's something else you should know," he said stubbornly. *Tell her all of it.*

"What's that?" she said, and she was looking at him as if not a single thing he could ever do or say could frighten her away from him.

Houston hesitated, searching for the words, framing them in his mind.

My father's getting out of prison. I don't know what to do. Somehow I feel that you'll know what to do, if I let you into my world. Did she want to come into this?

He drank her in, felt her hand still on his heart. The

softness in her face, the utter desire to love him, could make a man take a sledgehammer to his own defenses, knock them down, not be worried about what got out. Wanting to let something else in. Wanting to let in what he saw in her eyes when she looked at him.

A place where a man could rest, and be lonely no more. A place where a man could feel cared about. A place where he could lay down his weapons and fight no more. A place where he could be seen. And *known*. For who he was. All of it. She would want him to answer that letter from his father. He knew a man who was going to be worthy of loving her would be able to do that.

Would be able to believe that love could heal all things, just as she had said.

For a moment he was completely lost in thought, the look in her eyes that believed him to be a better man than Houston Whitford had ever believed himself to be. A man could rise up to meet that expectation, a man could live in the place that he found himself. Funny, that he would come this close to heaven in Clinton.

Suddenly the hair on the back of his neck went up. He was aware of something trying to penetrate the light that was beginning to pierce his darkness. And then he realized he was not free from darkness. This world held a darkness of its own, not so easy to escape, and he foolishly had brought her here.

They weren't alone on this street. The hair rising on the back of his neck, an instinctual residue from his days here, let him know they were being watched.

He glanced over Molly's shoulder, moved away from her hand still covering his heart. With the focused stare of a predator, a man in a blue ball cap nearly lost in the shadow of the liquor store's doorway was watching them. He glanced away as soon as Houston spotted him.

What had Houston been thinking bringing her here? Flashing his watch and his custom suit like a neon invitation. He knew better than that! He should have known better than that.

That man pushed himself off the wall, shuffled by them, eyed Houston's watch, scanned his face.

Houston absorbed the details. The man was huge, at least an inch taller than Houston, and no doubt outweighed him by a good fifty pounds. He had rings on his hand, a T-shirt that said Jay on it, in huge letters. His face was wily, lined with hardness.

"What's going on?" Molly asked, seeing the change in Houston's face. She glanced at the man, back at him.

But Houston didn't answer, preparing himself, his instincts on red alert.

"Got the time?" "Jay" had circled back on them.

The certainty of what would happen next filled Houston. Mentally he picked up the weapons he had thought it was safe to lay down. Without taking his eyes off Jay he noted the sounds around him, the motion. The neighborhood was unusually quiet today, and besides, people here knew how to mind their own business.

Molly was looking up at the thug, smiling, intent on seeing the good in him, just as she was intent on seeing the good in everyone. *Even a man who had come into her life to bring changes she hadn't wanted.*

Except falling in love. She'd wanted that. The bridal gown should have warned him. He should have backed away while he still could have. Because Molly was about to see something of him that he had not intended to show her. That he thought he had managed to kill within himself.

She looked at her wrist, gave "Jay" the time. Houston was silent, reading the predatory readiness in that man's body language, the threat.

Silently he begged for Molly to pay attention to her intuition, to never mind hurting anyone's feelings if she was wrong. He wanted her to run, to get the hell out of the way. To not see what was going to happen next.

"How bout a cigarette?" the man asked.

The first doubt crossed Molly's features. Houston could feel her looking at him for direction, but he dared not take his eyes off "Jay," not for a second.

"I don't smoke," she said uneasily.

Adrenaline rushed through Houston. In one smooth move he had taken Molly and shoved her behind his back, inserted himself between her and the threat.

"He doesn't want a cigarette, Molly," he said, still not taking his eyes from the man.

"Ain't no watch worth you dying for," the man told him, and Houston saw the flash of a silver blade appear in his palm.

"Or you," Houston said.

Molly gasped. "Just give him the watch."

But if "Jay" got the watch, then what? Then the purse? Then the wallet? Then Molly?

The watch might not be worth dying for. But other things were.

"Just give it up," the man was saying in a reasonable tone of voice. "No one has to get hurt."

Something primal swept Houston. He went to a place without thought, a place of pure instinct. Years on the speed bag had made him lightning fast.

He knew his own speed and he knew his own strength, and there was nothing in him that held back from using them both. He was outgunned, the man both taller and heavier than him. There could be no holding back. None.

He was aware his breath was harsh, but that he felt calm, something at his core beyond calm. Still. It felt strangely as if this was the moment he'd prepared for his entire life, all those hours at the bag, running on cold mornings, practicing the grueling left right combinations and jabs.

All for this. To be ready for this one moment when he had to protect Molly.

"Hey, man," the guy said, "give it up, I tell you."

But the phrase was only intended to distract. Peripherally Houston registered the silvery flash in the young thug's hand, the glitter of malice in his eyes. Houston was, in a split second, a man he had never wanted Molly to see, a man he had never wanted to see himself, even as he'd been aware of the shadowy presence within him.

This was what he had tried to outrun, the violence of his father, the primitive ability to kill thrumming through his veins. He was a man who had never left these streets behind him at all, who was ready now to claim the toughness, the resilience, the resourcefulness that a person never really left behind them.

His fists flashed. Left jab. Straight right. The man slashed at him once, but his heaviness made him less than agile, and Houston's fury knew no bounds. Jay went down under the hail of fists, crashed to the sidewalk.

Houston was on top of him, some instinct howling within him. *Don't let him get up. Not until you see the knife. Where is it?*

Pounding, pounding in the rhythm to the waves of

red energy that pulsed through him. The fury drove his fists into the crumpled form of Jay over and over.

Slowly he became aware that Molly was pulling at him, trying to get him off him, screaming.

"Stop, Houston. You're going to kill him."

"Where's the knife?"

And then he saw it, the silver blade under Jay's leg. The man had probably dropped it the minute he'd been hit.

Still, Houston was aware of his reluctance, as he came back to her, made himself stop, rose to his feet, tried to shake it off.

He was aware he had come here to show Molly where he was from, to see how she reacted to that.

Instead, he had found out who he really was. A thug. Someone who could lose control in the blink of an eye. He'd brought Molly down here to see if she could handle *his* reality. He was grateful this test that not even he could have predicted or expected had come.

They were not going to move forward. There was no relationship with Molly Michaels in his future.

What if he got this angry at her? The way his father had gotten angry at his mother? And claimed it was love.

And if anybody asked him why he had just pulverized that young man, wouldn't that be his answer, too?

Because he loved her.

And he would protect her with his very life.

Even if that meant protecting her from himself.

He had come so close to believing he could have it all. Now watching that dream fade, he felt bereft.

The man rolled to his side, scrambled drunkenly to his feet, sent a bewildered look back, blood splashing down a nose that was surely broken onto a shirt. The knife lay abandoned on the sidewalk.

Only when he was sure that Jay was gone did Houston turn to her. She stared at him silently. And then her face crumpled. A sob escaped her and then another. She began to shake like a leaf. She crept into him, laid her head against his chest and cried.

Just the shock of the assault? Or because she had seen something in him that she couldn't handle and that love could not tame, had no hope of healing?

Houston took off his jacket and wrapped it around her shoulders, pulled her close into him, aware of how fragile she was, how very, very feminine, how his breath stirred her hair.

There was that exquisite moment of heightened awareness where it felt as if he was breathing her essence into his lungs.

To savor. To hold inside him forever. Once he said goodbye.

And then, out of nowhere, heaven sent, a cab pulled up and he shoved her in it.

"B-b-but shouldn't we wait for the police?"

The police? No, when you grew up in these neighborhoods you never quite got clear of the feeling that the police were not your friends.

Besides, what if some nosy reporter was monitoring the scanner? What a great story that would make. CEO of successful company wins fight with street thug. But just a bit of digging could make the story even more interesting. A nineteen-year-old story of a bank robbery.

Loser, his mother had screamed when there was another lost job, another Friday with no paycheck. The look on her face of such disdain.

And the look on his father's.

I will win her. I will show her. I will show them all.

Except he hadn't. His father had been his mother's hero for all of two hours, already drunk, throwing money around carelessly. The police had arrived and taken him. An innocent bystander shot, but not, thank God, killed, during the bank robbery his father had committed. *Nineteen years of a life spent for an attempt to win what Houston realized, only just now, could not be won.*

"No police," he said firmly. "Give the driver your address."

It was a mark of just how shaken she was that she didn't even argue with him, but gave her address and then collapsed against him, her tears warming his skin right though his shirt. His hand found her hair. Was there a moment in the last few days when he had not thought of how her hair felt?

Touching it now felt like a homecoming he could not hold on to. Because in the end, wasn't love the most out of control thing of all?

And yet he could not deny, as he held her, that that's what the fierce protectiveness that thrummed through him felt like. As if he would die protecting her if he had to, without hesitation, without fear.

A feeling was coming over him, a surge of endorphins releasing like a drug into his brain and body.

He would have whatever she gave him tonight. He would savor it, store it in a safe place in his heart that he could return to again and again.

Once it was over. And it would be over soon enough. He did not have to rush that moment.

He helped her up the stairs to her apartment. Her hands were shaking so badly he had to take the keys from her.

"Do you have something to drink?" he asked, looking at her pale face.

"Zinfandel," she said. "Some kind of chicken zinfandel."

"And I always thought wine was made with grapes."

He hoped to make her laugh, but somehow his tone didn't quite make it. Tonight he had gone down there with an expectation of *maybe* there being some kind of chance for them.

For him to build a life different than the one of unabating loneliness he had always known. A life different than what his family had given him.

But that fury resided in him. And he was not sharing that legacy with her. Someday, if he followed that look in her eyes, there would be children, too. They did not deserve the Whitford legacy, either. Innocent. His unborn children were innocent, as once he had been innocent.

The ugly truth now? He had *liked* the feeling of his fist smashing into that man's face.

He would have liked to just leave, but he could tell she was quickly disintegrating toward shock.

"I think we need something a little stronger than chicken zinfandel," he suggested.

"I think there might be some brandy above the fridge. Chuck drank…" she giggled "…everything."

She was staring at him with something hungry in her eyes. She reached out and touched him, her hand sliding along the still coiled muscle of his forearm. There was naked appreciation in her touch.

He recognized in her a kind of survivor euphoria. He felt it sometimes after a sparring match. A release of chemical endorphins, a hit of happiness that opened your senses wide.

Tomorrow she would wake up and think of his hands smashing into that man, and feel the fear and doubt that deserved.

Tonight, she would think he was her hero.

He pulled his arm away from her, poured her a generous shot of brandy, made her drink it, but he refused one for himself.

One loss of control for the night was quite enough.

"Houston." She took a sip, stared at him, drank him as greedily as the brandy. And he let her. Drank her back, saved her every feature, the wideness of her eyes and the softness of her lips.

"I think you're bleeding," she gasped suddenly.

He followed her gaze down. A thin thread of red was appearing above the belly line on his white shirt. So, the knife had not dropped instantly. At some level, had the physical threat triggered his rage?

Excuses.

"You're hurt," she said, frightened.

If he was, adrenaline was keeping him from feeling it. "Nah. A little scrape. Nothing. A long way from the heart."

If his arm was hanging by a thread at the moment he suspected he would do the manly thing and tell her it was nothing.

"Let me see."

"No, I'm okay."

But she pointed at a chair, and because he was going to savor every single thing she gave him tonight—he sat there obediently while she retrieved the first aid kit. "Take off your shirt," she told him.

Who had he been kidding when he'd said his injuries were not close to the heart? It was all about the heart.

The walls he had tried to repair around it were crumbling again, faster than he could build them back up.

Now his heart was going to rule his head. Because he knew better than to take off that shirt for her. He was leaving. Why drag this out?

And he did it anyway, aware he was trying to memorize the kindness of her face, and the softness in her eyes, the hunger in her.

He undid the buttons with unreasonable slowness, dragging out this moment, torturing himself with the fact it would not be him who fed that hunger. He let the shirt fall open. He didn't need to take it off, but he did, sliding it over his shoulders, holding it loosely in one hand. The tangy scent of his own sweat filled the room, and he watched her nostrils flare, drinking him in.

She knelt in front of him, and her scent, lemony and clean, melted into his. Even though she was trying to be all business, he could see the finely held tension in her as her eyes moved over his naked chest.

It seemed like a long time ago that he had first seen her, known somehow she would change something about him.

Make him long for things he could not have.

But he could have never foreseen how this moment of her caring for him would undo him. Her tenderness toward him created an ache, a powerful yearning that no man, not even a warrior, could fight.

Not forever.

And he had been fighting since his hand had first tangled in her hair, had found the zipper on her wedding dress.

"Oooh," she said, inspecting the damage, a tiny thin line that ran vertically from just below his breastbone to his belly button. "That's nasty."

He glanced down. To him it looked like a kitten scratch.

"Are you sure we shouldn't call the police?" she said. "You've been stabbed."

"No police."

"I don't understand that."

"You wouldn't understand it," he said harshly. "All it would take would be for one snoopy reporter to be monitoring the police channel, and it could be front page news. What a nice human interest story. Especially if anyone did any digging. The son of an armed robber foils an armed robbery."

"Your father's shame isn't yours."

"Yes, it is," he said wearily. "You know after my dad was arrested, and my mom left, I got a second chance. A great foster home. For the first time in my life I had food and clothes and security.

"Then in high school there was a dance. I danced with a cheerleader. Cutest girl in the school. And some guy—maybe her boyfriend, or just a hopeful, I don't remember—came and asked her what she was doing dancing with a thug.

"And I nearly killed him. Just the way I nearly killed that man tonight. And I liked the way it felt. Just the way my dad must have liked the way it felt when he was hitting people, which was often."

"I don't believe that," she said uncertainly. "That you liked it. You just did what you had to do. He was huge. Any kind of holding back might have turned the tide in his favor."

He laughed, aware of the harsh edge to it. "That was the first two punches. He was already done when he hit the ground."

"Houston, you did an honorable thing tonight. Why are you trying to change it into something else?"

"No," he said softly. "Why are you?"

"I'm not."

"Yes, you are. Because you always want to believe the best about everybody even if it's not true."

"How come you haven't spent your life beating people up if you like it so darn much?"

"I learned to channel my aggression. Boxing."

"There you go."

"Not because I wanted to," he said, "but because I didn't like the way people looked at me after that had happened."

"You want to be a bad guy, Houston. But you're just not."

He got up even though she wasn't finished. He could not allow her to convince him. He knew what he was. He knew what he had felt when he hit that man. Satisfaction. Pure primal satisfaction. He tugged his shirt on. "I have to go."

"Please don't."

That man could see through her veneers as ruthlessly as he had disposed of his own. That man saw everything that she wanted to hide.

Her need was naked in her eyes, in the shallowness of her breath, in the delicate color that blossomed in her cheeks, in the nervous hand that tried to tame a piece of that wild hair.

Her gaze locked on to his own, her green eyes magnificent with wonder and hunger and invitation.

He was aware of reaching deep inside himself to tame the part of him that just wanted to have her, own her, possess her, the two sides of his soul doing battle over her.

He took a step toward the door. She stepped in front of him. Took his shoulders, stood on her tiptoes.

Her lips grazed his lips. He had waited for this moment since he had tasted her the first time. He felt the astonishing delicacy of her kiss, and the instant taming of that thing in him that was fierce.

Not all the strength of his warrior heart could make him back away. He had promised himself he would take whatever she offered tonight, so he would have something to savor in the world he was going back to.

So he took her lips with astounding gentleness and a brand-new part of him, a part he had no idea existed, came forward. It met her tenderness with his own. Exploring what she offered to him with reverence, recognition of the sacredness of the ritual he had just entered into.

This was the dance of all time. It was an ancient call that guaranteed the future. It was a place where ruthless need and tender discovery met, melded and became something brand-new.

His possession of her deepened. With a groan, he allowed his hands to tangle in her hair, to draw her in nearer to him. He dropped his head from the warm rhapsody of her mouth, and trailed kisses down the slender column of her throat, to the hollow at the base of it.

With his lips, he could feel her life beating beneath that tender skin.

"Please," she whispered, her hands in his hair, on his neck.

Please what? Stop, or go forward?

His lips released her neck, and when that contact stopped, it was as if the enchantment broke. Some rational part of him—the analytical part that had been his presenting characteristic, his greatest strength, his key to his every success—studied her.

The half-closed eyes, the puffiness of the lips, the pulse beating crazily in her throat.

Storing it.

But an unwelcome truth penetrated what he was feeling. He could not take what she had to offer, for just one night. You didn't just kiss a woman like her and walk away from it unscathed, as if it was nothing, meant nothing, changed nothing.

She would be damaged by such a cavalier *taking* of her gifts.

Besides, she was not fully aware of what she was offering. The brandy on top of the shock had made her vulnerable, incapable of making a rational decision. If there was ever a time the rational part of him needed to step up to the plate it was now.

He was not the hero she wanted to see.

"I'm going," he said.

"Please don't," she said. "I'm scared. I know it's silly, but I feel scared. I don't want to be alone."

Perhaps he could be a hero for just a little while longer, though it would take all that was left of his strength.

It was so hard to press her head into his chest, let his hands wander that magnificent hair. It was hard to move to the couch, to allow her to relax into him, to feel her shallow breathing become deep and steady, to let her feel safe.

He had another fault then, as well as fury that years had not tamed. He was no hero, but a thief, because he was going to steal this moment from her.

Steal it to hold in his heart forever.

After a long time, her grip relaxed on his hand, her

lips opened and little puffed sighs escaped. She had gone to sleep on him. He slipped out from underneath her sweet weight, laid her on the couch, looked for something to cover her with.

He tucked a knitted afghan around her, looked at her face, touched her hair one more time.

He glanced around her apartment, noticed the poster on the wall, and was mesmerized by it for a moment. He took a deep breath and moved away from all it represented.

Though he was now beyond weariness, he went back to his office, the one he would turn over to Miss Viv tomorrow.

There was a new stack of letters in defense of Prom Dreams. Just in case he wasn't feeling bad enough, he read them all.

A picture fell out of the last one. It was of a beautiful young woman, at her university convocation. The podium she was standing by said Harvard.

Dear Mr. Whitford:

I recently heard that Second Chances was thinking about canceling their Prom Dreams program. I would just like you to know that five years ago, my school was chosen to participate in that program. You may find this hard to believe, but being allowed to choose that beautiful dress for myself was the first time in my life that I ever felt I was worth something.

He set the letter down.

No, he came from the very neighborhood her school had been in. He knew how hard it was to feel as if you were worth something.

He knew, suddenly, that was as important as having a full belly. Maybe more. Because filling a belly was temporary. Making a person feel as if they were worth something, even for a moment, that was something they carried in them forever.

He could not have Molly. He had decided that tonight.

But still, he could live up to the man she had hoped he was. It could be a standard that he tried to rise to daily. Even as it was ending, something in him could begin.

It could start with leaving a note to Miss Viv, telling her that Molly should lead this organization into its new future, that she had gifts greater than his to give Second Chances. The ability to analyze was nothing compared to the ability to love that she poured into this place.

It could start with a few prom dresses.

And it could start with an answered letter to his father.

CHAPTER NINE

IT WAS way too soon to love him, Molly thought, walking up the street toward the office the next morning.

But there was no doubt in her mind that she was in love. Totally. Irrevocably. Wonderfully.

The whole world this morning felt different, as if rain had come and washed it clean, made it sparkle.

He had brought her to the place of his birth, thinking he risked something by showing her everything. Instead, she had seen him so completely it made her heart stand still, awed to be in the presence of a soul so magnificent, so strong.

She smiled thinking of how he thought it said something *bad* about him that he had dispensed with that horrible young mugger so thoroughly.

She suspected she would spend the rest of her life performing alchemy on him, showing him what he thought was lead was really gold.

Molly shivered when she thought of him last night *protecting* her. Prepared to die to protect her if he had to. And then running that act of such honor and such incredible bravery through the warp of something in his own mind, and making it *bad*.

He said he had lost control. But she didn't see it that way. He'd stopped. If he'd truly lost control, "Jay" would never have gotten up and scrambled away.

Houston didn't lose control.

If he did, last night would have ended much differently! Molly was aware of feeling a little singing inside of her as she contemplated the delightful job she was going to have making that man lose control.

She was pretty sure it was going to involve lots of lips on lips, and that she was up for the job. Even thinking about it, her belly did the most delightful downward swoop, anticipating seeing him today.

Maybe she'd dispense with the niceties, just close his office door and throw herself at him.

Wantonly. There was going to have to be an element of taking him by surprise to make him lose control.

Then again, today was a big day for them, a milestone, the unveiling of the new Second Chances that they had created together, that they would continue to create together.

Maybe she would hold off taking him by surprise until the open house was over. But she'd tease him until then. The odd little touch, her eyes on him, a whisper when he least expected it.

Her life felt so full of exciting potential. She could barely believe her life had gone from that dull feeling of same-same to this sense of invigorated engagement in such a short time.

That's what love did.

Brought out the best. Empowered. Made all things possible. And healed all things, too.

Molly could feel her heart beating a painfully quick

tattoo within her chest as she mounted the stairs, and went in the front door of the office.

Another day together. A gift. If things had gone differently last night they might not have this gift. It was a reminder to live to the fullest, to take the kind of chances that made a life shimmer with glory.

Tish was already at her desk. She looked up, beaming.

"There's a surprise for you."

Molly's eyes went to the huge bouquet of pink lilies on Tish's desk. She started to smile.

When she'd woken last night and found he had slipped away, she had thought maybe he planned to try to fight this thing. She put her nose to the flowers, and let subtle scent engulf her.

But no, they were on the same page. He was going to romance her. It was probably going to be hard for a realist like him, too! Because lovely as they were, flowers weren't going to cut it. They were the easiest form of romance.

Tish laughed. "Those aren't for you, silly. Those are from the next door neighbor congratulating us on our reopening. Your surprise is in Miss Viv's office."

He was waiting for her, then. Had some surprise to make up for the disappointment of a kiss not completed, of not staying the night with her.

She went to the closed office door, knocked lightly, opened it without waiting for an answer.

A sight that should have filled her heart to overflowing greeted her. Miss Viv sat behind her own desk.

Molly bit back the wail, *Where is he?* and rushed into the arms that were open to her. She had to fight back tears as Miss Viv's embrace closed around her.

"My word," Miss Viv said. "Isn't this incredible? Isn't the office incredible? You'll have to show me how to use this."

"I thought you didn't like computers?" Molly teased.

"There isn't anything here I don't like," Miss Viv declared happily.

"Where's Houston?" Molly asked, casually.

"I'm not sure," Miss Viv said. "I haven't seen him. Do you press this button to put the camera on? Molly, help me figure this out!"

Molly complied, pulled a chair up to Miss Viv's desk. Part of her was fully engaged in showing Miss Viv how to use the computer, hearing tidbits about her trip and the wonderful time she'd had.

Part of her listened, waited. Part of her asked, *Where is his office going to be, now that Miss Viv is back?*

She waited for the sound of the voice and the footsteps that did not come. For some reason, she thought of the time he had told her about waiting at the concert for his mother. This, then, was how he had felt.

The waiting was playing with her game plan. She was not going to be able to contain herself when she finally saw him. She was surely going to explode with joy. Everyone was going to know.

And she didn't care.

But by lunch he still had not come. Molly tried his cell phone number. She got the recording.

She listened to his voice, *greedily,* hung up because she could not think of a message to leave that could begin to say how she was feeling.

Eventually she and Miss Viv joined the rest of the office in getting ready for the open house. The flowers on Tish's desk had only been the first of many arrangements that arrived: from friends of Second Chances, neighboring businesses, well-known New York business people and personalities.

The caterers arrived and began setting up food, wine and cheese trays, while Brianna went into a tizzy of last minute arranging and "staging," as she called it.

At three, people began to trickle in the door. Invited guests, curious people from the neighborhood, the press. Information packets had been prepared for all of them: what Second Chances did, complete with photographs. Though no mention of a donation was ever made, each packet contained a discreet cream envelope addressed to Second Chances.

Molly felt as though she was in a dream as that first trickle of people turned into a flood. She was there, and not there. She was answering questions. She was engaged with people. She was laughing. She was enjoying the sense of triumph of a job well done. She was sipping the champagne that had been uncorked, nibbling on the incredible variety of cheeses and fresh fruits.

But she was aware she was not there at all.

Watching the door. Waiting.

Where was he? Where was Houston? This was his doing, the success of this gathering—and there was no doubt it was a success—was a tribute to his talent, his hard work, his dedication, his leadership. How could he not be here to reap the rewards of this, to see that basket on Tish's desk filling up with those creamy white envelopes?

Finally Miss Viv asked for everyone's attention. She thanked them all for coming, and invited them to watch a special presentation with her.

The lights were lowered, the voices quieted.

A screen came down from the ceiling.

Music began to play.

The office designer who had been in Molly's office closet the first day stood beside Molly. "Wait until you see this," she said. "Mr. Whitford always does the most incredible presentations." Then she cocked her head. "Hey, he's changed the music. That's interesting. It was Pachelbel before."

But it wasn't Pachelbel now. It was a guitar, and a single voice, soulful, almost sorrowful, filling the room, as black and white pictures began to fill the screen, one melting into the next one.

"You told me," the music said, "that I would know heaven."

But the pictures weren't of heaven. They were of dark streets and broken windows, playgrounds made of asphalt, boarded over businesses. They were of the places, that Molly had found out yesterday, where he had grown up.

The places that had shaped that amazingly strong, wonderful man.

The voice sang on, "You promised me a land free from want…"

And the pictures showed those who had newly arrived, the faces of immigrants, wise eyes, unsmiling faces, ragged clothes.

"I expected something different than what I got,
Oh, Lord, where is my heaven, where is my heaven?"

The pictures were breathtaking in their composition: a young man crying over the body of a friend in his arms, a little boy kicking a can, shoulders humped over, dejection in every line of him, a woman sitting on steps with a baby, her eyes fierce and afraid as she looked into the camera.

Then the pictures began to change, in perfect sync with the tempo of the music changing, the lyrics suspended, a single guitar picking away at the melody, but faster now, the sadness leaving it.

The pictures showed each of the stores, Peggy laughing over a rack of clothes at Now and Zen, the ultrasophisticated storefront of Wow and Then, a crowded day at Now and Again. Then it showed this office before the makeover, walls coming down, transformation.

And that voice singing, full of hope and power now, singing, *If we just come together, if I see you as my brother, Lord, there is my heaven, there is my heaven.*

Now there was a photograph of the green space that Molly recognized as her garden project, the only color in a block of black and white, the children at the daycare, the Bookworms bus.

Emotion was sweeping the room. Brianna was dabbing at her eyes with a hankie. "Oh, my God," she whispered, "he's outdone himself this time."

Something in Molly registered that. *This time.* Brushed it away like a pesky fly that was spoiling an otherwise perfect moment. Except it wasn't perfect. Because he wasn't here.

"Where is Houston?" Molly whispered to Brianna. She *needed* him to be here, she needed to be sharing this with him.

"Oh," Brianna said, "he never comes to the final day."

"Excuse me? What final day? He's the boss here." *We are going to be building a future together.*

And hopefully not just at work.

But Brianna was clapping now, keeping time. Every one was clapping, keeping time as that voice sang out, rich and powerful, full of promise, *"There is my heaven."*

A final picture went across the screen.

It was that little girl, the princess, kissing Houston on the cheek.

And Molly thought, as that picture froze in its frame, *there is my heaven.*

Over the thunder of applause, she turned to ask Brianna what she meant, about the final day. About Houston never coming to the final day.

Other thoughts were crowding her memory. She realized he had a relationship with all those workers who had come in, with Brianna. He hadn't just met them when he took over, hadn't just hired contractors and designers and computer geeks.

He'd known them all before.

He *never* came to the final day. He's outdone himself *this time.*

Houston Whitford had done all this before. That's why he'd been brought in to Second Chances. Because he'd done it all before. And done it well.

The applause finally died down. Miss Viv stood at the front of the room, beaming, dabbing at her eyes.

As she spoke, Molly felt herself growing colder and colder.

"First of all, I must thank Houston Whitford for donating his time, his expertise and his company, Precision Solutions, to all of us here. I know his team does not come cheaply. His donation probably rates in the tens of thousands of dollars."

The cold feeling increased. He'd been donating all

the renovations? He'd let her believe he was taking the money from Prom Dreams?

No, he'd never said that. He'd probably never told Molly an out-and-out lie. The more subtle kinds of lies. The lies of omission.

"Houston's not here today," Miss Viv said. "With any luck he's back to his real job. Personally I wish Precision Solutions was consulting with the president of the United States about getting this country back on track."

A ripple of appreciative laughter, only Molly wasn't laughing. There. It was confirmed. He was not an employee, not the new head of Second Chances. He had never planned to stay, he had known all along they were not building a future of any kind together.

The only one, apparently, who had not known that was her.

Little Molly Pushover. Whose record of being betrayed by every single person she had ever loved was holding.

Miss Viv was talking about the holidays she had just gone on, and how it had made her rethink her priorities. She had decided to retire. Then Miss Viv was thanking everyone for their years of support, hoping they would all show the same support and love to the new boss as they had shown to her.

"I'd like to introduce you now to our new leader," Miss Viv said, "the person I trust to do this job more than anyone in the world."

So, he was here after all. Molly allowed relief to sweep over her. She must have misunderstood. He was leaving Precision Solutions to head up Second Chances. Molly could feel herself holding her breath, waiting to see him, *dying* to see him.

So relieved because as the afternoon had worn on and

he had not shown up, a feeling of despair had settled over her. She had known *exactly* what he had felt like at that Christmas concert when his mother had not come.

He would not make someone else feel like that. Not that he cared about. He wouldn't. She thought of the look of fierce protectiveness on his face last night. He would never be the one to hurt her. He had almost died to keep her safe!

But now he was here. Somewhere. She craned her neck, waiting for Miss Viv to call his name. After the crowds had thinned, she would laugh with him about her misunderstanding. Kick closed that office door, and see what happened next.

But Miss Viv didn't call his name.

Her eyes searched the people gathered around her, until she finally found Molly. She smiled and held out her hand.

"Molly, come up here."

Molly tried to shrink away. Oh, no, she did not want to be part of introducing the new boss. She thought her feelings would be too naked in her face, she felt as if there was no place for her to hide.

But Miss Viv did not notice Molly trying to shrink away. She gestured her forward even more enthusiastically. She thought Molly not coming was because of the press of the crowds, and gave up trying to get her to the front.

The crowd opened for her. Somebody pushed her from behind.

Molly had no choice but to go up there.

"I'd like to introduce you to the new head of Second Chances," Miss Viv said gleefully. "Molly Michaels."

Molly stood there, stunned. There was no happiness at all. Just a growing sense of self-scorn. Until the very last minute, she had believed in him, believed the best in him. Just like always.

No doubt she'd be getting another postcard from some far off exotic place soon. To rub her face in her own lack of discernment.

Her own Pollyanna need to *believe*.

She had been lied to by the man she thought she had seen more truly than anyone else. He wasn't the boss and he wasn't going to be part of her future here.

Or anywhere else.

"I don't know that I'm qualified," Molly managed to say through stiff lips, in an undertone to Miss Viv.

"Oh, but you are, dear. That's one of the things our darling Houston was here to do. To find out if you were ready to take over for me."

Our darling Houston.

Molly had been falling in love, and he'd been conducting a two week job interview?

The front door opened, and a delivery man walked in, barely able to see over his arms loaded with long, white boxes. "Where should I put—" He stopped, uncomfortably aware he was the center of attention. "The dresses?"

"What dresses?" Tish asked.

"I hate to break up the party, but I got a truckload of prom dresses out there, lady, and I'm double parked."

Miss Viv put a hand to her heart. "Oh," she said, and her eyes filled with fresh tears. "My Houston."

And again, Molly felt no joy at all. *Her Houston. Darling Houston.* Houston Whitford was Miss Viv's Houston.

They had a relationship that preexisted his coming here. He had never thought to mention that in two weeks, either. Nor had Miss Viv mentioned it when she had first introduced him.

Molly had been lied to, not just by him, but by the woman she loved more than any other in the world?

Somehow Molly managed to get through the gradual wind-down of the festivities. She begged off looking at the dresses that had arrived. Someone else could do it. Prom Dreams seemed like a project suited to a desperate romantic, which she wasn't going to be anymore.

And she meant that, this time. That moment in the garden when Molly had thought she knew who she really was wavered like the mirage that it was.

Though there were still people there, Molly tried to get out the door unnoticed.

Miss Viv broke away from the crowd and came to her. "Wait just a sec. Houston left something for you."

She came back moments later with a long, narrow box, pressed it into Molly's unwilling hands.

"Are you all right?"

She was not ready to discuss the magnitude of how not all right she was. "Just tired," she said.

"Are you going to open it?"

Molly shook her head. "At home." The fact that it was light as a feather should have warned her what was in it.

She opened the box in the safety of her apartment with trepidation rather than enjoyment.

There was the feather boa she had worn on that day when they had danced at Now and Zen. Baldy's feathers. One of those fancy dresses, a diamond ring, flowers, somehow she could have handled a gift like that. Expensive. Impersonal somehow. A *thanks for the memories* brush off.

But this?

Molly allowed the tears to come. What she should have remembered when she was nourishing the ridiculous fantasy of him as the lone gunslinger who saved the town, was how that story always ended.

With the hero who had saved the town riding away as alone as the day he had first ridden in.

An hour ago watching Houston's face flash across the screen, that child kissing his cheek, Molly had thought, *there is my heaven.*

How was it that heaven could be so close to hell?

CHAPTER TEN

HOUSTON awoke with the dream of her kiss on his lips. If he closed his eyes again, he could conjure it.

It had been a month since he had felt her lips under his own, since he had known he had to say goodbye to her. Why were the memories of the short time they had shared becoming more vivid instead of fading?

Probably because of the choice he had made. He might have chosen to walk away from Molly—for her own good—but he had also chosen not to walk away from her lesson.

Every day he tried to do one thing that would make her proud of him, if she knew, one thing that somehow made him live up to the belief he had seen shining in her eyes.

He had sent a truckload of brand-new shoes to Sunshine and Lollipops. He had arranged scholarships for some of those girls who had written the earnest letters in defense of Prom Dreams.

Yesterday, he had rented an apartment for his father. It was just down the block from the garden project that would never become a parking lot. After he had rented the apartment, he had wandered down there, and looked at the flowers and the vegetables growing in cheery defiance of the concrete all around them, and he had known this would be a good place for his father to come to.

Then Houston had seen Mary Bedford working alone, weeding around delicate new spinach tops. He had gone to her, and been humbled by her delight in seeing him. He had told her his father would soon be new to the neighborhood. He had not told her anything that would bring out the drowning kitten kind of sympathy—for his father would hate that—but he had asked her if she could make him welcome here.

His phone rang beside the bed.

"Houston, it's Miss Viv."

"What can I do for you, Miss Viv?" *Please, nothing that will test my resolve. Don't ask me to be near her.*

"It's about Molly."

He closed his eyes, steeling himself to say no to whatever the request was.

"I have a terrible feeling she's involved herself in an Internet affair. You know how dangerous those can be, don't you?"

"What? Molly? That doesn't sound like Molly." Even though his heart felt as if it was going to pound out of his chest, he forced himself to be calm. "What would make you think that?"

"After I came back from my holiday, Molly just wasn't herself. She didn't seem interested in work. She wouldn't accept the position as head of Second Chances and seemed angry at me, though she wouldn't say why. She lost weight. She had big circles under her eyes. She looked exhausted, as if she may have been crying, privately."

Not an Internet affair, he thought, sick, *a cad.*

"But then, about a week ago, everything changed. She

started smiling again. I didn't feel as if she was angry with me. In fact, Houston, she became radiant. Absolutely radiant. I know a woman in love when I see one."

In love? With someone other than him? This new form of torture he had not anticipated.

"Then, just out of the blue, she announced she was going on holidays. I just know she's met someone on the Internet! And fallen in love with them. Houston, she's foolish that way."

I know.

"Did she say she'd met someone?" he asked, amazed by how reasonable he made his voice sound.

"She didn't have to! She said she's done experiencing her dreams through a picture on her living room wall! She said she was going to California for a while."

"What do you want me to do?" he asked.

"I don't know," Miss Viv wailed. "But I need to know she's safe."

That's funny. So did he.

"I'll look after it," he said.

"But how?" This said doubtfully. "California is a big place, Houston!"

He thought of the picture on Molly's living room wall. "It's not that big," he said.

Molly sighed with absolute contentment, and looked over the incredible view. The sun was setting over the Napa Valley. It was as beautiful as she had ever dreamed it could be.

Of course, maybe that was because she was in love.

Finally.

With herself.

Molly sat on a stone patio, high up on a terraced

hillside that overlooked the famous vineyards of the Napa Valley in California. The setting sun gilded the grapevines in gold, and the air was as mild as an embrace. She was alone, wearing casual slacks and a T-shirt from a winery she had visited earlier in the day.

She had the feather boa wrapped around her neck.

In front of her was a wineglass of the finest crystal, a precious bottle of Cabernet Sauvignon this Valley was so famous for producing.

For a while after Houston had gone, she had thought she would die. Literally, Molly had thought she would curl up in a ball in a corner somewhere in her apartment and die.

But she didn't. She couldn't.

Baldy needed her.

And then one day she went to Sunshine and Lollipops to do a routine visit for a report that needed to be filled out for a grant.

All the children, every single one of them, were wearing new shoes.

"An anonymous donor," one of the staff told her. "A whole truckload of them arrived."

Something in Molly had become alert, as if she was reaching for an answer that she couldn't quite grasp.

The next day there had been an excited message on her answering machine.

"Miss Michaels, it's Carmen Sanchez." Tears, Spanish mixed with English, more tears. *"I got a scholarship. I don't know how. I never even applied for one."*

And that feeling of alertness inside Molly had grown. And then, when the second call came, from another one of the girls who had written a letter for Prom Dreams, the alertness sighed within her, *knowing.*

And with that knowing had come a revelation: she had always known the truth about Houston Whitford.

It was her own truth that she had not been so sure of.

Even though he would never admit it, she could clearly see he understood love at a level that she had missed.

It didn't rip down. It didn't tear apart. It didn't wallow in self-pity. It didn't curl up in a corner and die.

Those who had been lucky enough to know it gave back. They danced with life. They embraced *everything:* heartbreak, too. They never stopped believing good could come from bad.

She had told *him* that love could heal all things.

But then she had not lived it. Not believed it. Not ever embraced it as her own truth.

Now she was going to do just that. She was going to be made *better* by the fact, that ever so briefly, she had known the touch and the grace and the glory of loving. She was going to take that and give it to a world that had always waited for her to *see.*

Herself.

So, she watched with a full heart as the light faded over the Napa Valley. She felt as if the radiance within her matched the golden sun.

Headlights were moving up the hill toward the bed and breakfast where she was staying, and she watched them pierce the growing blackness, marveled at how something so simple could be so beautiful, marveled at how a loving heart could *see.*

The car pulled into the parking lot, below her perch, and she watched as a man got out.

In the fading light and at this distance, the man looked amazingly like Houston, that dark shock of hair, the way he carried himself with such masculine confidence, grace.

Of course, who didn't look like Houston? Every dark haired stranger made her heart beat faster. At first, in her curl-up-in-the-corner phase, she had hated that. But as she came to embrace the truth about herself, she didn't anymore.

It was a reminder that she had been given a gift from him. And when she saw someone who reminded her of him now, she allowed herself to tenderly explore what she felt, and send a silent blessing to him.

To love him in a way that was pure because it wished only the best for him and asked for nothing in return.

It wasn't the same as not expecting enough of someone like Chuck, because really getting tangled with someone like Chuck meant you had not expected enough of yourself!

The man disappeared inside the main door far below the patio she sat on, and Molly allowed the beating of her heart to return to normal. She took another sip of wine, watched the vineyards turn to dusky gold as the light faded from the sky.

"Hello."

She turned and looked at him, felt the stillness inside her, the *knowing*. That love was more powerful than he was, than his formidable desire to fight against it.

"Hello," she said softly, back.

"Surprised to see me?"

"Not really," she said.

He frowned at her. "You made yourself damnably hard to find, if you were expecting me."

She smiled.

"Miss Viv was worried that you were having an Internet affair."

"And you? Were you worried about that?"

"Impossible," he whispered.

"Then why did you come?"

He sighed and took the chair across from her. "Because I couldn't *not* come."

They sat there silently for a moment.

"The feathers look good on you," he said after a while.

"Thank you."

"Where's Baldy?"

"I left him with a neighbor."

"Oh."

Again the silence fell. She noticed it was comfortable. *Full,* somehow.

"I owe you an apology," he said.

"No," she said, "you don't. I learned more from you walking away than I could have ever learned from you staying."

He frowned. "That's not what I was going to apologize for. We both know you're better off without me."

We do?

"No, I wanted to apologize for bringing you to the old neighborhood that night. And then for losing it on that guy, the mugger. For not being able to stop. I might have killed him if you hadn't stopped me."

She chuckled, and he glared at her.

"It's not funny."

"Of course it's funny, Houston. I weigh a hundred and thirteen pounds. And I could have stopped you? Don't be ridiculous. You stopped yourself."

"I'm trying to tell you something important."

"I'm all ears."

"I come from chaos," he said. "And violence. That is my legacy. And I am not visiting them on you."

"Why?" she asked softly.

He glared at her.

"Why are you so afraid to visit your legacy on me?"

"Because I love you, damn it!" The admission was hoarse with held in emotion.

"Ah," she said softly, her whole world filling with a light that put the gold of the Napa Valley sunset to shame. "And you're afraid you would hurt me?"

"Yes."

"You told me you hit a boy in high school once."

"True," he said tautly.

"And then what, fourteen or fifteen years later you hit another person? Who was attacking you?"

"I didn't feel like he was attacking me. I felt as though he was attacking you."

"And so defending me, putting your body between me and that threat, taking care of it, that was a *bad* thing? A pattern?"

"I lost control."

She would have laughed out loud at how ludicrous that assessment of himself was, except she saw what he was doing. He was trying to convince himself to climb back on that horse and ride away from her, back to those lonely places.

The thing was, she wasn't letting him ride off alone. That's all there was to it. Somewhere, somehow, this incredible man had lost a sense of who he really was.

But she saw him so clearly. It was as if she held his truth. And no matter what was in it for her, she was leading him back to it. Because suddenly, she understood that's what love did.

"He had a knife, Houston. He was huge. Don't you think you did what you had to do?"

"Overkill," he said. "Inexcusable."

"I'm not buying it, Houston."

He looked her full in the face.

"You're afraid of loving me."

"Yes," he whispered.

"You're afraid I will let you down, just like every other person who should have loved you has let you down."

"Yes," he admitted.

"You're afraid you will let yourself down. That love will make you do something crazy that you will regret forever."

"Yes," he said absolutely.

"There is a place," she said ever so softly, "where you do not have to be afraid anymore, Houston. Never again."

He looked at her. His eyes begged for it to be true.

She opened her arms.

And he came into them. She reached up and touched his cheek, with reverence, with the tender welcome of a woman who could see right to her gunslinger's soul. She could feel the strong beat of his good, good heart.

"You are a good man, Houston Whitford. A man with the courage to take every single hard thing life has handed you and rise above it."

He didn't speak, just nestled his head against her breast, and he sighed with the surrender of a man who had found his way down from the high and lonely places.

Over the next few days, they gave themselves over to exploring the glory of the Napa Valley.

They took the wine train. They went for long walks. They drove for miles exploring the country. They stopped at little tucked away restaurants and vineyards, book shops and antique stores. They whiled away sun-filled afternoons sipping wine, holding hands, looking at each other, letting comfortable silences fall.

They laughed until their sides hurt, they talked until their voices were hoarse.

Molly remembered the day she had first met him, looking at herself in that wedding dress, and yearning for all the things it had made her feel: a longing for love, souls joined, laughter shared, long conversations. Lonely no more.

It was their final morning in California when he told her he had a surprise for her. It was so early in the morning it was still dark when he piled her into the car and drove the mazes of those twisting roads to a field.

Where a hot air balloon was anchored, gorgeous, standing against the muted colors of early morning.

It seemed to pull against its ropes, its brilliant stripes of color—purple, red, green, yellow—straining to join the cobalt-blue of the sky.

She walked toward it, her hand in Houston's, ready for this adventure. Eager to embrace it. She let Houston help her into the basket.

As the pilot unleashed the ropes and they floated upward to join the sky, she leaned back into Houston.

"I have waited all my life for this," Molly whispered.

"For a ride in a hot air balloon?"

"No, Houston," she said softly.

For this feeling—of being whole and alive. In fact, it had nothing to do with the balloon ride and everything to do with love. Over the last few days, it had seeped into her with every breath she took that held Houston's scent.

The hot air heater roared, and the balloon surged upward. The balloon lifted higher as the sun began to rise and drench the vineyards and hillsides in liquid gold. They floated through a pure sky, the world soaked in misty pinks and corals below them.

"Houston, look," she breathed of the view. "It's wonderful. It is better than any dream I ever dreamed."

She glanced at him when he didn't respond. "Is something wrong?"

"I was wondering—" he said, and then he stopped and looked away. He cleared his throat, uncharacteristically awkward.

"What?" she asked, growing concerned.

"Would you like some cheese?"

He produced a basket with an amazing array of cheese, croissants warm from the oven.

"Thank you," she said. "Um, this is good. Aren't you going to have some?"

He was working on uncorking a bottle of wine.

It was way too early for wine. She didn't care. She took a glass from him, sipped it, met his eyes.

"Houston, what is wrong with you?"

"Um, look, I was wondering—" he stopped, took a sudden interest in the scenery. "What's that?" he demanded of the pilot.

The pilot named the winery.

"Are you afraid of heights?" she breathed. This man, nervous, uptight, was not her Houston!

"No, just afraid."

Only a few days ago he wouldn't have admitted fear to her if he'd been dropped into a bear den covered in honey. She eyed him, amazed at his awkwardness. He was now staring at his feet. He glanced up at her.

"I told you," she reminded him gently, "that there is a place where you don't have to be afraid anymore."

"What if I told you I wanted to be in that place, with you, forever?"

His eyes met hers, and suddenly he wasn't fumbling at all.

In a voice as steady as his eyes, he said, "I was wondering if you would consider spending the rest of your life with me."

Her mouth fell open, and tears gathered behind her eyes. "Houston," she breathed.

"Damn. I forgot. Hang on." He let go of her hand, fished through the pocket of the windbreaker he had worn, fell to one knee. He held a ring out to her. The diamonds turned to fire as the rays of the rising sun caught on their facets.

"Molly Michaels, I love you. Desperately. Completely. With every beat of my heart and with every breath that I take. I love you," he said, his voice suddenly his own, strong and sure, a man who had always known exactly what he wanted. "Will you marry me?"

"Yes," she said. Simply. Softly. No one word had ever felt so right in her entire life.

It was yes to him, but also yes to herself. It was *yes* to life, in all its uncertainty. It was *yes* to disappointments being healed, *yes* to taking a chance, *yes* to being fully alive, *yes* to coming awake after sleeping.

And then they were in each other's arms. Houston's lips welcomed her.

Their kiss celebrated, not the miracle of a balloon rising hundreds of feet above the earth, defying gravity, but the absolute miracle of love.

He kissed her again with tenderness that *knew* her. And just like that they were both home.

At long last, after being lost for so long, and alone for so long, they had both found their way home.

EPILOGUE

HOUSTON WHITFORD sat on the bench in Central Park feeling the spring sunshine warm him, his face lifted to it.

The park was quiet.

Peripherally he was aware of Molly and his father coming back down the park path toward him. They had wandered off together to admire the beds of tulips that his father, the gardener, loved so much.

Houston focused on them, his father so changed, becoming more shrunken and frail every day. Molly's arm and his father's were linked, her head bent toward her beloved "Hughie" as she listened to something he was telling her.

Houston saw her smile, saw his father glance at her, the older man's gaze astounded and filled with wonder as if he could not believe how his daughter-in-law had accepted him into her life.

This is what Houston had learned about love: it could not heal all things.

For instance, it could not heal the cancer that ate at his father. It could not heal the fact that he woke from his frequent sleeps with tears of regret sliding down his face.

Love, powerful as it was, could not change the scar left on a nose broken by a father's fury, or the other scars not quite as visible.

No, love could not heal all things.

But it could heal some things. And most days, that was enough. More than enough.

Once, his father had looked at Molly, and said sadly, "That's the woman your mother could have been had I been a better man."

"Maybe," Houston had said gently, feeling that wondrous thing that was called forgiveness. "Or maybe I'm the man you could have been if she had been a better woman."

Now, the baby carriage that Houston had taken charge of while Molly took his father to look at the tulips vibrated beneath where his fingertips rested on the handle, prewail warning. Then his daughter was fully awake, screaming, the carriage rattling as her legs and arms began to flail with fury.

Like her mother in so many ways, he thought with tender amusement, redheaded and bad-tempered.

At the sound of the cry, Houston's father quickened his steps on the path, breaking free of Molly's arm in his hurry to get to the baby.

He arrived, panting alarmingly from the small exertion. He peered at the baby and every hard crease his life and prison had put in his face seemed to melt. He put his finger in the carriage, and the baby latched on to it with her surprisingly strong little fist.

"There, there," his father crooned, "Pappy's here."

The baby went silent, and then cooed, suddenly all charm.

For a suspended moment, it seemed all of them—his father, Molly, the baby, Houston himself—were caught in a radiance of light that was dazzling.

"I lived long enough to see this," his father said, his voice hoarse with astonishment and gratitude, his finger held completely captive by the baby.

"A good thing," Houston said quietly.

"No. More. A miracle," his father, a man who had probably never known the inside of a church, and who had likely shaken his fist at God nearly every waking moment of every day of his life, whispered.

Houston felt Molly settle on the bench beside him, rest her head on his shoulder, nestle into him with the comfort of a woman who knew beyond a shadow of a doubt that she was loved and cherished above all things.

"How's my Woman-of-the-Year?" he asked.

"Oh, stop," she said, but kissed his cheek.

She had taken Second Chances to the next level, beyond what anyone had ever seen for it, or dreamed for it. He liked to think his love helped her juggle so many different roles, all of them with seeming effortlessness, all of them infused with her great joy and enthusiasm for life.

Houston put his arm around her, pulled her in closer to him, touched his lips to her forehead.

His father was watching him, his eyes went back to Molly and then rested on Houston, satisfied, content, *full*.

"A miracle," he said again.

"Yes, it is," Houston, a man who had once doubted miracles, agreed.

All of it. Life. Love. The power of forgiveness. A

place to call home. All of it was a miracle, so sacred a man could not even contemplate it without his heart nearly bursting inside his chest.

"Yes," he repeated quietly. "It is."

* * * * *

BRIDESMAID SAYS,
'I DO!'
BARBARA HANNAY

*I wish to remember those who suffered
the devastation of the Queensland floods in
January 2011. Many homes and lives were lost
in the very places where this story was set.*

Reading and writing have always been a big part of **Barbara Hannay**'s life. She wrote her first short story at the age of eight for the Brownies' writer's badge. It was about a girl who was devastated when her family had to move from the city to the Australian Outback.

Since then, a love of both city and country lifestyles has been a continuing theme in Barbara's books and in her life. Although she has mostly lived in cities, now that her family has grown up and she's a full-time writer she's enjoying a country lifestyle.

Barbara and her husband live on a misty hillside in Far North Queensland's Atherton Tableland. When she's not lost in the world of her stories she's enjoying farmers' markets, gardening clubs and writing groups, or preparing for visits from family and friends.

Barbara records her country life in her blog, Barbwired, and her website is: www.barbara hannay.com.

CHAPTER ONE

It began on an everyday, average Monday morning. Zoe arrived at the office punctually at eight forty-five, clutching her takeaway coffee, a necessary comfort when facing the start of the working week. To her surprise, her best friend Bella was already at work.

Bella was usually a bit late, and as she'd just spent another weekend away visiting her father in the country Zoe had expected her to be later than ever. This Monday morning, however, Bella was not only at her desk *early*, but she had a huge grin on her face. *And* she was surrounded by a semicircle of excited workmates.

She was holding out her hand as if she was showing off a new manicure. No big surprise. Bella had a thing for manicures and she often chose very out-there nail polish with an interesting assortment of decorative additions.

But as Zoe drew closer, curious to check out her friend's latest fashion statement, she saw that Bella's nails were painted a subdued and tasteful taupe. And they were *not* the focus of everyone's attention.

The grins and squeals were for a sparkling ring.

On Bella's left hand.

Zoe's cardboard coffee cup almost slipped from her

suddenly weak grasp. She managed to catch it just in time.

She was stunned.

And a bit stung, too.

Struggling to hang on to her smile, she hastily dumped the coffee and her handbag on her desk and hurried over to Bella.

She told herself she was misreading this. Bella couldn't be engaged. Her best friend would most definitely have told her if wedding bells were in the air. Zoe knew for a fact that Bella wasn't even dating anyone at the moment. Together, they'd been commiserating about their date drought, and they'd talked about trying for a double date online.

They'd even considered going on an overseas holiday together—a reconnaissance tour, checking out guys in other countries. Deepening the gene pool, Bella had called it during one of their regular Friday nights together.

Admittedly, for the past three weekends in a row Bella had travelled to her country home on the Darling Downs, and Zoe had been beginning to wonder what the attraction was. Bella had said she was worried about her widowed father, which was totally understandable, as her dad had been in a miserable slump for the past eighteen months ever since her mum died.

Bella had also mentioned her close and supportive neighbours, the Rigbys, and their son, Kent—literally, the boy next door, whom she'd known all her life.

Was something going on with this guy? Had he given Bella this ring?

Bella hadn't breathed a *hint* about a romance with anyone, but it was abundantly clear that the sparkle on her friend's finger was most definitely a diamond. And the name on her lips was...

'Kent Rigby.'

Bella was grinning directly at Zoe now, an expectant light shining in her pretty green eyes.

'Wow!' Zoe managed, squeezing her cheek muscles to make sure she was smiling and not still looking like a stunned mullet. 'You're engaged!'

Bella dipped her head ever so slightly, as if she was trying to read Zoe's reaction, and Zoe cranked her smile another notch while she hunted for the right things to say. 'So—does this mean you and the boy next door have taken the plunge after all?'

She was trying not to sound too surprised, and she *hoped* she looked happy. She certainly didn't want the entire office to realise she was totally clueless about her best friend's romance.

Just in time, she remembered to give Bella a hug, and then she paid due homage to her ring—a solitaire diamond, very tasteful, in a platinum setting, and appropriately delicate for Bella's slim, pale hands.

'It's gorgeous,' Zoe told Bella with genuine honesty. 'It's perfect.'

'Must have cost a bomb,' commented one of the girls behind her in an awed voice.

Eric Bodwin, their boss, arrived then and an awkward hush fell over the office until someone piped up with Bella's happy news.

Eric frowned, dragging his bushy eyebrows low, as if an employee's impending marriage was a huge inconvenience. But then he managed to say 'Congratulations,' with a grunting nod in Bella's direction, before he disappeared into his private den.

He'd never been the type of boss who chatted with

his staff, so everyone was used to his gruffness. Nevertheless, his dampening presence put an end to the morning's excitement.

The semicircle of onlookers melted away. Only Zoe remained, her head so brimming with a thousand questions she was reluctant to go back to her desk. And she couldn't help feeling a tad put out that Bella had never confided in her.

'Are you all right, Zoe?' Bella asked cautiously.

'Of course, I'm fine.' Zoe touched Bella's ring finger. 'I'm stoked about this.'

'But you didn't reply to my text.'

'What text?'

'The one I sent you last night. Just before I left Willara Downs, I texted you with my good news.'

'Oh?' Zoe pulled a sheepish face. 'Sorry, Bell. I took myself to the movies last night, and I turned my phone off. Then I forgot to switch it back on.'

'Must have been a good movie,' Bella said dryly, but she was smiling again.

'It was. A lovely, mushy romance.'

Bella rolled her eyes, but they grinned at each other and Zoe was ridiculously pleased that she hadn't been left out after all.

'Meet me at The Hot Spot at lunchtime?' Bella asked next.

'Absolutely.' The busy little café on the corner was their favourite, and a meeting today was top priority.

Back at her desk, however, Zoe's spirits took another dive as she came to grips with the reality of Bella's startling news. She was losing her best friend. Bella would move back to the country to live with Kent Rigby and that would be the end of her close friendship—their mutual support over office grumbles, their lunchtime chats, their Friday night cocktails and joint shopping sprees.

It was definitely the end of their overseas holiday plans. And it was very puzzling that Bella had never confided in her about Kent. What did that say about their supposedly close friendship?

Glumly, Zoe retrieved her phone from her handbag and flicked it on to find two unread messages—both from Bella.

At 6.35 p.m. last night:

The most amazing thing! Kent and I are engaged. So much to tell you. B xx

And then at 9.00 p.m.:

Where r u? Gotta talk. x

Zoe winced. If she'd been available for a heart-to-heart chat last night, she'd know everything now and perhaps she'd understand how this engagement had happened so quickly.

Instead, she had to get through an entire morning's work before she received a single answer to her thousand and one questions.

'You're getting *married*?'

'Sure.' Kent pitchforked fresh hay into the horse stall, then angled a meaningful glance to his mate Steve who leaned on the rails, watching. 'Why else would I be asking you to be my best man?'

Steve's eyes widened. 'So you're dead-set serious?'

'I'm serious.' Kent grinned. 'Getting married isn't something to joke about.'

'I guess it isn't. It's just that we all thought—' Steve stopped and grimaced.

'You all thought I'd carry on playing the field for ever,' Kent supplied.

'Maybe not for ever.' Steve's grin was sly. 'But heck man, you never gave the impression you were planning to settle down just yet, even though plenty of girls have tried their hardest.'

Kent's jaw tightened as he thrust the pitchfork back into the hay bale. He'd anticipated Steve's surprise—and yeah, maybe his disbelief—but his friend's reaction still rankled. It was true that he'd dated plenty of girls without getting serious. In the past. But those days were over now. He had responsibilities to shoulder.

Steve's ruddy face twisted into a baffled smile, and he scratched at the side of his sunburned neck. 'Crikey.'

'You're supposed to say congratulations.'

'Of course, mate. Goes without saying.' Balancing a booted foot on the rail, Steve leaned into the stall, holding out his hand. His eyes blazed with goodwill. 'Congratulations, Kent. I mean it. Bella's an ace girl. She's terrific. The two of you will be a great team.'

He shook Kent's hand.

'Thanks.'

'I shouldn't have been so surprised,' Steve added, accompanying the words with a shrug. 'It makes sense. You and Bella have always been like—' He held up a hand, displaying his index finger and forefinger entwined.

Kent acknowledged this truth with a nod and a smile. He and Bella Shaw had been born six months apart to families on neighbouring properties. As infants they'd shared a playpen. As youngsters they had joint swimming and riding lessons. They'd gone to school together, travelling into Willara each day on the rattling school bus, swapping the contents of their lunch boxes and sharing the answers to their homework.

From as far back as Kent could remember, their two families had gathered on the banks of Willara Creek for regular barbecues. Their fathers had helped each other with shearing or mustering. Their mothers had swapped recipes, knitting patterns and old wives' tales.

When Kent was just six years old, Bella's dad had saved his life...

And now, with luck, Kent was returning the favour.

He felt OK about it. Honestly, he was happy with the future he and Bella had planned.

Just the same, Kent would have been relieved to get a few things off his chest to Steve. In the past few years his load had mounted steadily.

When his dad had hankered for an early retirement, Kent had taken on the bulk of the farm work. Then Bella's mother had died, and her father, the very man who'd saved his life when he was a kid, had started drinking himself to death. Desperately worried, Kent had helped out there as well, putting in long hours ploughing fields and mending neglected fences.

Bella, of course, had been distraught. She'd lost her mother and now she was likely to lose her father, and if these weren't enough troubles to bear, her family's property was rapidly going down the drain.

A host of heavy emotions was tied up in their decision to marry, but although Kent was tempted to confide in Steve he wouldn't off-load his baggage, not even to his best friend.

'I hear Bella's dad's in a bad way,' Steve said. 'He's been keeping very much to himself and he needs to slow down on his drinking.'

Kent's head shot up. Had Steve guessed things were worse than most people realised?

'Tom has the beginnings of heart failure,' he said slowly.

'That's a worry.'

'It is, but if he looks after himself, he should be OK.'

Steve nodded. 'And once you're his son-in-law, you'll be able to keep a closer eye on him.'

Clearly, Steve thought their decision was reasonable, but then his eyes flashed as he sent Kent a cheeky smirk. 'You and Bella are a sly pair though, keeping this under wraps in a gossipy town like Willara.' He snapped a piece of straw between his fingers and raised his eyebrows. 'So, when's the happy day? I suppose I'll have to wear a penguin suit.'

When Zoe burst into The Hot Spot, Bella was already there, waiting in their favourite corner booth with salad sandwiches and two chai lattes.

'That was the longest morning of my life,' Zoe moaned as she hurled herself into a seat. 'Thanks for getting lunch.'

'It was my turn.'

Reaching across the table, Zoe touched the diamond on Bella's left hand. 'This is real, isn't it? You're properly engaged. I'm not dreaming.'

'It's totally real.' Bella gave a crooked little grin. 'But I must admit I still have to pinch myself.'

'You, too?' Drawing a deep breath to calm her racing thoughts, Zoe asked carefully, 'So...you weren't expecting this engagement?'

'Not really,' Bella said, blushing. 'But it wasn't exactly a surprise either.'

Zoe blinked and gave a helpless flap of her hands.

'I'm sorry, I'm lost already. You're going to have to explain this.' She took a sip of her chai latte, but she was too intent on Bella's response to register the sweet and spicy flavour she usually loved.

'There's not a lot to explain.' Bella tucked a shiny strand of smooth blond hair behind one ear. 'The thing is…even when we were kids there was a lingering suggestion from Kent's and my parents that we might eventually—you know—end up together some day. They teased us when we were little, then toned it down later, but all the time we were growing up it was there in the background as a possibility.'

This was news to Zoe and she couldn't help asking, 'How come you've never mentioned it?'

Bella looked contrite. 'You must think I'm crazy, talking so much about guys without ever really mentioning Kent.'

'You spoke about him, but you said he was just a friend.'

'He was. For ages. We were just…neighbours…and good mates…' Her shoulders lifted in a casual shrug. 'To be honest, I'd never seriously thought about marrying him. But then—'

Zoe leaned closer. 'Is Kent the reason you've headed for home every weekend lately?'

Pink crept into Bella's cheeks and her green eyes took on a touching mistiness as she held out her left hand and admired her ring again. 'It sort of crept up on us. Kent's been so sweet.'

'Oh-h-h…' Watching the dewy smile on Bella's lips, Zoe was overcome by the romantic possibilities of her friend's situation. Her skin turned to goose bumps and she could picture it all: a wonderful, long-term friendship where a couple felt really comfortable with each other, and knew each other inside out—all the good bits and the bad. Then, suddenly, they were hit by a blinding and beautiful truth.

So different from Zoe's soul-destroying experience with Rodney the Rat.

'Out of the blue you just realised you were in love and meant for each other,' she said.

Bella nodded.

'And you definitely know Kent's Mr Right?'

Another nod.

Zoe couldn't believe the way her throat was choking up. 'I thought those blinding flashes of insight only happened in movies, but look at you. This is a real life friends-to-lovers romance!' To her embarrassment, a tear spilled down her cheek.

'So you understand?' Bella's smile was a mixture of sympathy and relief.

'My head's still trying to catch up, but I guess I understand here.' Not caring how melodramatic she looked, Zoe pressed a hand over her heart. 'I'm happy for you, Bell. Truly.'

'Thanks.' In a blink, Bella was out of her chair and the girls were hugging. 'I knew you'd understand.'

'Your dad must be thrilled,' Zoe said when Bella had sat down again.

To her surprise, a flood of colour rushed into Bella's face and she paled and then she looked down at the sandwich in front of her. She pulled at a piece of lettuce poking out from the bread. 'Yes, he's very happy,' she said quietly.

Puzzled, and just a little worried by the reaction, Zoe wasn't sure what to say next. Something wasn't right here.

Or was she imagining Bella's tension?

She wondered if Bella's dad had expressed mixed feelings. It would be bittersweet for Mr Shaw to watch his daughter's engagement blossom so soon after his wife's death. He'd miss having her there to share the joy with him.

Zoe thought about her own parents, settled at last, running their little music shop in Sugar Bay and raising her little brother, Toby. After Toby's unexpected arrival when Zoe was fourteen, her mum and dad had undergone a dramatic transformation. By the time she'd started work and Toby was ready for school, they'd given up their nomadic existence, travelling round the country in a second-rate rock band.

But becoming conventional parents hadn't dimmed their love for one another. They'd remained fixed in a crazy love-struck-teenager groove and, although their relationship had always left Zoe feeling on the outside, she couldn't imagine either of them having to manage alone. Not for ages, at any rate.

Poor Mr Shaw…

'Earth to Zoe. Are you there?'

Zoe blinked, and realised Bella had been talking, and by the look of frustration on her face she'd been saying something important. 'Sorry. I—ah—missed what you said.'

Bella sighed and gave a little, heaven-help-me eye roll. 'I said I was hoping you'd be my bridesmaid.'

Zap!

Zoe's heart gave a jolt, like a soldier jumping to attention. She'd been so busy getting her head around Bella's new status as fiancée, she'd given no thought to her actual wedding. But bridesmaid?

Wow!

She had a sudden vision of Bella looking lovely in

white, with a misty veil…and herself in a beautiful bridesmaid's gown…

There'd be bouquets…and handsome guys in formal suits…

She'd never been a bridesmaid.

Warmth flooded her and she felt quite dizzy with excitement. 'I'd love to be your bridesmaid. I'd be totally honoured.'

This was no exaggeration. In fact, Zoe was quite sure Bella could never guess how over-the-top excited she was about this.

She'd heard other girls groan about being bridesmaids. They seemed to look on the honour as a boring chore and they told war stories about having to wear horrible satin gowns in the worst possible colours and styles.

Talk about ungrateful! For Zoe, being a bridesmaid was a wonderful privilege. She would wear anything Bella chose—puce coloured lace or slime-toned velvet—she wouldn't care. Being Bella's bridesmaid was clear, indisputable evidence that she was someone's really close friend.

Finally.

Oh, cringe. Anyone would think she was a total loser.

Well…truth was…she'd actually felt like a loser for much of her childhood. She'd had so few chances to make close friends, because her parents had dragged her all around the country, living—honest to God—in the back of a bus. There'd never been time for her friendships to get off the ground.

Her best effort had been in the fifth grade when the band broke up for a bit and her parents had stayed in Shepparton for almost twelve months. Zoe had become really good friends with Melanie Trotter. But then the band had regrouped and her parents had moved on, and the girls' letter exchange had lasted six months before slowing to a trickle, then, inevitably, dried up.

It wasn't until Zoe started work at Bodwin & North and met Bella that she'd finally had the chance to form the kind of ongoing friendship she'd always longed for. And now, here was the proof—an invitation to be Bella's bridesmaid.

Zoe beamed at Bella. 'Will it be a country wedding?'

'Yes—on the Rigbys' property—Willara Downs.'

'Wow. That sounds utterly perfect.' Ever since her childhood, travelling through endless country towns, Zoe had known a secret yearning to drive through a farm gateway instead of whizzing past. Now, she wouldn't merely be driving through the farm gate, she'd be totally involved in the proceedings.

Wow, again. She could picture Bella's big day so easily—white-covered trestle tables on a homestead veranda. A ceremony beneath an archway of pale pink roses. Male guests with broad shoulders and suntans. Women in pearls.

'So…how many bridesmaids are you planning' She tried to sound casual, which wasn't easy when she was holding her breath. Would she be sharing this honour with six bridesmaids? Hadn't she read somewhere that a celebrity had eighteen attendants—all of them in purple silk?

'Only one,' Bella said calmly as she spooned fragrant froth from the inside of her glass. 'It won't be a big flashy wedding. Just family and close friends. I've never wanted a swarm of bridesmaids.' She smiled. 'I just want you, Zoes. You'll be perfect.'

Perfect. What a wonderful word.

'I'll do everything I can to make the day perfect for *you*,' Zoe said.

There was no question—she would try her utmost to be the *perfect* bridesmaid. She would research her duties and carry them out conscientiously. No bride had ever had a more dedicated wedding attendant. 'So, do we have a date? Is there a time line?'

'Actually, we were thinking about October twenty-first.'

'Gosh, that's only a few weeks away.'

'I know, but Kent and I didn't want to wait.'

How romantic.

Zoe supposed she'd hear the phrase *Kent and I* rather a lot in the next few weeks. She wondered, as she had many times, what it was like to be so deeply in love.

But then another thought struck. Leaning closer, she whispered, 'Bell, you're not pregnant, are you?'

'No, of course not.'

'Just checking, seeing you're in such a rush, in case my bridesmaid's duties involved knitting bootees.'

Bright red in the face, Bella slapped her wrist. 'Shut up, idiot.'

'Sorry.' Zoe smiled. 'Well, a tight deadline can focus the mind wonderfully.'

'It shouldn't be too hard to organise. Everything will happen at the homestead, so we won't need to book a church, or cars or a reception venue, and the local rector is a good friend of the Rigbys.'

'So you only have to buy a wedding dress and order a cake.'

'Yes. Too easy,' Bella said with a laugh, and then as they started on their sandwiches her face grew more serious. 'I've made an appointment with Eric Bodwin. I'll have to resign, because I'll be living at Willara, but

I was also hoping we might be able to arrange time off for you as well, so you can come out and help with all the last minute organising. I don't want to burden Kent with too much of the legwork. But I know the time off would eat into your holiday allowance—'

'That's fine,' Zoe said quickly. 'I'd love a week or so in the country.' She was feeling a bit down at the thought of Bella resigning, but then she grinned. 'As a bonus, I might have a chance to wangle a nice country romance of my own.'

Bella's eyes danced. 'Now that's a thought.'

It wasn't just an idle thought for Zoe. As a young girl, experiencing constant brief tastes of country towns before moving on, she'd developed something of a penchant for the jeans-clad sons of farmers with their muscular shoulders and rolling, loose-hipped strides.

'Mind you,' Bella said, 'I've grown away from country life since I moved to Brisbane.'

'But you're looking forward to going back and settling down as a farmer's wife, aren't you?'

Bella gave her lower lip a slightly troubled chew. 'It will certainly be an adjustment.'

'I think it sounds idyllic,' Zoe said honestly. 'But then I probably have a romanticised idea of life on a farm. I've never actually been on one.'

'Why don't you come home with me next weekend?' Bella suggested with a sudden beaming smile. 'We could go together after work on Friday. It only takes a little over an hour. You can meet Kent and I can show you where we're planning to have the wedding, and you can help me to nut out the details.'

'Wow. That sounds wonderful.'

'Actually, you know how hopeless I am at organising. I'll probably hand you pen and paper and a list of phone numbers for caterers.'

'That's OK.' No doubt it was pathetic, but Zoe loved to feel needed. 'I'd love to come. Are you sure there's room for me to stay?'

'Of course I'm sure. We won't stay with my dad. He hasn't been well and he'd get in a stew about clean sheets and things. We can stay at Willara Downs. The homestead is huge and Kent's a wonderful host. His parents live in town these days, but they'll probably come out and you can meet them, too. They'll welcome you with open arms.'

Again Zoe thought of all the times her parents had whizzed in and out of country towns when she'd longed to stay. She'd been constantly looking in from the outside, never really getting to know the locals.

Now, for a short time, for the *first* time, she would be an insider.

'I'd love that. We can take my car,' she offered, eager to help any way she could. 'It's so much easier than getting the bus.'

Already, in her head, she was compiling a list of her bridesmaid's responsibilities. Number one—she would support Bella and help her to stay calm through the next nerve-wrangling weeks. Perhaps she would also help her to address the wedding invitations, and then there would be a hen night to arrange…and a bridal shower…

It was going to be fabulous. She was determined to carry out every task to the very best of her ability. Her aim was nothing less than perfection.

CHAPTER TWO

THE next weekend, fifteen kilometres from Willara Downs, Zoe heard an unmistakable flap, flap, flap coming from her car's rear tyre. Her stomach took a dive. *Not now. Please, no!*

But it was useless to hope. She'd heard that flapping sound too many times in her childhood—her dad had always been changing flat tyres on their bus. Now she knew with sickening certainty that she had no choice but to pull over onto the grassy verge and try to remember what to do.

It wasn't fun to be alone, though, on the edge of an unknown country road at dusk on a Friday evening. Zoe wished she hadn't been so convincing when she'd assured Bella she'd be fine to drive on to Willara Downs by herself, while Bella visited her dad.

Two days ago, Bella's father had been admitted to hospital. Apparently, Kent Rigby had found Mr Shaw in a very bad state and insisted on rushing him in to Willara.

Understandably, Bella had been beside herself with anxiety and Zoe had dropped her in town.

'Kent's not answering his phone, so he's probably out on the farm, but he'll understand if you turn up alone,' Bella had assured her.

'And one of us will come back to pick you up in an hour or so,' Zoe suggested.

'Yes, that will be great.'

And so…after expressing the wish that Mr Shaw was much improved, Zoe had set off happily enough— at least she was driving her own car and she felt at ease behind the wheel. And apart from concern about Mr Shaw's illness, she was dead excited about this weekend away and getting to meet Bella's fiancé… seeing the wedding venue…being part of the planning.

The very last thing she needed was a flat tyre.

Damn.

Briefly, Zoe toyed with the idea of trying the Willara Downs number to see if Kent Rigby could help. But it was such a bad way to start the weekend, to be seen as a useless city chick who wouldn't even *try* to fix a simple problem by herself.

Resigned, she climbed out. The tyre was as flat as a burst balloon, and she went to her boot to hunt for the jack and the thingamabob that loosened the wheel nuts.

Mosquitoes buzzed as she hunted. The jack was, of course, buried under all the luggage—two overnight bags, two make-up bags, two sets of hot rollers.

'You never know, there *might* be a party,' Bella had said.

Now, with their belongings scattered haphazardly on the side of the road, Zoe squatted beside the wheel, positioned the jack and got on with turning its handle.

So far so good…except she didn't really know how high she was supposed to raise the car. And once that was done…she wasn't certain she was strong enough to loosen the wheel nuts. They looked mighty tight. And even if she did get them off, would she be able to tighten them up again?

Zoe's unhelpfully vivid imagination threw up a picture of her car driving off with the back wheel spinning free and bouncing into the bush, while she struggled with an out-of-control steering wheel.

Maybe she *should* try to ring for help.

Standing again, she reached into the car for her handbag. As usual, because she really needed it, her phone had slipped from its handy side pouch to the very bottom of her bag, so she had to feel around among movie tickets, keys, lipsticks, pens, old shopping lists, tissues...

She was still fumbling when she heard the sound of a vehicle approaching. Her spirits lifted. This *might* be nice, friendly country folk only too happy to stop and help her.

The thought was barely formed, however, before Zoe felt a shaft of hot panic. If only she hadn't watched all those horror movies. Here she was—totally alone in the silent, empty bush wondering if the driver was an axe murderer, an escaped prisoner, a rapist.

She made a final, frantic fumble in the bottom of her bag, and her fingers closed around her phone just as a white utility vehicle shot around the curve.

There was only one person in the ute and all she could see was a black silhouette, distinctly masculine. He was slowing down.

Zoe's nervous heart gave a sickening thud as his ute came to a complete stop and he leaned out, one strong, suntanned forearm resting casually on the window's rim.

In panic, she depressed the call button on her phone and glanced quickly at the screen.

No signal. She was out of the network. *Oh, terrific.* There was no hope of a rescue.

'Need a hand?' the driver called.

At least he had a friendly voice—mellow and warm with a hint of good humour.

Zoe gulped, and forced herself to look at him properly. She saw dark, neatly trimmed hair and dark eyes. Not threatening eyes, but genial, friendly, and framed by a handsome face. Nicely proportioned nose, strong jaw and a generous mouth.

Already his door was swinging open, and he stepped out.

He was wearing a crisp blue shirt with long sleeves rolled back from his wrists and pale cream moleskin trousers. His elastic sided riding boots were tan and well polished. Zoe had always fancied that look—clean cut with a hint of cowboy. Surely, an axe murderer wouldn't go to so much trouble?

'I see you've got a flat,' he said, coming towards her with the easy loose gait of a man of the land. 'That's rotten luck.'

He smiled and his eyes were deep, coffee-brown— friendly eyes, with a spark of fun, and with laughter lines fanning from the corners.

In spite of her fears, Zoe couldn't help smiling back at him. 'I've just about got the car jacked up, but I wasn't sure how far I should take it.'

'I'd say you have it just right. The perfect height.'

Perfect. It was fast becoming one of her favourite words.

Suddenly, she couldn't remember why she'd been scared of this fellow. There was something about his smile and about his face that was incredibly, importantly *right*.

In fact…Zoe felt as if a gong had been struck deep inside her, and it took a magnificent effort to force her attention away from this stranger to her problem. 'I was—um—about to tackle the wheel nuts.'

'Would you like a hand with them?' He was smiling again and her skin tingled deliciously. 'If that doesn't offend you.'

'Why would I be offended by an offer of help?' *From a gorgeous man*, she added silently.

He shrugged. 'Thought you might be like my little sister—the independent type. She hates it when guys assume she needs help when she doesn't.'

'Oh, I see.' The mention of his sister relaxed Zoe even further. Actually, she was so relaxed she was practically floating, and she offered him a radiant smile. 'I'd love to say I could manage this tyre on my own, but, to be honest, I'm really not sure I *can* manage. I was just about to phone for help.'

'No need. It won't take long.'

'That's awfully kind of you.' Holding out the wheel thingamajig, she hoped her saviour didn't get grease on his clothes.

Clearly not sharing her concern for his pristine trousers, he hunkered down beside the wheel and began working smoothly and efficiently.

Nice hands, Zoe noticed. He was nice all over, actually. Tall and muscular. Not too lean, not too beefy. She suppressed a little sigh, and told herself she was a fool to feel fluttery over the first country fellow she met. Before this wedding was over she'd meet tons of cute rural guys.

But there was something special about this man, something totally entrancing about the warmth in his brown eyes and the quirk of his smile, a subtle *something* that made her heart dance and her insides shimmy.

Strange she could feel so much when all his attention was focused on her car's rear wheel.

'Now for the spare.' Having loosened the wheel, he was standing up again, and he glanced Zoe's way.

Their gazes linked and...

He went very still. And a new kind of intensity came into his eyes. He stared at Zoe...as if he'd had a shock, a pleasant, yet deeply disturbing shock.

Trapped in his gaze, she could feel her face glowing hot as a bonfire, and she was struck by the weirdest sense that she and this helpful stranger were both experiencing the same awesome rush. Deep tremors—happy and scary at once—as if they had been connected on an invisible wavelength.

This can't be what I think it is.

Back to earth, Zoe.

She realised that the stranger was frowning now and looking upset. Or was he angry? It was hard to tell. His brow was deeply furrowed and he dropped his gaze to the ground and his throat worked as he stared at a dried mud puddle.

Zoe held her breath, unable to speak or even think, and yet incredibly aware that something beyond the ordinary had happened.

Then her rescuer blinked and shook his head, as if he was ridding himself of an unwanted thought. He cleared his throat. 'Ah—the spare tyre. I guess it's in the boot?'

Turning away from Zoe, he made his way to the back of the car, skilfully stepping between the scattered pieces of luggage.

'I'm sorry,' Zoe spluttered, struggling to shake off the unsettling spell that seemed to have gripped her. 'I should have fetched the spare tyre and had it ready for you.'

'No worries.' He spoke casually enough, but when he looked back at her he still seemed upset, as if she'd done something wrong. But then, without warning, he smiled.

His smile was warm and friendly again, and once more Zoe was electrified. Instantly. Ridiculously. She found herself conjuring a picture of him in a farmhouse kitchen, smiling that same yummy smile across the breakfast table at her, after a night of delicious love-making.

Good grief. Next minute she'd be imagining him naked.

Could he guess?

'Excuse me.'

His voice roused her. Blushing, she stepped out of his way as he carried the new wheel and hefted it into position. But, heaven help her, she was mesmerised by the strength of his shoulders and the sureness of his hands as he lined up the wheel as if it weighed no more than a cardboard button, and fitted it into place.

'You've done this before,' she said.

'So many times, I could do it in my sleep.'

Zoe wasn't sure it was wise to let her mind wander in the direction of this man's sleep. Better to keep the talk flowing.

She said, 'I've watched my dad change tyres on country roads enough times. I should have picked up a few more clues.'

He looked up at her, clearly surprised. 'Which country roads? You're not from around here, are you?'

'No. My parents were in a band and they toured all around the various country shows.' She hoped any resentment she felt for those nomadic gypsy years hadn't crept into her voice.

'Which band?' he asked, pausing in the middle of tightening a nut.

'Lead the Way.'

'You're joking.'

Laughing, Zoe shook her head. 'No, I'm afraid I'm serious.'

'Were both your parents in Lead the Way?'

'Yep. My dad was the lead singer and my mum was on drums.'

'So you're Mick Weston's daughter?'

'His one and only.' It wasn't an admission Zoe needed to make very often. Since she'd started work in the city she'd hardly met anyone who'd heard of her parents or their band.

'Amazing.' To her surprise, he threw his head back and laughed. 'Wait till I tell my old man. He's a huge fan of Mick Weston. Never missed a Lead the Way performance in Willara.'

Fancy that. Zoe beamed at him. It was heartening to be reminded that her dad had been very popular out here.

But, heavens, now she and this stranger had something in common and she found herself liking him more than was sensible. Perhaps encouraging conversation wasn't such a bright idea.

She busied herself with securing the punctured tyre in the boot and restowing all the bits and pieces of luggage.

By the time she'd finished, her good Samaritan was removing the jack. 'That's done,' he said, straightening and dusting off his hands.

'Thank you so much. It's incredibly kind of you. I

really am very grateful.' *And just a little sad that we'll have to say goodbye now...*

He stood with his feet apart, hands resting lightly on his hips, watching her with an enigmatic smile. 'What about you?' he asked. 'Do you sing or play the guitar?'

''Fraid not.' Zoe returned his smile—seemed her face was permanently set in smile mode. 'The musical genes totally bypassed me.'

'But you inherited your dad's talent for flat tyres on country roads.'

'Yes...unfortunately.'

Wow. Instead of rushing off, he was making conversation with her. And Zoe loved it. She was no longer bothered that he was a stranger. She was too busy enjoying this amazing experience—the most awesome sensation of being swept high and pumped full of excitement, as if she were riding a magnificent, shining wave.

Were her feet still touching the ground?

She'd never felt like this before. Not with a complete stranger. Not with this bursting-from-a-geyser intensity. Rodney the Rat didn't count. He'd been a work colleague and she'd known him for twelve months before he asked her out.

Truth was—Zoe usually lacked confidence around guys. She guessed it was part of an overall lack of confidence, a problem that stemmed from her childhood when she'd always been the new girl in town, always arriving late in the term when all the friendship groups were firmly established. She'd grown up knowing she'd never quite fitted in.

But this man's gorgeous smile made her feel fabulously confident and suddenly her biggest fear was that he would simply drive away—out of her life.

'I'll tell my dad I met the son of one of his fans,' she told him.

'Do you have far to go?' her helper asked.

'I don't think it's much farther. I'm heading for Willara Downs.'

He stiffened. 'Willara Downs?'

'It's a property near here—a farm.'

'Yes, I know.' Now, he was frowning again. 'It's my property.'

His property?

Really?

A sudden chill swept over Zoe. He wasn't…

He couldn't be…

'You're—you're not—a Rigby, are you?'

'I certainly am.' He smiled, but it was a shade too late, and with only a fraction of its former warmth. 'The name's Kent Rigby.' His smile wavered as he asked uncertainly, 'Should I know you?'

Oh, God, he was Bella's Kent…Bella's boy next door.

Kent's been so sweet, Bella had said.

No wonder he was nice. He was the man her best friend was about to marry.

A cool breeze made icy goose bumps on Zoe's skin. The purple tinged dusk crowded in and she felt suddenly, terribly weary. And wary.

'We haven't met,' she said quietly, hoping she didn't sound as ridiculously disappointed as she felt. 'But we'll soon have a lot to do with each other. I'm Zoe. Bella's bridesmaid.'

Kent Rigby's eyes darkened and his features were momentarily distorted, as if he tried to smile but couldn't quite manage it.

But if he'd been caught out, he was very good at covering it up. 'Sorry, I should have guessed,' he said,

speaking smoothly once more, with no hint of distur-
bance. 'But I expected you to be with Bella.'

Calmly, he held out his hand.

Unhappily, she felt the warmth and strength of his
hand enclose hers in a firm clasp. 'Hello, Kent.'

'Hi, Zoe.'

'I dropped Bella off at the hospital. She tried to call
you to explain that I'd be arriving on my own.'

Kent had forgotten to let go of her hand. 'I'm actually on my way back from seeing Tom myself,' he said.

'How—how is he?'

'Slightly improved, thank God.'

Suddenly he realised he was still holding her hand.
Letting go, he cracked a slightly embarrassed grin, then
thrust his hands into his jeans pockets. He straightened
his shoulders, then looked to the sky in the east where
a huge full moon was already poking its golden head
above a dark, newly ploughed field. 'I guess Bella will
ring when she's ready to be picked up.'

'Yes.'

'We'd better get going, then. Would you like to follow me? I'll keep you in my rear vision, so I'll know
you're OK.'

'Thanks.'

As Zoe followed Kent Rigby's ute she tried to laugh
at herself. What a fool she'd been, getting all hot and
bothered about a stranger she'd met on a road side.

Shouldn't she have guessed that a hot-looking guy
like Kent would have already been taken? Hadn't she
learned anything from her experience with Rodney?

OK, so she was feeling ridiculously disappointed
right now, but she'd get over it. She'd been looking forward to this weekend too much to let anything spoil
it. She'd been so excited about Bella's wedding and

being her bridesmaid. She'd wanted to be the *perfect* bridesmaid.

That was still her goal. Having a fan-girly moment over the bridegroom had been a minor hiccup, but she'd recover in no time.

In the fading light of dusk, which just happened to be Zoe's favourite time of day, the track she and Kent were driving along emerged out of a purple-shadowed tunnel of trees onto sweeping lawns, dusky and magical in the twilight.

Zoe saw an archway of rambler roses and a weeping willow...an elegant, Federation-style house, long and low, with lights already glowing on the veranda.

The car's wheels crunched on white gravel as she pulled up behind Kent's ute in front of smooth sandstone steps flanked by garden beds filled with agapanthus and lilies. When Kent got out, she saw him silhouetted against the backdrop of his home. Damn. It was such an attractive image—but she had to stop thinking like that.

She had no choice. This gorgeous man was Bella's future husband and there was no way she would let her silly imagination give into any more reckless fantasies.

'I'll show you to your room,' Kent said with the gracious charm of a perfect host, which showed that he at least knew exactly what *his* role was.

Zoe followed him down a hallway past an elegant lounge room with deep squishy sofas and rich Oriental rugs to a pretty bedroom that was the epitome of comfort and tasteful country-style décor.

With her things stowed, she was taken out to a wisteria-scented back veranda, and soon found herself sitting in a deep cushion-lined cane chair, sipping chilled white wine while she and Kent looked out in the fading light to the most beautiful view of fields and distant hills.

She suppressed an urge to sigh. Everything about Kent Rigby's home was as gorgeous as he was. And it was all so beautifully presented she supposed he must have a housekeeper and a gardener. Lucky Bella wouldn't be a slave to housework.

As a child, looking out of the bus window, Zoe had dreamed of living in a lovely farmhouse like the Rigbys', but she'd never been the jealous type and she wasn't about to start now.

Very soon Bella would return from the hospital and take her rightful place at Kent Rigby's side. And Zoe's silly road side mistake would be a thing of the past.

Clutching an icy glass of beer as if his life depended on it, Kent struggled to ignore the girl sitting beside him. Not an easy task when he was her host and hospitable manners had been ingrained in him from birth.

Problem was, he was badly rattled and he couldn't really understand how he'd got this way. Anyone would think he wasn't used to meeting new girls—when the truth was quite the opposite.

He could only assume the problem arose because he hadn't adjusted to his newly engaged status. No doubt that would explain the crazy chemistry that had gripped him from the moment he set eyes on Bella's bridesmaid.

Why the hell hadn't he introduced himself to Zoe Weston as soon as he stepped up to help her? If he'd known who she was, he could have avoided those telling moments—those shocking spellbinding seconds when he'd felt drawn to her, as if a bizarre spell had been cast over him.

Chances were, he'd never have noticed her inexplicable appeal, that special *something* in her eyes, and in the sheen of her hair or the tilt of her smile—a quality that rocked his easy-going nature to its very foundations.

How crazy was that? He'd exchanged nothing more than a few glances with her.

Kent knew it was nothing more than an illusion. A mistake. It was more than likely that every man experienced a similar difficulty in his pre-wedding weeks. Commitment to one girl didn't automatically stop a guy from noticing other girls. Learning to ignore their appeal was part of the adjustment to being engaged or married.

In Kent's case, his commitment was binding on all kinds of levels, and there was no going back. No regrets. He was a man of his word.

Besides, if he was rational about this, there wasn't even anything particularly special about Zoe Weston. Her brown hair and blue eyes and slim build were nice enough, but her looks were average. Surely?

The imagined attraction was merely a blip, and now he could put it behind him.

That settled, Kent took a deep, reassuring draft of beer, pleased to realise he'd been overreacting.

It wasn't as easy as Zoe had hoped to relax while sitting beside Kent on his veranda. She found herself crossing and uncrossing her legs, fiddling with the stem of her wine glass, or sneaking sideways glances at her host's stare-worthy profile. Hardly the behaviour of a perfect bridesmaid.

Desperate to stop this nonsense, she jumped to her feet and leaned on the veranda railing, looking out at the parklike sweep of gardens that stretched to a timber fence, and fields of golden crops and grazing animals.

Concentrate on the wedding—not the groom.

Casually, she asked, 'Are you planning a garden wedding, Kent?'

He looked surprised, as if the question had caught him out, but he responded readily enough. 'An outdoor ceremony would be great and the weather forecast is promising. What do you think?'

Rising from his chair, he joined her at the veranda's edge, and once again Zoe was struggling to ignore his proximity. Now there was the tantalising whiff of his cologne to deal with as well.

She concentrated on the lawns and banks of shrubbery. 'A garden wedding would be perfect. Would you hire a caterer?'

'That's one of the things we need to discuss this weekend. But Bella's a bit…distracted.'

'Yes, her dad's health is a big worry for her.'

Kent nodded, then let out a heavy sigh.

'You're worried, too,' Zoe said, seeing the sudden tension in his face.

'I have to be careful what I say around Bella, but I'm angry with her dad.' Kent sighed again. 'Don't get me wrong. Tom Shaw's a wonderful guy. In many ways he's been my hero. But his wife died eighteen months ago and he dropped his bundle. He started drinking heavily, and now he has the beginnings of heart failure.'

'From drinking?'

'From drinking and generally not looking after himself.' Kent's hand fisted against the railing. 'Bella's beside herself, of course.'

'I hadn't realised his health was so bad,' Zoe said with concern. 'Poor Bell.'

'Don't worry.' Kent spoke quietly, but with unmistakable determination. 'I'll look after her. And I'm damned if I'll let Tom kill himself.'

Wow, Zoe thought. Kent had sounded so—so *noble*; he really was Bella's knight in shining armour.

And clearly he was happy in that role. He was turning to Zoe now with a smile. 'Bella said you're going to be a great help with the wedding.'

'I—I'm certainly happy to do all I can to help.'

'She claims you're a fabulous organiser and list-maker.'

'I suppose I can be. I've never organised a wedding, but I quite like planning our office Christmas party. A smallish wedding won't be too different.' To Zoe's dismay, her cheeks had grown very hot. She shot a quick glance out to the expanse of lawn. 'I imagine you'd need to hire tables and chairs.'

'Yes, definitely.'

'And table cloths, crockery, glassware et cetera.'

'I dare say.' Kent flashed a gorgeous crooked smile. 'If you keep talking like that you'll land yourself a job, Zoe.'

And if he kept smiling at her like that she wouldn't be able to refuse.

CHAPTER THREE

IT WAS late on Sunday night before the girls arrived back in Brisbane. As Zoe drove they discussed practical matters—the style of wedding gowns and invitations, and the things they needed to hire for the garden reception. They were both tired, however, and, to Zoe's relief, they spent much of the journey in reflective silence.

She dropped Bella off at her flat in Red Hill, declining her invitation to come in for a drink with the excuse that they both had another Monday morning to face in less than ten hours.

'Thanks for spending the weekend with me,' Bella said as she kissed Zoe's cheek. 'And thanks for offering to help Kent with organising the reception. Well, you didn't actually offer, but thanks for agreeing when I pleaded. We all know I can't organise my way out of a paper bag.'

'That's OK,' Zoe responded glibly, hoping that she sounded much calmer than she felt about ongoing communication with Bella's fiancé—even if it was only via email or telephone.

'And thanks for taking your car, Zoe. So much better than bumping along in the old bus.'

'My pleasure.' However, Zoe couldn't possibly share Bella's opinion on this matter. If she hadn't taken her car, she wouldn't have had a flat tyre and she wouldn't have had a private meeting with Kent. And her weekend would have been a darned sight easier.

'Thanks for inviting me, Bell. It was—wonderful. You're going to have the most gorgeous wedding ever.'

'I know. I'm so lucky.' Bella's green eyes took on a wistful shimmer. 'You do like Kent, don't you?'

Zoe's heart took a dive, but she forced a bright smile. 'Of course. What's not to like? He's lovely. Perfect husband material. You should have snapped him up years ago.'

Bella smiled, looking genuinely happy now, as if she'd needed this reassurance. Then she grabbed the straps of her overnight bag, slammed the door and called, 'See you in the morning.'

Zoe watched as Bella hurried up her front steps, pale hair shining in the glow cast by a streetlight, then she drove on, feeling the last of her strength ebb away.

All weekend she'd held herself together—remaining upbeat and excited for Bella's sake, while keeping a lid on her own private turmoil. Dropping any interest in Kent had proved much harder than she'd expected, and now the ordeal was over she was totally drained. She just wanted to crawl into her own little space and let go.

Finally, she reached her flat in Newmarket, let herself into the kitchen, dumped her bag in the corner.

She loved her little home. For the first time in her life she had a proper place to call home that had four walls instead of four wheels.

First she checked her goldfish—Brian, Ezekiel and Orange Juice. They'd survived beautifully without her. Then she dashed out onto her balcony to make sure her pot plants were still alive.

Zoe had always kept pot plants, even when they

were in the bus. Her mum said she'd inherited Granny Weston's green thumb, and Zoe saw it as a sign that she was meant to have her own plot of land.

One day.

Back in the kitchen, she reached for the kettle. First priority was a comforting mug of tea, accompanied by a long soak in a warm bath. She could sort out her laundry tomorrow night after work. For now, she was going to be totally self-indulgent.

Five minutes later, warm, rose-scented water enveloped her, and at last she could set her thoughts free.

Unfortunately, her thoughts zeroed straight to Kent Rigby.

She let out the loud groan she'd been holding in for two whole days, ever since the road-side revelation on Friday evening. All weekend, honest to God, she'd tried unbelievably hard to stop liking Kent.

It should have been easy. He was her best friend's fiancé, and Zoe had already dated a previously engaged man. She'd been burned. Horribly. After she'd dated Rodney for several months and helped him to get over his break-up, he'd moved in with her and she'd been deeply in love with him. Then she'd come home unexpectedly early one evening and found him in bed with Naomi, his former fiancée.

Rodney the Rat.

Never again would Zoe set herself up for that kind of heartache.

So why hadn't she found the 'off' switch for her attraction to Bella's fiancé?

It was ridiculous, as if she'd contracted a mutant strain of a virus that was resistant to all known treatments.

The truth was that deep down she was genuinely

thrilled for Bella. Willara Downs was the lifestyle her friend had been born into. Bella's parents had always lived in the district. Her father would soon be out of hospital and home on his farm, and her grandfather still lived in an aged care facility in Willara township. On top of that, the Shaw and Rigby properties were adjoining and so Bella and Kent had the whole dynasty thing happening.

Beyond all these practical considerations, Bella and Kent were so sweet together, and so very at ease. Maybe they weren't all touchy-feely, but that was to be expected when others were around. Just the same, it was clear as daylight that they belonged together.

Without question, Bella fitted in. She'd found where she belonged, while once again, as always, Zoe was the outsider.

Oh, God.

Zoe dunked her face under the water to wash away her stupid tears. She had to get a grip. Had to stop this nonsense now.

Curse that flat tyre.

This problem would never have arisen if she and Bella had driven to the homestead together. If Bella had been there, from the moment Zoe met Kent she would have known who he was, and the first thing she would have seen was Kent embracing his bride-to-be. She would have been excited for Bella, and her heart would have stayed safely immune to Kent's charms.

Instead, cruel fate had delivered her a punctured tyre and twenty minutes alone with a wonderful man who'd arrived like a gift from heaven.

She kept reliving that thrilling moment—only a few seconds admittedly—when their gazes had connected. She could have sworn something huge and earth-shattering had passed between them.

Had it all been in her stupid head?

She hated to admit that she'd deluded herself, but there was no other explanation. Thank heavens Kent hadn't noticed.

His behaviour had been beyond reproach. He'd been unfailingly polite and friendly to Zoe, and he'd been wonderful about her damaged tyre, organising a replacement to be sent out from a garage in Willara and then fitting it for her.

Appropriately, he'd devoted the bulk of his attention to Bella. There'd been no sign that he was remembering the moment when he and Zoe had looked into each other's eyes and the world had stopped.

And she was going to be just as sensible.

It was time for self-discipline and maturity. Time to get a grip on reality.

Kent-slash-man-of-her-dreams-Rigby was going to marry her best friend in less than two months and she, Zoe Weston, was going to be their happy, loyal, non-jealous, and perfect-in-every-way bridesmaid.

Kent couldn't breathe. Pinned at the bottom of a dark muddy pool, he could feel his lungs bursting, his legs thrashing. He couldn't see a thing. Couldn't hear anything either, just a dull roaring in his head.

Fear, blacker than the night, pressed down with a weighty and smothering hand.

He fought, struggling, gasping…shooting awake out of a tangle of sheets.

He dragged in air. His heart raced, but he wasn't panicking. He knew it would slow down soon. He was used to this dream. He knew its familiar pattern, even though he had no real memories of almost drowning in Willara Creek.

The dreams were based on what his family had told him—that he'd been pinned under a rock and Tom Shaw had saved him, and that little Bella had been there, white-faced and sobbing.

Don't let Kent die. Please, please don't let him die...

It was years later, in his teens, that the dreams had begun. By then it had finally sunk in that all life was tenuous and that Kent's own life had nearly ended when he was six years old.

A kid showing off. All over red rover. Then a man with good instincts diving down and dragging him free.

Tom Shaw had given Kent a second chance at life, and with that gift had come responsibility.

The dreams never let Kent forget. He owed. Big time.

To: Kent Rigby<willaraKR@hismail.com>
From: Zoe Weston<zoe.weston@flowermail.com>
Subject: Caterers etc.
Dear Kent,
Thanks for your kind hospitality on the weekend. It was great meeting you and having the chance to see where the wedding will take place.

I'm sure you'll be pleased to hear that my spare car tyre held up splendidly, so thanks for your help with that as well.

As you know, I had a good chat with your mother about the best caterers to approach for the wedding and I've rung them all and am sending you their quotes as an attachment for your perusal.

I showed the quotes to Bella, but she has enough to think about with finding her dress and worrying about her dad and she's more than happy to leave the planning details to us.

I thought the menu supplied by Greenslades sounded delicious and it also provides a range of dishes to suit most tastes, but they're a little more expensive than the others.

I'm also sending a link to a website with the table settings that Bella and I think will be perfect. If you like them, I'll go ahead and place an order.

Oh, and are you still happy to use the homestead verandas if there's a threat of rain, or would you like me to look into hiring a marquee?

If there's anything else I can do to help, please let me know.

Kind regards,

Zoe Weston

To: Zoe Weston<zoe.weston@flowermail.com>
From: Kent Rigby<willaraKR@hismail.com>
Subject: Re: Caterers etc.

Hi Zoe,

Thanks for your email with the quotes and the link. Has it occurred to you that you may have missed your calling as a wedding planner?

I agree that the Greenslades menu is a standout, so let's go with them, especially as they're based in Toowoomba and they can send out a mobile kitchen. Great find.

The table settings look terrific—I'm happy to go with whatever you girls choose.

Zoe, you might be Bella's best friend, but I think

you've just become mine, too. Such a load off my mind to have this sorted so quickly and easily.
Cheers
Kent
P.S. I was wondering—do you have a favourite colour?

To: Kent Rigby<willaraKR@hismail.com>
From: Zoe Weston<zoe.weston@flowermail.com>
Subject: Re: Caterers etc.
Dear Kent,
All the bookings are made and both Greenslades and the Perfect Day hire company will be sending you their invoices with details about deposits etc.

Ouch. I hope you don't get too much of a shock.

I'm leaving the ordering of drinks to you. Bella and I will look after the flower arrangements and decorations. So now the major details are planned, but I'd also like to have a bridal shower and a hens' party for Bella, so there's a bit more to be sorted. I guess you and your best man will be having a bucks' night?

As Bella has probably told you, she's found a dress she loves, so it looks as if everything is coming together.

I can't imagine why you want to know my favourite colour. I'm not even sure I can answer that question. It depends if you're talking about a colour to wear, or a colour to look at. It can make quite a difference, you know.
Regards,
Zoe

To: Zoe Weston<zoe.weston@flowermail.com>
From: Kent Rigby<willaraKR@hismail.com>
Subject: Re: Caterers etc.
Hi Zoe,
Once again, thanks for all your help. I can't imagine how this wedding could have happened without you.

As for the question about your favourite colour, I'm afraid I can't really explain. It's a small but pleasant task Bella has assigned to me.

That's a fascinating observation you've made about colours. For now, could you give me both your favourite colour to wear and your favourite colour to look at?
Cheers
Kent

On the following Saturday morning, Bella bought her wedding dress. Zoe had been with her when she'd first seen the dress on the previous Saturday, and they'd loved it. Twice during the week Bella had been back to the shop to look at it again, and now she'd dragged Zoe along with her to approve her final decision.

'Each time I see it, I love it more,' Bella had confided, and as Zoe watched her parade across the store's plush carpet she totally understood why. The floor-length gown was very simple, but its elegant lack of fussiness totally suited Bella's blond, country-girl beauty. Its style, with beautifully embroidered straps and Grecian draping, was perfect for an outdoor country wedding.

'Kent will adore you in this,' Zoe said as she pictured Bella coming across the lawn to her waiting bridegroom. 'You'll stop him in his tracks.'

She was proud that she said this with a genuine smile, although putting the Kent nonsense out of her thoughts hadn't been as easy as she'd expected. Emails in which he asked about her favourite colour hadn't helped.

She still hadn't answered that one. It was silly of her, but it felt too…personal.

'This is definitely the dress for me,' Bella said, giving a final twirl to admire her reflection in the full-length mirror.

She paid for her dress with her credit card, then linked her arm through Zoe's. 'OK, it's your turn now. We have to find something really lovely for you.'

Abruptly, in the middle of the salon, Bella stopped. 'Have I told you how incredibly grateful I am for everything you're doing to help? Kent told me how brilliant you've been.'

'I've enjoyed it,' Zoe said honestly. 'So far, it hasn't been a huge job. Really.'

'But it's such a relief to know it's all in hand,' Bella said. 'Since my dad got sick, I've been rather distracted.'

'That's why I was happy to help.'

'You're one in a million. You know that, don't you?'

It was hard not to bask in the warmth of Bella's smile. Zoe found it incredibly reassuring to be appreciated, to feel needed and important.

Businesslike once more, Bella turned to a rack of dresses. 'I thought if we chose something that didn't scream bridesmaid, you'd be able to wear it afterwards. Colour-wise, I was wondering about—'

Bella paused, looking at a row of dresses, and Zoe waited. Even though she hadn't answered Kent's question about colours, she rather liked pink. She knew lots of girls avoided pink like the plague, but she'd always thought the colour brought out the rosy tones in her skin and went rather well with her dark hair. So, she was thinking of a pretty shade of pink when Bella said, 'Green.'

'Green?'

Bella nodded emphatically. 'I can really see you in green, Zoe. It suits you beautifully. And it's so fresh, just right for a country wedding.'

Yes, green was fresh, no doubt about that. But it was also the colour of grass and trees, and there were rather a lot of both in the country. In the outdoors, green would work like camouflage, wouldn't it?

Worse, wasn't green the colour of jealousy? *Oh, cringe.* Zoe had worked extremely hard to rid herself of any jealousy. Even so, *green* was the last colour she wanted to wear to *this* particular wedding.

Bella was frowning at her. 'Don't you like green? I thought you loved it. That long green scarf of yours looks stunning with your black winter coat.'

But I won't be wearing my black winter coat, Zoe wanted to remind her. *We're supposed to be choosing a dress for a spring garden wedding. If not something with a hint of pink, why not a pretty pale primrose?*

Not that Zoe would actually say any of this out loud, not when she was still, in spite of her minor problem re the groom, trying to be the perfect, considerate bridesmaid.

With a pang of guilt, she remembered the Monday morning, almost two weeks ago now, when Bella had asked her to be her bridesmaid. She'd been ready to wear anything then, even a black plastic garbage bag.

Somewhat ashamed, she said, 'I'm sure a pale apple green could be very nice.'

'Hmm.' Bella was looking less certain now. 'I must admit I hardly wear green myself.' Already, she was heading over to a rack of pretty pastels. 'Our high-school uniform was green, so I had an overdose of it in my teenage years.'

'Oh,' Zoe gasped and smacked the side of her forehead. 'I'd almost forgotten until you mentioned your high school. I had a message on Facebook from one of your old school friends.'

'Really?' Bella was already at a rack, reaching for a coat hanger with a rather pretty pink dress.

'I posted a message on Facebook, you see, about how excited I was to be a bridesmaid at a country wedding near Willara. I didn't actually mention Willara Downs and I didn't give full names, but I said the bride was my best friend, Bella. I hope you don't mind, Bell.'

'No, of course I don't mind. So who was it?'

'A guy. I think he's been living somewhere overseas, but he said he used to know a girl called Bella Shaw at Willara High and he wondered if she was my friend getting married.'

Bella was suddenly very still and she shot Zoe a strangely nervous glance.

'I haven't replied to him,' Zoe said, cautiously.

'What's his name?' Bella's voice was barely above a whisper now.

'I'm trying to remember. I think it might have been David. No, that's not right. Maybe Damon? Yes, I'm pretty sure it was Damon.'

'Damon Cavello?'

'Yes, that's it. I—' Zoe stopped, shocked into silence by the sight of Bella's deathly pale face and the coat hanger slipping from her hands, landing on the bridal salon's white carpet in a sea of frothy pink chiffon.

'Bell?' With a pang of dismay, Zoe bent down to pick up the fallen gown before any of the store's assistants noticed. 'Bella?' she repeated as she slipped the gown's straps onto the hanger and returned it to its rightful place on the rack. 'What's the matter?'

Bella gave a convulsive little shudder, then the colour rushed back into her face. 'Nothing. Nothing's the matter,' she said quickly. 'I just got a surprise. It's so long since I've heard from D-Damon.'

As she stammered his name her cheeks turned deep pink.

'Who is he?' Zoe had to ask. 'A high-school sweetheart?'

With a startled laugh, Bella whipped her gaze back to the rack, and began, rather distractedly, to check out the dresses. 'God, no. We were just friends.'

'Right.' Zoe frowned as she watched Bella's hands, with their smart navy-blue nail polish and sparkling diamond engagement ring, swish along the coat hangers.

Bella turned to her, eyes extra bright. 'When did you say Damon wrote to you?'

'I found his message when I got home from work last night.'

'But you haven't written back to him?'

'Not yet. I thought I'd better check with you first. I wasn't sure he was someone you wanted to know.'

'Of course you can answer him. There's no problem. Damon's—fine.'

Bella sounded calm enough on the surface, but something wasn't right. Zoe could sense her inner tension.

'Damon was always a bit of a daredevil.' Bella spoke a little too casually, as if she needed to prove she was mega cool about this subject. 'He moved back to Brisbane in the middle of his final year, and he went on to study journalism. He's been overseas for years— as a foreign correspondent, specialising in all the worst trouble spots.'

'He sounds like an adventurer.'

Softly, Bella said, 'I hate to think of the things he must have seen.'

Zoe nodded, still puzzled by the tension Bella couldn't quite disguise. 'I think he might be heading back to Australia,' she said. 'Or he could even be on his way already. So is it OK to pass on your email address?'

'Of course.' This time Bella gave an offhand shrug, as if Zoe had been trying to make Mount Everest out of a molehill.

Lifting a very pretty coffee-and-cream floral dress from the rack, she said, 'If Damon's back in Australia, he's bound to come out to Willara. His father doesn't live there any more, but his grandmother's in the same old folks' home as my grandad, and I'm sure he'll want to visit her. They've always been close. His gran shows me all the postcards he sends her.'

'That's nice.'

Bella bit her lip and gave an uncertain smile.

'Would you invite him to the wedding?' Zoe asked.

'Heavens, no.' A strange snorting laugh broke from Bella. 'He wouldn't be interested in my marriage.' Then her eyes met Zoe's and she frowned. 'Don't look at me like that, Zoe. Damon's not the type to enjoy a romantic country wedding.'

'OK. Just asking. I thought he might have been an old friend of Kent's, that's all.'

She heard the hiss of her friend's sharply indrawn breath.

'Well, yes,' Bella admitted, almost reluctantly. 'Kent and Damon were mates at one time, so I suppose I should tell Kent.' She sighed. 'Actually, he'll probably want to include Damon.'

Then, as if deliberately changing the subject, she held out the coffee-toned dress. 'Now, why don't you try this one on? I can see you in it already.'

It was pretty obvious that Bella wanted to drop the subject. 'All right.'

In the changing cubicle, however, Zoe took one look at herself in the pretty bridesmaid's dress, and she forgot about Bella and the old school friend.

The colour was perfect—tawny flowers on a creamy white background that totally flattered her complexion. But her first thought was not to wonder how she looked.

But— *Would Kent like me in this?*

This was getting tedious.

On Tuesday evening, Zoe was in the middle of important, toenail-painting research when the phone rang. She and Bella were wearing toe peepers to the wedding, and each night, following Bella's instructions, Zoe was trying out a different colour. Serious comparisons were made the next day in their lunch hour.

This evening, when the phone rang, Zoe had toe separators in place and three nails painted with rosy minx, so she was grumbling as she screwed the lid on the bottle and hobbled over to the phone. 'Hello?'

'Hi, Zoe.'

The caller was male with a smooth as molasses country drawl that she instantly recognised. Her heart tried to leap clear out of her chest.

He said, 'Kent Rigby here.'

Why was he ringing? Several scenarios flashed before Zoe. All of them impossible. *Good grief. Calm down.* He'd be ringing about another planning detail.

But when she tried to speak, she sounded distinctly breathless.

'Zoe, are you OK?' Kent sounded genuinely concerned.

'I'm perfectly fine,' she managed to insist, although it came out in a choked whisper. 'Just a bit puffed. I had to—' *quick breath* '—come running in from outside.'

Great. Now she could add dishonesty to her list of sins. Grimacing, Zoe willed herself to calm down. Developing high blood pressure before the wedding was not on the bridesmaids' list of duties.

She took another breath, deeper and slower, aiming for a tone that was friendly, but as businesslike as possible. 'What can I do for you, Kent?'

'I wondered if you've made a decision about the hens' night. I hear you're in charge of that, too.'

'Oh, right, do you want an invitation?' she teased.

Kent chuckled at her weak joke. 'My best man, Steve, has been pressuring me about a bucks' night, and I didn't want it to clash with your arrangements.'

'Actually, I sent you an email about it earlier this evening.'

'Sorry. I haven't checked my emails. I've been out on the tractor since the early hours and I just got back. Thought I'd give you a quick call while my dinner's heating up.'

Zoe pictured Kent up before dawn, out ploughing the fields as the sun rose. Farmers worked such long hours. She wondered if Bella would be the sort of wife who took her farmer husband a Thermos of coffee and a snack. Maybe they'd share a quick cuddle behind the machinery shed?

Oh, God. Stop it!

Assuming her briskest, most businesslike voice, she said, 'We'd like to have the hens' night in Willara, on the weekend before the wedding—that's the same weekend as the bridal shower. Bella's friends from Brisbane don't mind trekking off to the wilds of the country for two weekends in a row, but I think three would be expecting too much.'

'Fair enough.'

'So the girls are planning to book into the Willara pub—that is, unless you want to have your bucks' night there.'

'No, you stay with that arrangement. We'll have the bucks' party on the same night, but we'll go over to Mullinjim. It's not far out of town.'

'Great. That sounds like a plan.' Zoe let out a nervous, huffing laugh. 'So it looks like the wedding's all coming together?'

'Like clockwork. Piece of cake, thanks to you, Zoe.'

A small silence fell and Zoe was shocked to hear her heartbeats, still galloping away like a cattle stampede. She would rather keep talking than risk Kent hearing them, so she asked the question that had been on her mind for days.

'Has Bella mentioned Damon Cavello, the old school friend who made contact?'

'No,' Kent said slowly. 'She hasn't.'

There was no mistaking the surprise in his voice. A beat later, he asked, 'So…what's the wild boy up to these days?'

Zoe could quite believe why Kent had called Damon a wild boy. She'd checked out photos of him on the internet and he had the dark, scruffy, bad-boy looks of a rock-and-roll star. It wasn't a look that appealed to her—

she'd seen enough of guys like that hanging around her parents' band while she was growing up—but she knew bad boys were considered very sexy by girls confident enough to attract them.

'Damon's on his way back to Australia,' she told Kent. 'Coming from Afghanistan, I think.'

Another small silence.

'Is he OK?' Kent asked.

'As far as I know, he's fine.'

'That's a miracle.' Kent spoke with uncharacteristic cynicism, but then he quickly corrected himself. 'Don't get me wrong. I'm relieved to hear that he's in one piece. But with Damon, there's always a risk of—' He left the sentence dangling. 'Do you know if he's likely to be around for the wedding?'

'I think there's a good chance.' Zoe hoped she wasn't breaching Bella's confidence. But then, because she was curious, she couldn't help adding, 'He sounds rather mysterious.'

'Yeah.' There was a barely concealed sigh on the other end of the phone line. 'He's always been a bit of a puzzle, but Bella knew what drove him better than any of us. What did she tell you?'

'Not much at all—just that he left Willara High in Year Twelve and ended up becoming a foreign correspondent. I got the impression he's attracted to danger.'

'No doubt about that,' he muttered.

She could hear definite tension in Kent's voice now, the same tight caution she'd sensed in Bella. What was it about this Damon guy that put everyone on high alert?

'How did Bella react to the news?' Kent asked carefully.

This last question was a curly one. Zoe sensed she was on dangerous ground, and, no matter what she thought of Kent, her loyalty lay with Bella. She certainly wouldn't tell him that Bella had been rather edgy and strange when she'd heard about Damon Cavello.

'Bella said—ah—that she'd talk to you to see if you wanted to invite him to the wedding.'

'But she didn't invite him straight out?'

'No. I'm sure she wants to talk to you first. Does Damon—um—pose a problem, Kent?'

'No, not at all. I didn't mean to give that impression.' He spoke almost too smoothly. 'Bella's right. He's just an old school friend, and it'll be great to catch up with him. Actually, I'd like his email address if that's OK. I presume Bella's already made contact with him?'

Kent sounded relaxed enough, but as they said goodnight and Zoe hung up she couldn't help wondering. And worrying.

She wished she'd left it to Bella to tell him about this Damon guy. A bridesmaid was supposed to be tactful and diplomatic. Instead, she'd opened her big mouth and she had the awful feeling she'd stirred up unnecessary trouble.

CHAPTER FOUR

GRABBING a beer from the fridge, Kent snapped the top off, then went out to the back veranda.

The night was hot and still and silent. Low clouds hid the moon and the stars, and the air was heavy and stifling, as if a thunderstorm was brewing.

Tipping back his head, he downed the icy liquid, hoping to wash away the sense of foreboding that hunkered inside him.

Foreboding wasn't an emotion Kent Rigby enjoyed, and it wasn't something that normally troubled him. Most times he was too busy working hard or playing hard. Besides, he liked to keep his life on an even keel and he left the rocking of boats to others. Like Damon Cavello.

Hell.

Kent downed another icy slug, and leaned his shoulder against a timber post, staring out into the black, fathomless night. Talk about lousy timing. Why the blue blazes had Cavello come back now, just when he and Bella had everything sorted and settled?

They hadn't heard from him in years.

Sure, they'd seen his news reports on television, delivered on battlefields while he was dodging explosions and bullets, or emerging from the rubble of an earth-quake, covered in dust and grime.

Damon had made no personal contact with either of them for years. And now Kent and Bella had planned a future together, and they were doing it for all the right reasons.

Everything was working out so well. Tom Shaw was out of hospital and if he continued to follow his doctor's instructions, he'd be OK. He was looking forward to the wedding and walking his daughter down the aisle.

The rosy future Kent had planned was falling into place.

But now this Cavello bombshell had exploded.

Why now?

Zoe sat for ages after she hung up the phone. Curled in an armchair, she almost fell into her old habit of nibbling at her thumbnail. Actually, she did chew on the corner before she remembered that she had to keep her nails pristine for the wedding. So she chewed on the inside of her lip instead. And pondered.

The vibes for this wedding weren't as upbeat as she would have liked. There were so many undercurrents, not just her own silly crush on the groom—which she *so* hoped no one had guessed—but now, with the arrival of Damon on the scene, there were Bella's and Kent's subtle but unmistakable tensions.

Zoe wished they could all snap out of it. She wanted everything to be rosy and wonderful on planet Bella-and-Kent.

Guiltily, she felt an urge to run away for a bit, but, apart from the fact that she was needed at Willara next weekend, she didn't really have anywhere to go. It was a pity her parents didn't live closer. She would have loved to see her little brother, Toby—to go and watch him play soccer on Saturday afternoon perhaps, or to go surfing with her dad, help her mum make her habitual Friday night curry.

She wondered if Toby knew how lucky he was to live in a cosy house with parents who stayed in one place with a steady job now their dad ran a music store.

One thing was certain. If she ever found the right man, she definitely wanted to settle down and to stay in one place. She wanted her children to go to school with friends they'd known since kindergarten, and she wanted them to play sports together, to make memories together...

Just as Bella and Kent had, and as their children would, too...

Zoe sighed as jealousy coiled unpleasantly inside her. Immediately she felt ashamed of herself. It wasn't as if poor Bella enjoyed a perfect family life. She'd lost her mother. She had no brothers or sisters, and her only family consisted of her ill and grieving father, and a grandparent in an old people's home.

Was it any wonder Bella had turned to gorgeous, steady Kent Rigby and his happy, well-balanced family?

Zoe launched to her feet before she had a chance to feel the lurch of pain that followed any thoughts about Kent. Tonight she was more determined than ever to get over that nonsense. This wedding would be fantastic and she would be the best possible bridesmaid.

Her job for this weekend and over the next few weeks was clear. She had to steer Bella through any muddy waters that surfaced—including old flames—until she arrived safely beside Kent at the altar.

Yes, Zoe felt better now that plan was reaffirmed.

But as she reached for the kettle she saw her hand. Damn! She'd chewed her thumbnail to a nub.

Stripped to the waist, Kent was bending under an outside water tap, cleaning up the worst of the day's grime, when he heard the squeaky hinges of the backyard gate. He looked up, blinked water from his eyes, and saw Zoe Weston poised uncertainly just inside the gate.

She was dressed in city clothes, as if she'd come straight from the office, and her crisp white blouse and charcoal pencil skirt looked totally out of place against a backdrop of gumtrees and grazing land. Kent, however, found himself helplessly captivated.

Stunned might be a better word. He couldn't stop staring.

Zoe's office clothes emphasised her neat, slim curves, and her legs, in sheer stockings and shiny high heels, were—there was only one word—*sensational*. Her dark hair was pulled back beneath a narrow velvet band into some kind of knot, and she looked sophisticated and serious and—heaven help him—astonishingly sexy.

His reaction was as bad as last time. No, worse.

When he'd met her by the road side she'd been wearing a T-shirt and blue jeans. Ever since then he'd worked hard to stop thinking about her unique qualities—not just her sensible calm manner, but the cute tilt of her head, and the blue of her eyes, and the softness of her mouth.

Now, there was something else—something about the sight of her in her smart city clothes that grabbed him by the throat and sent a jolt arrowing south.

Hell.

Why was she here? Alone?

Where was Bella? Weren't Zoe and Bella supposed to be staying at Blue Gums this weekend with Tom Shaw? Tom was so much better now and he'd started going into Toowoomba to the AA meetings.

What had happened?

Shaking off his unwanted reaction, Kent called to her, 'Hello there.'

Zoe still hadn't moved. In fact, she seemed to be as transfixed as he was—watching him with a worried, staring gaze and with a hand pressed to the open V of her snowy-white blouse.

Hastily, Kent snapped off the water and reached for his discarded shirt, using it to dry his bare shoulders and chest as he hurried over to her.

'I wasn't expecting you,' he said, stating the obvious as he thrust his arms into the sleeves of the damp and crumpled shirt. 'Is everything OK?'

'I—' Zoe began, gulping and looking uncomfortable. 'Bella asked me to come here. We were supposed to stay at her father's place, but he's—' She grimaced, and looked embarrassed.

'Oh, no. Tom isn't drunk, is he?'

Zoe nodded. 'He's in a pretty bad way, I'm afraid.'

Kent swore and slammed a balled fist against his thigh. 'Tom was doing so well. He seemed to be on the mend.' He let out a heavy sigh. 'I'm sure Bella's upset.'

'Yes. She begged me to come over to your place, while she stayed with her dad.' Zoe's eyes were round with worry. 'I hope she's OK.'

'She won't come to any harm. Tom's never violent, and he'll certainly never hurt his daughter. Not physically.' Kent pulled the limp fronts of his shirt together, and started to fumble with the lower buttons. 'Just the same, I'll phone her straight away.'

Zoe glanced at his chest and then looked away, her colour deepening.

'Come inside,' he said, doing up another button, then nodding towards the house. 'You look like you could use a cuppa, or maybe something stronger.'

'Thanks. I'd love a cuppa.'

As they walked across the lawn to the screen door at the back of the house Kent's thoughts were for Bella and her devastation over Tom's lapse. He forced himself to ignore the slim, sophisticated woman walking beside him. He paid her no attention. He couldn't afford to think about her curve-hugging skirt and her long legs sheathed in filmy stockings, or her high city heels sinking into the grass.

Sitting at the granite island bench in the Rigbys' farmhouse kitchen, Zoe wrapped her hands around a mug of hot, sweet tea, closed her eyes and drew a deep breath.

From outside came the creamy vanilla scent of wisteria mixed with the danker scent of hay and a faint whiff of animals. But the pleasant country aromas did little to calm her. She was still shaken by the scene she'd witnessed at Blue Gums.

The sight of Bella's father, staggering and incoherent, had been beyond awful, and poor Bella had been so embarrassed and upset. She'd shooed Zoe out of there as quickly as she could.

But Zoe's arrival at Willara Downs had brought an equally disturbing close encounter with Kent's naked, *wet* torso.

OK, a man without his shirt should *not* have been a big deal. Zoe had seen plenty of bare male chests. Of course she had, but this was the first time she'd had a close encounter with Kent Rigby's smooth, bulky muscles, and tapering, hard-packed abs. Not to mention the enticing trail of dark hair heading downwards beneath his belt buckle.

It was an experience destined to rattle any girl senseless. What hope had Zoe?

For pity's sake, she'd gone into mourning over the closure of his shirt buttons…

In fact, Kent had been doing up his buttons crookedly and she'd *almost* offered to help him get them straight. How sad was that? Thank heavens she'd stopped herself just in time.

Now she cringed as she imagined the surprise and disapproval in his eyes if she'd actually reached out and touched him.

It's OK. I didn't do anything stupid. I'm calming down. I'm fine. I'm back in control.

Zoe took another sip of tea and then a bite of the scrumptious shortbread that Kent's mother had thoughtfully left in his pantry. Yes, she was definitely feeling calmer now. And sanity certainly returned as she heard the deep rumble of Kent's voice down the hall. He was talking to Bella on the telephone, and she could imagine him making sure Bella was OK and that her dad was fine, too. He would be reassuring Bella and telling her he loved her.

While their conversation continued, Zoe flicked through a country life magazine with articles about kitchen gardens and new breeds of chickens, and fabulous recipes using all kinds of cheese.

Zoe tried to imagine Bella reading one of these country magazines, and being inspired by the articles. Somehow, she couldn't quite picture her friend getting her beautifully manicured hands dirty in a veggie garden, or rolling pastry, or saving her kitchen scraps to feed to the chooks.

Bella had never actually talked about her future as a farmer's wife. In fact she seemed very much a city girl these days with a fondness for beauty salons and coffee shops rather than hay bales and farmhouse cooking. But then Bella was a bit of a dark horse. She'd never talked about her father's problems with alcohol either.

Clearly there were many strands to Bella's life, and the city office girl who loved high fashion and fancy nail polish was quite possibly a brave front. Now, more than ever, Zoe could understand why her friend had chosen a steadfast and reliable partner like Kent. A good, rock-solid husband. A loving man who knew all about her, a guy who would help to shoulder her worries about her father.

There was no doubt about it. Kent was Bella's perfect match in every way.

Right. OK.

Fortunately, Zoe locked in that thought scant seconds before she heard Kent's footsteps returning down the passage to the kitchen. She had her smile fixed in place before he entered.

Even so, she felt a zap of reaction the instant she saw him. There was something impossibly appealing about Kent Rigby, something about his tanned profile, about his dark, friendly eyes and the flash of his smile that made Zoe feel as bright and shimmering as a sunrise.

Which proved how very foolish she was. Apart from the very important fact that the man was taken—by her best friend, no less—she should have enough bad memories of Rodney the Rat to douse any sparks of unwanted libido.

'How's Bella?' she asked Kent.

'She's upset, of course, and mad as hell with her dad. He'd started going to AA and we thought he was going to be fine now.'

'Perhaps he's just had one slip and he'll be back on the wagon tomorrow.'

'Let's hope so.' Kent let out a sigh. 'Tom had problems with grog when he was young, but he was dry the whole time he and Mary were married. Since her death, he's been on a downhill slide.'

'Poor man. And poor Bella. She must feel so helpless.'

Kent nodded. 'It must have been a shock for you, too, coming across him like that.'

'Well, yes, it was, but only because it was so unexpected. And Bella was so upset.' Zoe lifted her now empty mug. 'Thanks for the tea. It was just what I needed.' She stood. 'I guess you'll want to get over to Bella's place straight away.'

'Later. Tom's asleep right now and Bella wants a bit of time to sort the place out.' Kent went to the fridge, opened it and stood staring at its contents. 'I'll fix a meal for us first.'

'For us?'

'Yep—we're on our own tonight.'

'B-but you don't have to feed me.' Zoe was stammering, rattled by the possibility of a meal alone with this man. 'I can go into town. I'll stay at the pub and grab a meal there.'

'Zoe, relax.' Shutting the fridge once more, Kent grinned at her. 'You're president and secretary of our wedding planning committee. Of course, you're very welcome here. You can stay the night, and you can have the same room as last time.'

She was about to protest again, when she realised it

might come across as rude. Kent was keeping up his reputation for country hospitality. He might be upset if she refused.

'Thanks,' she said. Then, to cover any giveaway signs of attraction, she surveyed the kitchen with her most businesslike glance. 'So what can I do to help you?'

'If we dig out the sheets now, you can make up your bed while I throw a couple of steaks in a pan.'

Already Kent was heading out of the kitchen and Zoe hurried after him. The linen cupboard was in a hallway, and he flipped the louvred doors open, releasing a faint scent of lavender.

'This is where I run into trouble.' A small smile made attractive creases around his dark eyes. 'I haven't a clue which sheets I'm supposed to give you.'

Zoe gulped. Discussing bed sheets with Kent was her wickedest fantasy rolled into her worst nightmare. 'I think I used those pink striped sheets last time.'

'Terrific.' He was already lifting them from the shelf. 'I'm sure they'll do.'

His wrists brushed against her as he handed her the sheets. It was a relief to disappear into the guest room and get busy making the bed.

Once this was done, she freshened up in the bathroom, brushed her hair and changed into shorts and a T-shirt. If only she could switch off her hormones as easily as she changed her clothes.

The scent of frying steak and onions greeted her when she came back into the kitchen. And the rather fetching sight of Kent standing at the stove, changed into a clean white, correctly buttoned shirt.

He sent her another of his flashing smiles, but then

his smile went super still, and he continued to stare at Zoe, a slight frown now warring with his grin.

'What's wrong?'

'You've let your hair down.'

Zap! A bushfire scorched her skin. She fingered her hair, dark and straight like her mum's, and now skimming her shoulders. 'I didn't know it was a crime for a girl to let her hair down on a Friday evening.'

'Course it isn't.' Kent shrugged and turned back to the steaks, flipping them over. Without looking at her, he said, 'It looks great either way. In your bridesmaid's outfit you're going to knock the local yokels for six.'

The comment warranted another very stern lecture to herself. His compliment would go to her head. It should be possible to have a normal conversation with him without overreacting to every second sentence.

Desperate to appear cool and unaffected, she said glibly, 'That's reassuring to know. I'm on the lookout for a spare farmer.'

'Are you?'

It wasn't the flippant or teasing response she'd expected from Kent. His head had jerked around and his dark eyes were surprisingly intense.

Now she was more flustered than ever. 'Of course I'm not serious,' she said tightly. 'That was my poor attempt at a joke.'

Time to put an end to this subject. She looked around her. 'What can I do to help? Why don't I make a salad to go with the steak?'

Kent's thoughts were apparently elsewhere and he took a moment to answer her.

'Sure,' he said at last, and then, after a beat, his usual

smile was back in place. 'Trust a girl to want to spoil a good steak with rabbit food.'

They ate on the back veranda, looking out at the idyllic view of the soft, velvety hills and fields as they were slowly enveloped by the shadowy night.

Zoe wondered what she and Kent would talk about now. Given her recent gaffes, she wasn't sure she could cope with a conversation about Bella and the wedding. She wanted to ask Kent about the property. That was safe, and she was genuinely curious about the crops and grazing herds. Details of farm life had always fascinated her.

But it seemed Kent had other ideas. As he speared a tomato cube and a chunk of cucumber he said, 'So, tell me about yourself, Zoe.'

'Me?'

'Why not?' His smile was relaxed and easy once more and when she hesitated, he said, 'You're Bella's best friend and your friendship's not going to come to an end when we're married. I expect you'll be an important part of our lives for a very long time.'

Would she? Zoe had been hoping that her life beyond the wedding would be Kent-free. How else could she get back to normal? How could she stand the strain of an ongoing friendship with Bella and Kent if they remained close friends way into the future? Good grief, surely she wouldn't still be a jangling wreck when she was eighty?

It was an alarming prospect. Added to that, Zoe didn't really enjoy talking about herself. As a child she'd been forever arriving at new schools and answering the same old questions over and over. 'I've already told you about my parents and how I spent most of my childhood on the road.'

'But your parents have stopped touring now, haven't they?'

She nodded, then took a sip of the chilled white wine Kent had poured for her. And as she put the glass down she found herself telling him about the music shop in Sugar Bay and her little brother, Toby. And then, because he smiled so encouragingly, she told him about Toby's soccer ambitions and his endless experiments and their family's Saturday night barbecues when her parents had jam sessions with old mates.

'Sounds like they're a lot of fun,' Kent said sincerely. 'Would you like to live at the bay?'

'I—I'm not sure.' Zoe pulled a face. 'If I'm honest I feel a bit resentful that Mum and Dad waited till Toby came along before they settled down. He's having a very different childhood from mine.'

She shrugged. 'The bay's a great place to visit, but I like Brisbane, too.' *And the country.* But she wouldn't tell Kent that. 'I have to make my own life, don't I?'

'Of course.' He was watching her carefully again. 'And the world's your oyster,' he said quietly.

'Well, yes… Actually, I'm thinking about heading overseas.'

'You'll love it,' he said, but now his smile was tinged with a bewildering hint of sadness and for the first time Zoe wondered if he felt trapped at Willara Downs.

Curiosity prompted her to say, 'I've often wondered what it's like to grow up in one place and know you'll spend your whole life there.'

'Do you think it sounds boring?'

'No, not at all. Quite the opposite, actually.'

A frown furrowed Kent's brow and his dark eyes registered something very close to dismay.

Fearing she'd said too much, Zoe took a quick sip of her wine.

But whatever had bothered Kent passed and he was soon relaxed again. 'I love living here,' he said. 'It's not just the land and the lifestyle. For me, it's the strong feeling of continuity. My family's been here from the start. My great-great-great-grandfather looked after the horses on one of the earliest explorations and he fell in love with this district and settled here more than a hundred and fifty years ago.'

'Wow.' Zoe looked out at the view that had almost disappeared. 'All that history.'

Kent nodded. 'My grandfather and my great-grandfather both went away to the wars, and while they were gone the women and children ran the farms for them.' Across the table Kent's eyes met Zoe's. 'The responsibility of continuing those traditions means a great deal to me.'

'I'm sure it does. I feel goose bumps just thinking about it.' Zoe loved the idea of such permanence and such a deeply rooted sense of belonging.

'But that doesn't mean I don't love travelling as well,' Kent added with a twinkling smile.

'Have you travelled very far?'

'When I was nineteen I had a year off—backpacking with Steve, my best man, around Europe.'

'What was your favourite place?'

'Prague,' he answered without hesitation.

'That's interesting. Most people choose Paris or London or Rome. Even Barcelona.'

'Or Venice.'

'Yes.' She smiled, pleased that Kent was relaxed

again. When he looked at her with his serious expression, the world seemed to tilt ever so slightly, but everything felt in the right balance again now. 'So what did you love about Prague?'

Kent laughed. 'If Steve was here, he'd rave about the Czech beer. But for me it was the old city at Christmas time. It was snowing and unbelievably beautiful—the buildings, the pavements, the cafés, the restaurants. Everything in Prague is so old and dripping with history. Not a plastic Christmas tree in sight.'

'That sounds lovely. I must remember to try to be in Prague at Christmas.'

'Yes, do that.' For a moment there was a flicker of something in Kent's eyes. It might have been regret, but then he cracked a grin. 'And send me a postcard.'

'I will. I promise.'

'By the way,' he said, 'you still haven't told me your favourite colour.'

'And you haven't told me why you want to know.'

'Patience, Zoe. All in good time.'

'What if said I don't have a favourite?'

He laughed. 'I'd believe you. Neither do I.'

They laughed together then, and for a heady few seconds their gazes reached across the table and locked. For Zoe, it was like the moment beside the road when her entire being had felt connected to Kent's.

Then Kent broke the spell by looking away and deliberately reaching for his beer. And Zoe thudded back to earth. To reality.

She was such an idiot.

After that, they both turned their attention to their meals, but, although Zoe's steak was tender and the salad crisp, she seemed to have lost her appetite. She took another sip of wine and vowed to keep her thoughts firmly fixed on the painful truth.

How could she be so hopeless, when poor Bella was stuck at Blue Gums, caring for her dad? It was Bella who should be here, alone with Kent, and having this nice romantic dinner.

Zoe felt a little better when she and Kent left the veranda and returned to the kitchen to rinse their cutlery and plates and stack them in the dishwasher.

'I hope Mr Shaw will be OK in the morning,' she said.

'Don't worry about Tom.' Kent gave an offhand shrug. 'I'm sure he'll be fine in the morning. He'll be full of remorse and Bella will give him an earful about following doctor's orders.'

Zoe nodded. 'There was a fellow in Lead the Way with a drinking problem. He wanted everyone to turn a blind eye.'

Kent's eyes widened with interest, then abruptly he let out a sigh. 'Got to admit, it's really hard to watch Tom sink into such a state. He used to be such a fine man. He was my hero for many years. He saved my life when I was a nipper.'

'Really?' Zoe couldn't resist asking, 'What happened?'

'I was acting the fool down at the local waterhole, dived in at the wrong spot and hit my head on a rock.' With a sheepish smile Kent leaned closer and pointed to a faint thin scar on his forehead.

Zoe caught the clean, male scent of his skin, mere inches from her. She could see the scar, but his proximity also gave her the chance for a close-up study of the rest of his face, the length of his eyelashes, the graininess of his jaw, the sexy curve of his lips.

Oh, man.

Perhaps Kent sensed her indecent interest. His expression took on a strange frowning tension, and the air around them seemed to pulse. It seemed like ages before he pulled back, and he let out a strangled laugh. 'Lucky I didn't break my flaming neck. I certainly would have drowned if Tom hadn't been there. He got me off the bottom, dragged me out and revived me.'

'Thank God he did.' Oh, heavens, that sounded far too fervent. Quickly, Zoe asked, 'Was Bella there, too?'

'Yes, she witnessed the whole thing. We've both looked on her dad as a hero ever since.'

Kent's voice was so rough and solemn as he said this that Zoe knew deep emotions were tied to the statement.

'I'm sure he'll get over this road bump,' she said gently.

She was also sure it was time for Kent to leave. Regrettably, their time together had been way too pleasant.

She made a shooing motion towards the door. 'Now, thanks for a lovely dinner, but you should get going over to Bella's.'

'Yes, I'll head off now. You know where the tea and coffee are, don't you? And the TV remote.'

'Yes, thanks. I'll be fine. Don't worry about me. I'm used to living on my own. Now, go, Kent. Get out of here.'

He went.

I'm used to living on my own...

Standing at the kitchen window, Zoe watched the twin red eyes of Kent's tail lights disappearing into the black night, and she discovered a huge difference between being alone and being consumed by horrible loneliness.

Dismayed, she went through to the lovely lounge room. Like the rest of the house it was elegant yet relaxing, with deep comfy sofas, brightly coloured throw pillows. With a feminine touch, there'd be cut-glass vases filled with flowers from the garden.

For a brief, unwise moment, she indulged a childhood fantasy and imagined being the mistress of a beautiful country homestead like this one—cutting and arranging flowers from her garden, baking hearty meals for her drop-dead gorgeous, farmer husband and their children, attending meetings of the local growers' association, waking each morning to fresh air and open spaces...

And waking to the drop-dead gorgeous, farmer husband in bed beside her.

OK. Fantasy over. Back to reality. Fast.

Zoe flicked on the TV, made herself comfortable, and settled to watch one of her favourite comedies. A good dose of on-screen hilarity would soon cure her of any lingering self-pity.

But unfortunately the usually lively script was dull and unfunny this evening, and Zoe couldn't raise a chuckle. Her thoughts kept drifting...

She was picturing Kent's arrival at Blue Gums...and Bella's happy, open-arm welcome.

Stop it. Stop it. Stop it.

The couple on the TV screen were embracing, and again Zoe thought about Kent and Bella. Right about now, Bella would probably be undoing the buttons on Kent's shirt, running her hands over his lovely, hard muscles...

Oh, good grief. Enough!

Snapping off the TV, Zoe jumped to her feet. She was *not* going to succumb to this nonsense. She needed to keep busy, to keep her mind occupied with something constructive. But what could she do in a stranger's house?

Heading for the kitchen, she prayed for an answer.

CHAPTER FIVE

KENT was in a black mood. His experience at Blue Gums this evening had been depressing to say the least. Disturbing, too, as he hadn't been able to offer Bella much comfort. She'd been distracted, not her usual self and troubled by more than her father's illness. And yet she wouldn't confide in Kent, wouldn't let him help.

After the pleasant dinner conversation he'd enjoyed with Zoe, his fiancée's reception had been like a bucket of icy water. He was sure it had been a relief for both of them when he left early.

Now, home again, he approached the kitchen and saw...

Candles.

Everywhere.

On every bench top and flat surface in the state-of-the-art kitchen his mother had so faithfully designed, small candles sat, glowing warmly. And in the middle of the dancing candlelight stood Zoe, looking lovely, yet wide-eyed and cautious, rather like a naughty angel caught playing with the devil.

'I'm going to shift all this,' she announced hurriedly as soon as she saw him. 'I was planning to tidy everything before you got back.'

Black mood gone, Kent suppressed a smile as he stepped through the doorway into his kitchen.

'I—I know I've been a little carried away,' she hastened to add. 'I wanted to see how these candles looked, but I wasn't expecting you so soon, Kent. You're early, aren't you?'

'Bella's...worn out,' he said quietly.

'Oh.' Zoe frowned. 'Well, I know you weren't expecting to come home to forty-eight candles, but they're for the wedding. What do you think?'

'They're beautiful.' He gave in to the smile tugging at his mouth. *And you're beautiful, too...*

The thought sprang unbidden, and the words trembled on his lips, but thank goodness he resisted the impulse to voice them aloud.

'I wanted to get the full impact,' Zoe was explaining earnestly. 'I thought the candles would be lovely for the wedding reception. I'd like to put them in little paper bags filled with sand and they should look lovely outside in the garden. But don't worry—they're battery powered, so they're not going to burn your house down.'

'That's a relief.' Stepping closer, Kent lifted a little candle. 'And they can't blow out either.'

'No. They're called smart candles.'

'Good name.' He smiled at her, and he couldn't help adding, 'Smart candles for a smart girl.' Too late, he realised how softly he'd spoken, almost seductively, as if a weird kind of spell had taken hold of him.

In response, Zoe's blue eyes grew wider, clearly surprised. Her lips parted in a small moue.

Kent found himself staring at her soft pink lips... gazing into her lovely, expressive blue eyes...until he was lost in those eyes...

He was in free fall...

And all he could think was how badly he wanted to kiss Zoe. Now. In the middle of his kitchen. Surrounded by the glow of her candles.

He would start by sweeping her into his arms and kissing her sweet, pouty lips, and then he would sample the pale, fine skin at the base of her throat.

But perhaps Zoe could read his mind. She dropped her gaze and a deep stain spread over her cheeks. Her hand shook as she pressed it to her forehead, pushing back a strand of hair with a small sound of dismay.

Kent blinked. What the hell had come over him? Why couldn't he shake off this strange feeling of enchantment?

Zoe was the bridesmaid, for crying out loud. He had to forget about kissing her. *Say something about the candles.*

With a supreme effort, he dragged his attention away from her. What had she said? Something about putting these candles in little bags of sand?

'Do you have the sand you need?' he asked.

Zoe shook her head. 'I—I'm really mad with myself. I meant to call in at a craft shop and I forgot.'

'A craft shop? For sand?'

'In Brisbane the craft shops sell lovely, fine white sand.'

At that, he couldn't help laughing.

'What's so funny?'

'You don't need to buy sand at a craft shop, Zoe. Willara Creek is full of it.'

She shook her head, clearly unimpressed. 'But creek sand is damp and dirty and full of little twiggy bits.'

'Not all creek sand. Why don't I take you down there tomorrow and you can see what you think?' When she hesitated, he said, 'If it's not up to scratch, no harm done.'

'Bella and your mother are both coming over tomorrow. We're going to be busy with all the preparations.'

'We'll go first thing in the morning, then. If you don't mind an early start. How about a quick trip down to the creek before breakfast?'

There was more than a slight hesitation this time, but then Zoe nodded. 'Thank you,' she said, although she didn't smile. Instead she became businesslike. 'I'll shift everything out of here now.' Already she was turning off the candles.

Sitting in bed, Zoe stared into the darkness, unable to sleep.

Hugging her knees, she rocked slightly, something she only did when she was worried.

Or puzzled.

And confused.

The foreboding she'd felt about this wedding was deepening. Something *really* wasn't right—and she was pretty sure it wasn't just her feelings about the bridegroom getting in the way.

She knew Bella wasn't happy and the unhappiness wasn't only related to her father's health problems. Now Zoe was beginning to suspect that Kent wasn't happy either.

This possibility shocked her.

How could such a gorgeous, successful man, who could no doubt have his pick of any girl in the district, allow himself to walk, with his eyes wide open, into a marriage that wasn't gloriously happy?

It was the kind of question that would keep a conscientious bridesmaid awake all night. Pity she'd agreed to be up at the crack of dawn.

When Zoe woke to Kent's knock the next morning she felt more like a sleep deprived bridesmaid than a conscientious one. The thought of leaving her nice comfy bed to look at sand in a creek bed held no appeal.

But Kent had brought her a mug of tea and a slice of hot toast with strawberry jam, and Zoe couldn't help being impressed by this, so she soon found herself in his ute, bumping down a rough dirt track to Willara Creek.

To discover the creek was stunningly beautiful.

Majestic twisted and knotted paperbarks and tall river gums stood guard above water that was quiet and still and cool, and edged by boulders entwined with grevillea roots. Wind whispered gently in the she-oaks.

Charmed, Zoe watched a flight of wild ducks take off from the water. 'It's so beautiful and peaceful,' she said in an awed whisper.

Kent smiled at her. 'I thought you might like it.'

As she climbed out of the ute she heard birds calling to each other as they hunted for honey in the bright red grevillea flowers.

'And here's the sand,' she said, almost straight away seeing a small beach of nice white quartz-like grains.

'There's even better sand over here.' Kent was pointing farther along the bank.

Sure enough, he was right. Trapped among rocks, the sand was so white it glistened. Kneeling, Zoe studied it more closely and saw flickers of gold—pale golden specks, shining brightly. 'Kent, that can't be real gold?'

'No, I'm afraid it's only fool's gold. Its technical name is pyrite. But it's pretty enough for what you want, isn't it?'

'It's perfect. Absolutely gorgeous for a wedding.'

With impressive efficiency, Kent filled a couple of good-sized buckets and stowed them in the back of his ute.

Zoe took a deep breath of the fresh morning air as she looked about her at the deep pool of cool, inviting water, the smooth boulders and magnificent trees. 'I guess we'll have to go back already, but what a pity. It's so beautiful here. It almost looks as if it's been landscaped.'

'We don't have to rush away.' Kent left the ute and squatted on the bank, looking out across the still water. 'This place has always been special. We've always kept the cattle out of here and we pump water up to troughs for them.'

'It must be amazing to have a place like this that you actually own. You'd feel a very close affinity to it.'

To Zoe's surprise, Kent didn't respond straight away. Picking up a handful of polished river stones, he skipped them out over the water, watching them bounce. As the last stone plopped he said, without looking at her, 'This is where I nearly ended my young life.'

Oh, God.

A pang of horror arrowed through Zoe, and she had a sudden picture of a little boy with dark hair and dark eyes recklessly diving and hitting his head…

This lovely man had nearly died.

Here. In this idyllic setting.

Her throat stung and she might have cried, if Kent hadn't been watching.

He sent her a grin.

She blinked away the tears. 'So this is where Bella's dad saved you?'

He nodded. 'It was nearly a year before I got back in the water.'

'I'm not surprised.' And then, she *had* to ask, 'What was it like, Kent? Can you remember? Did you know you'd nearly died?'

As soon as the questions were out she felt embarrassed by her nosiness, but Kent, to her relief, didn't seem to mind.

'I have no recollection at all of diving in, but I have a very vivid memory of opening my eyes from a deep and terrible, dark dream where I was choking. I looked straight up into Tom Shaw's face, and beyond him I could see the vivid blue sky and the tops of the river gums.'

'Did you know what had happened?'

Kent nodded slowly. 'It's weird, but I seemed to understand that I'd been given a second chance at life.'

He'd only been six—so young to be confronted with something so profound.

'I'm surprised you're still happy to come down here,' she said.

'I love it here,' Kent replied quietly. 'This place always makes me think about survival. And fate.'

'And Tom Shaw.'

His dark eyes studied Zoe's face intently, and again she felt an unwilling connection, a silent *something* zinging between them. Quicksilver shivers turned her arms to goose bumps.

'And Tom Shaw,' Kent said quietly. 'I'll never forget that debt.'

* * *

Shortly after they got back to the homestead, Bella rang.

'How are things at your place this morning?' Kent asked her.

'Dad's fine, thank heavens. He slept in late, but he's just eaten a huge recovery breakfast. And he seems really well. No coughing or shortness of breath. And of course, he's full of remorse and promises.'

'Good. So you'll be coming over here soon?'

'Actually…' An awkward note crept into Bella's voice. 'That's what I'm ringing about. I've been thinking I really should scoot into town to see Paddy.'

'Your grandfather?' Surprise buzzed a low warning inside Kent. 'But Zoe's here. Don't you two have all kinds of jobs lined up for this weekend?'

'Well…yes…but I thought I could squeeze in a *very* quick trip to town. It's just that I haven't seen Paddy for ages and you know how dreary it can be in the old people's home.' Almost as an afterthought, Bella asked, 'Is Zoe at a loose end?'

Kent glanced through the open doorway across the veranda to the garden. His mother had driven out from town to discuss wedding plans and she and Zoe were deep in conversation. They were pacing out sections of lawn and, judging by their arm-waving movements and general nodding and jotting-down of notes, they were discussing the table and seating arrangements.

They'd started over coffee this morning, chatting about the bridal shower—something about making a wedding dress from wrapping paper. Then they'd moved on to the flowers for table centrepieces at the wedding, and the kinds of pot plants that looked best in the gazebo. Zoe had wondered if there should be little lights entwined with the greenery.

The two of them were getting on like a bushfire.

But Kent knew damn well that it should be Bella who was out there in the garden with his mother. Surely, the bride should be involved in all this planning.

Renewed uneasiness stirred in him. He did his best to suppress it. Bella had always been upfront with him. She would tell him if there was a problem.

'Zoe's certainly not at a loose end,' he told her now. 'She and my mother are pretty busy, actually. If you're not careful they'll have the whole wedding planned before you get here.'

'Wonderful,' Bella said with a laugh.

'Wonderful?' Kent tried not to sound too concerned, but he couldn't shake off the troubling sense that something was definitely off kilter. Last night when he'd gone over to the Shaws' place, Bella had been moody and despondent, but that was excusable. He'd understood how upset she was about Tom.

But this morning was different. Tom was on the mend again, and Bella seemed to be leaving all the arrangements for the wedding to Zoe. Surely she should be here?

'You know me, Kent,' Bella said smoothly. 'I've never been much of a planner. Remember how I always used to leave my assignments until the last minute.'

'Yeah, I remember. But I think *you* should remember that Zoe *is* a planner, and hosting a wedding with dozens of guests is hardly the same as a school assignment. Zoe's your only bridesmaid, for heaven's sake, and she's doing an incredible job, but you can't leave it all on her shoulders.'

'Kent, you're right. I'm sorry.' Bella's lowered voice was suddenly contrite. 'I mustn't leave everything to Zoe just because she's so capable. Look, I promise to be out there very, very soon. I'll just race into town, say a quick hello to Paddy, and I'll come straight over. I'll bring a cherry pie and some of that lovely stuffed bread from the Willara bakery for lunch.'

Still worried, Kent hung up and stood with his hand resting on the receiver. He frowned as he looked through the doorway to his mother and Zoe out in the garden.

They were examining a bed of roses now, heads together—one a shower of silver curls and the other a silky, dark brown fall. The two of them were talking animatedly and doing rather a lot of smiling and nodding.

Zoe leaned forward to smell a lush pink rose bloom, and her hair swung forward with the movement. She was wearing knee-length khaki shorts and sandals, and a soft floral top with a little frill that skimmed her collarbones—so different from yesterday afternoon's pencil-slim skirt, stockings and high heels, and yet every bit as appealing.

The women moved on, and his mother became busy with her secateurs, tidying, trimming, and apparently explaining something to Zoe. Every so often, a tinkle of feminine laughter floated over the lawn.

Watching them, Kent thought that any stranger, coming upon the idyllic scene, could be forgiven for assuming that Zoe was his mother's future daughter-in-law.

His bride.

Hell. A dangerous flame leapt in his chest. Hell no. Not Zoe. It was ridiculous. Impossible. Never going to happen.

Bella should be here. Now.

* * *

As it turned out, Zoe also made a trip into Willara that morning. Having settled on their plans for the bridal shower, she and Kent's mother needed several items from the newsagent, so Zoe volunteered to collect them.

'Perhaps Kent could go with you for company,' Stephanie Rigby suggested.

Out of the corner of her eye, Zoe saw Kent tense, and felt an answering whip-crack reaction. *No.* No way could she risk spending any more time alone with her best friend's bridegroom.

Without chancing another glance in Kent's direction, she said, 'Thanks, but I know Kent's busy, and I'll be fine on my own.'

To her relief, there was no argument.

'You never know your luck,' Stephanie said serenely. 'You might run into Bella and you could double check her preferences before you buy the ribbons and the paper daisies.'

'That's a good idea. I'll keep an eye out for her. I guess Willara's so small, it's quite possible to run into people on the main street.'

Stephanie laughed. 'It happens all the time.'

'Your best chance of catching Bella will be at the Greenacres home or the bakery,' Kent suggested in a dry, unreadable tone that made Zoe wonder if he was in a bad mood.

'OK, I'll try the home, then the bakery.'

Zoe had never visited a home for the aged. Her grandparents were still quite fit and healthy and lived in their own homes, so she was already a bit nervous when she pulled up at Greenacres on Willara's outskirts. Then she walked through sliding doors into the large, tiled foyer, and came to a frozen, heart-thudding halt.

Bella was standing on the far side of the reception

area, deep in conversation—an animated, intense conversation—with a young man.

Zoe took one at Bella's companion and immediately recognised the wild, dark hair and strong stubbled jaw from the photos she'd seen on the internet. Damon Cavello.

She felt a punch of shock in the centre of her chest, but she told herself she was overreacting. Damon was an old friend of Bella's and Kent's from their school days— and a chance meeting with him in an aged care home was perfectly harmless. It wasn't as if she'd caught Bella indulging in a sly assignation. This was no big deal.

So maybe they were leaning subtly towards each other and gazing intently into each other's eyes. And maybe their body language suggested a deep, mutual interest that locked out the rest of the world…

Or maybe Zoe was totally misreading the whole situation.

Unable to contain her curiosity a moment longer, she stepped forward. 'Bella!'

Her friend jumped and turned, and when she saw Zoe she blushed like litmus paper.

'Zoe, f-fancy seeing you here.' Bella shot a hasty glance to the man at her side, then back to her friend. 'Are you looking for me? Nothing's happened at home, has it?'

'There's no problem,' Zoe reassured her. 'I came into town to buy a few things from the newsagent, and I ducked in here first. We knew you were here and we'd like to have your approval on—'

Zoe hesitated, uncomfortably aware of Damon Cavello's steely and not particularly friendly gaze. 'We wanted to check on one or two—matters—for the wedding.'

'Oh, right.' Bella was her normal colour again, and she straightened her shoulders and lifted her chin, drawing dignity around her like armour. She smiled carefully as she turned to the man beside her. 'Damon, this is my bridesmaid, my wonderful friend, Zoe Weston.'

Despite the tension zinging in the air, Zoe was aware of a warm swelling of pride when she heard herself described in such glowing terms.

'Zoe, this is Damon Cavello, an old school friend.'

'Of course.' Zoe held out her hand and favoured him with her warmest smile. 'You contacted me on Facebook. Hi, Damon, nice to meet you.'

'How do you do, Zoe?' Damon shook her hand firmly, but his smile didn't quite reach his eyes. 'And thank you for engineering this chance to hook up with the old gang.'

He nodded towards Bella and his silver-grey eyes seemed to smoulder, but his voice was relaxed enough, so it shouldn't have been an awkward moment. Zoe, however, could feel unmistakable vibes of tension. And yikes, she could practically see the electricity sparking between this pair.

'Damon has been visiting his grandmother,' Bella said.

'And you ran into him while you were visiting your grandfather. What a lucky coincidence.'

'Yes.'

An elderly woman, shuffling past with a walking frame, beamed a radiant smile on the three of them.

'Well…as I said, I was on the way to the newsagents,' Zoe continued. 'So if you two have more catching up to do, I can wait for you there, Bella.'

'It's OK. I'll come with you now. Damon and I have said our hellos.'

Damon frowned and Zoe sent him another friendly smile. 'Will we see you at the wedding?'

'Sure.' He swallowed uncomfortably as if there was a painful constriction in his throat. 'Kent kindly emailed an invitation. Asked me to the bucks' party as well.'

'Great. We should run into you again, then, either some time next weekend, or on the big day.'

'Absolutely.'

The girls had driven into town in separate vehicles, so there was no chance for an in-depth conversation during their shopping jaunt or on their separate journeys back to Willara Downs. And for the rest of the weekend they were so busy, making decorations, or party favours, or cooking sweets and canapés to be stored or frozen that they didn't have time for an in-depth talk.

It was Sunday afternoon when they were heading back down the highway to Brisbane before they were alone and the subject of Damon could be properly aired.

Not that Bella was in a talkative mood. From the moment they left Willara, she seemed to slip lower and lower in the passenger seat, slumped in despondent silence.

'Missing Kent already?' Zoe asked tentatively.

Bella gave a guilty start and she frowned like a sleeper waking from a dream. 'Sorry…what did you say?'

'I asked if you were already missing Kent.'

'Oh…yes…of course.'

'At least you'll only have to wait two more weeks and then you can be with him all the time.'

'Yes,' Bella said softly.

Zoe had used every ounce of her inner strength to remain upbeat and supportive about Bella's good fortune, despite all the worrying niggles. Surely her friend could try a bit harder to act happy. Instead of rallying, however, Bella seemed to sink into even deeper misery.

By now, they were heading down the steep Too-woomba Range, and Zoe couldn't take her eyes off the road, but she had the horrible feeling that Bella was on the verge of crying. Then she heard a definite sob.

Casting a frantic sideways glance, Zoe saw tears streaming down her friend's face. Her heart gave a sickening lurch.

'Bell,' she cried, keeping her gaze fixed on the steep, winding road. 'What's the matter?'

'I'm OK,' Bella sobbed. 'I'm just being an idiot.'

Zoe couldn't help wondering if Damon was somehow the cause of these tears, but she had no idea how to ask such a probing question. Besides, it was her duty to keep Bella focused on Kent.

'It must be awful to have to say goodbye to Kent every weekend.'

'Oh, Zoe, don't,' Bella wailed.

Don't? Don't talk about Kent?

Thoroughly alarmed, Zoe held her tongue as she negotiated a particularly sharp hairpin bend. Out of the corner of her eye, she was aware of Bella pulling tissues from the bag at her feet and wiping her eyes and blowing her nose.

It wasn't till they reached the bottom of the range and the road levelled out once more that Zoe stole another glance Bella's way. Her friend was no longer crying, but her face was pale and blotchy and she still looked exceedingly unhappy.

'I really don't want to pry, Bell, but is there any way I can help?'

Bella released a drawn-out sigh. 'I don't think so, thanks.'

'I mean—tell me to shut up, but if you want to talk—about—*anything*—it's the bridesmaid's job to listen.'

This was greeted by a shaky little laugh. 'Oh, Zoe, you're such a sweetheart.'

A nice compliment, but not exactly true. A sweetheart did not fall for her best friend's fiancé.

A few minutes later, Zoe tried again. 'So…I suppose it's just tension. You have so much on your plate just now—worrying about your dad, and so many jobs crowding in with the wedding so close.'

Bella turned away to look out of the window at rows and rows of bright sunflowers standing with their heads high like soldiers in formation.

Clearly, she wasn't looking for a chance to talk about her problem, so Zoe drove on in silence…wondering… worrying…

Then out of the blue, as they approached Gatton, Bella sat up straighter. 'Zoe, I think I do need to talk. I can't deal with this on my own. Can we pull over?'

CHAPTER SIX

ZOE took the next ramp leading off the highway and parked beneath a jacaranda tree in an almost empty picnic area. At a distant table, a family were gathering up their tea things and packing them into a basket. The mother was calling to her little girl who was scooping up fallen jacaranda blossoms.

Suddenly needing air, Zoe lowered her window and dragged in deep breaths, catching the dank scent of newly turned earth from nearby fields and the sweeter scent of the flowering trees.

Her stomach churned uncomfortably and she unbuckled her seat belt. She was dead-set nervous now that Bella was about to confide her problem. Her friend's tears pointed to a serious dilemma, and Zoe wasn't confident she had the wisdom or the strength to advise her.

Honestly, could she trust herself to put her own silly, unwanted emotions aside?

Praying she would get this right, she said gently, 'I'm ready whenever you are, Bells.'

Bella pulled another tissue from her bag and blew her nose noisily, then, after only a moment's hesitation, she took the leap. 'There's no point in beating about the bush. I'm in a mess about this wedding.'

'Ah-h-h.'

Bella shot Zoe a sharp glance. 'So you're not surprised?'

'Not entirely. I must admit I've been waiting for you and Kent to show more—er—emotion about—well—everything. And right from the first time Damon made contact, it was pretty clear he made you edgy.'

Bella nodded. 'I know. Seeing Damon again has been a kind of wake-up call.'

'You mean you really care about him?'

'Oh, I don't really know, Zoes. He sends me kind of crazy. It's like I'm still in high school. Up and down and all over the place.'

'I'm sorry. I should never have posted that rave about your wedding on Facebook. It's my fault Damon found you.'

'Gosh, don't blame yourself. I think he heard about the wedding from other people as well.' Bella was pulling the tissue in her lap to shreds.

'Damon's not trying to stop you getting married, is he?'

Zoe had a sudden vision of Damon Cavello calling out in the middle of the wedding—at that moment when the minister asked the congregation to speak up or for ever hold their peace.

Bella shook her head, then, with another heavy sigh, she kicked off her shoes and drew her feet up onto the seat, hugging her knees. 'The thing is, when Damon rang me on Saturday morning, I had to see him. I thought if I saw him just once in the flesh—if I spoke to him, I'd get the old memories out of my system. But as soon as we met—'

Hairs stood on the back of Zoe's neck as she watched the flush spread across Bella's face. She tried to make light of it. 'So your heart took off like a racehorse? Your knees gave way?'

Bella nodded, then covered her face with her hands. 'What am I going to do?'

It was a question Zoe didn't want to answer. But poor Bella hadn't a mother to turn to and she was her best friend. Praying for wisdom, Zoe took a deep breath before she spoke. 'I—I guess it all depends on how you feel about Kent.'

At first Bella didn't answer. When she did, her voice was soft, wistful… 'That's my problem. I'm so worried that Kent and I are marrying for all the wrong reasons.'

'But he's stop-and-stare gorgeous,' Zoe suggested miserably.

Bella shot her a sharp, surprised glance.

'Just stating the obvious.' Zoe's shoulders lifted in a defensive shrug, and a dull ache curled around her heart.

'Well, I'm not going to argue with your good taste,' Bella said with a watery smile. 'But I just wish Kent and I had been in some sort of long-term relationship, or had at least been dating. The truth is, we haven't really seen very much of each other since I moved to Brisbane. We only caught up again properly when I started coming home, because Dad was so sick. We were both so worried about Dad and the farm, and Kent's gone out of his way to help.'

And he feels he owes your dad big-time for saving his life, Zoe wanted to say, but she kept the thought to herself.

Instead she said, 'I never totally understood how your engagement came about. It seemed a bit out of the blue to me. What made you say yes in the first place?'

Bella looked down at her diamond engagement ring

and her stunning, dark berry fingernails—enviably dramatic and gorgeous. 'It was a bit of an emotional whirlwind. It's not all that long since I lost my mum, and then it looked like I was losing my dad as well. The farm was going to rack and ruin. I felt like I was going under, too.'

'And yet you never mentioned anything about it to me.'

'Well…to be honest, I was a bit ashamed about my dad's drinking.'

Zoe gave a guilty sigh. If she'd been a better friend, the *right* kind of friend, Bella might have felt more comfortable about sharing her worries.

'I was coming home every weekend,' Bella went on. 'And I started seeing more and more of Kent, and he was so sweet, so supportive. He's been running our property as well as his own. And of course we have a deep bond that goes way back. Then one weekend, he just looked at me and said "Why don't we just do it? Why don't we get married?"'

Bella was smiling at the memory. 'In a flash, it all seemed to make wonderful sense. It was the perfect solution, and you should have seen the smile on Dad's face when we told him. He was *so* relieved I was being taken care of.'

To Zoe it was now blindingly obvious why Bella and Kent were marrying. Kent felt a huge debt to Tom Shaw. Bella was in danger of losing her family, her farm— losing everything, in other words. Bella and Kent had a long history, a shared background that made them suited to each other in every way. Duty and friendship had won, and Kent had saved the day.

Everything might have been fine if Damon hadn't arrived on the scene, no doubt reawakening Bella's school-girl fantasies of passion and romance...

Oh, man... Zoe's thought winged back to Friday night when Kent arrived home to find his kitchen filled with candles. Her skin flamed at the memory of the way he'd looked at her...

The flash of fire in his eyes had shocked her. Thrilled her. As had the roughness of emotion in his voice.

And next morning, there'd been another moment of connection down on the creek bank...

No, she mustn't think about that now. She mustn't let her own longings confuse Bella's situation.

In fact, Zoe knew she mustn't do or say anything to influence Bella right now. She had no similar experience to draw on, no wisdom to offer. Her role was to listen...

But surely Bella must see all the benefits of this marriage? Her life could be fabulous if she went ahead with it. Kent was perfect husband material. Gorgeous looks aside, if you factored in his easy manner, his beautiful home and garden, his prosperous farm and country lifestyle in a friendly, close-knit community, Willara Downs was like the closest thing to heaven.

Then again, Zoe knew that her nomadic childhood had given her a longing for security and a love of being settled that Bella might not share.

And yet, for Bella there was the added advantage that, with Kent as her husband, her father would almost certainly recover and grow stronger. Every day he would see his daughter happily married and living close by. It was such a strong incentive for Tom to throw off his bad habits and take care of his health.

Surely these were weighty plusses.

Bella, however, was sighing. 'I was so emotional at

the time Kent came up with the wedding proposal. But I know he only made the offer because he was worried about Dad, and he felt he owed something to my family. He's always had a highly developed sense of doing the right thing.'

'So he was being heroic instead of romantic?'

'Yes,' Bella admitted in a small voice.

A marriage of convenience. The thought suffocated Zoe.

Again, she forced her own longings aside. She had no doubt that Kent possessed the necessary strength of character to make a success of anything he set his mind to. Even if his marriage wasn't based on passion, he would be a loving and loyal husband.

'But the marriage could still work,' she said softly.

Bella turned to her, her eyes wide with dawning hope. 'That's true, Zoe. Even arranged marriages can work out happily.'

'So I've heard,' Zoe agreed, trying not to sound deeply miserable. Perhaps it was melodramatic of her, but she felt as if she were saying goodbye to her own last chance for happiness.

Bella was looking down at her sparkling engagement ring. 'So…you think I should go ahead and marry Kent?'

An agonising pain burst in Zoe's throat and she swallowed it down. She opened her mouth to speak, but changed her mind, afraid she might say something she'd regret.

Bella sat up straight. 'It *is* the right thing to do,' she said with sudden conviction. 'Kent's no fool. He wouldn't have offered to marry me if he wasn't happy about it.' She shot Zoe a pleading glance. 'Would he?'

Tension made Zoe tremble. She could feel the sharpened claws of her jealousy digging deep, but she forced a shaky smile. 'From where I'm looking, you'll have a wonderful life with Kent.'

She held her breath as Bella sat, staring through the windscreen, her eyes bright and thoughtful. Outside the car, the light was fading. A gust of wind sent jacaranda bells fluttering onto the windscreen.

'But you're the only one who can make the final decision,' Zoe said at last.

'You're right. I shouldn't be putting pressure on you like this.' Nevertheless, a smile dawned on Bella's face, as pretty as a sunrise. She took Zoe's hands and squeezed them tightly. 'I know what I must do. Damon threw me off track. He's always been dangerous like that. But Kent and I made our decision for all the right reasons and we should stick to our original instincts.'

Leaning forward, Bella kissed Zoe's cheek. 'Thank you for helping me to sort this out.'

Tears stung the backs of Zoe's eyes and she blinked madly to hold them back. 'No problem. Point thirty-nine in the bridesmaid's handbook. Lots of brides have second thoughts as the big day approaches.'

'I'm quite normal, then. That's a relief.'

Zoe tried to crack another smile, but couldn't quite manage it.

It didn't matter. Bella's arms were around her, hugging her tight. 'I'm so lucky,' she whispered. 'I have the best bridesmaid in the world.'

CHAPTER SEVEN

To KENT's relief, his bucks' night wasn't too extreme. He'd heard of bridegrooms being tied naked to a pole in the main street, or bundled into a crop-dusting plane and transported to a remote outpost.

Fortunately, his best man, Steve, wangled just the right tempo. He'd done a great job of rounding up Kent's mates and the party was a blast. Not a city-style bash with strippers and pranks—just blokes enjoying themselves in a quiet country pub. Actually, the quiet country pub was growing rowdier by the minute, but the revelry was harmless enough.

There were the usual games with drinking penalties. Right now, anyone who raised taboo topics—cricket or football, the bride or her bridesmaid, the share market or politics—had to down his drink in one go. Merriment by the bucketful.

Later they'd sleep it off in the Mullinjim pub, and there'd be a few sore heads in the morning, but at least there was still a full week before the wedding.

Of course there were all kinds of comments flying about Kent's last chance for freedom.

It was a phrase that made him distinctly uneasy— but he wasn't prepared to dwell on that. He imagined most guys felt the cold snap of an iron noose about their throats whenever they thought too hard about the doors closing behind them when they stepped up to the altar.

One week to go...

He'd be glad when the tension was behind him, when he and Bella were safely settled...

Tonight, however, he had to put up with the good-natured ribbing from his mates, had to laugh as he agreed that his days as a carefree bachelor were numbered. But he wondered what the others would think if they knew how often his thoughts trailed back to earlier this evening when he'd driven through Willara and caught a glimpse of the girls at the pub.

Already in party mode after the bridal shower, Bella's friends had all been there, in shiny strapless dresses in a rainbow of colours. Looking like gaudy beetles, they'd wolf-whistled and waved glasses of pink champagne at Kent as he drove past.

He hadn't seen Bella, but she would have been in the mob somewhere, no doubt sporting a mock bridal headdress concocted from a piece of mosquito netting and a plastic tiara.

The girl he *had* seen and noted was Zoe.

She'd been standing in a doorway, chatting with a friend, and she was wearing a dress of striking tangerine silk, an exotic colour that highlighted her dark hair and slim elegance.

For a split second as Kent flashed past her eyes had met his. Startled, she'd half raised her glass.

He'd only caught that fleeting glimpse of her in the bright dress with one shoulder bared, but the image had shot a scorching flame through him. He'd remembered her in his kitchen, surrounded by four dozen smart candles and he'd felt that same thrust of longing he'd felt then.

Now, Kent consoled himself that this was the doppelgänger that haunted most men about to be married—the alter ego taking a final backward glance at freedom before diving into monogamy.

Get over it, man.

But even now, as he chatted and joked with his mates, his brain flashed to the memory.

Of Zoe. Not Bella.

Damn it, if he'd seen Bella at the pub he wouldn't be plagued by these memories now. He'd be thinking only of Bella, not Zoe with her shiny dark hair and soft smile. But now, instead of focusing on his bride, a treacherous part of his brain kept pressing rewind, kept replaying a picture of Zoe's slender curves encased in a sunburst of silk.

Why the hell now? Why tonight?

'Kent, old mate. Need to have a word.'

The voice behind Kent brought him swinging round.

Damon Cavello, glass in hand—a double shot of neat whisky by the look of it—greeted him with a morose smile.

They'd talked earlier, fighting to be heard above the hubbub, but it had been a superficial catch-up, skimming over the past decade in half a dozen carefully edited sentences. Now Damon held out his hand.

'I've overlooked congratulating the lucky bridegroom.'

'I'm sure you said something earlier.' Kent accepted the handshake uneasily, wondering if he'd detected a hint of stiffness in Damon's manner.

'You know you're a very lucky man,' Damon said.

'I do indeed.'

'You deserve her, of course.'

'Thank you.'

Why did he have the feeling that Bella's old flame was testing him? Rattling his antlers, so to speak.

Damon offered a mirthless grin. 'Bella's a—'

'Hold it!' Kent laughed as he raised his hand. 'There's a penalty tonight if you mention the bride's name.'

'Damn, I forgot.'

Before Kent could let him off the hook, Damon tossed down the contents of his glass.

Kent inhaled sharply, imagining the fire lacing the other man's veins.

'So, where was I?' Damon asked as he set the empty glass on the bar. 'Ah, yes.' Folding his arms across his chest, he sized Kent up with a knowing smile. 'I was agreeing that you've made an excellent choice of bride. You and your future wife will be the toast of Willara.'

Kent accepted this with a faint nod.

Damon's gaze shifted to a point in the distance beyond Kent's shoulder. His chest rose and fell as he drew in a deep breath, then exhaled slowly.

To Kent's dismay, the other man's eyes betrayed a terrible pain. 'I was a fool,' he said, his voice quiet yet rough with self loathing. 'I was the world's biggest fool to head off overseas, leaving her behind.'

A nightmare weight pressed down on Kent, crushing the air from his lungs and stilling his blood. He pulled himself together. 'That may be true, mate,' he said slowly. 'You were famous for doing crazy things back then. You were legend.'

'I was, but I regret it now.'

What was Damon implying? Was this some kind of mind-game strategy?

'Are you trying to tell me something?' Kent challenged in a deliberately exaggerated country drawl. 'Are you saying that you would have married young and settled down with a mob of kids in quiet old Willara?'

'Who knows? We can't turn back time.' Damon squared his shoulders, looked about him at the happy crowd, then whipped back to Kent. 'Promise me one thing.'

Kent eyed the other man levelly, refusing to be intimidated. 'What's that?'

Temporarily, Damon lost momentum. Dropping his gaze, he tapped a short drumbeat on the smooth timber-topped bar. When he looked up again, his grey eyes were blazing ice. 'Just make sure you don't have any doubts, my friend, not the slightest shadow.'

The words struck hammer blows, but Kent refused to flinch. 'Thanks for your advice,' he said coolly. 'It's heartening to know there's another man in town who understands how lucky I am to be marrying Bella Shaw.'

Looking Damon in the eye, Kent downed his drink.

It was well past midnight when Zoe heard the tap on her door. She hadn't been asleep, although her body was worn out from the huge effort of running both the bridal shower and then the hen night. The functions had been proclaimed a great success, but now her brain couldn't stop buzzing.

When the soft knock sounded, she slipped quickly from the bed, went to the door and opened it a crack. Bella was outside in the dark passageway, wild eyed and wrapped in a pink-and-blue kimono.

'Can I come in for a sec?' she whispered.

'Sure.' Zoe readily opened the door, but threads of fear were coiling in her chest. All night she'd been watching Bella with mounting alarm.

While the bride had laughed and chatted and joined in the silly, light-hearted party games, Zoe had been aware of the underlying pulse, a ticking time bomb of tension. Plainly, things still weren't right for Bella. The strain showed in her eyes, in her smile.

Luckily, all the other party girls had been too busy drinking and having a good time to notice. But Zoe, who'd taken her hen night responsibilities seriously, had mostly drunk tonic water.

Clear-headed, she'd noticed plenty and she'd worried plenty. Most especially, she'd worried that Bella still wasn't happy with the decision she'd reached last week.

Now, her friend collapsed into the only chair in the room. 'I've just had a text from Kent,' she said. 'He wants to see me. To talk.'

'Tonight?'

'Yes, but I said it was too late. I rang back and talked him into leaving it till first thing in the morning.'

'Do you know what he wants to talk about?'

'He wants to make sure I'm totally happy about—' Bella let out a soft groan. 'He wants to discuss the wedding.'

Zoe's heart thudded. 'I assume this isn't just a planning meeting.'

'No. I'm pretty sure he wants to double check that we're both still on the same page.'

'About getting married?'

Closing her eyes, Bella nodded.

'What are you going to tell him?'

A sob broke from Bella. 'I have to be totally honest, Zoe. I don't think I can do it.'

CHAPTER EIGHT

FOR ages after Bella went back to her room, Zoe tossed and turned, her sheets damp with sweat, her thoughts rioting. Eventually, she got up and shut the window and switched on the air conditioning, but, although the system was efficient and the room cooled quickly, she couldn't settle down.

Everything was spinning round and round in her head. Bella's distress, Kent's ultimatum, the mystery surrounding Damon—and, of course, the beautiful wedding reception she'd planned....

Time crawled. It took for ever for dawn to finally arrive as a creamy glow around the edges of the curtains. Giving up any pretence of sleep, Zoe rolled out of bed and opened the curtains to a view down Willara's main street. At this early hour the little town was empty and silent, and it looked a little faded, too, like a ghost town in an old black-and-white movie.

Was Kent already on his way?

She showered and shampooed her hair, then blow-dried it and packed her bags, shoving all the leftover party glitter, shredded cellophane, cardboard and felt pens into an outside pocket. She had no idea why she was saving this stuff, couldn't imagine ever using it again.

There'd been no special arrangements made for breakfast—all the hen-night girls wanted to sleep off the party after-effects. But Zoe's room had started to feel like a jail cell. She knew Bella wouldn't eat until after she'd spoken to Kent, so she decided to go downstairs to dine alone.

As she went past Bella's door she thought she heard the soft murmur of voices. Perhaps, even now, Bella and Kent were making a decision. Just thinking about it made Zoe's eyes and throat sting with hot tears.

The hotel's dining room was old-fashioned with dark panelled walls and vases of bright flowers on the tables. It was still very early, and the room was empty, but a girl was there, ready to take orders.

Zoe glanced at the menu. It offered a full country breakfast with bacon, scrambled eggs, mushrooms and fried tomatoes, but, while she'd been ravenous an hour ago, her anxious stomach rebelled now.

She ordered tea and toast and sat in a sunny corner near a window. She was drinking her second cup of tea and eating hot buttered toast spread with local orange marmalade when a tall, broad-shouldered figure appeared at the dining-room doorway.

Kent.

Zoe's knife clattered to her plate.

Had he already spoken to Bella? If he hadn't, what was she supposed to say?

Kent came across the room, weaving past the empty tables covered by clean white cloths. He sent her a cautious smile, but it was impossible to gauge his mood.

He didn't look utterly heartbroken, but perhaps he was very good at masking his feelings. He was definitely paler than usual and there were shadows under his eyes, as if his night had been as restless and as tormented hers.

'I was hoping I'd find you,' he said when he reached her.

'Have you seen Bella?'

'Yes. We've been talking in her room for the past hour.'

A chill skittered over Zoe's arms. She was still unsure how to handle this.

'Can I join you?' Kent asked.

Zoe nodded, and once he was seated she realised she'd been holding her breath. The tension was unbearable. What had they decided?

Kent placed his hands squarely on the table. 'I wanted you to be the first to know. Bella and I are calling off the wedding.'

Zoe's heart gave a painful thud. Even though this wasn't totally unexpected, she felt as if she'd stepped from solid ground into thin air. 'I'm so sorry.' Tears stung her eyes and her throat. 'I can't begin to imagine how you must be feeling right now, Kent.'

'It had to be done,' he said with a shaky smile.

Zoe didn't know how to respond to that. She was dazed—and shell-shocked.

No wedding.

After all the excitement and planning and busyness of the past few weeks—now, nothing. *Nada.*

'How's Bella?'

'She's worn out from over-thinking this whole deal, but she's OK, I guess, or at least she will be after a good night's sleep.'

'I should go upstairs to see her. She might want some friendly support.'

'Actually, she's not here.' Kent lifted his hands in a

don't-ask-me gesture. 'She had to rush off to Green-acres. There's been some sort of problem there.'

'No...not her grandfather?'

'I think so.'

'Oh, God. Poor Bella. As if she hasn't had enough to worry about.'

'I offered to go with her, but she said she wanted to handle it herself, which was understandable, I guess.'

'Maybe there's something I can do?' Zoe was already rising from her chair.

'I told Bella to ring if we can help.'

As Zoe sat once more she let out a sigh. Her mind flashed to her excitement when Bella first asked her to be a bridesmaid. Who would have thought it would come to this?

The waitress appeared at Kent's side. 'Would you like to order breakfast, sir?'

'Ah, no...but perhaps some tea. Zoe, shall we order a fresh pot?'

Considering the awkwardness of their situation, Zoe found his politeness and self-control impressive. As soon as the girl had left she reached across the table and squeezed Kent's hand. It was meant to be a comforting gesture, but for her the brief contact still sparked the usual silly electricity.

'Thanks for being such a good friend to Bella,' he said.

Zoe gave a rueful shake of her head. 'My big chance to be a bridesmaid. Gone down the tube.'

'You would have been perfect,' he said warmly.

'Well, for that matter, I thought you and Bella would have been the perfect couple.'

'Did you really?'

Tension shadowed his lovely dark eyes as he waited for her answer.

Zoe found herself suddenly flustered. 'You had so much in common.'

'Maybe that was the problem.'

The waitress returned with the tea and a fresh cup and saucer for Kent, so they became busy with pouring and helping themselves to milk and sugar.

When they were alone again, Kent said, 'Zoe, the decision to call the wedding off was mutual.'

She was almost giddy with relief. 'Gosh, I'm— I'm—'

'Mad with us both for messing you around?'

'No, I'm not mad. If I'm honest, Kent, I've been worried for ages. The vibes weren't right between you.'

Kent grimaced and rubbed at his jaw in a way that was intensely masculine.

'But for what it's worth,' Zoe added, 'I think your motives for proposing were honourable.'

'What do you know about my motives?'

'I don't want to say anything out of place, but I'm guessing you wanted to look after Bella, and you wanted to put Tom's mind at ease.'

Kent's mouth tilted in a lopsided smile. 'You're not just a pretty bridesmaid, are you?'

Despite everything, Zoe drank in the sight of him sitting opposite her in his moleskin trousers threaded with a crocodile leather belt.

'The truth is,' he said, after a bit, 'I had a revealing chat with Damon last night. We started off toe to toe like two duelling bucks, all bluster and bravado. But then I started really listening to the guy. He was talking about Bella, and I watched his face, his body language. I heard the depth of emotion in his voice...'

Kent paused and his impressive chest expanded as he drew a deep breath. 'I don't know if he's the right man for Bella, or if she even wants him, but last night I found myself questioning—everything. I realised that I was denying Bella—denying both of us the chance to have a marriage based on something *more* than friendship.'

He was looking directly at Zoe and she felt heat spreading over her skin. She told herself to stop it. Just because Kent was no longer marrying Bella, she couldn't start imagining he was going to dive into a new relationship. And even if he did, why would he choose her?

Suddenly, with her role as bridesmaid swept away, her old insecurities were rushing back.

She was relieved when Kent returned to practicalities.

'I've told Bella I'll take the heat as far as the wedding's concerned. I'll talk to our families and friends.'

What a task. Zoe pictured the girls upstairs. They'd be getting up soon and would have to be told the news, and there were so many others who would need to know. It was all going to be awkward and embarrassing, and Kent was shouldering the load. She felt a rush of sympathy for him, another layer to add to the emotional storm inside her.

'Perhaps I could help with ringing the caterers and the hire people?'

Kent considered this. 'I'd like to say don't worry. You've done more than enough, and I'll take care of it. But with all these other calls to make, I'd really appreciate your help, Zoe. As it is, I think I'll be spending all day on the phone.'

On cue, Kent's mobile phone rang and he quickly retrieved it from his pocket. 'It's Bella,' he said as he checked the caller ID.

Zoe watched the concern in his eyes as he listened. She tried not to eavesdrop, but she couldn't help catching his rather alarming responses.

'Do you think that's wise, Bella?… What about the police?… Yes, I've spoken to Zoe. I'm with her now. Yes, sure.'

To Zoe's surprise, he handed her the phone. 'Bella wants to speak to you.'

'What's happening?' she whispered.

He rolled his eyes. 'Big drama. Bella will explain.'

Heavens, what else could go wrong? Zoe lifted the phone. 'Hi, Bella.'

'Zoe, I'm so sorry I dashed off, but you won't believe what's happened. My grandfather and Damon's grandmother have taken off.'

'Taken off?' Zoe almost shrieked. 'You mean they've run away from Greenacres? Together?'

'Yes. They've taken Damon's grandmother's car.' Bella's sudden laugh was almost hysterical. 'It's ridiculous, I know. It might only be a prank, and they're not senile or anything, but we can't let them drive off together without knowing what they plan to do. We have a lead, so Damon and I are going after them.'

'Far out. That's—that's incredible.'

'I know. I can't believe it either. But, Zoe, I'm really, really sorry to be abandoning you. I wanted to talk to you this morning, to explain everything.'

'Don't worry about me.' Lowering her voice, she said, 'Kent's explained about the wedding.'

'Is he OK?'

Zoe sent a glance Kent's way. Catching her eye, he gave her another crooked smile and she felt a flash of useless longing. 'He seems to be bearing up.'

'Zoe, can you look after Kent? Keep an eye on him?'

'I—I—' Zoe was so thrown by the thought of ongoing contact with Kent that she wasn't quite sure what to say. And yet, she couldn't overlook the pleading in Bella's voice. 'Yes, yes, of course I will.'

'Thank you. Thanks for everything, Zoes. I'm so sorry you're not going to be my bridesmaid after all, but at least we can be thankful we chose a dress you can wear to a nice party.'

Zoe rolled her eyes. The last thing on her mind was her dress.

'I'll stay in touch,' Bella said. 'But I've got to dash now. Talk soon. Bye.'

'Bye. And, Bella—'

'Yes?'

'Be careful, won't you?'

'Um…yeah, thanks for the warning.' Bella spoke softly, as if she knew very well that the warning was mostly about Damon Cavello.

Dazed, Zoe handed the phone back to Kent. 'I'm beginning to think I must be dreaming. Runaway grandparents, for crying out loud! None of this is happening, is it?' She held out her arm. 'If someone pinched me now, I'm sure I'd wake up.'

Laughing, Kent took her arm, and his warm fingers encircled her, creating a bracelet of heat. Instead of pinching her, however, he stroked a feather-light caress on the fine, pale skin of her inner wrist.

A tremor vibrated through her, and she gasped. Had he felt it?

His dark eyes flashed a message—inchoate and thrilling—unmistakable.

Her heart thundered. *Don't be an idiot.*

He was still watching her as he released her. He smiled. 'I'm quite sure you're wide awake.'

Then, as if to correct himself, he became business-like once more. 'Now,' he said. 'It's time to get cracking. We have a wedding to cancel.'

Rusty hinges squeaked as Kent pushed open the old timber gate that led to the tangle of shrubbery and weeds surrounding the Shaw family's homestead. Even on a pleasant spring afternoon, the unkempt jungle looked depressing—a far cry from the beautiful, prize-winning garden that had been Bella's mother's pride and joy. Mary Shaw would roll in her grave if she could see this mess now.

Kent called out, partly in greeting, partly as a warning. 'Tom, are you home?'

Tom's faithful border collie appeared, eyes eager and bright and tail wagging happily. Mounting the front steps, Kent greeted him. 'Where's your boss, Skip?'

'I'm in here,' called a deep male voice. 'In the kitchen.'

Relieved, Kent made his way down the hall, but his gut clenched as he thought of the task ahead of him.

He'd already broken the news about the wedding to his parents and they'd coped surprisingly well. His mother had made a gentle complaint about all the money she'd spent on her outfit.

'Where am I going to wear a brocade two-piece in Willara?' she'd demanded, with a rueful smile, but she hadn't really looked unhappy.

His father had given his shoulder a sympathetic thump and muttered that he was proud of Kent's courage.

And Bella had spoken to Tom, of course, so Kent wasn't about to drop a bombshell.

Just the same, as he entered the big, airy kitchen at the back of the old timber Queenslander it was hard to shake off the feeling that he'd let Tom Shaw down.

Kent looked about the kitchen filled with windows and painted sunshiny yellow. It had always been his favourite room in this homestead. In his primary school days, he'd regularly dropped in here for afternoon tea.

There'd always be home-made macadamia or ginger cookies and milk, and he and Bella had eaten them at the scrubbed pine table, or sometimes they'd taken their snack outside to sit in their cubbyhouse beneath an old weeping willow.

Now, Kent found Bella's father standing at the greasy stove, thin, unshaven and pale, with heavy shadows under his eyes. At least he appeared to be sober, which was something, and he was stirring the contents of a pot with a wooden spoon.

This Tom Shaw was such a different figure from the man Kent had known and admired for most of his life. It had been a rude shock to watch this man slide downhill so quickly and completely after his wife's death. He'd hated to stand by and witness his hero's self-destruction.

So, yeah…the wedding plan had been all about propping Tom up again. Now, Kent squared his shoulders.

'Evening,' Tom greeted him morosely.

'Evening, Tom.' Kent stood with two hands resting on the back of a kitchen chair, bracing himself.

'Bella rang and she explained about the wedding.'

'Yeah.' Kent swallowed. 'I'm sorry it hasn't worked out.'

'Well…actually—' Tom smiled wryly '—I'm relieved, son.'

'Relieved?'

Tom nodded. 'I know I was excited at first. It's true I was thrilled with the notion of you taking care of my Bella and Blue Gums. I could die happy. But it wasn't long before I realised something was missing. Something really important.'

Turning the flame down beneath his cooking pot, Tom folded his arms and leaned back against a cupboard. 'I've been in love, Kent. I had a great marriage, full of spark.' He fixed Kent with knowing eyes. 'That's the thing. There has to be a spark—something beyond friendship. Something to set your soul on fire.'

Kent knew he was right. This lack of a spark was exactly what he and Bella had finally acknowledged. They were very fond of each other. They were great mates. But deep down they knew the passion they both yearned for was never going to materialise.

'I'm ashamed that you were both prepared to take that huge step for my sake,' Tom said. 'Heck, Kent, marriage is a gigantic step.' His eyes took on a little of their old fire. 'I couldn't bear to think you were tying the knot to repay me for yanking you out of the flaming creek all those years ago.'

'But I owe you my life.'

'I happened to be on the spot, and I just did what anyone would have done.' Tom shook his head. 'Thank heavens you and Bella have come to your senses.'

Kent took a moment to digest this. He had a sneaking suspicion that his parents were as relieved as Tom was, although they hadn't expressed their views quite so strongly.

'I'm glad you understand,' he said quietly. 'But while we're being honest, there's something else I need to get off my chest.'

'What's that?' The other man's eyes narrowed.

Kent's grip on the chair tightened. 'It's your turn to wake up, Tom. I know it's been hard for you these past eighteen months, but you need to accept that no one else can take responsibility for your health. I can plough your fields and mend your fences, and I can even offer to marry your daughter, but none of that will help you if you can't give up your bad habits.'

Tom dropped his gaze, jaw stubbornly jutted. 'You're dead right. In fact, I'm one step ahead of you.'

'Have you rejoined AA?'

'I have and I won't miss another meeting. That last time I put on a turn in front of Bella's friend was my wake-up call. I really let Bella down.'

Kent gripped Tom's hand. 'That's great news, mate. Well done.' Now he was grinning widely. 'Doc King gave you plenty more years if you conquered the grog and worked on your fitness.'

'Yeah, so that's the plan. I want to be around to see my grandkids.' Tom gave Kent's shoulder a hearty bang. 'And your nippers, too.'

At the end of the day Zoe stood on the back veranda at Willara Downs, looking out at what had fast become her all-time-favourite view. She'd had a huge weekend and was almost dead on her feet, and Kent had insisted that she couldn't possibly drive back to Brisbane this evening.

So while he'd gone to talk to Tom Shaw, she'd prepared dinner—lamb baked with garlic and rosemary and lemon.

For an afternoon, she'd been living her fantasy—fussing about in a farmhouse kitchen, cooking a tasty dinner for the handsome farmer who belonged there.

Which only proved how foolish she was. It was time to put this episode behind her, time to forget about Kent.

The emotional connection she felt towards him and his beautiful home was out of all proportion to her true relationship. She was nothing more than Kent's former fiancée's *almost* bridesmaid.

OK. So maybe she'd promised Bella she would 'look after' Kent, but surely the kindest thing she could do was to leave quickly and without any fuss. Later she would stay in touch via email. Emails were safe.

Even though she knew all this…for now, she was enjoying her last look at this lovely view. Beyond the fence bordering the homestead's lawns and gardens stretched fields of sun-drenched golden corn and green pastures dotted with grazing cattle. Beyond that again, distant low hills nestled in a purple haze.

For Zoe there was something magical about it, especially now when it was tinged by the bronzed-copper glow of the late afternoon.

When she was small, she used to look out of the window of her parents' bus at views like this. At this time of day she would see farmers on their tractors, turning away from the chocolate earth of their newly ploughed fields and heading for home.

As the bus trundled down the highway she would watch the lights coming on in farmhouses, spilling yellow into the purple shadowed gardens. She'd watch wisps of smoke curling from chimneys into skies streaked with pink and gold and lavender. Sometimes she caught glimpses through windows of families gathered around kitchen tables.

Most evenings, shortly after dusk, her parents would turn in at a camping ground. Zoe and her mum would need a torch to find their way to the shower block, and they'd hurry back, damp and sometimes shivering in their dressing gowns. Her parents would cook a meal on their portable gas stove, and Zoe would do her homework, or read a book, or listen to the radio.

The bus was cosy enough at night, but oh, she'd coveted those warm, sturdy farmhouses. For Zoe, the simple ripple-iron-roofed dwellings surrounded by crops and fields were more beautiful and desirable than any fairy-tale castles.

Remembering those days now, she leaned on the veranda railing, drinking in details to keep them stored in her memory. The scent of newly cut grass. The deepening shadows creeping over the fields. The soft lowing of cattle. And coming from behind her, the fragrant kitchen aromas.

'I thought I might find you out here.'

Zoe turned, deliberately slowly, and smiled as Kent came to rest his arms on the timber railing beside her.

'Now everyone who needs to know knows,' he said. 'I had to leave messages for one or two folk, but at least they've all been informed.'

'How did Tom take the news?'

'Surprisingly well.'

'Wow. You must be relieved.'

'Very.' He turned, folded his arms and regarded her with a quizzical smile. 'Dinner smells good.'

'Yes, you have impeccable timing. The roast is due out of the oven right now.'

Together they went into the kitchen and Kent opened a bottle of wine. It felt incredibly domesticated and intimate to Zoe. But then, she was in full fantasy mode, while Kent was getting over a huge ordeal.

Nevertheless, he looked very much at home, pouring wine, wielding a carving knife, slipping a light jazz CD into the player. And he was lavish with his compliments for Zoe's cooking.

'I had farm-fresh ingredients,' she said. 'How could I go wrong?'

Across the table, Kent sent her a smile. 'Pity you're heading back to Brisbane tomorrow.'

It was silly to feel flustered, but there was a glitter in his dark eyes and a husky rumble in his voice that set Zoe's pulses dancing a crazy jig.

'So what are your plans for the rest of your week off?' he asked.

'Actually, I've been thinking that I might as well go back to work.'

Kent's eyebrows shot high. 'And waste the chance to take a holiday?'

'I'm not in the mood for a holiday now, and I can save this week for later. For when I go overseas.'

'Ah, yes. Christmas in Prague. Is it all planned?'

'No. I need to start booking my flights as soon as I get back.'

Kent frowned and dropped his gaze. A muscle jumped in his jaw.

'What about your plans, Kent? I know you had time set aside for a honeymoon. Are you still going to take a break?'

He shrugged. 'Not much point really. Besides, it's

the dry season and I need to keep the feed supplements up to the cattle. There's more than enough to keep me busy around here.'

Zoe was quite certain he was making excuses, but she understood. Under the circumstances, he wouldn't enjoy a holiday on his own. For her, getting back to work was about keeping busy and stopping her mind from revisiting endless if onlys...

It would be the same for Kent, magnified one hundred times.

Zoe left Willara Downs after breakfast the next morning. For the last time, she stripped the pink-and-white sheets from the bed in the pretty guest bedroom, and looked around fondly at the space she'd foolishly begun to pretend was hers.

Now it was time for reality. Back to the city. She needed to get over her silly crush on Kent, and the only way to achieve that was to stay well away from him.

Her car was parked at the side of the house, behind a hedge of purple-flowering duranta, and Kent insisted on carrying her bags, while she carried the bridesmaid's dress.

After laying it carefully along the back seat, she stepped back and took a deep breath. Time to say goodbye. *No tears, now.*

She offered Kent her best attempt at a smile.

But to her surprise he was staring at the dress, which was now a filmy river of coffee and cream chiffon on the back seat. 'You would have looked so lovely in that,' he said in a strangely choked voice.

Zoe tried to laugh. 'It's ridiculous how badly I wanted to be a bridesmaid.' She shook her head at her own foolishness.

'You've been perfect anyhow, a perfect *almost* bridesmaid.' He flashed a brief quarter-smile. 'Bella couldn't have had better support.'

'Nice of you to say so.' Zoe squeezed the words past the tightness in her throat. 'But if we talk about all that now, I'm going to make a fool of myself.'

Determined not to cry, she opened the driver's door, tossed her shoulder bag onto the passenger's seat, and slipped the key into the ignition. She was blinking madly, trying so hard to be strong.

'Zoe,' Kent said softly, and his hand closed around her arm.

She ducked her head, hoping he couldn't see her struggle.

'Zoe, look at me.'

He spoke with such convincing tenderness she couldn't bear it. She was swiping at her eyes as he turned her around.

'Hey…' With the pads of his thumbs, he dried her tears.

Electrified, she was zapped into stillness by his touch. He was so close now she could see the tiny flecks in his eyes—fine streaks of cinnamon combined with hazelnut—could see his individual eyelashes…

'There's something I need to give you,' he said and he produced from his jeans pocket a slim gold box.

'What is it?'

'Your bridesmaid's gift.'

Shocked, Zoe clapped a hand to her mouth. She shook her head.

'Come on,' he said, smiling as he pushed the box into her free hand. 'You've earned this, and I went to a lot of trouble to get the right colour.'

'Oh.' Her hands were shaking.

'Here, let me open it for you.'

She watched as Kent's big hands lifted the dainty lid to reveal a bracelet made of beautiful, translucent beads of every colour.

'They're made of hand-blown glass designed by a local artist.'

'Kent, they're gorgeous.' Each bead displayed a uniquely different rainbow of colours, but the overall effect was one of beautiful harmony. 'I love it. Thank you so much.'

Setting the box on the bonnet of her car, Kent took her wrist. Oh, the intimacy of his hands, of his warm strong fingers brushing her skin. A wave of longing and regret crashed over Zoe and she was in danger of crying again. She closed her eyes to hold the tears back. Then, to her utter surprise, she felt Kent's hands cradle her face, tilting it ever so slightly towards him.

Her eyes flashed open and for breathless seconds they stared at each other, and she saw surprise—the same surprise she was feeling—mirrored in Kent's eyes.

Surprise and disbelief...

And knowledge...

And helplessness...

And then he was kissing her.

Or Zoe was kissing him.

Or perhaps they simply flowed together, drawn by a potent, irresistible magnetism, as if by some miracle they shared the same aching need, the same unspoken longing.

Zoe's senses revelled in the scent of Kent's skin, and the dark taste of coffee on his lips, the thrilling strength of his arms wrapped around her. She was quite sure she'd never been kissed with such wanting, and she certainly knew she'd never returned a kiss with such fervour.

When they drew apart, at last and with great reluctance, they stood facing each other, panting and flushed and slightly self-conscious.

When Zoe spoke, she tried to sound a thousand times more composed than she felt. 'That was unexpected.'

'For me, too. But I'm not complaining.'

No. Zoe wasn't complaining either, but she felt compelled to offer reasons…excuses… 'It's been an emotional weekend. I—I guess I needed a hug.'

'I guess you did,' Kent agreed with a smile.

'And I—ah—should be going.' She turned back to the car again. Already the magic was fading, and the reality of their situation was rushing back. They'd both been under amazing strain and the kiss was an emotional finale to an incredibly emotional weekend.

Nothing more. Certainly nothing to weave dreams around.

What could she say now? *So long, it's been good to know you?* If she looked at Kent again, she might make a fool of herself, so she spoke without turning back to him. 'I'll let you know if I hear from Bella.'

'Thanks, and I'll pass on any news from my end.'

'Emails are probably the easiest.'

'Sure.'

Deep breath. 'Goodbye, Kent.'

'Bye.'

He took a step closer, and dropped another warm kiss on her cheek. Zoe's insides were doing cartwheels. 'See you later. Maybe,' she choked.

'Make that definitely,' Kent corrected quietly.

She didn't reply and closed the car door. He tapped

on her window with his knuckle, and they waved to each other.

Her eyes welled with tears, but she blinked them clear. *Enough of this nonsense.* They'd finished this story. This was…

The End.

She took off, watching Kent in her rear vision mirror. He stood with his feet firmly planted, his hands sunk in his pockets…watching her…and when she reached the end of the drive and was at last enveloped by the tunnel of trees, he still hadn't moved.

CHAPTER NINE

To: Zoe Weston<zoe.weston@flowermail.com>
From: Kent Rigby<willaraKR@hismail.com>
Subject: The Runaways
Hi Zoe,
I hope you had a safe trip back and that everything was fine when you got home. Just wanted to thank you once again. I don't think you truly realise how big a help you've been.

Also, I've had a text from Bella, and she and Damon are still on the trail of the grandparents. They're heading north—staying in Rockhampton tonight, I think.

Are you determined to go back to the office tomorrow?

Seems a shame you can't have a decent break.
Cheers,
Kent

To: Kent Rigby<willaraKR@hismail.com>
From: Zoe Weston<zoe.weston@flowermail.com>
Subject: The Runaways
Hi Kent,
Thanks for your email and for asking if everything

was OK, but I'm afraid I came home to a minor disaster. I asked my neighbour to take care of my goldfish while I was away and she overfed them, so my poor goldfish, Orange Juice, was floating on the top of a very murky tank. By the looks of it, Anita dumped half a tin of fish food in there.

I didn't think to warn her that you can't do that with goldfish. Thank heavens I wasn't away all week or I would have lost Brian and Ezekiel as well. As it is, they look a bit peaky.

I know you must be thinking I'm a screw loose to be so upset about a goldfish, but they're the only pets I can have in this flat, so they're important. Now, I've spent most of the evening cleaning the tank.

But, yes, to answer your question, I'll be back at the office in the morning.

Bella sent me that text, too. It's a weird situation they've found themselves in, isn't it? We can only hope it all works out happily.

Best wishes and thanks again for your hospitality, Zoe.

To: Kent Rigby<willaraKR@hismail.com>
From: Zoe Weston<zoe.weston@flowermail.com>
Subject: Thank You

Kent, you shouldn't have. Honestly. It was so sweet of you to have a goldfish delivered to the office.

The delivery boy caused quite a stir when he appeared in the doorway with a huge grin on his face and a plastic bag with a goldfish in his hand.

As if the office gossip wasn't already flying thick

and fast this morning. Quite a few of the girls were at the hen party, so of course the whole staff wanted details.

Luckily, when the delivery came I got to the door first, so no one else saw the docket and realised it came from you. That would certainly have put the cat among the goldfish, and everyone would have been jumping to the wrong conclusions.

But I'm very grateful, Kent. According to a magazine article on feng shui, three goldfish in a tank are always better than two, so your gift has restored my chances of inner peace and prosperity.

And I'm sure you'll be pleased to know that the new fish is very pretty, with lovely white markings and delicate fins. I've decided she's a girl and I've called her Ariel.

Brian and Ezekiel are very impressed.

Thank you again, and warmest wishes,

Zoe

P.S. I'm off to book my overseas trip tomorrow—with Christmas in Prague as a must.

To: Zoe Weston<zoe.weston@flowermail.com>
From: Kent Rigby<willaraKR@hismail.com>
Subject: Re: Thank You

I'm so pleased the delivery arrived safely. Sorry that it caused a stir in the office, but at least feng shui has been restored in your household. I hope you enjoy your new fish.

No news from the northern adventurers, but I'm assuming they're still hot on the trail.

Hope the travel bookings go smoothly. I'm jealous.
Cheers
Kent

The confession of jealousy was no lie. As Kent pressed send he could think of nothing he'd like more than to take off for Europe again. With Zoe.

He imagined showing her all the places he'd discovered—taking a ride on the London Eye and drinking a pint in a quaint old English pub. Dining out in Paris, or walking through the Latin Quarter. In Spain they would visit art galleries and sample tapas bars. They'd walk Italy's magical Cinque Terre. Experience Christmas in Prague.

Together.

He'd decided that Zoe would be a perfect travel companion. She was organised and yet easy-going, adaptable and fun. Sexy.

Yeah, if he was honest, he was utterly absorbed with the idea of kissing Zoe in every location. Their farewell kiss replayed in his head on an almost continuous reel.

He tried to tell himself that he was overreacting, riding on a tidal wave of relief now that he was no longer marrying someone out of a sense of friendship and duty.

So, OK, there'd been plenty of sparks. With Zoe he'd experienced the very fireworks that had eluded him and Bella. Serious sparkage that left him hungry for more than mere kisses. But Zoe was back in Brisbane now, and soon she'd be heading overseas. A man with a grain of common sense would look elsewhere.

Problem was, this man had experienced his fill of common sense. Now he wanted nothing more than to indulge in fantasies. And he kept remembering Zoe

surrounded by dozens of smart little candles, kept picturing her on the bank of Willara Creek, her face soft
with emotion and empathy, wanting to understand. He
saw her on the road side struggling with a flat tyre. In
the pub on the hens' night, in a sexy dress, bright as a
flame. He remembered drying her tears just before he
kissed her. Goodbye.

Zoe knew it was silly to keep checking her private
emails at work and then to rush to her laptop as soon
as she got home. Silly to be disappointed when there
was no new message from Kent.

She wanted to move on and to put the entire Willara
experience behind her, so Kent's silence was a step in
the right direction.

Now that she was home, and had a little distance,
she could see how dangerous her penchant for Kent
had been. After her painful, harrowing heartbreak over
Rodney, she was mad to hanker for another man who'd
just called off his engagement.

Even though Kent and Bella's relationship had been
very different from Rodney and Naomi's, the patterns
were too close for comfort.

Besides, she suspected that Kent wasn't looking to
settle down. She'd heard talk at the hens' night that
he used to play the field, and, of course, he'd recently
pulled out of commitment to Bella. It was true; he'd
been gallant to the end. Just the same, he certainly
wouldn't be ready to leap into a new, serious relationship.

Once and for all she had to move on. Kent's kiss
had been nothing more than a spontaneous outburst of
feelings at the end of an extremely emotional weekend.

And his thoughtfulness in sending the goldfish was just another example of his general niceness.

His email silence, on the other hand, simply meant there was no news from Bella—and it was a perfect opportunity for Zoe to move forward.

His silence was a desirable result. Honestly.

Very slowly, over the next twenty-four hours, the straightforward sense of this started to sink in. Zoe focused on planning her holiday.

It was going to be quite different travelling solo instead of travelling with Bella as she'd once hoped. Quite an adventure, really.

On Friday evening when Zoe arrived home from work, she was deliberately *not* thinking about Kent Rigby. She most especially concentrated on *not* thinking about him when she heard a knock on her front door.

Having just kicked off her shoes, she answered the door in stockinged feet—a distinct disadvantage when her caller was six feet two. No doubt that was why she blurted out inhospitably, 'What are you doing here?'

Kent had the grace to look a little embarrassed. 'I had business in the city and I was passing by.'

It might have been the lamest of excuses, but Kent Rigby in the flesh could obliterate Zoe's protests and doubts with a single warm smile.

One glance into the twinkling dark depths of his eyes and all her resolutions to forget him flew out of the window.

'So,' she suggested, trying to subdue her happy grin. 'I suppose you've dropped by to see how Ariel's settling in.'

'Ariel?'

'Your thoughtful gift. My new goldfish.'

Kent laughed—a lovely, sexy masculine rumble. 'Of course. I've had sleepless nights wondering. How is she?'

Zoe stepped back to let him through her doorway, conscious of his height and size and her lack of shoes and the supreme smallness of her living room. The fish tank sat rather conspicuously at one end of the low set of shelves that also held her television set.

With a wave towards it, she said, 'Ariel's the pretty one with the dainty white fins.'

Kent sent a polite nod towards the tank. 'She's a very fine specimen.'

'As you can see, she's quite at home now.'

'She is. That's great.' But he immediately switched his attention from the fish and back to Zoe. 'I know this is a bit last minute. I would have called at the office earlier today, but you were worried about wagging tongues.'

'You could have telephoned.'

'Yes.' His smile tilted. 'But I wanted an excuse to see you.'

Not fair. Zoe's resistance was melting faster than ice cream on a summer's day. Desperate to hang on to her diminishing shreds of common sense, she said, 'I haven't heard from Bella, have you?'

'Yes, she rang this morning.'

'So they're still heading north?'

'Yes, and there's an awful lot of coastline, so heaven knows how long it will take.'

Standing in the middle of her living room, Kent was watching her, unabashedly letting his eyes rove over her work clothes, her legs...

Self-consciously, she fiddled with the bridesmaid bracelet at her wrist. Unwisely, she'd taken to wearing

it constantly. She rubbed one stockinged foot against
the other.

He smiled again. 'So...how are you now, Zoe?'

'I'm—I'm fine.' What else could she say? She could
hardly admit to feeling up and down and all over the
place after one goodbye kiss. 'More importantly, how
are you?'

'I'm OK. Surprisingly OK, actually.'

Memories of their kiss hovered in the air. Recklessly,
Zoe thought how easy it would be to drift towards him
again, to find herself in his arms, tasting that lovely,
seductive mouth.

She struggled to remember all the reasons it was
wrong. *He's free to play the field now. Don't get hurt.
Remember Rodney!* She found refuge in her duties as
a hostess. 'Would you like to sit down, Kent? Can I get
you a drink?'

Instead of answering, he asked, 'Am I interrupting
your plans for Friday night?'

'I—I was planning to have a quiet night in.' She'd
been looking forward to a stress-free weekend for a
change.

'So I can't tempt you to a quiet dinner out?'

Oh.

Zoe's mouth worked like her goldfish's. She'd spent
the past week listing all the reasons why she must stop
swooning over this man. Rodney the Rat had featured
high on that list. Kent's own reputation as Willara's
most dedicated bachelor was another point worth remembering. But now—*shame on her*—now that he'd
asked, she couldn't think of anything she'd like more
than to go out with him.

Besides, she'd promised Bella she'd keep an eye on

Kent—and going out with him tonight was simply doing Bella a favour, wasn't it?

'Dinner would be lovely,' she said, trying to strike the right note between polite and casual. 'Why don't you make yourself at home while I change into something more—?' Zoe bit off the word *comfortable*… It was such a cheesy cliché and she didn't want to give Kent a whiff of the wrong idea.

'Let me get you a drink,' she said instead. Her kitchen led off the living area and she went to the fridge and opened it. Unfortunately, she hadn't been in the mood for shopping this week, so there was half a bottle of rather old white wine, the heel of an ancient block of cheese and a handful of dried apricots.

Thinking of the bounty at Willara Downs, she felt extremely inadequate in the hostess department.

'I don't need anything now. I'm happy to wait till dinner,' Kent said, watching her from the doorway. 'And you don't need to change. If you don't mind coming as you are, I think you look great in that outfit.'

'In this?' Zoe repeated, amazed. She was still in her work clothes—a dark green skirt and a cream blouse with pintucking and neat little pearl buttons.

Kent's eyes twinkled. 'Yes, in that. You have no idea how good city clothes look after a steady diet of jeans and Akubras.'

Given her own love of all things rural, Zoe had quite a fair understanding of how the trappings of a very different world might appeal.

So, five minutes later, having once again donned her high heels and given her hair and make-up a retouch, she was in Kent's ute and heading for her favourite suburban Thai restaurant. Fleetingly, she wondered if she should be wary or on guard, but such caution seemed impossible. She was ridiculously happy.

Apart from the huge fact that she was being escorted by a gorgeous guy who caught every woman's eye, she'd always loved this particular eating place. She loved coming through the swing glass doors to be enveloped by the fragrant and exotic aromas wafting from the kitchen. And she loved the sumptuous yet relaxing ambience—rich pink walls adorned with mirrors in dark, intricately carved wooden frames, and tables covered in cloths of peacock and gold.

She enjoyed the little rituals, too, like the basket of pale pink prawn crisps that came along with their menus. This evening, sharing one of her favourite places with Kent, she was filled with bubbling excitement.

They decided to choose exotic steamed fish, and chilli and ginger paste chicken. Then their drinks arrived—a glass of chilled white wine for Zoe and an icy beer for Kent—and they nibbled the prawn crisps and sipped their drinks. And they talked.

Wow, how they talked.

To Zoe's surprise, Kent did *not* bring Bella or the wedding into their conversation. He started by asking her more about her travel plans, and he told her about the places he'd enjoyed most when he'd been overseas. They moved on to movies and discovered they both loved thrillers. They talked about books, but Kent preferred non-fiction, so there wasn't quite so much common ground there.

They might have moved on to music, but their meals arrived in traditional Thai blue-and-white bowls and they soon became busy with helping themselves to spoonfuls of fluffy jasmine rice. The delicious fish had been baked in coconut milk with slices of ginger, and the chicken had been stir-fried with masses of vegetables.

Everything was wonderfully hot and spicy and at first they were too busy enjoying themselves to talk about anything except the food, but then Kent asked, out of the blue, 'Are you very ambitious, Zoe?'

Ambitious? Thrown by the question, she stared at him. Her most recent goal had been to be a perfect bridesmaid. Apart from that, she wanted to travel, but her biggest ambition was to find the right man, to settle down and start a family, which was the last thing she'd admit to this man.

Fleetingly, she remembered her childish dream to live in a farmhouse that sat safely and squarely in the middle of green-and-gold fields. She hastily dismissed it.

'Actually, I don't think I can be very ambitious,' she said. 'I like my job and I want to be good at it, but I have no desire to smash through glass ceilings.' She pulled a face. 'Don't tell your feminist little sister.'

Kent grinned. 'Your secret's safe with me. Perhaps you're content.'

No. Content she was not, especially since she'd met Kent. Lately, restless yearning had been her constant companion.

She doubted that Kent would want to hear her true ambition—to settle down with the right man, to put down roots, raise a family.

'My parents have never been go-getters,' she told him instead. 'Lead the Way might have been a huge success, if they'd had a bit more tooth and claw.'

'And you might have been the child of celebrity rock stars.'

'Imagine.' Zoe rolled her eyes. 'Actually, I think my

parents would have hated all the celebrity fuss that goes
with being famous. I can't imagine my mother being a
diva, stamping her foot because the limo wasn't pink.'

She laughed at the impossibility of the picture. 'What
about you, Kent? Are you ambitious?'

'I have big visions for the farm—projects like land
management and tackling environmental issues. It's
easier to try new methods now I'm managing Willara
on my own. My dad wasn't keen to change and Tom's
just as bad. They want to keep doing things the way
they always have. Pair of dinosaurs, both of them.'

There was passion in his voice, which surprised Zoe.
'I must admit every time I was at Willara I was always so caught up with the wedding I didn't give much
thought to the business and management of your farm.
But it must be quite an enterprise. You're like a CEO
of your own private company.'

'Yes, and it keeps me busy.'

'But you love it.'

'I do.'

Kent smiled that special way of his that launched Zoe
into outer space. Yikes, she had to calm down. Tonight
was all about friendship.

Sure, there were sizzles and sparks that zapped her
whenever she looked across the table. And yes, there
were dark flashes of appreciation in Kent's eyes. And,
most certainly, she was aware of a deepening sense of
connection when they talked.

But this wasn't a date. Kent hadn't once tried to flirt
with her, or to touch her, or to offer her the over-the-top
compliments that Rodney had trotted out on their first
date. This evening was humming along at a nice, safe,
just-friends level.

Reassured by this success, Zoe found herself asking

recklessly, 'Are there any other ambitions? Do you still plan to marry and have a family one day?'

Kent stiffened with obvious surprise.

Oh, good grief. What an idiot she was.

He concentrated on helping himself to a final spoonful of fish. 'Right now I can't imagine ever lining up for another wedding.'

'And who could blame you?' Zoe said fervently.

To her relief, her awkward question didn't ruin the night. As they left the restaurant and walked into the sensuous magic of the warm spring night the scent of frangipani and honeysuckle hung in the humid air. From a pub down the road a band was sending out a deep pulsing beat.

Kent reached for Zoe's hand, threaded his fingers through hers. 'Thanks for bringing me here. It was a fabulous meal.'

'My pleasure,' she said softly, while her skin tingled and glowed from the contact.

When they reached his car, he opened the passenger door for her, and she was about to get in when he said, 'Wait a minute.'

She turned and he gently touched her cheek. 'I just wanted to tell you—you look lovely tonight.'

Her skin flamed with pleasure. 'Thank—'

Her reply was cut off by his kiss.

Which wasn't exactly a surprise—all night she'd been teased by memories of their other kiss.

This kiss was different and yet utterly perfect. Beyond friendly—oh, heavens, yes—but not pushy. Just slow and sexy and powerful enough to make Zoe hungry for more.

She was floating as she settled into the passenger seat, and it wasn't till they pulled up outside her flat that she came to her senses. It was time for a polite, but hasty exit.

A kiss was one thing, but becoming more deeply involved with this man was way too risky. He might be the most attractive man she'd ever met, but tonight he'd admitted that his long-term goals were the polar opposite of hers. She wanted to settle down. He didn't.

It was all very black and white.

'Thanks for a lovely evening, Kent.' Already, her fingers were reaching for the door handle.

'Zoe, before I forget, I have something for you.' Reaching into the back seat, Kent picked up a brown-paper packet.

'Another gift? But you've given me a bracelet and a goldfish.' She hoped this wasn't going to be chocolates or flowers—the clichéd trappings of seduction.

'It's just a book,' he said. 'I thought it might come in handy.'

She caught the dark gleam of his eyes as he smiled at her through the darkness. A book, a nice safe book. Tilting the packet, she let it slip onto her lap. It was a hardback with a glossy cover. They weren't parked near a streetlight, but there was just enough light for her to make out the title.

'A book about Prague. Gosh, how thoughtful of you.'

Flipping it open, she saw beautiful, full-page co-loured photographs, but the dim light couldn't do them justice. It seemed rude not to invite Kent inside.

'I need to make you coffee before you tackle the long drive back,' she explained in case he got the wrong idea.

So they ended up on the sofa, poring over pictures of Prague while their mugs of coffee cooled on the low table in front of them. The pictures were gorgeous—

soaring cathedrals, fairy-tale castles, steep-roofed houses, a horse and carriage in the snow...

'It's so old world and so very civilised,' Zoe said.

'I know. I couldn't think of any place more different from Queensland.'

'I can't believe I'm going to see it all. I'm booked into a small hotel just around the corner from the Old Town Square.'

Kent was silent for a bit. Frowning, he said, 'I hope you won't be too lonely spending Christmas overseas on your own.'

Zoe wondered if he was teasing her, but he looked quite genuine, and if she was honest she *was* a little worried about being on her own. But now with Bella unavailable it was a matter of travelling solo, or not at all. She looked sideways to find Kent still watching her with a troubled expression.

'I'll be fine,' she said. 'I've been doing some research, and, from what I've read, solo travellers have a much better chance of meeting people. There's always someone to share a meal or a bus ride.'

'I dare say that's true.' Kent picked up her hand and turned it over.

At the unexpected contact, Zoe's breath hitched and her heart picked up pace. 'What are you doing?'

'I'm reading your palm,' he said calmly.

She should have resisted, should have pulled her hand away, but it was already too late. She was mesmerised by his touch, by the scent of his aftershave, by the inescapable fabulousness of having him so close beside her.

Instead of protesting, she found herself playing his game. 'And what do you see in my palm?'

His eyes sparkled. 'Travel to far away places.'

'Fancy that. How perceptive.'

'And romance.'

Her palm curled instinctively. The warmth of his hands and the mellow teasing in his voice wove silken threads of longing deep inside her.

Fighting the hot urges, she challenged him. 'I thought palm readings only told you how long you're going to live and how many children you'll have.'

Kent's eyebrows lifted. 'Is that right? I'd better take another look, then.'

OK...she really should stop this nonsense. She tried to pull her hand away, but Kent was holding her firmly.

'Yes, of course,' he said. 'I can see a very long and happy life here.' With his forefinger he traced a shiver-sweet line across the centre of her palm. 'And a whole tribe of children.'

'A tribe?' Her breathlessness was caused more by his touch than his words. 'How many children are in a tribe?'

'Oh, I'd say around ten or eleven.'

'Far out.' Zoe tried to sound appalled, but she spoiled it by laughing. 'I think you'd better give up reading palms and stick to farming.'

Sure that her face was glowing bright pink, she switched her attention back to the book, still lying in her lap. It was open at a double page, showing Prague in the soft blue light of dusk. Four beautiful, ancient bridges spanned the Vltava River, and the sky and the water and the distant hills were all the exact same shade of misty blue. Even the splashes of yellow from street-lights and windows were soft and fuzzy. So pretty.

'Willara Downs is as lovely as this at dusk,' she told Kent.

To her surprise, he closed the book and set it on the

coffee table, then he took her hands, enclosing them in both of his. 'Zoe, I have a confession to make.'

Her heart skidded as if she'd taken a curve too fast.

'Would you be shocked if I told you that I fancied you *before* Bella and I called off the wedding?'

'Yes.' Of course she was shocked. Her heart was thumping so hard, she could hardly hear her own voice.

'Believe me, I was shocked, too. But I couldn't shut off my feelings.'

'But you didn't—' She pressed a hand to her thumping heart. She was scared and excited. Confused. 'You didn't call off the wedding because of me.'

'No, I didn't.' Smiling, Kent tucked a strand of her hair behind her ear. 'You don't have to feel guilty. It was only afterwards that I allowed myself to think about what had been happening. By then, I realised that I fancied you like crazy.'

She closed her eyes, searching for the strength to resist him. Kent had fancied lots of girls. This wasn't a confession of love. But even though she knew this, his words were unfurling fiery ribbons of need inside her. His touch was clouding her thoughts.

When his thumb brushed gently over her lips, she couldn't think of anything but kissing him again, of throwing herself into his wonderful, strong arms, of climbing brazenly into his lap…the bliss of skin against skin…

'You're lovely,' he whispered.

'Kent, don't say that.' She dragged herself back from the magnetic pull of his touch. 'You mustn't. We can't.'

'Why can't we?'

Remember Rodney.

But Kent was nothing like Rodney. He wasn't up and down in his moods as Rodney had been. He'd been engaged to Bella for noble reasons and he'd been very considerate of everyone's feelings when he'd broken that commitment. He was a man who took responsibilities seriously.

Even so, by his own confession, he still wasn't the marrying and settling down type.

Maybe I can simply enjoy the moment?

In a few weeks she was going to Europe, and Kent knew that, so a liaison now could only be temporary. Temporary flings were safe. They couldn't break a girl's heart. She could look on her trip overseas as her escape route.

Besides…heaven help her, she wanted this man… wanted him to kiss her, wanted his kiss so badly she was trembling. Every nerve in her body was quivering.

Kent dipped his head till his lips were almost touching hers. She looked into his eyes and saw the dark urgency of her longing mirrored there. A soft gasp escaped her, an embarrassing, pleading sound.

His mouth brushed hers, slow but insistent. 'Tell me why this is wrong,' he murmured against her lips.

She couldn't answer. If there had ever been a reason to say no, she'd lost it. His lips caressed hers again, and the last warnings in her head crumpled like tissue paper thrown on fire. She couldn't think of anything but returning Kent's kiss. Already she was winding her arms around his neck…and she kissed him.

Kissed him and *kissed* him.

Somewhere in the midst of kissing him, she kicked off her shoes and wriggled into his lap. And this time it was he who gasped. Then his hands traced the silky shape of her legs encased in tights. He dropped a fiery line of kisses over her skin from her collarbone into the V of her blouse. Then their mouths met again, and

their kisses turned molten as they tumbled sideways—
a blissful tangle into the deep red cushions.

Out of habit, Kent woke early, but this morning, instead
of bouncing out to face a day's farm work, he lay in the
soft light watching Zoe sleep. She was on her side, facing him, her dark hair tumbling over the white pillow,
her dusky eyelashes curving against her soft cheeks, her
mouth pale and slightly open. She looked so innocent
and vulnerable now, so different from the fiery, sensuous woman who'd made love to him last night.

Last night…

When he'd knocked on Zoe's door, he hadn't known
what to expect. Hadn't dared to hope that he might end
up spending the night with her. And yet, he couldn't
deny he'd been on fire since their farewell kiss at
Willara.

Even so, last night had defied all logic. He and Zoe
had shared a mere explosion of passion and excitement,
but there'd been astonishing tenderness, too. The same
kind of emotional connection he'd felt before—over
dinner conversations or on the creek bank. An amazing sense of rightness. A certainty that some kind of
miracle had been set in motion.

Briefly, as he lay there, he wondered if such thoughts
were fanciful. But then Zoe stirred beside him, opened
her bright blue eyes and smiled, and he was flooded
with a wonderful sense of buoyancy. Perhaps his life
was taking a turn in a very good direction.

CHAPTER TEN

ZOE'S new version of heaven was waking up beside Kent Rigby on a Saturday morning and knowing they had the whole, delicious weekend to spend together.

They rose late, and went out to have breakfast at a pavement café that served great coffee and luscious, tasty mushrooms on thick sourdough toast. Afterwards, they walked beneath flowering jacarandas on the banks of the Brisbane River, enjoying the sunshine, and sharing happy, goofy smiles.

In the afternoon they went to a suburban cinema to see a creepy thriller movie. Like teenagers they stole popcorn flavoured kisses in the dark, and on the way home they stopped off at a supermarket and bought ingredients for a pasta dish to make at home.

In Zoe's kitchen they sipped wine while they chopped and cooked. Every chance they had, they touched and smiled and hugged and kissed. They were, in a word, entranced.

Wrapped in a bubble of bliss, Zoe wouldn't let anything intrude. No negative thoughts, no questions, no doubts. If the slightest misgiving about history repeating itself reared its ugly head, she told herself this time was nothing like her disaster with Rodney. Rodney had moved in. Rodney had promised for ever.

With Kent, she was merely enjoying a fab weekend. At the end of two days he would go back to Willara, knowing that she was about to leave for overseas. For now she was trusting her instincts and her instincts felt *fantastic*!

Their pasta sauce was bubbling beautifully and Kent was stealing yet another kiss from Zoe when the phone rang. She grabbed the receiver and trilled 'Hello-o-o,' in a super-happy singsong.

'Zoe, how are you?'

'Bella?' Zoe shot a startled glance to Kent and watched his eyebrows hike.

Bella laughed. 'Don't sound so surprised.'

'Sorry. I wasn't expecting you, Bella, and I was—um—distracted for a moment.'

'Are you all right, Zoe?'

'Absolutely fine. Why?'

'I don't know. You sound—different somehow.'

'I don't think I'm different. More importantly, how are you?' Zoe flashed another glance Kent's way.

His eyes were more cautious now, as if he felt as awkward as she did. It would be so hard to explain this to Bella. A week ago, Zoe had been focused on being the perfect bridesmaid. Last night she'd slept with the bridegroom. Admittedly, those roles were now defunct, but how would Bella react if she knew they were together so soon?

And just like that, with Bella on the other end of the line, Zoe saw her wonderful weekend in a whole new light—as an outsider might—and her brain flung up words like *impetuous, cheeky, reckless…*

Bella said, 'I'm fine, thanks. I'm in Port Douglas with our grandparents. There's been a cyclone, would you believe? But we're all OK. Just garden damage.'

'That's really bad luck about the cyclone. How's everything…going…with…Damon?'

'OK,' Bella said in a sharp, *don't-go-there* tone. 'I was actually ringing to see if you've been in touch with Kent.'

'Oh?' Zoe was instantly nervous. She widened her eyes at Kent. Pointing to the phone, she mouthed, *'Do you want to talk to Bella?'*

Frowning, he shook his head.

She swallowed. 'Yes, I've had *some* contact with him.'

'I tried his mobile, but he's switched it off, so I rang the homestead and he wasn't there either so I rang his parents and Stephanie told me he's away for the weekend.'

'Did you want Kent for anything important?'

'Not especially. I guess I just wanted to make sure he's OK. You know the wedding would have been happening right about now.'

Oh, gosh. Zoe glanced at the clock on her kitchen wall and saw that Bella was right. At this very moment, Bella and Kent should have been exchanging their marriage vows. How on earth had it slipped her mind?

'I would have liked to make certain that Kent was OK,' Bella said.

'I'm sure he's fine. He's probably decided not to dwell on the wedding too much.'

'Yes, that would be best, wouldn't it? I hope you're right.'

On the stove the sauce began to boil and spit. Zoe gestured frantically, but Kent had moved to the window and was standing with his back to her, studiously looking out into her backyard. His shoulders were squared and his back very straight. Sure signs of tension.

Zoe tried to attract him with a stage whisper. *'Pssst, can you turn that sauce down?'*

'Do you have someone there?' Bella asked.

'Yes—just—a friend over for dinner.'

'Oh, that's nice. I won't keep you, then.' But instead of hanging up, Bella lowered her voice. 'Would this friend be male by any chance?'

Zoe made the mistake of hesitating for a shade too long.

'Zoe, it's a guy, isn't it? That's why you sounded so different—sort of bubbly and excited. Who is he? Anyone I know?'

'Bell, I'm sorry. The dinner's burning, and I've got to go. But it's been fantastic to hear from you and to know you're OK.'

'All right.' Bella laughed. 'I can take a hint. But if you hear from Kent, tell him that I rang and, apart from the weather, I'm fine.'

'I will, and I'll tell him you were thinking of him.'

Zoe hung up and rushed to rescue the sauce. Kent turned from the window, and she sank back against a cupboard, letting out a groan. 'That was awful. I felt terrible lying to her.'

'You weren't exactly lying.'

'No, but I was hiding the truth and that's just as bad.'

Zoe felt sick. Hands clenched, she paced across the kitchen. And to her horror, all the reasons she shouldn't be with Kent rushed back to taunt her. What was she doing leaping into bed with another man who'd just broken off an engagement?

Spinning around, she challenged him. 'Had you re-membered that you should have been getting married right now?'

He looked uncomfortable. 'Is that why Bella rang?'

'Yes. She was worried about you. She tried the Willara Downs number and your mobile.'

Pulling his phone from his pocket, Kent thumbed a button or two. 'It's not that I don't want to talk to her. I didn't want to embarrass you. I'll call her back now.'

'Actually…I'm not sure that's a good idea. If you call back straight away, she'll probably guess you're with me. She's already figured I have a guy here.'

Grimacing, Kent stood looking down at the phone. It looked tiny in his big brown work-roughened hand. His throat rippled as he swallowed. 'I'm sure Bella will understand if I explain.'

Zoe gave a choked laugh. 'How are you going to explain that you ended up spending the weekend with her bridesmaid? It'll sound so—' she swallowed, grasping for a word '—tacky.'

'Tacky?' Kent repeated, shocked.

'Hasty, then. Indecently so.'

In two steps, Kent was across the room and grabbing Zoe's arm. 'Is that what you think? That last night was tacky?'

'No.' Suddenly, Zoe was trembling and fighting tears. 'Oh, Kent, you have to admit it might be viewed by many as indecent haste.'

He pulled her in to him, holding her against his broad chest, kissing her hair. 'Whatever's happening between us is *good*.' Gently, he tucked her hair behind her ear and kissed her brow. 'And it's no one else's business.'

Zoe closed her eyes and let her head sink against his shoulder. She loved being with this man so much— loved the way he smelled of sunlight and clean shirts, loved the hard strength of his body, and the warm reassurance of his arms wrapped around her. Loved who he was.

But she had loved Rodney, too. She'd adored him. She could never have believed he might hurt her.

'How did we let this happen so soon?' she asked Kent.

For answer, he hugged her closer, but even as warmth and pleasure seeped through her the impact of Bella's phone call remained, lifting the lid on all the difficult questions she'd doggedly resisted for the past twenty-four hours. And one thing was certain—she couldn't find answers to these questions while she was in Kent's arms.

With enormous reluctance she pulled away, went to the window and opened it, letting in a fresh breeze as if, somehow, that might clear her thoughts.

'I never meant this to happen,' she said. 'After that kiss goodbye last weekend I decided we shouldn't get too involved. It's all too soon. Too convenient.'

She looked down at her hands—rubbed the rough edge of a thumbnail. The real issue here was that Kent didn't want to settle down. He'd said so last night. She, on the other hand, wanted nothing more than to marry and start a family—to be the bride, not the bridesmaid. And Kent was exactly the sort of man… No, he was the *only* man she wanted to settle down with.

She couldn't tell him that. There was no point. 'I can't help worrying that this weekend has been a mistake,' she said instead.

'You mean you're feeling pressured?'

'Well, yes. I tried to tell you last night that we shouldn't…' She shot him an accusing glance. 'I'm sure you remember.'

'Oh, yes, I remember.' Kent's slow smile made her wince.

No doubt he was remembering the way she'd shamelessly climbed into his lap and kissed him as if there were no tomorrow. She was so hopelessly weak around him and last night she'd foolishly given in to that weakness.

Now she was determined to be strong. 'The thing is, I've been through something like this before, Kent.'

He frowned. 'How do you mean?'

'I fell for a guy who'd recently broken off an engagement. He was a work colleague and I'd known him for about twelve months. I'd even met his fiancée, Naomi, at parties. A few months after their break-up he asked me out, and I conscientiously tried to cheer him up. All went well. He moved in with me and we lived together for another six months. Until—'

Zoe paused for dramatic emphasis.

'Until he let you down,' Kent suggested.

'Yes. I came home one Friday evening and found him in *my* bed with Naomi.'

He scowled. 'That's a low-down act.'

'That's why I call him Rodney the Rat.' Zoe closed her eyes at the memory. 'He made me feel used and stupid and conned and hurt and angry. You name it—I felt it. I was devastated.'

And now…she wouldn't run the risk of being hurt again, surely? She'd been a fool to let herself fall for Kent so quickly and easily, when she'd spent the past week telling herself that it wasn't wise.

'Zoe, I swear I would never do anything to you like that.'

'I know you wouldn't hurt me intentionally, but I can't help feeling vulnerable.' Impatiently, she swept a lock of hair from her eyes. 'Maybe I'm jumping the gun. We haven't even talked about what we want from—from this. Are we having a fling—or—or—?'

'I thought we were getting to know each other.' He came to stand beside her again, and with his hands on her shoulders he turned her to look at him, trapping her with the dark, frank depths of his eyes. 'We were honest with each other when we made love, weren't we?'

Zoe couldn't deny there'd been a special openness and sincerity about last night. But that was the problem. To her, it had felt like so much more than a temporary fling and just thinking about it brought her to the edge of tears.

She took a deep breath. If she played this the wrong way, she would lose Kent, and live to regret it deeply. But her bigger fear was that she'd keep seeing him for several more weeks and *then* the novelty would wear off for him. To spend more time with him and then lose him would be so much worse. Unbearable.

The hard truth was that every moment she spent with Kent was dangerous. She'd been falling more deeply in love with him since the moment she'd met him beside the road side. If she didn't apply the brakes now, before she was in any deeper, she could end up *very* badly hurt. Again.

It was important now to list her extremely valid concerns.

'Kent, until last weekend, you were all set to marry my best friend. You were ready to vow to love her till you were parted by death.'

A muscle jerked in his jaw. 'But you know why we called it off.'

'Yes, I do. And I can understand why you want to move on with your life. But I'm not sure it's a great idea to move straight on to the bridesmaid, as if I was there, ready and waiting—like the next cab on the rank.'

Zoe knew it was a cheap shot, and a sound like a

growl broke from him. Anger flashed in his eyes and he looked so unlike his calm, easy-going self that she almost backed down and apologised. But then where would she be? In his arms with nothing sorted? Nothing solved?

Kent's eyes narrowed. 'Are you asking me to leave?'

No, no, no. That wasn't what she wanted at all. How could she let him go? She'd been so looking forward to this evening—to their shared meal, and the long night after—and then, all of Sunday still ahead of them. And their future...

She dropped her gaze to the floor. It was too hard to think when Kent was standing right there all gorgeous and frowning in front of her.

Be strong, Zoe.

She took a deep breath before she spoke. 'Perhaps we just need space to sort things out—a sort of cooling-off period.' She hoped she didn't sound as miserable as she felt.

Kent remained very still, and his dark eyes, usually so warm and sparkling, remained severe and narrowed. 'Cooling-off period? So what's that? Forty-eight hours? Four weeks?'

I don't know! she wanted to wail.

Kent, however, had made his decision. 'It's clear I should go.' Stepping forward, he dropped a light kiss on her cheek. 'I'll be in touch, then.' And just like that, he was heading out of her kitchen.

Zoe wanted to call him back.

Don't you want dinner? It's a long drive back to Willara. She shot a desperate glance to the sauce-spattered stove. They'd cooked all this pasta.

But what about your things? she almost called out, until she remembered that Kent hadn't brought any luggage. He'd slept naked, and used her spare toothbrush—because he hadn't planned to stay...

Everything that had happened this weekend had been wonderfully spontaneous and...

And now she'd spoiled it.

Stumbling behind him through the flat, she swiped at embarrassing tears. When they reached her front door, Kent turned to her again, looking so desperately stern and handsome Zoe could barely breathe.

'I guess I need to get this straight,' he said. 'While we're cooling off, what exactly are we sorting out?'

Zoe gulped. Her mind was swirling. What could she say? Was this the time for painful honesty? What else could she offer him? 'I'm worried that I'm not the right girl for you, Kent.'

He stood, wary-eyed, waiting for her to continue.

Now that she'd started, she had no choice but to confess. 'I'm afraid I'm very keen on you, keener than you realise. And I don't think you'd want to deal with that right now.' Taking a deep breath, she rushed on. 'To be honest, I'm in love with the whole picture of you and your farm and your country lifestyle.'

Kent didn't speak. Perhaps he was stunned, or simply puzzled.

And Zoe realised, now, too late, that it had been a mistake to mention any of this, but she felt compelled to explain. 'It started when I was little, living in a bus and always looking out of the window at snug farmhouses in the middle of neat, tidy fields. I thought they looked so wonderful and I developed this fantasy of marrying a farmer one day.'

'So I'm a fantasy?' he queried, looking uncomfortable. 'Along with a country wedding?'

Oh, God. Too much information.

'I'm making a hash of this,' Zoe said. 'I didn't mean that the only reason I like you is because you're a farmer.'

'OK.' He lifted a hand as if to put a stop to the conversation. 'This is getting way too complicated.'

'I'm sorry.'

'Don't apologise, but I take your point about a cooling-off period. I guess it's a good idea.'

Thud. It was ridiculous to be disappointed as soon as he agreed to the very thing she'd asked for. Zoe's throat was suddenly a scalding knot of unshed tears.

Already he was turning to leave, but she couldn't speak, was too busy keeping her lips pressed together to hold back embarrassing sobs.

'Take care,' he said gently, before he went swiftly down her steps to his ute.

Driving west against the fierce glare of the setting sun, Kent had never felt less like cooling off.

He was fired up. Burning.

Angry with himself.

Last week he'd been a step from marrying Zoe's best friend, and a week later he'd leapt straight into her bed. What was he thinking?

Of course it was a hasty, rash and thoughtless act. If one of his mates had behaved the same way, Kent would be wondering if the guy's actions were driven by a bruised ego, or by his brains dropping below his belt!

Zoe had every right to ask questions—questions he should have asked himself.

What did he want from this relationship? Was it a casual fling? Did he expect to follow his old pattern, to date her for a month or so, and then drift away?

He certainly hadn't been thinking about the long term.

After last week's close brush with the responsibility and permanence of matrimony, he'd been set free, so to speak. He was free to embrace his old ways and his plan was to prolong his bachelorhood for as long as he could.

But did he honestly expect a conscientious girl like Zoe to treat their relationship lightly? After her past weeks of hard work and dedication, shouldn't he have known better? After she'd made love with such breath-taking spontaneity and touching emotion, shouldn't he have known their liaison was already complicated?

Hell. Zoe had told him about her rat of a boyfriend, and he'd been so self-righteous.

I would never do anything to you like that. What a fool he was.

Selfish, too. He'd wanted a little fun after the tension and drama of the past weeks, and Zoe had been available. How had she put it? The next cab at the rank.

And yet—that wasn't how he thought of her. Zoe was special, amazing in so many ways—the kind of girl he could, quite possibly, marry one day…if he'd had plans to settle down.

Maybe he shouldn't have been so surprised by her confession that she had feelings for him and wanted to marry, that she'd always wanted to be a farmer's wife, for heaven's sake.

But he hadn't seen it coming, and now, instead of relaxing after a pleasant weekend, he had a lot to think about. Too much. Not a chance of cooling off.

CHAPTER ELEVEN

IT WAS ten-thirty when the delivery boy arrived at the office doorway. At least, Zoe assumed it was the delivery boy, although all she could see of him were his jeans and his grubby green and yellow sneakers. The top half of him was entirely obscured by the biggest bunch of flowers she'd ever seen.

As the flowers appeared there was a collective gasp from every female in the office. The girl at the desk nearest to Zoe stopped a phone conversation in mid-sentence. Someone else gave an excited little squeal.

Mandy, whose desk was closest to the door, got out of her seat and practically tiptoed in awe towards the mountain of blooms.

Zoe was as curious as anyone else as she exchanged smiles with her workmates. She knew everyone was trying to guess who the lucky recipient could be. Emily had recently announced she was pregnant. Joanne was turning forty soon. Jane had acquired a new and, apparently, ultra-romantic boyfriend.

At least, Zoe knew the flowers couldn't be for her. The only person who might send them was Kent and he'd embraced her cooling-off suggestion with depressing enthusiasm. It was three weeks now since she'd seen him. Three desperately miserable weeks.

In all that time, she'd made no attempt to contact him and he'd only been in touch once to report that, despite the terrible weather in the north, Bella and Damon were apparently OK. There'd been nothing personal in his message. Not a breath of romance.

The silence had been awful. At times Zoe had felt so miserable, she'd almost weakened and begged him to forget everything she'd said.

Fortunately, she'd restrained herself. She'd done enough damage last time when she'd talked about loving him. Of course she'd frightened him off.

If she'd handled everything sensibly, they would have continued to see each other on weekends and who knew what pleasing developments might have occurred?

Now, in just a few days, she would be leaving for Europe, so there was no point in even thinking about what might have been with Kent. Instead, she was hoping and praying that the exciting new foreign sights and experiences would cheer her up, and help her to put the whole Willara experience behind her.

At any rate, she could relax right now. There was absolutely no chance these flowers were for her.

At the doorway, the floral Mount Everest was handed over to Mandy, who had to turn sideways to see where she was going as she made her way carefully back into the centre of the office.

'Help, someone!' she called. 'I'm sure there's a card pinned on here, but I can't possibly reach it.'

Zoe jumped to assist her. The bouquet was so huge, it took a few moments to locate the small white envelope, but she finally found it pinned beneath a cascade of lavender orchids.

'Here!' she cried, triumphantly waving the small white envelope above her head like a trophy.

'Who's it for?' cried several voices.

All eyes in the room were on Zoe. She saw smiles of amusement, wistful faces filled with hope, others wide eyed with genuine tension. The air was shimmering with palpable excitement.

Suddenly the centre of attention, Zoe felt her heartbeats begin a drum roll as she deliberately took her time looking at the name on the envelope. Then she dropped her gaze to the white square of paper. And her heart stopped beating altogether.

There…on the envelope in clear blue ink…

Zoe Weston.

There was a painful thump in the centre of her chest, and then her heart began to pound savagely. She hadn't expected, hadn't dreamed… The paper in her hand was shaking.

Everyone was watching her.

'Oh, gosh.'

'Who's it for?' Mandy demanded.

Almost apologetically, Zoe said, 'Me.'

At first there was silence. Then a voice cried, 'Oh, wow! Congratulations!' But for Zoe this was almost drowned out by her thundering heartbeats.

Her hands were shaking so badly, she had a hard time getting the little card out of the envelope, but finally she was able to read it.

I'd like to talk. How about you?

Kent xx

A thrill burst inside her like fizzing champagne.

'Who's it from?' called Jane.

Zoe hesitated. Many of these girls had been to

Willara Downs for the bridal shower. 'Just a guy,' she said lamely. As you did.

The response was a predictable group groan.

'If a guy sends a bouquet the size of a house he must be asking you to marry him at the very least,' someone said.

'Or perhaps he's been a very, very bad boy and he's very, very sorry,' said someone else.

Zoe shook her head, but she wasn't about to tell them: *he just wants to talk.* She was still trembling as she took the flowers from Mandy and stumbled off to hunt for a bucket to put them in.

In a back room she found a metal waste-paper bin, and she filled it with water. With the flowers taken care of, she sank back against a filing cabinet and read Kent's note again.

I'd like to talk. How about you?

Every possible emotion raged war inside her. Joy. Hope. Fear. Uncertainty.

Kent was opening a door, trying to reconnect, and she couldn't think of anything she wanted more than to see him again.

But in a few days she would be flying to the other side of the world, and she'd be away for a month. Surely her sudden impatience to see him was foolish.

Just because he's sent me a bunch of flowers?

But I love him.

Did she? Really?

She'd had enough time to think about it, to try to work out if she was actually in love with the real man and not with an embodiment of her childhood fantasy.

She found herself asking how anyone ever knew for certain that they were truly in love. In three weeks her longing to see Kent had been agonising. Was that love?

Was love ever safe and certain, or was it always a great big gamble?

She reminded herself again, as she had so often in the past three weeks, of her headlong rush into love with Rodney. She'd been so certain he was The One.

She'd been such a diligent girlfriend, so anxious to please Rodney, cooking his favourite meals, hiring his favourite DVDs. She'd been so busy showing him how devoted she was, she'd never stopped to make sure he felt the same way.

Being dumped by him had awoken every one of her insecurities. Once again she'd been an outsider, without a best mate.

Lately, she'd even wondered if she had poor judgement when it came to men. Perhaps it would be much more sensible to wait to talk to Kent after she got back from her travels. Mightn't she gain a clearer perspective with the benefit of further time and distance?

At lunchtime, Zoe divided the flowers into smaller bunches and handed them out among her surprised work colleagues.

'There's no point in taking them home to my place,' she explained over and over. 'I'm leaving for Europe on the weekend. You may as well enjoy them.'

The only flowers Zoe saved were the lavender orchids, which she took home and placed in a vase on the shelf beside the fish tank.

That was the easy part. Deciding how to deal with Kent was the difficult bit. She had to ring him to thank him, and there shouldn't be any harm in a phone call. Just the same, she had to be careful not to say too much. Now, when she was about to leave, she certainly couldn't let on how much she'd missed him.

No, she would have to be very strong and in control

of this conversation. Most definitely, she mustn't allow Kent to say or do anything to spoil her holiday plans.

The phone's shrill ring sent a jolt of adrenalin punching into Kent. He willed himself to stay calm. Almost certainly, this would be yet another phone call from a wedding guest, calling to cheer him up, or to invite him over for a meal. There'd been many such calls during the past month.

Even so, Kent knew the flowers must have arrived in Brisbane, and he was picturing Zoe as he picked up the receiver. He imagined her on her sofa in her Newmarket flat, with her long legs tucked neatly beneath her, her shiny hair a dark splash against the vivid red of her sofa's upholstery. Her eyes the blue of the morning sky…

He forced a smile into his voice as he answered. 'Hello. Willara Downs.'

'Hi, Kent, it's Zoe.'

Twin reactions—elation and alarm—tightened like lassos around his chest. It was so good to hear her voice and he couldn't believe how much he'd missed her. For these past three weeks he'd spent far too much time thinking about her, missing her smile, her touch, her company.

But he couldn't believe how worried he was, too. Worried she would read too much into this gesture. He simply needed to see her again. From their first meeting, he'd been aware of a fatal chemistry, and he'd tried his best to ignore it, but it was still tormenting him like a constant ache.

He'd given in, sent the flowers and a request to make contact, and now he forced a smile into his voice. 'Hey, Zoe, it's great to hear from you. How are you?'

'I'm fine, thanks.'

She didn't sound fine. She sounded nervous, as nervous as he was.

'Your flowers arrived,' she said. 'Thank you so much, Kent. They're beautiful. There were so many of them.'

'Not too over the top, I hope. I ordered them over the phone and just named an amount. Anyway, I'm glad you liked them.'

'All the girls in the office were jealous.' After a small pause, she asked, 'How—how are you?'

'Fighting fit.' He swallowed a sudden constriction in his throat. 'But I've missed you, Zoe.'

'Oh.'

Oh? What was that supposed to mean? He needed to know if she was pleased or disappointed. 'I was wondering if you'd had enough of this cooling-off period.'

'It hasn't been much fun,' she said softly, but then added almost straight away, 'but I still think it's a sensible idea, don't you?'

'I'm not sure it's possible to sort out a relationship in isolation. I was hoping we could talk.'

She made a noise that sounded like a sigh. A sad sigh that chilled him. 'I'm leaving for Europe on Saturday, Kent.'

'So soon? But Christmas is a month away.'

'I'm going to London and Paris first. Ten days in each city, and then on to Prague.'

A curse fell from his lips before he could bite it back. He didn't want to wait another month. He'd had enough of waiting while his thoughts went round and round the same worn track. Solitary contemplation hadn't helped.

He couldn't make decisions about their relationship in a vacuum.

He wanted action. He needed to be able to touch Zoe, to share meals and conversations, to make love to her.

If they waited another month, Zoe would have all kinds of opportunities to meet suave, silver-tongued Continental Casanovas. Hell. Had she already dismissed him?

Surely she owed him another chance? He had to see her. 'I'll come down to Brisbane.' Kent glanced at his watch. It was too late tonight. 'How about tomorrow night?'

'Sorry, Kent, my parents will be here. They're coming up to Brisbane to collect the goldfish and my pot plants.'

Curse the goldfish. Why had he ever thought it was a good idea? 'What about Friday night, then?'

There was another, longer pause. 'I—I'm not sure that's a good idea. I'll be leaving early on Saturday morning. Maybe we should let this go till I get back.'

'Sorry, Zoe. That's not an option. I have to see you. I'll come to the airport. What's your flight number?'

'Honestly, there's no need to see me off.'

'You can't keep stalling.' He was bulldozing her, but he didn't care. He'd heard a quiver in her voice that hinted at her inner battle, and in that instant he'd decided there was no way he could let her leave for the far side of the world without seeing her.

'Just tell me the flight and I'll be there.'

'OK, but I'll need to make a condition though, Kent.'

'What is it?'

'Promise you won't try to talk me out of going away.'

'Agreed,' he said, with a reluctance that disturbed him.

* * *

Zoe's boarding pass was tucked into her handbag and her suitcase was already on its way down the conveyor belt as she scanned the international terminal, searching for Kent.

Despite her best efforts to remain calm, her insides were flapping like bait in a net. She couldn't wait to see him, couldn't believe he was driving all the way from Willara Downs to Brisbane airport to spend a few short minutes with her.

How amazing was that? She'd given him a chance to cool off and it seemed that he hadn't cooled.

Of course, she hadn't cooled either. She was desperate to see him. And yet she was scared. For three and a half weeks, she'd kept her feelings for Kent carefully tied up in tight little parcels, and now, when she was about to head overseas, she wanted them to stay that way.

This trip was important to her. She was looking forward to the exciting new sights and sounds and smells of foreign places.

More importantly, she was hoping that time and distance would offer her an excellent chance to sort through her emotions and get a new perspective on her hopes and dreams. It would give Kent time, too.

Right now, however, she was scared. Scared that seeing him again would unravel her tightly bound feelings. Scared that one look into the deep brown warmth in his eyes could too easily break her resolve. How awful if her emotions spilled out all over the airport, like luggage bursting from an over-stuffed suitcase.

I can't let that happen. I have to be strong.

It would be so much easier to leave now without seeing him. All she had to do was walk through the exit doors into the secure Customs area and Kent wouldn't be able to follow her. Then she could keep herself together until she was safely out of reach. Should she leave? Now?

'Zoe.'

His voice came from behind her, spinning her around, a smile already flooding her face.

Oh, wow! He looked even more wonderful than she'd remembered. He was so tall and broad shouldered and his skin was darker, as if he'd spent a lot of time outdoors.

They stood, just staring at each other. Not touching.

'I'm late,' he said. 'The traffic was insane. I was afraid I'd miss you.'

'It won't be long before I have to go.'

'That's OK. At least I'm here now.' He smiled.

Heavens, his smile was gorgeous.

Dangerous. Zoe wanted to lean in to him, to touch him, to smell him.

Instead she searched for safe conversation. 'How's everything on the farm?'

'All running along smoothly.'

'Who's looking after the garden?'

Kent smiled again, but his eyes were watching her with hawklike attention. 'I have my work cut out running the farm, and my mother's busy planting up her new cottage garden, so, for now, the garden's looking after itself.'

'That's a shame.' There would be so many weeds, and the roses would need dead-heading. All the lilies and irises would be out now, but there'd be no one to truly appreciate them.

'I might get someone in,' he said, still watching her.

Zoe nodded and told herself to forget Willara Downs.

Kent said, 'You're going to have a fabulous trip.'

She was grateful that he wasn't going to try to stop her from leaving. She hoped he had no idea how easily he could.

His eyes searched her face, again, worried now. 'You'll be careful, won't you, Zoe?'

'Of course. Don't worry. My dad's given me all the lectures about a girl overseas on her own... I have a long list of instructions. Use a money belt. Keep enough money for the day in my pocket. Stay away from the lonely spots.'

'All very good advice.'

'And I've scanned my travel documents and emailed them to myself.'

'Great. And remember to keep in touch,' Kent added.

'That, too.' She smiled. 'I have international texting on my mobile phone.'

'And you have my number, I hope.'

'Yes. I'll text you.'

'Promise?'

The dark intensity in his eyes made her heart stumble. 'I promise, Kent.'

His shoulders visibly relaxed, and it was only then that she realised how very tense he'd been. 'Text me as often as you like, Zoe. If you're having a great time, or—or a not so great time.'

'I will.' She smiled. 'Don't look so worried.'

'I can't help it. I'm letting you go.'

She didn't know what to say. She hadn't expected him to be quite so...so protective...and she was scared she'd start to cry. 'I should head off now.'

He touched her elbow. 'You can't rush off without a decent goodbye.'

It was a warning, Zoe realised, not a request. But

Kent gave her no chance to deny him. In a heartbeat, he'd gathered her in, and he was kissing her.

Not hungrily, as she might have expected after their three-week stand-off, but with devastating tenderness. And heaven help her, she couldn't even pretend to resist. He only had to touch her and her will power evaporated like mist in sunlight.

Now, he'd barely sipped at her lower lip and, already, she was trembling.

His lips brushed her top lip. A kiss, as teasing and as light as air. Heartbreaking in its sexiness. He pressed another kiss to the corner of her mouth.

Wherever his lips touched her, Zoe melted.

Her knees threatened to give away as he took the kiss dizzyingly deeper, and she had no choice but to cling to him, grabbing handfuls of his T-shirt to steady herself. Now she was truly melting all over. Melting from head to toe. Dissolving right there. In the busy airport.

The bustling crowds and the voices over the intercom faded as Zoe became lost in the deep, dark mystery of Kent's kiss. Her impending flight no longer mattered. The whole world was happening right here. In Kent's arms.

When he released her, she wanted to cry.

Gently, he tucked a strand of her hair behind her ear, and his eyes betrayed a mix of sadness and triumph. 'So, Zoe…about this cooling-off idea.'

Right now, the cooling off was quite obviously the most ridiculous idea she'd ever had.

Then again, this kiss only proved how very badly she needed a safety net. She was so susceptible to this man. She lost her head whenever he was near. His kisses made her want to cancel her flight, tear up her ticket and toss her passport in the nearest waste bin.

Snap out of it, Zoe. For heaven's sake pull yourself together. Now.

She squared her shoulders. 'I—I don't think we should change our current status before I get back.'

Kent was smiling, damn him. 'So I guess this farewell kiss was an exception.'

Somehow, miraculously, Zoe kept her face poker straight. 'Under the circumstances, it was an excusable infringement.' With deliberate brusqueness, she checked the time on her phone. 'I'm sorry. I really must go now.'

To her surprise, Kent nodded. 'Yes, you must. I hope you have a safe journey, Zoe.'

'Thanks.'

It was happening. Kent was letting her go. Why couldn't she feel relieved?

His eyes were burning and serious. 'Remember to stay in touch. Your messages can be as cool as you like, but keep them coming.'

'All right.'

She thought he might kiss her again. And he did. He dropped one last, sweet, too-tempting and too-brief kiss on her lips, and then he stepped away from her, his throat rippling.

He lifted his hand.

Zoe's vision blurred and when she tried to walk her shoes were filled with lead.

CHAPTER TWELVE

AT FIRST, Zoe managed quite well. In London and Paris there were so many famous sights she wanted to see, so many beautiful art galleries, and amazing, historic buildings. So many wonderfully enticing shops to explore. She managed to keep busy every day and she found each new experience thrilling and exciting.

She also discovered definite advantages to solo travelling—total freedom to decide what she wanted to see and where she should stay, or when and where she should eat. And she met lots of interesting fellow travellers from all over the world.

But of course, she missed Kent and thought of him often.

Too often.

No way could she pretend she didn't miss him. He was always there, as an ache beneath her breastbone, a tightness in her throat. Her solo travels would have been a thousand times better if he'd been there to share everything with her.

Even so, she was very disciplined. She restricted her text messages to Kent, allowing only one message every second day, and she kept them brief and cheerful. No mushy stuff.

Kent's responses were disappointing—often arriving much later than Zoe would have liked, even taking the time difference into consideration. And when he replied, his tone was cool and utterly lacking in anything even slightly mushy or romantic.

Clearly, he was taking her request to extend their cooling-off period seriously, and she knew she should be grateful for that. But there was always the chance that his interest in her was fading, just as she'd always feared.

Zoe hated how sick this thought made her.

She tried to cheer herself up by conjuring memories of their farewell kiss at the airport, but what an unhelpful exercise that was. She found herself missing Kent more and more every day.

It was dark when Kent got back to the homestead. He fed his dogs on the back veranda, then went into the kitchen to heat up a can of tomato soup for himself. He knew it was lazy, but it was already after eight, and he was too weary to bother about cooking a proper meal. Since Zoe left, he'd been working long hours, seven days a week, hoping that the self-imposed labour would act as a sedative.

It hadn't worked.

Nothing in his life felt right. Each night he fell into bed exhausted, but then couldn't sleep. His solitary existence, which had never bothered him before, was now suffocating.

He couldn't stop thinking about Zoe in Europe, wishing he were there. Worse, he kept reliving all the times they'd been together. Not just the lovemaking—all the everyday moments, like the evening she was here in his kitchen, making a salad while he flipped steaks, on another afternoon, preparing a roast, or sharing a sunset.

He remembered the meals they'd enjoyed on the back veranda, the conversations. Recalled Zoe's enthusiasm for the garden, remembered the morning she'd gone down to the creek with him to collect sand—the soft empathy in her eyes when she'd asked him about the accident.

Each small recollection had become painfully sharp and clear. So important.

Now that Kent had too much time to think, he realised that he'd been so caught up with the wedding plans that he'd never really noticed how perfectly Zoe fitted into life on Willara Downs. Now, despite his best attempts to ignore such dangerous thoughts, he knew that his plans for a lengthy bachelorhood were fast losing their charm.

It was not a comforting discovery. Small wonder he couldn't sleep.

For Zoe, things went from not so great to downright dismal when she arrived in Prague.

As her plane touched down she looked out at the banks of snow lining the cleared runway, and her first, her *only* thought was—*Kent should be here*.

Riding in the taxi from the airport, she couldn't stop thinking about him. She'd brought his beautiful book with her, and now the same gorgeous pictures she knew by heart were unfolding before her. She kept thinking about the night they'd shared dinner on the back veranda at Willara Downs, when Kent had first told her about Christmas in Prague.

If only he were here.

Impulsively, she sent him a text message.

1.30p.m.: I'm in Prague!!!!!!! My first glimpse of the fairy-tale skyline. Prague castle silhouetted against a winter-white sky. It stole my breath. So pretty and timeless.

She'd only come to Prague because Kent had told her about it, and now she was here, surrounded by its ancient, wintry beauty, she wanted him to be here with her. So badly. How could she enjoy the snow, the castles and the Christmas markets without him?

Loneliness descended like the snow.

She remembered all the overtures Kent had made before she left—the enormous bunch of flowers, the offers to visit her at her flat, the trip to the airport to say goodbye. Each time he'd tried to restart their relationship she'd blocked him.

Now, she had to ask why.

Why? *Why?*

Why had she been so fixated on keeping him at bay?

She was left with unanswered puzzles. She was surprised that he still seemed keen even though she'd spilled her dreams about settling down. Not that this meant he was ready to marry her. Perhaps he'd hoped to win her around to accepting a freer relationship. To Zoe, in her present lonely circumstances, that seemed to be a reasonable compromise.

However, her fixation with Kent annoyed her. She'd come away, hoping that distance and time would clear her head and her heart. But now, here she was in Prague on the far side of the world, and she still spent her whole time thinking about one man.

She missed his smile, missed his friendly brown eyes, the warmth and power of his arms about her. Missed his smell, his voice, his kisses, his touch...

And she had to ask why she'd insisted on an extension of their cooling off.

Her initial caution, so soon after the cancelled wedding, had been sensible. But was her request to continue it really such a good idea?

Suddenly, it made no sense to ration her text messages.

She had to make contact with Kent. If he couldn't be here, she needed to share her experiences by the only means she had. Opening her phone, she began to type.

4.15 p.m.: It's already dark and it's snowing and I'm wearing a new red woollen hat I bought in Paris.

5.45 p.m.: I'm in the Old Town Square. So many sounds. Church bells, a brass band playing carols, the chiming of the famous astronomical clock.

6.01 p.m.: Now I'm walking across Charles Bridge. There's a busker playing a violin. Magic.

7.10 p.m.: Goulash for dinner with five white dumplings to mop up the yummy rich beef gravy.

7.30 p.m.: Have just had my first drink of grog—a mix of rum and tea. Miss you heaps. Xx

By the time Zoe went to bed she'd had no reply from Kent. She told herself this was to be expected given the time differences, but it didn't stop her from feeling depressed and lonely and sorry for herself.

She knew it was pitiful, but she couldn't help feeling

down. She cried herself to sleep, and she slept fitfully, waking often to check her phone for messages.

There was only one, which arrived at 3.00 a.m. From her mum.

Next morning, Kent still hadn't replied, and Zoe found reasons—he'd risen early and taken off on his tractor without checking his phone. Or perhaps his phone's battery had needed recharging. She knew there were all sorts of logical explanations.

Just the same, she waited on tenterhooks. And to cheer herself up, she kept sending messages.

8.05 a.m.: From my apartment window, I look out at steep rooftops covered in snow and I can see Prague castle.
    Don't you wish you were here?

8.35 a.m.: The cars are covered in snow. The statues have snow on their shoulders. The tree branches are sagging beneath the weight of the snow. There are children tobogganing.
    What's it like at Willara?

9.15 a.m.: I'm trying to catch falling snow in my mouth. Can you tell snow's a novelty for me?

10.00 p.m.: Kent, I've been in Prague a whole day. Where are you?

At midnight, Zoe sat on her bed, wrapped in a warm quilt, staring forlornly at her phone. She'd written another message, but she wasn't quite brave enough to press Send. Kent's silence had made her desperate, but the message was so—*revealing*—and sending it was far too risky.

Heartsick, she read it again.

11.53 p.m.: Kent, I miss you so much. This cooling off isn't working any more. When I get back home, I hope we can talk.
I love you,
Zoe xxx

She'd changed the last part of the message a dozen times, had deleted and then rewritten those three telling words— *I love you.*

She knew this wasn't what he wanted to hear. How could she make such a rash confession? In the weeks since she'd left home, he hadn't given her any fresh reason to hope.

At twenty past midnight, Zoe was still huddled on the bed, but she decided she'd been too cautious for too long. What the heck? It was time to be brave.

Taking a deep breath for courage, she pressed the send button, and then she slipped beneath the covers, and tried to sleep. Her heart was pounding.

Next morning there was still no answer from Kent, and Zoe had never in her life felt as bereft as she did now.

She stood at the window looking out at the postcard-perfect scene of Europe's fairy-tale city. Overnight it had snowed again and all the rooftops and the streets were coated with glistening white. She didn't care. She didn't want to be in Prague. It was almost Christmas and she was alone and heartbroken and on the wrong side of the world.

How could she have been such a fool? How had she ever thought she could enjoy this alone?

But even if she paid the extra money to change her flights in the middle of the festive season, she didn't want to fly back to Australia if she couldn't be sure Kent would welcome her. That would be unbearable. Better to stay here in Prague and try to make the best of a bad situation.

She should try to put Kent out of her mind.

This morning she would go to the markets and buy Christmas decorations. She would school herself to live in each moment, to enjoy the ancient cobbled streets, and the old Gothic architecture, and the brightly decorated wooden huts selling handicrafts and wooden toys. Instead of dwelling on her misery, she would think of others. She would buy presents. Lots of presents. Her little brother, Toby, would love those cheeky wooden puppets.

But as Zoe walked from stall to stall she was painfully conscious of the small solid weight of her phone in her coat pocket. All morning, even though she knew it was the middle of the night in Australia, she remained on edge, waiting for the phone to vibrate against her hip, to tell her there was an incoming call.

In the afternoon, she joined a tour of Prague Castle and St Vitus Cathedral. The buildings were beautiful, and the history was epic and fascinating. The views of the city and the elegant bridges over the Vltava River were truly picturesque. Zoe soaked up the atmosphere and told herself how lucky she was to be having such memorable experiences. She told herself this over and over.

Her phone didn't ring.

By the time she'd finished the walking tour, darkness was closing in, but she didn't want to go back to her hotel room. She stayed out in the streets where the music and pretty lights were designed to lift everyone's spirits.

The air was thick with the warm smell of cinnamon and she admired the enormous, brightly lit Christmas tree which, according to the hotel concierge, had been brought down from the Sumava Mountains.

Every ten minutes or so, desperation drove her to take her phone out just to check that she hadn't missed a call.

She hadn't.

By now, her legs were leaden and aching from walking all day in the freezing cold. Her stomach was hollow with regret and self-recrimination. Her last message had been too strong. Kent didn't know how to answer her.

Or worse...

Kent had been in an accident. He was ill.

Stop it.

She would go mad if she kept this up. She should eat. The market stalls sold all kinds of wonderful hot food—corn on the cob, crumbed mushrooms and spicy sausages. Perhaps she should buy a cup of the hot mulled wine that everyone else seemed to be enjoying so much. The wine certainly looked and smelled yummy—spicy, with floating pieces of apple and orange.

At least it would keep her warm.

Slipping her phone into her coat pocket, Zoe gave it a small pat. Silently, she said: *That's it—I'm done with you for tonight.*

The thought was barely completed before she felt, through the soft kid of her glove, a gentle vibration against her fingers.

Her heart banged hard against her ribs. And then her phone began to ring in earnest.

This wasn't a mere text message. On the tiny screen she saw a name.

Kent Rigby...

Her hand was shaking as she held the phone to her ear.

Kent said, 'Zoe—'

And at that very moment a brass band struck up a noisy rendition of 'Good King Wenceslas', drowning out Kent's voice as it blasted the carol into the frosty night air.

'Sorry,' Zoe cried to him, running across the cobblestones with the phone pressed to one ear and her hand covering the other. 'I can't hear you. Hang on, Kent. Are you still there? I'm going to have to get away from this music.'

Around a corner, in a small, narrow street, she sank against a stone wall. 'Sorry,' she puffed. 'That's a little better. Are you still there?'

'Yes, I'm here.' His voice was rippling with warmth and a hint of laughter.

'Are you OK? It seems ages since I heard from you.'

'I'm fine, Zoe. How are you?'

'I'm OK. Everything's lovely here. But it's so good to hear your voice.'

'Are you homesick?'

'I am a bit, yes.' Nervously, she chewed her lip. 'Have my text messages been getting through to you?'

'They have.' There was a tiny pause. 'Thank you.' His voice sounded deeper, rougher, thick with emotion.

Zoe held her breath, wondering if he would explain his recent silence, or if he'd comment on her last message.

At least *I love you* hadn't frightened him away.

'It's beautiful here,' she said lamely.

'Where are you exactly?'

'I'm not sure. It's a little side street off the Old Town Square. Why?'

'I was hoping you weren't too far away.'

She laughed. 'Yeah, right. Like I'm just around the corner from Willara Downs.'

'I'm not at Willara Downs.'

'Where—?' she began, then froze as she heard the triumphant notes of a brass band. The music was coming from…

Inside her phone.

Surely she was mistaken?

No, she wasn't.

'Kent?' Zoe was so tense she was sure her skin had snapped. 'Where are you?'

'Right behind you.'

Heart thumping, she spun around.

And there he was.

On the street corner in a heavy winter coat, outlined by the bright lights from the markets.

She tried to lift a shocked hand to wave, but already Kent was coming towards her, and then, as fast as her shaky legs would allow, Zoe was stumbling over the snowy cobblestones.

Into his open arms.

She buried her face in his shoulder and he held her. She was crying, laughing and snuffling with happiness.

'What are you doing here?' she asked when she got her breath back.

'Looking for you, of course.'

'Kent, that's insane.' A huge sob burst from her. 'Oh, God, I've missed you so much.'

'And I've missed you.' Kent wiped her tears with a gloved hand. 'You wrote that you missed me on your first day here, and I jumped straight on the very next plane.'

Stunned, she pulled back to look into his face. His dearly loved, beautiful face. And in that moment she understood exactly why she loved him.

It had nothing to do with his farm, or his lovely homestead. Or his country shirts and his riding boots. She loved him for something else entirely. Something warm and powerful and steadfast and strong that she found shining in his beautiful brown eyes.

'Thank you for coming,' she said softly.

'Thank you for missing me,' he answered, kissing the tip of her nose.

Arm in arm and warmed by mulled wine and hot corn cobs, they walked through the snowy night to Zoe's hotel. Kent was insanely happy. *Insanely. Over the moon.*

They collected his backpack and went up the narrow stairs. In Zoe's room, they peeled off their gloves, hung up their woollen hats and coats, and removed their heavy, damp boots.

Zoe, looking all kinds of gorgeous in a soft crimson sweater and pale blue jeans, turned to him, her eyes shining with happy expectation.

He wanted nothing more than to scoop her in to him, but he remembered, just in time, that he had something even more important planned for this moment.

He said, with a rueful smile, 'Can you hang on a tick?'

'No, Kent, I can't.' Zoe was laughing and impatient,

rising on tiptoes to nuzzle his jaw. With her lips against his skin, she growled, 'I can't wait another second.'

OK, it was a whacky plan anyway, and Kent knew he couldn't wait either. He needed this. Now. Needed Zoe wrapped in his arms, needed her sweet mouth locked with his, needed the soft silk of her skin under his palms, needed her eager and hungry and loving…

Later…

Everything else could wait till later…

'So what was it?' Zoe asked much later as she lay with her head cradled against his bare shoulder.

Kent yawned. 'What was what?'

'Earlier tonight, when we got back here to the room, you asked me to hang on. What was that about? Were you going to show me something?'

'Yeah,' he said sleepily, and then he yawned. 'But it can wait.'

Gently, she ran her fingers over his chest. 'Poor Kent. You've flown all this way and you must be so jet-lagged.'

'Mmm.'

Kent slept, and Zoe lay awake. After the strain of the past few days, she should have been exhausted, but she was too happy and excited to close her eyes.

Kent had come to her as soon as she told him she missed him. How wonderful was that?

Faint moonlight spilled from the window across their bed and she watched him sleep and thought how amazing, how unbelievably perfect he was.

Her happiness was astonishing, as if she'd been living in a grey world that was suddenly flooded with colour.

Of course, in a deep corner of her heart there was still a niggle of disquiet. When Kent had swept her into his arms he hadn't promised love or marriage. But perhaps it was time to put her dreams aside. Time to put Rodney behind her and to take another risk. Didn't loving someone always involve a risk?

Bella had taken a huge risk when she dashed off to Far North Queensland with Damon Cavello. Kent had taken another big risk by travelling over here on the strength of a text message...

Anyway, why should she worry now simply because Kent hadn't actually told her in so many words that he loved her? He'd flown all this way to be with her, and he'd made love to her with a passion that made her blood sing.

Really. On a night like this, just having him here was enough.

Kent kissed Zoe awake. 'Morning, Sleeping Beauty. I've brought you coffee.'

To her surprise it was already past ten.

'Gosh, you're the one with jet lag. I should be bringing you coffee.'

Kent smiled and sat on the edge of the bed. 'Did you know you're at your most beautiful when you've just woken up?'

'I can't be.'

'But you are. I love the sleep-tumbled look.'

For a moment she thought he was going to say he loved her—no matter how she looked.

It doesn't matter. I don't need words.

Outside, the day was sunny, crystal clear and gleaming white, but they stayed in until lunchtime, making leisurely love. When they eventually went out, they ate food from a market stall, then took a train ride to Karlstejn Castle.

The castle was stunningly beautiful, and Zoe decided that Cinderella, Snow White and Sleeping Beauty had all spent time living within those spectacular walls at the top of a snowy mountain.

From the castle ramparts, the view was truly majestic. They could see for miles, and Zoe wondered—just briefly, as she had earlier that morning—if *this* setting might prompt Kent to tell her he'd changed, that he loved her and wanted to spend the rest of his life with her…

It didn't happen.

But that was OK. Nothing could spoil her happiness as they took the train back to Prague, or as they walked to Wenceslas Square to a café that served coffee and sensational apple strudel with home-made ice cream.

'Save room for dinner,' Kent warned her. 'I'm taking you somewhere special.'

So they walked off the strudel, then went back to their hotel to change. Kent had made reservations at the most gorgeous restaurant where the food was so divine it could easily have inspired a brand-new 'Bohemian Rhapsody'.

Over dinner they talked about Prague and what they knew of Czech history, and the whole time Kent's eyes were lit by a special light that kept Zoe's heart zinging.

All right, all right…

There was no talk of love. *But who needed words?*

Back at the hotel, Zoe took a long hot bath and told herself that she had to stop waiting for Kent to say *something*.

He was a farmer, a doer, a man of action, not words.

He'd bought her a bracelet and he'd sent her goldfish and flowers and given her a book. He'd rushed to the airport to farewell her. And he'd flown all this way from Australia. Why would he do all that if he didn't really care for her?

Just the same…tonight, she would pluck up the courage to mention her last revealing text message. She needed to know how he felt about it…

After drying herself, Zoe rubbed moisturiser all over her body, then slipped into the luxuriously thick towelling robe supplied by the hotel. She opened the bathroom door…

And gasped when she saw their room…

Candles…

Candles everywhere. Candles on the coffee table, on the bookcase, on the bedside tables, on the deep stone window sills. Candles on every available surface. Dainty, *little* candles.

Candles that looked strangely familiar.

Kent was standing in the middle of the room, watching her. In the flickering light, he sent her a shy, crooked smile. 'This was supposed to happen last night.'

'Wow.' Zoe pressed a hand to the jumping pulse in her throat. 'They look so lovely.'

The candles were more than lovely. They were gorgeous. Dazzling. The room danced and glowed with romantic light, while darkness hovered outside and white snowflakes fell soundlessly against the window pane.

Kent grinned. 'You probably recognise these little guys. I have to confess I borrowed your smart candles.'

Of course. Now she knew why they were so familiar. They were the same candles she'd planned to put in sand-filled paper bags for Bella's wedding. 'You brought all of them? All this way?'

'Yes. Four dozen smart candles in my backpack.' He smiled boyishly. 'I brought them to help me.'

Help him? Why? Zoe held her breath. Her heart began to thump.

Kent stepped closer and reached for her hands. 'I wanted to tell you how special you are, Zoe, but I wasn't sure I could convince you with words alone. The candles are my back-up.' His eyes shimmered. 'They stand for everything I love about you. They're bright and—'

'Wait,' she said. 'Please, don't rush over that bit.'

'What bit?'

'The—ah—bit you just said.'

'About loving you?'

'Yes.'

Kent smiled gorgeously. 'Darling girl, that's why I'm here.' His hands framed her face. His eyes shone. 'I love you so much. So much it kills me.'

She was so happy she was going to cry. But she still mustn't get her hopes up. She had to stay sensible. 'But—but this isn't a proposal or anything, is it?'

'It certainly is.'

Her heart almost leapt clear out of her chest. 'But you—you said—'

'I know what I said about long-term commitment, but that was before.' Kent's throat rippled and his eyes shimmered. 'Everything changed when you stepped on that plane, Zoe. I watched you walking out of my life, and it was like I was drowning all over again. Every moment I'd spent with you flashed before my eyes—from the first time we met by the road side and you had the flat tyre, and all those other times at Willara, and then in Brisbane.'

He took a deep breath. 'I've been falling for you from

the start, but I was planning the wedding to Bella, and I couldn't let myself think about you.'

Lifting her hands, Kent pressed them against his chest and she felt the thud-thudding of his heartbeats. 'I've missed you so much. And I've come to my senses at last. Of course, I want what you want, Zoe. I want your help with running the farm, and I want our own little family.'

It was too, too wonderful to take in. To Zoe's dismay, fat tears rolled down her cheeks and she had to blot them on Kent's shirtfront.

When she looked up again, his dark eyes burned with an intensity that made her tremble. 'Don't ever doubt that I love you, Zoe. You're exactly like these candles. You're beautiful and smart and you set me alight.'

'And you brought all forty-eight of them all this way to prove it.' Smiling, she snuggled closer and wound her arms around his neck. 'I do love a man of action.'

'So does that mean you'll marry me?'

Would she? Would she marry the most gorgeous farmer in the world and live in his lovely farmhouse set solidly and safely amidst spreading fields?

Would she embrace her most cherished dream?

For answer Zoe kissed him. 'Yes,' she said, and she gave him another kiss. 'Yes, please, I'd love to marry you.' Then she kissed him again while forty-eight candles glowed warmly in the midwinter night.

* * * * *

THE DOCTOR'S
SURPRISE BRIDE

FIONA McARTHUR

Mother to five sons, **Fiona McArthur** is an Australian midwife who loves to write. Mills & Boon® Medical Romance™ gives Fiona the scope to write about all the wonderful aspects of adventure, romance, medicine and midwifery that she feels so passionate about—as well as an excuse to travel! Now that her boys are older, Fiona and her husband, Ian, are off to meet new people, see new places and have wonderful adventures. Fiona's website is at www.fionamcarthur.com.

CHAPTER ONE

'ARE you OK?' Dr Jack Dancer, Medical Director—in fact, only doctor at Bellbrook Hospital—tilted his head. He tried to bring together this city woman's list of qualifications and experience—then reconcile it with her youth and the tiny package she came in. Actually, Eliza May looked like a garden fairy with attitude. Her shoulders were tense, her head tilted and she glowered fiercely at him through slitted eyes.

This woman looked ten years too young to qualify for half of her résumé and, with Mary going, the hospital needed every skill this city woman was supposed to have.

He'd thought his cousin's agency recommendation extraordinarily glowing and he wondered what fanciful planet his cousin had been on when she'd recommended this woman.

'I'm fine.' Her voice was not loud but contained an element of self-confidence that made him look at her again. She straightened and the movement added a desperately needed few centimetres to her height. Now he could see her eyes.

Jack felt a ripple shimmer down his back and his breath stuck somewhere behind suddenly sensitive ribs.

Good grief. Her eyes were amazing—vibrant green, alluring eyes that dared him to step out of line and taste the consequences. Even the jagged gold circles around her pupils seemed to glow and shimmer and draw him in. He couldn't look away.

Jack forced his diaphragm back into action, and dragged his gaze lower to accelerate past memorable lips and a determined little chin, but knew he was in trouble when he skimmed too low and had to bounce his attention out of her tightly restrained cleavage. What on earth had got into him?

'Lead on, Dr Dancer.' Now she was decisive and he felt the earth shift again under his feet. No fluttery fairy here. He quietened his reservations—and his libido. Energy vibrated and the new Eliza May held such promise for Bellbrook Hospital that he would never risk jeopardising her suitability with unwanted attention.

Perish the thought.

Whatever shock wave had belted him was past now and he wouldn't think like that again.

Realistically they had no one else, and apparently she was multi-skilled and dynamic, though a bit of a chameleon. Still, they all required diversity when Bellbrook bestowed some of those moments of unusual interest and everything went haywire.

He had a full waiting room in his surgery at the side of the hospital and his sister-in-law, Mary, had been due to start maternity leave a month ago. His cousin *had* said Eliza was reliable.

'Right, then.' He didn't look at her again. 'As soon as we find our matron, she'll show you around. I won't see you until later when I do my evening round at the hospital.'

'Good,' Eliza said quietly, but with emphasis, and Jack blinked. Did she mean good she didn't have to see *him* till later, or good that the departing matron would show her around?

Strangely, both explanations piqued him and he glanced down at her as they made their way to the front of the hospital. This new matron came up to his shoulder yet her smaller legs didn't seem to have any trouble keeping up with him.

Her hair shone with red glints as they passed under a light and her fringe swung across her face as she turned her head to look up at him. She floated beside him on invisible wings and matched his speed.

'Where's the fire?' She lifted one finely arched brow as she dared him, and he couldn't help smiling at her.

'Touché,' he said and slowed. 'I forgot your legs were smaller than mine.'

'Thought you might have,' was all she said, and he realised she jangled his nerves and wasn't overawed by him at all. Well, that was good. Wasn't it?

Jack was pleased to see Mary up ahead.

Matron Mary McGuiness was round-faced and round-bodied, though, of course, most of her abdomen belonged to the baby inside her. Mary *was* the hospital.

The staff, and Jack, had a problem imagining anyone else in her position. He hoped Eliza May could do half as good a job in the time she was here.

After the introductions Jack was eager to get away. Most of his eagerness had to do with his waiting patients and a backlog of paperwork, but a percentage had to do with a sudden need to ring his cousin and find out a few more facts about Bellbrook's new Acting Matron. Something about Eliza bothered him.

In fact, several things about her bothered him in a way he hadn't been bothered for years.

He turned to Mary. 'I'll leave Eliza with you, but after showing her around I want you signed off, and with your feet up. Doctor's orders, Mary!' He nodded at Eliza. 'Good luck. You can phone my office if you're worried about anything.'

Eliza smiled blandly. Not if she could help it, Eliza promised herself grimly. Thank goodness he was going. Dr Jack Dancer had everything she wanted to keep away from in a man, let alone one she'd have to totally rely on.

Eliza regretted another bad decision. She may as well rip the heart out of her chest and tear it in two. All he needed was some psychological disaster that kept him from forming a relationship and he'd be irresistible to her twisted mind. After eight weeks with *her* he'd be ready to marry—someone else.

She watched Dr Jack Dancer stride away and Eliza dispassionately imagined she could hear the creak of the fabric stretching across the strong muscles of his long legs and taut backside. Then there were his shoulders.

The man's physical presence was too much. Any woman cradled in Jack Dancer's arms wouldn't be afraid of falling—until he dropped her.

'This will be your office.' Obviously Mary McGuiness hadn't been sidetracked by Jack's physique and Eliza knew *she* was immune. Unobtrusively Eliza dug her nails into her palms to remind herself.

'Do I need an office?' Back on track, Eliza couldn't help returning the other woman's friendly smile because there was something about Mary that warmed the cold parts in Eliza left by too many people over the years. Mary would never let anybody down.

Mary nodded sagely. 'Rosters, hunting up staff if someone is off sick, stock ordering, company reps, interviews with the local newspaper. Heaven forbid—disaster control.'

'Good grief.' Eliza laughed and then stopped, surprised at herself. She hadn't laughed freely for a while. There was such a different feel to this little hospital, a warmth and genuineness that probably radiated from the woman in front of her.

'I'm sure most of those occasions will wait for your return but I can see the need for a private space.' Eliza looked out the door and into the corridor with the clinical areas. 'You say most of my work is hands on?'

'I think you're pleased about that.' Mary smiled again and drew Eliza out of the office. She pointed at doorways as they walked the length of the small building.

'On the semi-acute side, we have two two-bed wards and four single rooms, each with their own bathroom.

We were fortunate to build this wing with a bequest from a grateful former client.'

The rooms were light and airy and all the fittings sparkled with good care. Only two of the rooms held patients.

The first room held two men. 'Meet the new matron, gentlemen. This is Eliza May.'

In the bed beside the door, a man in his early thirties had both arms bandaged to the shoulder with just the tips of his fingers poking out the ends.

Mary stopped beside his bed. 'Joe came off worse when he lit a bonfire with too much petrol.' Mary shook her head at his folly.

'Because Joe's hands and arms are involved he needs help to care for himself. He should be in Armidale Hospital but Dr Dancer has a lot of experience with burns and they let Joe come home if he stays here for another few days.'

'Hi, Joe.' Eliza smiled. 'When I was six I fell off my horse and broke both my arms. For six weeks it was hell with no hands. I have a lot of sympathy.'

Joe sighed with relief. 'Reckon you understand, then.'

'Next to Joe is Keith.' Mary smiled at a seventy-ish-looking man with leathery skin and crinkled stockman eyes. 'Keith's supposed to be going home tomorrow. He ruptured his appendix without telling anyone. He wouldn't come in to see the doctor and nearly paid the ultimate price. We've kept him a few extra days to make sure he doesn't work too hard.' Mary narrowed her eyes at the old gentleman. 'I'm not sure he's right yet.'

'Now, Matron.' Keith had a slow drawl and his lilting

voice brought back memories to Eliza's mind of her father, as did the seriousness of the old man's expression.

He held out his hand to Eliza. 'Good to meet you, new Matron. I'll shake for Joe and me.'

His work-roughened hand felt cool and welcoming in Eliza's and she began to recall the sweeter side of country towns. These were the facets to country life that the city missed—that she missed—and she had never realised the fact before. Of course she'd never miss anything enough to move from the city permanently and there were aspects of country life that terrified her.

Small towns, gossip, everyone related to everyone else. Eliza had grown up in such a place and shuddered at the memory of when her mother had left them. Her father had closed his door on the wagging tongues, and incidentally Eliza's friends, and she'd never been so lonely. But she didn't want to think about that.

And she didn't want to be drawn into some tiny niche of a town where they would all know her business and invade her personal life.

She'd even told her friend, Julie, at the agency that. 'Bellbrook might be a little too warm and fuzzy for me, the way I'm feeling at the moment,' she'd said, but Julie had seen a benefit that had escaped Eliza.

'There's only one doctor you have to work with.' Julie had avoided Eliza's eyes when she'd said that, now that Eliza came to think of it.

'Hope you enjoy your stay, Matron.' The old man's

kind words penetrated Eliza's reflections and she thanked him and moved on with Mary.

They moved on to the next room and Mary spoke to their only maternity patient. 'This is Janice, and her son Newman.' The baby squawked as if he'd recognised his name and the three women smiled.

'Newman was born two days ago in Armidale by Caesarean, and Janice arrived this morning to convalesce here for the next few days. Meet our new matron, Janice. Eliza May.'

'Congratulations, Janice. He's gorgeous.' Eliza stroked Newman's tiny wrist. She'd read the patient notes later and find out the rest because there'd be a Caesarean story there. She'd always enjoyed her stints in Maternity.

Eliza's not-so-great ex-fiancé, Alex, had been reluctant to even speak of babies and months ago Eliza had decided she'd be better sidetracked by more illness-orientated nursing until her fiancé was ready to discuss children. But she'd missed working in Maternity.

Midwifery was such a fascinating area of nursing. If she wasn't going to get married, maybe she could just enjoy other people's babies.

'He's such a good boy.' Janice's delight in her new son touched Eliza and she saw Mary rest her hand over her stomach. Of course Mary would be anxious for the birth of her own child. Eliza narrowed her eyes as she tried to estimate when Mary's baby was due. Here was an obstetric case right beside her that she needed to keep an eye on.

To Eliza, Mary looked ready to go into labour today!

Maybe that was why Julie had been so keen for Eliza to come here?

They moved on and Eliza glanced in the doors of two empty rooms. 'So do you have many maternity patients?'

Mary nodded. 'We normally have three or four post-delivery patients a month. Each stays for a day or two, sometimes longer.'

'Do you ever have emergency deliveries?'

Mary smiled as if at an amusing memory. 'We can manage if we have to but Jack is so busy with everything else he doesn't feel he can give the care needed and refers any obstetric case on.'

The two women set off again and turned a corner to enter a large dining area with rooms off the other wing. 'Our older residents are on this side of the building and enjoy their meals in the communal dining room when they're well enough.'

They paused at the nurses' station where two identical-looking dark-haired women stood in civilian clothes, waiting to be introduced to Eliza. Another younger woman came up to the desk as introductions were started. They all shook hands and smiled but Eliza had the feeling they were measuring her against Mary. Height wasn't the only thing they were measuring.

Mary continued as her comforting self. 'We have four wonderful enrolled nurses who rotate as the second person on for each shift.' She gestured to a dark-haired young woman. 'This is Vivian, who will be on with you for the rest of the day.'

Eliza smiled at Vivian. A patient call bell rang and Vivian said, 'Nice to meet you.' Then scooted away to answer the summons.

'Rhonda and Donna are our dynamic duo. One of them is your night sister while the other is on days off. They also do the two days on call to cover when you're off. The rest of the week you're the third pair of hands if needed at night.'

Both women nodded and smiled so Eliza gathered she'd passed muster, at least today. 'I'm going home to bed,' Donna said. 'Nice meeting you.'

'I'm off, too. Ditto.' added Rhonda, and they hugged Mary and left.

Mary watched them go and she smiled. 'I'm going to miss this place.' She sighed and then blinked mistily at Eliza and moved on.

Mary cleared her throat. 'Across the hall we have our admissions office and medical records, and in here we have our small emergency room.'

Mary entered the neat mini-theatre and treatment room. 'Of course, very occasionally we have larger emergencies and sometimes use the wards if we need more space.' She gestured to the labelled shelves. 'I'm a big believer in labelling so you shouldn't have any trouble finding things.'

'This is going to be great.' Eliza leant across and rested her arm briefly around Mary's shoulder in a spontaneous gesture of comfort. 'I know I'll love it here, Mary, and you're not to worry. I'll take good care of your hospital until you come back.'

A bell rang overhead and they both glanced up.

'What's the bell for?' Eliza asked, and then frowned as Mary stopped and rested one hand low on her stomach.

'That's the casualty bell. At least I'll get to run you through an outpatient card.'

Eliza inclined her head towards Mary's stomach. 'I'll do this. If you're going into labour I'll write a card for you, too.'

'The tightness will go.' Mary smiled ruefully but didn't deny she had some discomfort as she gingerly led the way round the corner towards the main admissions desk, where a young mother leant on the desk with her frightened daughter by her side.

'Asthma,' the clerk said. 'I'll do the admission without her.' She gladly handed over her charges, along with a dog-eared card.

Eliza glanced at the name. Mia Summers. A good choice by the admissions clerk, Eliza thought as she helped the woman up the hallway until she met Mary with the wheelchair. They wheeled Mia into the assessment room where Eliza sat her on the edge of the bed. Mary hovered at the door, ready to help if Eliza needed her.

At least the woman had been able to stand and hadn't fallen unconscious in the car. It hadn't been that long since Eliza had been present at a young man's tragic death from asthma, and that had been in a big city emergency department with more doctors than they'd needed, but it hadn't been enough. Asthma was a killer if people didn't take the early warning signs seriously enough, and Eliza was on a crusade for education of patients at the moment because of that.

'Hello, Mia. I'm Eliza. Have you got your Ventolin on you?'

Mia opened her mouth to answer but was far too breathless to talk.

'Mummy's puffer is here but she can't seem to breathe it.' The little girl prised the small cylinder from her mother's clenched fist.

Eliza glanced at the label of the puffer and nodded as she slipped the pulse oximeter on the woman's finger and noted the low oxygen saturation of the woman's blood. She suspected Mia wasn't far from unconsciousness.

'What's your name?' Eliza asked the little girl as she reached up into the cupboard to pull down a Ventolin mask.

'Kristy. I'm eight.'

'I'm Eliza. I think you'll make a great doctor or nurse one day, Kristy, the way you've looked after Mummy. Where's Daddy?'

'Daddy's in the far paddock and Mummy said we had to go now. I left a note.'

'That was clever and Mummy was right.'

While she was talking, Eliza's hands were busy. 'This mask gives Mummy oxygen and makes the stronger asthma drug into a fine mist and that helps Mummy to breathe.'

Eliza broke open the plastic ampoule, squirted the pre-mixed drug into the chamber of the nebulising mask and fitted the now misting mask over Mia's face.

She continued talking to the little girl but really she was talking to the frightened young woman beside her. 'Inside Mummy's lungs, all her little breathing tubes are blocking up with thick slime. This medicine helps the slime get thinner so Mummy can cough it out of the way and breathe better again, and the oxygen makes mummy feel better.'

The little girl nodded and Eliza rested her hand on the woman's shoulder. 'Just close your eyes, Mia, and let the medication do the job.' Eliza fitted the blood-pressure cuff around the woman's arm and began to pump it up. 'Do you have an asthma plan sheet and a spacer?'

Mia shook her head tiredly and Eliza nodded. 'We'll talk about it later because I think it would help a lot in your case.'

Eliza glanced at Mary. 'She needs IV access, corti-sone and probably IV salbutamol. Would you like to ring Dr Dancer to come around? I'll pop a cannula in to save time.'

Mary nodded and reached for the phone on the wall while Eliza swiftly prepared her equipment. 'I'm going to put a little needle in Mummy's arm. It looks like it would hurt but it's really not much more than a mos-quito bite. Mummy needs some other medicine that works really quickly if we put it in through the needle. Do you want to look away when I do it?'

Kristy shook her head. 'I'll hold Mummy's other hand.'

'You have a wonderful daughter, Mia.'

Mia nodded as she started to cough. Already her oxygen saturation had improved. Eliza glanced at Kristy to see if she was upset by her mother coughing.

'So the slime in Mummy's lungs is getting thinner, isn't it Eliza?'

'Yep.' Eliza slid the cannula into Mia's arm and taped it securely. Then she began to assemble the flask and line and draw up the drugs in preparation. 'Next time Mummy's fingers go this blue or she can't talk, she'd better come in the ambulance because they can give her this medicine in the mask and put the needle in on the way to the doctor. Do you know how to ring an ambulance, Kristy?'

Kristy nodded. 'I ring 000, or 911 in America or 999 in England.'

'Wow. Even I didn't know that.' Eliza felt like hugging the little girl. 'Tell them Mummy can't breathe and then answer all the questions.'

When Jack arrived he could see that Eliza had everything under control. Mia could manage a few words, and after he approved the intravenous drugs Eliza had ready, Mia was stable enough to go by ambulance to Armidale, where she'd have to stay overnight, at the very least, for intensive observation.

'Rhonda's coming in as escort in the ambulance with you, Mia.' Jack squeezed the young woman's shoulder. 'If all goes well, I'll see if they'll transfer you back to us here at Bellbrook tomorrow or the day after.'

Mia's husband arrived. Jack reaffirmed Mia would be better in Armidale, at least overnight, and after goodbyes Mr Summers took their daughter home.

Jack watched Eliza clear the benches and restock the room in record time. He shook his head. Good was an understatement. He wasn't sure he was used to someone telling him what he needed to give a patient, but he'd have to get over it. Eliza had certainly been instrumental in saving Mia's condition from becoming perilous, and that was the important thing.

He cleared his throat and wondered why the words stuck a little. 'You did well, Eliza. Mia hasn't had an attack that severe before.'

Eliza stopped what she was doing and met his eyes. He watched her smile spread to her eyes at his compliment and he could feel himself responding. She was like a sunrise. Boom—explosion of light as she smiled. She blew him away again just like she had when he'd first met her.

'Thank you,' she said quietly. 'So this is what a sleepy country town is like.'

The moment extended and his smile broadened. She was gorgeous in an understated way and his diaphragm imploded again. Unconsciously he took a step forward towards her, as if it was the most natural thing in the world to want to be closer to her.

Then she changed and the corners of her mouth drooped. The expression in her beautiful eyes grew distant and she broke eye contact as she looked away. The angry fairy wasn't quite back but there were glimpses.

Eliza spoke to the package she lifted into the cupboard. 'Mia said she doesn't have an asthma plan or a spacer. Are the plans not something you do here?'

'Not really.' Jack didn't concentrate too much on what she was saying because he was wondering why she'd created such reserve and backed away from being friendly. He refocussed on her question. 'If someone becomes a moderate asthmatic, I usually send them to a specialist in Armidale or even the respiratory clinic in Newcastle, and the specialists do all that.'

She twisted her neck and looked at him from under her brows. 'I'll have some forms sent from the Asthma Foundation. They'll send us an info pack and a pad of plans that you could look at. I've helped generate plans before and believe they give the patient back control of their asthma. Spacers make it easier for the patient to take their Ventolin, especially during an attack.'

Her tone was icy and he couldn't help the drop in warmth in his own voice. It was almost as if she'd engineered the whole estrangement of their brief rapport. Something else was going on here, something ill-defined, and he didn't like it, but he had to get back to his surgery. If she didn't want him here, he could take a hint!

'Thank you, Matron May. I've actually seen such plans and I know what a spacer is,' Jack said dryly. 'I'll certainly consider your suggestion.' He glanced at the door where Mary was an interested bystander. 'I thought you were going home, Mary?'

Mary raised placatory hands and bit back a smile. 'I just need to finish the round I've started with Eliza. I'll be gone soon.'

'Well, I *am* gone,' Jack muttered. 'Matrons,' he said

mockingly, and inclined his head at Eliza. Then he took himself back to his surgery.

Eliza watched him go. What on earth had got into her? Lecturing Jack! It wasn't part of her job and she didn't need to alienate her boss for the next eight weeks.

And why was she thinking of him as Jack and not Dr Dancer?

The problem was, the guy was too tall, too handsome and too sure of himself, and he made her feel all weak and feminine and things she'd promised she wasn't going to feel again. What really worried her was whether coming here had been another bad decision. She'd made a few of those in her life.

'I'm afraid I've put his back up,' Eliza said.

'You don't look too upset about it. It won't kill him to have someone not in awe of him.' Mary changed the subject. 'You seemed to find everything you needed for Mia easily.'

Eliza glanced around at the now tidy room. Back to reality and escape from the distraction of Dr Jack Dancer. 'You've stored everything in the most obvious place, Mary, and the labelling is fantastic. This is such a bonus. As an agency nurse, finding the equipment is the hardest part.'

'I'll bet.' Mary tilted her head. 'So how did you get into agency work? I bet a few hospitals would love to hire you full-time with your qualifications.'

Eliza met Mary's eyes. 'It's a new direction for me. I like being unattached. It gives me the choice to move when I want to.'

'Fair enough,' Mary said. 'We'll move on ourselves before Jack discovers me here on his next round.' She smiled and swayed out of the room to waddle further down the hallway.

'Where was I? Basically, you do five days a week, eight hours normal and four hours overtime, then you're on call at night except for weekends. Think you can handle that?'

'Fine by me.' Eliza shook her head at Mary. 'How on earth did you have time to fall pregnant?'

Mary twinkled back. 'My husband is the local fire captain, amongst other things, so we know there's twenty-four hours in a day. We both enjoy being busy. He's away at a conference at the moment.'

Mary shrugged. 'When Mick's home he's home and when he's not I spend a lot of time here. We both like it that way. He used to be in the navy.' She answered the question Eliza didn't ask. 'Mick will be home in a few days and stick around more when my baby is due.'

'And if baby comes early?' They both glanced down at Mary's stomach.

'He'll have to fly home quick smart!'

Eliza shook her head at Mary's calmness. 'Mary, I think you're Wonder Woman.'

Mary shrugged. 'I'll be Bored Woman for the next few weeks. I wondered if you'd like to drop around in a day or so. I'm sure you'll have questions and I'll be dying to know how you settle in.'

And that's how country towns worked. Eliza knew that from past experience. It wasn't what she'd planned when she'd hoped to keep a city-dweller's distance from the townsfolk. She'd seen the effect of gossip and everyone knowing her business, but she couldn't offend Mary. Bellbrook's matron was too genuine.

Trouble was the next thing would be an in-depth conversation with the publican's wife when she went back to the hotel tonight. Then there'd be the corner shop purchases tomorrow and the visit to the post office, by which time everyone in the valley would be aware of her arrival, the car she drove and enough physical features to be picked out at a hundred paces.

She'd better not do anything noteworthy or Jack Dancer, who seemed to be related to everyone, would be the first to hear about it.

CHAPTER TWO

BY LUNCHTIME Mary had departed to rest as ordered by her doctor.

Eliza glanced around at the eight elderly patients seated at the dining table to eat their lunch. She'd handed out the medications and done a ward tidy with Vivian.

If Eliza looked on the workload as just a normal ward with diverse patients, and not a whole hospital, there was nothing she hadn't done before.

By six-thirty that evening she'd found most things she could possibly need, had had in-depth conversations with all the inpatients, as well as read their medical records and helped with the evening meal.

She'd glanced through the rosters to see how they worked and spent ten minutes on the phone to Julie, her friend at the nursing agency, to say she was settling in.

Now all she had to do was a ward round with the distracting Dr Dancer and she'd be finished for the day.

Eliza glanced at the clock again and drummed her fingers on the nurses' station desk.

He was late.

She was getting more unsettled by the minute with a waiting-for-the-dentist kind of tension and Eliza wished he'd just arrive. Surely Dancer wasn't so spectacular he'd turned her into a bundle of nerves?

Apparently he was. When Jack breezed in he brought more devastation to her peace of mind than she needed. So much for saying her imagination had been over-active. His wavy black hair was tousled as if he'd been dragging distracted hands through it all day, and he'd even jammed a couple of curls behind his ears. That was when she noticed he had a tiny diamond in his right ear lobe. How on earth had she missed that this morning?

'Ready for the round?' He seemed very businesslike and Eliza allowed some of the tightness to ease from her shoulders. Businesslike sounded good. He'd want to get home, too. The brusquer the better, Eliza thought gratefully.

'Let's go.' She picked up a notebook in case she needed to take notes.

He glanced across at her briefly, and she saw he had dark chocolate eyes, not black, as she'd previously thought, a strange thing to notice when she was supposed to be immune.

'So how was your day?' Jack was brief and Eliza even briefer.

'Fine.' She picked up the pace to get the next few minutes over as quickly as possible. Noticing too many things about this man, Eliza, she thought grimly.

'Are we racing again?' Laughter in his voice and

Eliza felt her face stiffen. Please, don't let him be nice to me or flirt with me or in any way endear himself to me, she prayed. There was something about him that pierced her skin like a poison dart and was just as irritating. She was not playing man games any more.

'I just know you'll be emotionally scarred and unable to have a worthwhile relationship,' she muttered.

Jack stopped walking and Eliza carried on a few more steps before she realised she'd said what was on her mind out loud! She closed her eyes and then opened them again. Oh, boy!

He tilted his head. 'I'm sorry? What did you say?'

She glanced down and then lifted her chin resolutely. 'Sorry. Ignore that.'

He looked stunned.

She shrugged. 'Look, I may seem mad, but I've had the worst run of luck with men and I'm still spinning from the last one. I seem to have a penchant for poor sods who have been a victim of some unscrupulous woman. They find me, I heal their poor broken hearts, and then they happily marry someone else. I usually get invited to the wedding. For some bizarre reason, I don't want to play that game any more.'

She was sure his eyes were glazing over but it was imperative she make this clear. 'This may seem more than you need to know, but I am trying to explain my stupid comment.'

He moved his lips a little but didn't actually say a word. Eliza sighed. 'Forget I spoke and we'll do the ward round.'

Jack felt as if someone had just popped a paper bag

in his unsuspecting face. He'd known there was something odd about her. The chameleon fairy was mad and Mary was gone. What the heck were they going to do? He'd had a hell of a day already.

After the dash out for Mia's asthma attack, he'd returned to his office and realised today was the anniversary of the worst day of his life. He hadn't been able to believe it had slipped his mind for a few hours.

After he'd fought his way out of that depression, a desperate young couple, distant relatives on his mother's side, had miscarried their second IVF baby. Then one of his uncles had come in for results on a mole he'd excised last week, and the specimen had proved to be a particularly vicious melanoma.

Now this!

The new fairy matron was a man-hating elf with issues.

He heard her voice from a long way off. 'It's OK,' she said. 'Forget it.'

He blinked, the hallway came into focus again, and he shelved her replacement problems for a minute. Deep breath, Jack, he suggested to himself.

She was still talking as if nothing had happened. 'You should have a look at Keith's wound. I know he's supposed to go home tomorrow but I believe he's brewing an infection.'

Jack blinked. He'd just play along with her until after the round. 'Fine. I'll look at that. How's Keith's temperature?'

'Creeping up, and it spiked to thirty-nine this afternoon before it went down again.'

Jack glanced at the chart the madwoman handed him from the end of Keith's bed and he saw that she was right. Blast. They'd have to start intravenous antibiotics again because Keith had little reserve to fight infection after his brush with peritonitis.

She'd pulled the curtains and had Keith supine in the bed with his shirt up before Jack could ask, and when she removed the dressing, tell-tale red streaks were inching away from Keith's wound.

He glanced at Keith's face and realised his patient did look more unwell than this morning. 'Sorry, Keith. No home until we sort this out.'

Keith sighed with resignation. 'Matron warned me it could be that way.'

Eliza spoke from beside his shoulder. 'Do you want me to put an intravenous cannula in?' Jack saw that she had the IV trolley waiting and she'd probably decided which antibiotics Keith should be on, too. Just who was the doctor here? He couldn't help the bite in his voice. 'Have you drawn it up as well?'

He should have known she'd be immune.

'Almost,' she said. Was there a hint of laughter in her voice?

Jack scowled. She went on, 'What would you like him started on?'

She had two choices there for him and they would have been first and second if he'd chosen them himself. What was wrong with him? He wanted her efficient. 'We'll go with the Ceftriaxone, but see if you can get a wound swab before the first dose.'

She didn't look at him and he couldn't tell if she was smiling. 'Did that earlier when I took today's dressing off,' she said, as she prepared the antibiotic before laying it down and assembling the cannulation equipment.

'Shall I pop the cannula in?' Eliza glanced at him.

Jack almost said, I'll do that thank you, but he changed his mind. 'Let's see how good you are,' he said out loud. Nothing like a bit of pressure to put someone off. He knew from bitter experience that Keith's veins were nowhere near the young bulging ones that Mia had. Matron May was too darned cocky.

'Just a sting for a second, Keith,' Eliza soothed as she slid the needle into an almost invisible vein with disgusting ease. She seemed to have three hands as she juggled cannulas, bungs and even took blood. 'Did you want blood cultures?' She taped the line securely and stood back. They both glanced at the antibiotic waiting to be injected.

'Can I do this?' He sounded petty and she made a strange sound that he hoped wasn't her laughing at him. He normally wasn't like this and he needed to get a grip. He looked at her to apologise but realised she *was* amused. Amused!

Today had been anything but amusing. He didn't say a word, just gave the antibiotic, wrote up the orders and patted Keith's hand carefully. 'Sorry, mate. You'll probably be in for another couple of days yet.'

Keith nodded. When they pulled the curtain back Jack was surprised to see that Joe was asleep. He frowned and raised his eyebrows at Eliza and she drew him from the room.

'I found out today he hasn't been taking any pain relief. He didn't want Keith to think he was a baby,' she said quietly, and shrugged. 'I spoke to Joe when Keith was out of the room and we've come to an agreement. Since the first lot of medication he's been asleep and Keith tells me Joe's hardly slept.'

Jack frowned and then nodded. 'OK. Let's get on, then.'

They completed the round and had a quick look at Janice and her baby in less than ten minutes. There was very little conversation between them.

As he was leaving, Jack looked back and paused. He had been abrupt. 'Matron?'

Eliza glanced up from the notes she was making. 'Yes, Doctor?'

'Well done with the cannula, and Joe as well. If I seem brusque, I've had a wild day.'

'No problem.' The woman seemed to be staring at some point over his left shoulder and disinclined to talk, so Jack forced himself to leave. It was surprisingly hard to take that first step away. He was more confused about her than ever and he didn't like it. Until today his world had been pleasantly uncomplicated.

He'd put the horror of three years ago behind him and he'd immersed himself in work. He'd assumed he'd get married again someday but hadn't dated a woman since Lydia had died.

And he wasn't thinking of dating this one—but she certainly unsettled him.

* * *

Eliza headed back to the hotel. Except for a young blonde woman reading in the corner, the bar was quiet as she walked past the door.

'So you're the new matron,' the blonde drawled, and Eliza's step slowed to a stop.

'Hello.'

'Staying here will get a little noisy on a Friday night.'

'I'll be fine.' Eliza smiled and crossed the room to hold out her hand. 'I'm Eliza May.'

'Carla.' There was something elusively appealing about this too-thin girl-woman and then there was the ice that frosted the outside of her glass in the cloying heat.

Eliza licked dry lips and put her handbag down on the stool beside the girl. 'It's hot this evening.'

'Always is this time of the year.' Carla stood up, walked behind the bar and filled a glass with ice. Then she opened an under-bar fridge and removed a beaded bottle of lemon squash and unscrewed the lid. 'I should ask you first.' She grinned. 'But you'd like a squash, wouldn't you.'

Eliza grinned back at her. 'Dying for one! Thank you. Do you work here?'

'No. Rob's gone to the loo. I'm just minding the bar for a minute.'

Carla glanced out the door and back. 'I'm off for a swim in the river when I finish my drink. If you want, I'll show you a spot you can swim in when the days are like this.'

'Local knowledge.' Eliza smiled as she put two dollars down on the bar for her drink. She remembered local knowledge as a child, it had usually got her into trouble.

'Something like that.' There was a hint of fun which dared Eliza to take her up on the offer. After the unease she'd felt round Jack Dancer, it would be nice to loosen up and get cool.

Eliza downed her squash. 'I'll slip up and grab a towel.'

The swimming hole was through two fences at the back of the pub but worth the climb down a steep bank to get to. It was under a cliff face and two large weeping willows shaded the pool. There was an aging PRIVATE PROPERTY sign, adorned with a few grass necklaces from previous floods, prominently displayed near the edge.

Carla ignored it. The water looked too good to forgo.

Eliza yanked down the sides of her bathers—they seemed to like crawling too high on her leg and up her bottom. She stood hesitantly at the edge. She hated wearing swimming costumes because they made her feel so self-conscious. Carla was already in and the water looked wonderful.

The first step wasn't too bad and the temperature of the water grew colder the further out through the reeds Eliza walked.

'It's freezing,' Eliza gasped. The shock on her face when she finally forced her whole body under the water made Carla laugh when Eliza surfaced beside her.

'Yep.' Carla swam languidly across the pool and

Eliza watched her for a moment before she turned on her back and floated with her arms out. The icy water was gorgeous against her heated skin. This had been an excellent idea.

'Get out of there!'

Eliza recognised that voice and the enjoyment drained out of the moment as if he'd pulled the plug.

'You know better, Carla.' Jack Dancer was cross, there was no doubt about that, Eliza thought, and her heart pumped as if she were a ten-year-old again caught crossing a forbidden field.

'You're such a sourpuss, Dr Jack,' Carla said as she drifted languidly to the shallow water.

'It would serve you right if you got bitten by a bull-rout. Smithy was stung here yesterday and you wouldn't be so relaxed if you'd seen his face as I filled him up with morphine. But you shouldn't have put Eliza at risk—she'd from the city and probably doesn't know what a bullrout is.'

'I know what a bullrout is,' Eliza said quietly. The camouflaged fresh-water fish could look like a rock and wore three venom pouches on its spines. Its sting was excruciating. She glanced warily at the reeds as she followed Carla out of the water. The spot was lovely but not worth those kinds of stings. Eliza wrapped her arms around her blatant nipples. Well, the water had been cold, for crikey's sake. Now she had to get out of here, wet, bathers glued to her too-generous curves, and all under the gaze of that man. The day just kept getting better and better. Eliza compressed her lips.

Finally both women stood at the edge of the inno-cent-looking water wrapped in towels. They both glared across at the man on the opposite bank.

Carla tossed her hair and turned her back on Jack. 'You can go home happy, now, you grump. You've spoiled our swim so you can relax.'

Jack didn't say anything or seem perturbed by Carla's rudeness, and Eliza stood indecisively. She resisted her own impulse to emulate Carla but had the maturity to realise it was a response to being caught in the wrong. Even worse, she hated being caught in her bathers. It was too late to worry now. She half waved to a still waiting Jack and followed Carla up the bank.

When they got to the top, Eliza was almost as hot as when she'd started and not all of it from the sun. She should have gone with her instincts and avoided the local knowledge.

'Sorry about that.' Carla held up her hands in an I-didn't-mean-for-that-to-happen gesture. 'No one's been stung there for two years. I didn't know about Smithy. It's such a top spot if Dr Jack doesn't catch you.'

'So Jack polices the waterholes as well as does the doctoring?' Eliza could see the amusing part of being caught by Jack—just.

'He owns the land on both sides of the river,' Carla said as she headed back to the pub. She glanced over her shoulder to Eliza. 'But nobody owns the river.'

The next day every person Eliza met in the hospital mentioned her being caught by Jack down at the rout waterhole. She knew there was a reason she'd avoided returning to the country.

Apparently Carla's friend Rob from the pub thought it a hilarious story and had mentioned it to everyone who'd come into the hotel. They'd passed it on to anyone they'd seen in the next twelve hours and by the time Eliza came to work the story had been embellished to include her and Carla topless with a few men from the pub watching.

'Spare me.' Eliza closed her eyes and shook her head. Janice tried to stifle her giggle so as not to wake her baby but she was having a hard time of it.

'The topless bit was from old Pat, and nobody really believes him, but it seems you've made a name for yourself as a good sport already.'

'Well, I hope nobody believes "Old Pat". If I meet that delightful old gentleman for a tetanus shot, he's in for a larger-than-normal-gauge needle.'

Janice dissolved into giggles again and Eliza had to smile at her, but the smile disappeared when Jack Dancer walked into the room.

The memory of him watching her as she'd left the water yesterday warmed her cheeks and she fought the sudden urge to fold her arms again. She was too darned aware of this guy and survival meant he wasn't to know.

'All well in here, ladies?' Jack's face was expressionless but Eliza suspected a twinkle behind those pseudo black eyes of his. The swine.

'Eliza was just saying how hot it was yesterday,' Janice said cheekily, but Jack wasn't playing.

'Yes, it was. How's Newman this morning, Janice?'

Eliza tried to let her relieved breath out unobtrusively as Jack concentrated on his patient.

Janice went on. 'Fine. We're both fine. My mum arrives from Melbourne today so he's going to meet his nana when she comes in to visit.'

'Say hello to your mum for me if I don't see her.' He stepped back from the cot. 'I've a lot on this morning so I'll leave you in Matron's capable hands.'

Eliza followed him out of the room. She hoped he didn't think she'd been discussing yesterday. 'I didn't tell her. Apparently it's all over town that you chased us out of the river.'

Jack glanced up from the notes he carried. 'Bellbrook is a small town. People find out and embellish all the time.' He looked at her fully and she saw the wicked twinkle in his eyes. 'I particularly enjoyed the naked version, with me throwing you a towel.'

Eliza rested her hand over her mouth as she felt the heat rise again in her face. Then she surprised herself with a tiny gurgle of laughter as the funny side of the situation tickled her again.

Just when he thought he had her on the back foot she surprised him again. Jack had spent most of the night trying to rid himself of delightful memories of Eliza, tiny but perfectly packaged, as she'd stepped from the water.

Intriguingly, her breasts had been stunningly full and globular beneath the wet one-piece costume as she'd bent to pick up the towel. Even now that day-old snapshot in his mind made his mouth dry.

Her breasts hadn't jumped out at him yesterday morning, he mused, and then his own sense of humour caught up with him. Impossible fantasy. He pulled himself back under control and tried to quieten the sudden increase in his heart rate. Now she was giving him palpitations. What on earth was the matter with him?

'Most people from the city would have a problem with being the object of small-town gossip,' Jack said without looking at her.

'I'm not "most people",' she replied calmly, and began to talk about Keith, but he didn't believe her. Her cheeks were just a little too rosy.

By the end of the round Jack was again impressed with Eliza's ability to manage situations. She'd steered him back onto the job, calmed Keith despite the older man being bitterly disappointed he'd be laid up for probably another week, managed the most painless removal of Joe's dressing they'd had yet, and was obviously a favourite with the seniors on the wing.

'You're doing a great job, Matron. It feels like you've been here for much longer than a day and a half.'

'It feels like that to me, too,' Eliza said dryly.

Jack wondered at her parting comment as he walked around the side of the hospital to his surgery. The woman intrigued him far too much and he didn't think she was immune to him either.

CHAPTER THREE

THE next day Jack had meetings in Armidale after the morning round and wouldn't be back until late. The day was uneventful for Eliza and she felt unsettled after the shift had finished. So much so that she decided to go for a drive.

Eliza glanced down at the directions Mary had pressed on her and judged she was nearly there. The powerful vehicle purred along the dirt road and hugged the uneven surface with ease.

The Mustang was almost forty years old and a classic. With the top down she could blow all her worries into tomorrow. She loved this car. It had been her father's pride and joy and she'd taken it to Sydney with her when she'd moved there.

She refused to think about Jack Dancer because she'd spent the last hour beating herself up over wondering if he'd make it for the last round after all. He had.

She wasn't sure if visiting Mary was the most sensible thing to do if she wanted to stay immune to involvement in this town. Though Mary seemed to be one of the few people who wasn't related to Dr Jack. And Eliza had promised an update of her first few days.

The Mustang pulled up outside the McGuiness property and Mary was at the door before Eliza could walk halfway to the front steps.

Mary's smile was almost as big as her pregnant tummy. 'How are you? Is everything going smoothly? How are you coping with Jack?'

Eliza stood there, felt her face freeze and wished she hadn't come. And the worst thing was, Mary picked it up immediately. Her grin faltered. 'I'm sorry, Eliza. Come in and I promise I won't ask about anything else. I was just so excited about getting a visitor.'

Eliza had to smile. 'So you've had thirty-six hours of maternity leave and already you're feeling socially isolated?'

'Pathetic isn't it?' Mary led them into a sunny room that faced west. There was a long purple mountain range in the distance and Mary's house perched on a rise overlooking a huge dam. Most of the sprawling garden comprised hardy native plants and birds darted in and out of the low foliage.

'It's beautiful here.'

'Yes, it is. But now that I'm having a baby I wish we were closer to town.' Mary showed her to a rose-patterned lounge suite and they both sat down.

Eliza sank into the cushions and sighed as she felt the tension from Jack's latest hospital round ease away into the soft upholstery.

She looked across at Mary perched on the adjacent

chair, a little forlorn-looking. 'Can't your husband come home earlier?'

'He could but then he'd have to travel sooner after our baby is born and we want as much time as a family in the early months as we can.'

'That makes sense. I think. So what are you going to do with your bundle of joy when you go back to work?'

Mary smiled. 'That's what's so special about Bellbrook. I'll take my baby with me. The hospital isn't really much more than a large family home and there're always plenty of hands ready to help if I need.' They both laughed and Eliza began to enjoy herself.

'Come for a walk in the garden,' Mary said, 'before the sun goes down. It's a lovely time of the evening.'

Eliza followed Mary out onto the patio and the scent of bush roses drifted up from the path. She'd often enjoyed long walks with her father around the farm.

Three black cockatoos took off from a gum tree and their raucous cries almost drowned Mary out as they flew away.

Eliza said 'Three days' rain' at the same time as Mary, and then laughed. 'So you're superstitious, too?'

'Aren't we all?' Mary sidestepped a ladder against the wall and they both had the giggles again.

'I always thought country people seem more prone to superstitions than city folk,' Eliza mused.

Mary looked up with interest. 'So are you really a country girl at heart?'

'My dad loved the country. I didn't mind it.'

'And your mother?'

Eliza shrugged. 'She left because of it. And the gossip, my dad said.'

Mary nodded. 'This place thrives on gossip.'

'Then I supposed you heard about Carla and I being hunted out of the river by Jack?'

Mary's eyes twinkled. 'I was hoping you'd mention that!'

Eliza held up both hands and shook her head. 'I'm innocent, I swear.' And then she started to laugh at the memory of herself cowering in the river. 'People even said I was naked and Jack threw me a towel.'

'You mean that didn't happen?' Mary looked crestfallen but couldn't hold the expression long enough for Eliza to believe she was serious. They both laughed again.

'Gossip comes because a lot of people are related in small towns—even if only by marriage.'

Eliza remembered the speed of the informants. 'So how many people are related to Jack Dancer?'

The question seemed to come from nowhere but it was too late for Eliza to call it back. She hoped Mary wouldn't assume she was becoming interested in Jack because she had the feeling matchmaking was a latent facet of Mary's personality.

Mary shrugged. 'Most of us are related in some way.'

Eliza nodded and rolled her eyes. 'So I've noticed. Does that mean you're a part of Jack's enormous family circle?'

Mary sighed. 'I'm not really. Originally, I was from Sydney.' There was sadness in Mary's voice and Eliza refrained from asking the obvious question.

'Jack's great-grandparents started it all when they had ten kids and most of them settled here. Jack has more cousins than a dog has fleas.'

Eliza had a sudden vision of a giant Jack with cousins crawling all over him, and she smiled. 'So why isn't Jack married with ten kids?'

'That's the crux of his problem. He was. Jack married my sister. She died three years ago.' Mary trailed off for a moment then shook her head to jolt herself out of the melancholy.

'Lydia didn't like the life in Bellbrook and went back to Sydney. She and their unborn baby boy were killed in a car crash a month later.'

Eliza felt the breath catch in her throat. Poor Jack. 'That's sad for everyone. It must have been hard for both you and Jack.'

Mary gazed in the direction of the distant hills. 'Jack looked after me. My husband, Mick, hadn't really liked Lydia, and when she left Jack, Mick washed his hands of her. Jack always has had that caring quality that forgives and shoulders responsibility, and I guess that was some of what my sister saw when she married him.'

Mary went on slowly. 'Lydia was different from me. Beautiful, spoiled by my parents, a talented arts major. And she hated Bellbrook. Then she hated being pregnant. In the end, she hated Jack.'

Mary looked down at her bulging belly and smiled.

'I love pregnancy and I love Bellbrook and…' Mary smiled softly, '…like a brother, I love Jack.'

Mary's face softened even further with a whimsical

smile. 'Thanks to Jack, I met my husband, Mick. He was best man at Jack and Lydia's wedding. We fell in love and married in about three days. I've felt at home here ever since. Life is funny with what it deals out.'

So there were good love stories out there, Eliza sighed. Mary looked so content with her life and her love. Lucky Mary. Eliza herself *definitely* wasn't interested in taking any more chances with love.

But she was curious about the dashing Dr Dancer's wife. How could any woman hate Jack? 'What did your sister do here?'

'Nothing. We tried to get her involved in community activities, tennis, I suggested she run an art class for the town but she wasn't interested. She was bored silly and became very bitter at wasting her life, as she called it. Before Lydia died, I'd even decided it hadn't been a bad thing she'd left, because she had made Jack so unhappy. I think Jack was leaning that way too, until the crash.'

Mary shook her head sadly. 'I went to pieces. Jack and I both felt so guilty because maybe we should have supported Lydia more. Jack was devastated about the loss of his son as well. He blamed himself and Lydia's pregnancy for making her temperamental, as if if he'd paid more attention to her she wouldn't have left and his son would be alive today.' Mary sighed.

'Jack studied up on maternal trauma and resuscitation of pregnant women for months afterwards, wondering if the hospital she had been taken to should have done anything different when Lydia was brought in barely alive.' She looked at Eliza.

'I think it's still all locked away inside him behind his carefree smile. I guess that's why he's not in a hurry to marry again.'

Mary patted her stomach. 'He said he'd leave all the hassle of kids to me and be a doting uncle. I think it's a shame—and watch out. Everyone in town agrees.'

Eliza felt a flicker of panic at Mary's hint. 'Don't look at me. I'm off men.'

Mary looked across at Eliza. 'That doesn't matter. You'd better be prepared for some matchmaking uncles and aunts because they'd all like nothing better than to see Jack settled with a family here.'

As they turned towards the back door the sound of a car pulling up outside coincided with the ringing of the telephone. Mary looked torn and Eliza shrugged. 'I'll get the door, you take the phone.'

Eliza wished she'd taken the phone because she was still affected by the conversation with Mary and the visitor was Jack.

'What are you doing here?' They both spoke and Eliza shook her head. Her whole life was a cliché.

'Snap!' She shrugged and stood back so he could enter. 'Mary's on the phone. She shouldn't be long.'

Jack's mouth twitched wryly. 'Unless it's her husband, in which case the record is three hours and ten minutes.'

Eliza whistled. She did not need three hours and ten minutes of Jack. Just looking at him jangled her nerves, and with all the new insight from Mary she didn't know how to cope with him. 'Tell Mary I'll come back another day. I'm tired anyway.'

He looked out the window to Eliza's car and grimaced. 'Is that your Mustang?'

Eliza's gaze shifted to the now dusty red duco of her car. 'That's my baby.'

'How much fossil fuel does it use?'

She glanced in the direction Mary had disappeared but relief wasn't in sight. There were undercurrents. 'That depends how I drive it, Doctor.'

When she looked back at him his face was hard. 'And how do you drive it?'

She shook her head. 'What possible interest could that be to you?'

She thought he wasn't going to answer that one but he did and she almost wished he hadn't. 'I don't like waste of life and a car like that just isn't as safe as the modern vehicles of today.'

'I'll be at work tomorrow. Don't worry.' She put her hand in her pocket and pulled out her car keys. 'Please, tell Mary I'll catch up with her later. Goodnight.'

Eliza didn't gun the engine but she would have liked to. Jack Dancer, emotionally scarred human being— she'd known it. Someone up there was plotting against her, although she had to admit Jack had had a tough couple of years.

Jack watched the dust ball disappear down the road just as he'd watched another car when his wife had left him to settle back into the city. He turned at the sound of Mary's footsteps and she crossed to his side and kissed his cheek.

'I think she'll be good for the town,' Jack said.

'She could be good for you,' Mary said slyly.

His emotions were still too mixed when it came to Eliza May. 'I didn't come here to talk about Eliza.'

'Why not? We talked about you.'

Jack lifted his brows but refused to bite. Mary lowered herself into a chair. 'So why did you come?'

'To see you.'

'And why has Eliza gone?'

'She said she'll come back another time.' He turned to face Mary. 'Workwise, she's good. If she stays, we'll manage fine until you feel like coming back.'

'You *are* being nice to her, aren't you, Jack?'

Jack shrugged. 'Not too nice. I think she has a lot of emotional baggage.'

'And you don't?'

His face hardened again and he changed the subject. 'I can't stay. Just wanted to see how you like being on maternity leave.'

'Putting my feet up is bliss but I think I'm going to go stark raving mad without something to occupy my brain. Stay and have tea with me. I was planning on persuading Eliza to stay but you chased her away.'

'I didn't chase her away,' he said, but he wondered if that was wholly true. He had to admit that so far the new matron had not brought out the best in him, and maybe that was because she scared him a little. Not physically—tiny bundle that she was—but at some deep instinctual level that he didn't want to think about. Maybe he owed Mary his company.

'Fine. Tea would be great. I've had a less-than-perfect day and not having to cook the evening meal will brighten the end of it.'

'I've told you before. You should get a housekeeper and she could prepare your meal before she leaves for the day.'

'I know, but I like my privacy, and you know what this town is like.' He followed Mary into the kitchen and tried to make his next comment seem inconsequential. 'I rang Julie again today and apparently she and Eliza are friends. She said she's very reliable.'

Mary tilted her head at him and he knew what she was thinking before she said it. 'Now, why would you do that? I thought you said you were satisfied with her work.' Trust Mary to question his motives.

'I decided to listen to my instincts.'

'Well, my instincts say that there is a wonderful woman inside Eliza May, and already I count her as a friend.' She looked at him as if daring him to comment, but he wasn't that silly. When he kept his peace, she nodded. 'Let's eat. I was thinking we might dine outside because it's such a lovely evening.'

'Good morning, Matron.'

Jack was all *bonhomie* this morning, Eliza thought sourly. Her back and legs ached from a third night on the lumpiest mattress in the southern hemisphere but that wasn't the real reason she hadn't slept. Her eyes felt scratchy from lack of sleep.

'Morning.' She turned from his scrutiny but he was observant.

'You don't look like you slept well.'

'I'll make the hotel a present of a new mattress.'

'Like that, was it?' He seemed determined to be nice and Eliza could feel herself softening more towards him—no doubt because she'd tossed and turned thinking over Mary's revelations last night.

'Hmm,' she said, and changed the subject, opting for safety. 'Keith looks a little better this morning so I gather the antibiotics are kicking in.'

They walked down the hallway together and now she was aware of his height beside her and when he smiled and even the sound of his feet quietly pacing beside her. She couldn't switch off her awareness of him. This was not good. She began to edge away from him.

He seemed oblivious. 'I'm pleased. And did Joe sleep better than you did?'

What was with the personal comments this morning? She remembered his tone last night when he'd been anything but friendly—of course, she'd left him with Mary so he'd probably had instructions to lift his game. Please, don't encourage him, she prayed to the absent Mary.

Eliza needed to create some space, quickly, until she could build her defences again. 'Did Mary tell you to be nice to me this morning?'

He actually blushed. Eliza felt mean, but he did withdraw. Ironically, a part of her regretted his distance now but the sensible Eliza sighed with relief.

They crossed to the little maternity room. Janice had Newman floating in the baby bath with the back of his neck draped across his mother's wrist. Mother and baby both looked relaxed.

'You're an old hand at this, Janice,' Jack said. He stared down at Newman, who floated with his eyes open, staring up at his mother. He was a cute little fellow, Jack thought, and this time the pain of his own loss didn't follow as strongly as it usually did.

'He loves his bath.' Janice smiled as she glanced up.

'How're your tummy stitches? Not too painful?' Janice seemed to be standing up straight enough, Jack thought.

'No. I'm fine. Eliza gave me some tablets earlier so I could enjoy giving Newman his bath, and we're both going to have a sleep after this.'

'How's he feeding?' On cue, Newman burped loudly and they all laughed.

'Piggy,' his mother said, and she grinned up at Jack. 'He feeds like there's no tomorrow. There'd better be a tomorrow because we'd like to go home then. Afternoon if we can?'

Jack glanced at Eliza and she nodded. He had no trouble reading Eliza's wordless message that Janice was ready to leave. 'You must take it easy.'

'Janice's mother is staying for a week.' Eliza said. 'I've suggested she shouldn't go home until after her mother's been there for at least a day.'

Janice chuckled softly. 'Peter is a terrific farmer but not much of a housewife. Eliza reckons I'd be better to wait till Mum's had a chance to sort the mess.'

'Sounds like a plan to me. I'll do the newborn check

tomorrow morning and see your sutures. If all's well you'll be right to leave after lunch.'

'Thank you.' She lifted her son out of the water carefully and wrapped him in the fluffy towel Eliza had spread out beside the bath. The baby whimpered at the sudden change in temperature but quietened as Janice snuggled him, wrapped tight, up against her shoulder.

Jack caught a look of wistfulness on Eliza's face and stamped down a sudden desire to find out more about his new matron. He hadn't thought that fairy queens went clucky.

Before he could even think about investigating that concept, Eliza had moved on to the two-bed ward and she began to pull the curtains around Keith's bed.

The streaks on Keith's stomach had paled a little but the old man's cheeks were still flushed. 'How's the pain?' Jack was glad to focus on the old man and noted Keith's rapid respirations and elevated pulse rate.

'Not too bad.'

Jack hadn't expected Keith to say anything else but they'd keep a weather eye on him. 'I think we caught the new infection in time, Keith. Hopefully you'll feel better this afternoon. The wound looks a little less angry. I'll leave you in Matron's capable hands.'

'I'll be fine then, Doctor. She doesn't miss much.'

Jack rested his hand on Keith's shoulder. 'So I'm learning.'

'Seems a shame such a good woman isn't married.' Keith winked at Jack who stepped back from the bed as if he'd seen a snake. 'Don't start, old-timer. I'll see you tomorrow.'

They crossed to the other bed and Jack smiled at his patient. 'You've lost the dark circles under your eyes, Joe. I'm glad the pain is more under control.'

'Felt a bit of a wimp.' Joe shrugged his shoulders gingerly with a rueful grin. 'Matron put the wind up me and I have to say the sleep hasn't gone astray.'

'You'll actually get better faster if you have reasonable pain relief,' Jack said. 'Pain is there to tell you something is wrong. Once we know why it's there you don't need to put up with the discomfort any more.'

'That's what Matron said. She's a good woman.' Joe glanced slyly between Jack and Eliza, and Jack had the feeling his able assistant was hard-pressed not to laugh. He admired her for her control. In fact, he admired her far too much for his own peace of mind but it was purely a physical attraction and he knew better than to listen to his libido, or his patients, in his own back yard.

'So, home tomorrow, Joe?' Jack smiled at the younger man's belongings all neatly lined up beside the bed. Joe's hands were out of bandages except for a four-inch strip just past both elbows where the petrol had splashed and burnt the deepest.

'Your fingers are healing well, even though they're pink—that's all new skin growth. You'll have to keep them clean and out of the sun. Remember I told you the new skin has no protection. Lots of sunscreen every couple of hours if you're outside—OK?'

Joe's eyes were shining with anticipation. 'Will do,

Doc. My sister will pick me up. She's lending me one of her sons to stay at my place to do the dirty work for the next few weeks.'

'That's great. Stay away from the bushfires—it looks like we're in for a bad couple of weeks. If fires come your way, you're to pack what you can and come straight back into town and join the sandwich brigade. No firefighting. OK?'

'If you say so, Doc.'

Jack lifted his hand in farewell and glanced at Eliza. He thought she'd paled a little and he narrowed his eyes.

'You OK?'

'Fine,' she said, 'I had a bad experience with a bushfire once, but that was a long time ago.'

'Can I do anything to help?' He'd thought there was something, and she'd looked quite distressed. He followed her out of the room.

She paused and waited for him to catch up, and he caught the drift of her soap, or shampoo, or whatever it was that seemed to linger in his mind after he'd left her.

The scent played havoc with his concentration. Plenty of people smelt like herbal soap, and he didn't take a scrap of notice. Why should she be any different?

Jack frowned his mind back into gear. 'So what happened?'

'I don't want to talk about it. What did you think of Keith's wound?'

He didn't say anything for a moment, just looked at her, and then he shrugged and followed her lead. 'The wound may look better but I'm not happy with Keith.

If you're concerned or the night girls get worried, give me a call. If he gets any worse, stop all food and fluids and watch for paralytic ileus. The infection could slow down his gut. We'd have to send him back to Armidale if his bowels shut down, and he doesn't like being that far from home.'

Eliza nodded. 'Keith's worried about Ben, his cattle dog. The neighbour's looking after him but Keith's still fretting.'

'He'll have to wait a day or two longer.'

There was silence as they both contemplated Keith's problem. Jack led the way to the aged wing and they managed a thorough round with time to spare before he was due to start his surgery day. He was consistently surprised how cheerfully Eliza was greeted after only a few days. It seemed the older residents were more than happy with their new matron.

'You seem to have your finger on the pulse here already.'

Eliza rolled her eyes. 'Is that a pun?'

'Definitely.'

She groaned and almost laughed. 'Don't. My father used to tell puns all the time up until...' She stopped and frowned. 'Never mind. Tell all the puns you want, it's your hospital. I'll phone you if we have any worries.'

Eliza watched him go and reminded herself she needed to be careful not to care too much for Jack. He unsettled her and made her feel like blurting things out, and that was something she'd never done—or had even had the opportunity to do. She'd always been the listener, the one who attracted needy people, but suddenly Jack felt like a father confessor. He was opening old wounds she'd had sealed off for years, and it was scary how easily he could do it.

She regretted she'd come here. Then she thought of Mary and how she'd have just kept working on despite her pregnancy with no one to relieve her, and Eliza couldn't wish that back.

She must have ended up here for a reason and she'd guess she'd find out why. She just hoped it wasn't so that Jack Dancer could be emotionally healed at her expense and she'd pay the price again.

'I said, my piles are getting worse, Doctor.'

Jack roused himself from remembering the way Eliza had looked that morning and concentrated on the elderly woman seated in front of him.

'I'm sorry to hear that, Mrs Rowe. Have you been taking those paracetamol and codeine tablets again?'

The elderly lady avoided his eyes. 'I might have had a couple in the last few days, now that you come to mention it, Doctor. Would they hurt my piles?'

'Not directly they won't, but the codeine in the tablets will make you constipated, and all that straining is sure to make your haemorrhoids worse. So something else must be troubling you. Where are you getting the pain?'

'Only in my piles.'

Jack blinked. 'Why are you taking the pain tablets, then?'

'To be honest, Doctor, it's my Jem. His snoring is that

loud, I can't sleep. If I pop two of them tablets, I sleep like a baby.'

Jack shook his head. 'I'll give you a prescription for a mild sleeping tablet and ask Jem to come and see me. I'll have a look down his throat and we might see about booking him into a sleep lab for his snoring. He could be having some breath-holding while he's asleep.'

Mrs Rowe sat up and her eyes brightened. 'You wait till I tell Norma. To think my Jem could be sick when he's never had a sick day in his life. Well, I never.' She sat back with a thoughtful expression on her face. 'Would that make him tired? He's always saying he's tired these days.'

'It could.' Jack stood up and handed Mrs Rowe the prescription he'd just printed out on his computer. 'Take one or two of these tablets at night until we sort Jem out.'

Jack came around from behind the polished desk and opened the door for his patient. He suppressed a yawn. Jem wasn't the only one who wasn't sleeping well.

Since Eliza May had come to Bellbrook he was doing some tossing and turning of his own. It seemed a long time until six o'clock tonight and he could go home. Maybe he needed some fairy dust to get to sleep. The thought brought a fleeting smile to his lips until he realised he was grinning like an idiot.

CHAPTER FOUR

IN THE early hours of the morning, Keith's temperature soared. The night sister, Rhonda, concerned and unsure of what to do, rang Eliza to come until the doctor arrived. Jack had been called out to a croupy child.

When Eliza arrived Keith was flushed and muttering as he pulled his sheet over his shoulders and shifted in the bed.

Eliza turned his pillow and tucked the cotton in around the old man's thin shoulders. 'How are you, Keith?' He looked dreadful to her.

Keith squinted one eye open and tried a smile. 'Been better. Thought I saw the Grim Reaper standing beside the bed before.' He was only half joking. His eyes narrowed as he tried to concentrate. 'You're early. Is it morning already?'

'Not quite. Rest and I'm here if you want anything. I'm going to sit beside you until Dr Jack gets back from his callout and can come and see you.'

Keith turned his face fully towards Eliza and weak tears formed at the edges. He grabbed her fingers.

'Don't let him send me away to one of them city hospitals. I don't want to die away from home.'

Eliza squeezed his shoulder with her other hand. 'You're not going to die, Keith, we won't let you. As for being transferred, you know Dr Jack won't transfer you out unless he absolutely has to.'

'If anything happens to me, will you look after my dog, Matron?' The old man's grip tightened on her fingers and she soothed him.

'Nothing is going to happen to you, Keith, but I'll look out for Ben. Now, you rest quietly until these antibiotics can work.'

She eased her fingers out of his grip and wiped the sweat from his weathered face, then increased the intravenous infusion rate to compensate for the fluid loss. Eliza calmed him with her voice. 'Close your eyes and just drift off when you can. I'll natter on in the background so you know I'm here.'

She began to talk softly about her years growing up on her father's farm and the animals she'd had. When he fell into an uneasy sleep her voice fell silent.

As she watched, the old man twitched and turned, and the sweat trickled down his neck onto the pillow. She sponged him and changed his linen as necessary.

Tension mounted in the next hour for Eliza as the old man worsened. The sight of his fevered face brought back the last painful memories of her father.

Eliza had been eighteen and left in charge of the house while her father had fought a fire caused by a lightning strike at the bottom of the paddock. It had been weather similar to what they'd had the last few days and Eliza could still remember the smell of burnt eucalyptus in the air and the crackle of the fire in the undergrowth.

She'd blocked the house gutters and filled them with water and had been hosing the flower-beds around the house when the wind had suddenly picked up. She'd lost sight of her father when the treetop-high wall of fire had jumped the waterhole and engulfed her father, before racing up the hill through the whiskey grass towards her.

She remembered the spurt of water from the hose in her hand as it slowed to a dribble when the pump house was engulfed and killed her water supply.

Fear for her father froze her steps as she watched in horror as the fire came closer, easily devouring everything in its path. Before she had a chance to turn and run for the house she saw the vegetable garden and then the outside toilet catch light, and that was when she was sure she was going to die.

She thought the noise of her heart thumping was deafening even above the sound of the flames, until she realised the noise and vibration was coming closer and louder from above her head.

Suddenly a deluge of cascading water hit the ground in front of her and an inexplicable waterfall slid down the hill, extinguishing the fire front. The water helicopter soared away for a fresh load and Eliza could only stand there amidst the smoke and charred grass and sob towards the spot where she'd last seen her dad. Then she broke into a run.

She found him in the waterhole. At first she thought

he'd escaped injury, and externally he had. But the flames and heat had seared his lungs and Eliza clung to his hand while they watched the helicopter douse the last of the runaway flames before coming to land beside them on the paddock.

He was airlifted out of their country town to the city and he never came back. For the two days it took him to die she always assumed he'd return, and never quite forgave herself for surviving when he hadn't.

Usually she avoided thinking about that time because it brought back memories of her own helplessness the last time she'd seen him. Her lack of first-aid knowledge had been one of the main reasons she'd gone into nursing.

Isaac's funeral had also been the last time she'd seen her mother. Their meeting had wounded Eliza for years. Even now she didn't want to think about the bitter words that had flown between them—mostly from Eliza.

That was enough reminiscing for the night, she admonished herself and straightened in the chair. When she looked up, Jack was standing beside her.

He looked so solid and dependable and kind. She was glad to see him. 'You're back?'

He nodded at her obvious question and Eliza sighed with relief.

'How's Keith?' Jack's voice was soft in the dim light and she realised again what a caring man he was.

Eliza rotated her neck to release the kinks and consciously dropped her shoulders to ease the tension. Jack was here now, and it felt good to share the load. 'I'm hoping he's on the mend. He's a little more restful than he was half an hour ago.'

Jack stared and looked at the man shifting deliriously beneath the covers. 'That must have been exciting.'

'Just the sort I don't need,' she said dryly, and even she could hear the underlying tension she'd been making light of. Keith was a worry and she had a sudden urge to seek comfort in some physical way from Jack. Maybe lean her head down onto his chest or let him drape his arm around her shoulder for support.

Thankfully—of course she was thankful—Jack did none of those things and she steered her thoughts away with a report on Keith's condition. Jack stood beside her with his hands jammed into his pockets.

'Keith's temperature has come down a little and the last time I looked at his wound I thought he might benefit from probing to release the pressure.'

Jack nodded. 'Let's have a look, then.'

The next hour saw a slim improvement in Keith's condition and the antibiotics were added to again.

When they'd finished making Keith as comfortable as possible, Rhonda, who'd been hovering nearby, suggested they leave Keith with her while they revived themselves with coffee.

Eliza watched Jack stifle a yawn. She shook her head. 'I'll stay another half an hour but I think he's over the worst now. You should go home. I could ring you if he worsens.'

Jack glanced at his watch. 'You have to work in a few hours, too. We'll both stay and keep each other awake for just a little longer. It's been a busy night,' Jack said quietly, as he and Eliza settled in the tearoom.

'You must be exhausted if you've been out since midnight.'

Jack shrugged and glanced at his watch. 'No more than usual. I find I only need a couple of hours sleep.' He perched on the edge of the table and swung one muscular leg back and forth. Eliza busied herself with the kettle and tried to ignore the way her eyes kept straying towards him.

Jack smiled a blinding I-want-something smile and Eliza stiffened her resolve. She must not become entangled with this man. She could feel the hairs rise on her arms as goose-flesh covered her when her body ignored her sensible thoughts.

He spoke quietly but his voice came out deep and rumbling with interest. 'Tell me about yourself. How are you enjoying Bellbrook so far, Matron May?'

She felt the barriers go up this time. 'I'd prefer it if you didn't call me Matron. It's hard enough getting used to the patients calling me that. I know it's how they addressed Mary so I can't change it. But I get the feeling you're mocking me when you use that form of address.'

He raised his eyebrows. 'I'm far from mocking you.' He paused, and then did as she asked. 'Eliza.' A shiver ran down her neck and suddenly she wished he'd call her Matron again.

'Now you call me Jack.' The odd inflection in his voice made her look up at him.

She didn't answer and he smiled mockingly. 'Coward.' Then he said, 'Eliza is a lovely name. Is it a family name?'

Eliza felt like she was slipping down a hill backwards with this conversation. She couldn't find purchase in her descent into confusion. 'It's my middle name.' Eliza shook her head. 'I was named after my mother, Gwendolyn, but I dislike the name and changed to Eliza when I was eighteen.'

'Does that mean you don't get on with your mother?'

Eliza raised her eyebrows. 'I wouldn't know. I've only seen her once since I was seven.'

There was silence for a few minutes while Jack drank his coffee and digested her comments.

Good, she'd shocked him, thought Eliza as she pulled Keith's patient notes towards her to write up her latest observations.

Maybe Jack would stop asking such personal questions because he was doing dreadful things to her stomach when he looked at her like that.

It seemed not. 'If I've been insensitive, Eliza, it's because I find myself unexpectedly at ease with you, considering our rocky start.'

Eliza's pen skidded across the page in an untidy zigzag as she looked at him in shock. 'Well, you fooled me.'

'Don't worry.' He grinned wryly. 'You're safe from propositions. I learnt my lesson a long time ago and I'm not looking to find a soulmate this century.'

She couldn't help smiling. 'Well, seeing as it's only early in the century, I doubt you'll live for the next one.'

Jack acknowledged her wall of reserve. He could see the hurt reflection of himself, and it wasn't his job to rescue Eliza from her ghosts. He carried his own burden of loss and he had never forgiven himself for not being there for Lydia. The shell around Eliza rang bells of recognition and he wondered what had happened to make her so wary of opening herself to others.

Maybe he could make the reluctant Eliza laugh.

He persisted. 'So let's be friends. I could do with a Nice Safe Female Friend.'

'Sounds delightful. NSFF. What makes you think I'm safe?' Eliza looked less than impressed with the prospect.

'You told Mary you're off men. I think you're even less likely to be on the lookout for a marriage proposal than I am.'

He had that right, judging by the vehement nod of her head. 'Correct. The next man who wants to marry me had better fly me to Gretna Green because I'll be kicking and screaming all the way to the altar.'

He felt the same. 'So now that we have that out of the way, tell me what you want to do after you leave Bellbrook. What's your goal in life?'

It was four in the morning and Eliza suppressed a yawn. She probably thought that humouring him would keep her awake.

He watched her frown as she gathered her thoughts. 'I've almost paid off my flat in Randwick. Originally I bought there to be close to my training hospital, and when I'm clear on that I want to buy a mountain hide-away with a few acres and a creek. Somewhere not too far, so I can escape from Sydney on weekends.'

She'd surprised him. 'So you're not a dyed-in-the-wool Sydneysider?'

He wanted more information but she was reluctant. He wondered why she wasn't used to talking about herself. 'We need to get back to Rhonda,' she said.

'Soon,' he said, and didn't move.

'You're persistent,' she said dryly, and he suppressed a smile. He could see her wavering.

Jack lowered his voice, and tried for persuasion. 'Tell me about the man who let you down.' Maybe the softness of his request was a factor, but she answered him.

'Which one?' She looked surprised at herself when she answered.

Jack blinked. 'There's been more than one?'

Eliza shrugged. 'After my father died in a bushfire…' She looked up and he connected that with what she'd spoken earlier, then she went on.

'I had to go to Sydney to live and trained to be a nurse. At uni I met and fell in love with an older man with a tortured past and we seemed to be good for each other.'

'We—mostly he, but I didn't mind—decided to quietly slip away and get married without telling anyone. Strangely, I thought, he became more distant as the wedding approached. Until the day before the wedding when he called, thanked me for waking him up to life again and said he had fallen for another woman. He became the first of a pattern.'

Jack screwed his face up and shook his head. 'How could you make a pattern out of that? The guy was obviously a jerk.'

Eliza half smiled at his championing. 'My last fiancé, Alex, had been let down by his previous lover and again I thought we suited each other. We became engaged, again he didn't want people at work to know, so it was just between the two of us. Our plans were so much a secret that before we set a date for the wedding he ran off with my unit manager.'

She stared down at her ringless finger. 'I'd actually thought I'd finally found a man who didn't need to work out his psychological problems on me, but Alex capped off a less than inspiring love life. If I tie that to my parents' marriage failure and growing up with my recluse of a father, I have to agree with my psychologist.'

Jack tucked his chin into his chest and stared at her from under his brows incredulously. 'You have a psychologist?'

'Wouldn't you?'

Jack did his wide-eyed goldfish impersonation as he struggled for air, and Eliza swallowed a bubble of satirical laughter. Well, he'd asked for it, Eliza thought grimly. It may as well be all out on the table so he doesn't get any ideas.

'My psychologist says I suffer from disconnection because of my mother's abandonment, which leaves me with diminished self-worth. That's why I fall victim to the needs of others and for men who are emotionally scarred, and can't return unconditional love.'

'Good grief!' A smile tugged at the corner of his

mouth and Eliza glimpsed the humour in the telling. It was surprisingly therapeutic to laugh at herself.

Maybe saying this out loud wasn't too bad after all. 'My new goal is to skim through life without love or the danger of wasting energy on another useless man.' She sat back and actually felt lighter than she had for weeks.

Jack scratched his ear. 'Let me get this straight. Your parents broke up and you stayed with your father, so where did you actually grow up?'

'On a farm near Macksville.'

'That's not all that far from here.'

Eliza smiled but didn't comment. 'Dad home schooled me until I was twelve. When I went to high school I found it hard to make friends. The only people who would talk to me were the ones who nobody else would listen to. I became a good listener.' She grimaced and stood up. 'Except when I'm around you, it seems.'

'I'm not bored.'

'Well, I am.' She couldn't believe she'd told him so much. Eliza picked up the chart from the table. 'Let's relieve Rhonda.'

Jack had been pleased with their new rapport, and found himself even more intrigued by the screwed-up life of Eliza May. She'd left him with a lot to ponder.

When they returned to the bedside, Keith seemed more settled and Rhonda was happier with his condition. She promised to check on him every fifteen minutes for the rest of the night.

Eliza heaved a sigh of relief. 'I'm glad we can manage Keith here, though his wound will keep him in for another two weeks at least. He was worried you'd transfer him out.'

Jack nodded. 'I think he'll improve now. Just dress the wound as often as it's needed and we'll keep him on the IV antibiotics for another week. The sensitivities should be back tomorrow so we'll know if it's the right antibiotics.'

Eliza glanced at the closed curtains across the room. 'It's lucky Joe is going home tomorrow. If we are careful, do you think Joe can still visit Keith without endangering his own wounds?'

'I think he'll be fine.'

She nodded and led the way back to the nurses' station. 'I'll see you in the morning, then.'

'Goodnight, Eliza.'

There was a note in Jack's voice that she hadn't heard before, and it kept her awake longer than she wished when she finally crawled into bed. She'd have to be very careful to maintain her distance.

By the time Eliza had been in Bellbrook for two weeks she'd begun to socialise more. She filled in for the night social tennis with Carla and a group of younger women, but both times she appeared on the court, the next day on the round, Jack had been able to recite the scores and what time she'd gone to bed after the game.

'Do you seek this knowledge or is it forced on you?' Eliza shook her head at the things people told Jack.

Jack grinned. 'You're big news around here.'

'Only because everyone wants to matchmake me

with you.' Eliza shook her head in mock-disgust. It was fun to spar with Jack, maybe too much so, and they had to remember the whole town watched them and she at least didn't want them to get the wrong idea.

'I'm a great catch.'

'I can think of lots of catches to hanging around with you. Not interested. Sorry.'

He lowered his voice and leant towards her. 'That's why I enjoy being with you.'

Eliza looked over her shoulder but nobody stood near. That was all she needed—a rumour like that. 'Don't even joke about it.'

October had started warm and grew warmer—as did the rapport between Jack and Eliza. By the fourth of the month the weather was scorching. On the wards the heat was the favourite topic. The elderly were starting to worry about the approaching summer temperatures.

When the first pall of bushfire smoke rose in the hills, most of the patients made their way to the hospital veranda to shake their collective heads and predict disaster.

'The worst I've seen was back in fifty-six,' Keith sighed as he remembered. 'Four lives were lost, two of Jack's uncles and their sons. A whole branch of the family wiped out when they were caught by a wind shift up the wrong end of the gully.'

Joe was in, visiting, and he nodded. 'I wasn't born then but I remember my father talking about it.'

'We've a good man in charge now.' Joe turned to Eliza. Eliza blinked as she squashed the images of her father and her own brush with death. She hated bushfire season and had sworn she'd never put herself at risk there again. The city, or at least where she lived, didn't have bushfires. Another reason she shouldn't have come to Bellbrook.

'Matron Mary's husband is the fire chief,' Joe went on. 'Mick's had a lot of experience. He flies all over the state as an advisor. He was some big fire chief in the navy.'

By lunchtime the call had gone out for all available men to present to the brigade hall because the wind was pushing the flames down the hills towards the town.

Mary arrived at the hospital, ostensibly because she didn't want to be out at her house alone but really to help Eliza as the first of the minor casualties began to trickle in.

The radio was on in the background in every room and Eliza couldn't escape the updates. 'Thousands of acres lost, cattle dead, shedding and fences lost, but no homes yet.'

'No lives lost, thank goodness.' Keith repeated what was on all their minds.

The outpatient bell rang again as Eliza fixed the nebuliser to the face of their second asthma sufferer and Eliza smiled at Mary hovering beside her.

'You knew it would be like this, didn't you?'

Mary nodded. 'I thought it might. I'll go and see this next one, shall I?'

'Thank you.' Eliza couldn't leave the young girl she was with until she was sure the bronchodilator was going to work, and she suspected Mary was itching to have her hand in. Eliza just hoped Jack wouldn't blame her for Mary's reappearance.

Eliza knew Jack had been called to a house out of town for a middle-aged woman found unconscious by her distant neighbour, and he had to wait for the ambulance to arrive.

The day grew even hotter and a steady stream of elderly citizens arrived to help the residents make sandwiches in the main dining room for the firefighters. All of the volunteers sighed as they entered the air-conditioned coolness of the hospital.

When Jack arrived, Mary had finally been persuaded to lie down in the office on a folding bed. She'd only succumbed to Eliza's hourly imploring because of the doctor's imminent arrival.

When Jack walked in, order ruled alongside Eliza with all beds full with those she hadn't wanted to discharge home without seeing Jack.

He threw his car keys on the desk. 'Been busy while I was away?'

'Slightly. We've three asthmatic children exacerbated by the smoke, two minor burns, an infant who had a febrile convulsion and one suspected broken wrist from a pushbike altercation with a panicked kangaroo.'

'Good old Bellbrook,' he said with a grin. 'I'll bet Mary is livid she's missing this.'

Eliza met his eyes reluctantly. 'She hasn't missed much. She's been here hands on for most of the morning but I've persuaded her she needs a rest and she's lying down in the office.'

Eliza waited for the explosion but when she met his eyes Jack was staring down at her quizzically.

'Were you worried I was going to blame you for Mary being here?'

So he could read minds. 'I wondered.'

'Mary is her own boss—which incidentally is why she makes such a good matron. The downside is she's hard to keep at rest when you want her to. I have great confidence you will prevent her from doing anything silly. Am I right?'

'I should hope so.' Eliza felt as though she'd been given a reprieve, which was ridiculous.

Jack seemed to think everything was normal. 'Let's clear the beds, then, shall we?'

They set to and within the hour all the patients had been seen, Eliza's initial diagnoses and treatment confirmed and sent on their way. Most would come back tomorrow for review and/or dressing of the burns, and the fractured wrist was off to Armidale for X-rays.

'You've done well, Eliza.'

She glowed from those few words even though she warned herself she was a fool. 'Thank you, Jack. Mary helped.'

'And the responsibility was with you.' He sat down at the nurses' station. 'Now, the patient I've been with, Dulcie Gardner, is fifty-four and has been transported to Armidale with a mild left-sided stroke. Her condition and prognosis are good with only a little left-sided weakness and slurring of speech. After she is assessed by a neurologist, I'm hoping they'll allow her to convalesce here. One of my distant cousins is an occupational therapist on maternity leave and she'll come in and monitor her progress for the next few weeks. How do you feel about admitting someone long term and initially labour intensive at this time?'

Of course it wasn't a problem. 'Fine.'

He smiled and she wondered just how many times he'd got his own way with that strategy. 'I was hoping you'd say that. But there's more.'

'That serves me right for being eager to please. You sound like one of those television commercials. And what would the "more" be?'

His dark eyes twinkled at her. 'Are you feeling eager to please?'

'Don't push your luck, Dr Dancer.'

He seemed reluctant to start on his next request but finally got around to it. 'I wondered if you'd consider moving into Dulcie's house temporarily? I know it seems bizarre, but it's a lovely little cottage and it even has a creek. The main problem is Dulcie's menagerie.'

Eliza's eye's widened at the unexpected request but Jack went on.

'The animals in her back yard need feeding twice a day. She's also one of the few people in Bellbrook not related to anyone else, so I can't pull a cousin from somewhere to take over her pets. She has a daughter in Sydney somewhere but they don't talk. It was one of the things Dulcie spoke about before the ambulance came.'

Jack was talking about a house, almost a farm, with animals, to look after on her own? She wasn't sure if she was scared or excited at the thought which surprised her more. 'Why me?'

'Because you're here for the next six weeks or so and she'll probably be in hospital for some of that time at least. I know you hate your bed at the pub and you said you wanted a hide-away.'

He had it all figured out and the pub was driving Eliza batty with the noise on the weekends. It did sound peaceful. 'When did you want me to start?'

He sighed with relief. 'That's great. What about tomorrow afternoon, if you could? The neighbours will sort the animals in the morning. I fed them while I was there this afternoon and all should be fine overnight. There's a donkey, some rabbits and a few hens, as well as a goat or two. I think the cat and dog have enough dry food to last them until tomorrow as well.'

'Good grief! You weren't joking about a menagerie. What makes you think I could handle all those?'

His dark eyes crinkled. 'A farm girl like you? No problem.'

He'd certainly been listening while she'd babbled on that night. Eliza narrowed her eyes. 'And why can't you move in and mind the animals?'

'I have my own dependants and you're one of the few people in town without commitments.' He lowered his voice. 'Dulcie has a real feather bed in her guest room. You'd probably sleep like a baby in that.'

On Tuesday afternoon Eliza packed her few belongings at the Bellbrook Inn and transferred them to Dulcie's tiny cottage five kilometres out of town. It was a dream of a place with a white picket fence, a moon gate above the driveway and a multitude of flowering shrubs.

Jack followed her out in his car to show her where the feed was and introduce her to Dulcie's animals.

A large cross-cattle dog with mournful eyes and a pretty face licked Eliza's hand as she climbed out of her car.

'Did you send word ahead I was the hand that feeds, Dr Dancer?'

Jack laughed and stepped out of his four-wheel-drive. 'Roxy loves everyone. Not your most reliable watchdog but she did run two kilometres to the neighbours to tell them her mistress was sick.'

That was it for Eliza. 'You clever thing.' She crouched down and hugged the dog, who quite happily licked her face. Eliza pushed her away, laughing. 'I may think you are a hero, Roxy, but don't lick me! I'm here to see everyone. Lead on, sir.'

Jack gestured grandly with his arm. 'Poco, the donkey, is easy as long as you keep the water up to him. The goats graze fairly well, too, and I believe Dulcie divided the scraps between the rabbits and the hens. Goodness knows where the cat is, but I'm sure she will turn up for dinnertime.'

Eliza darted backwards and forwards, peering at animals and doling out food. He smiled at her enthusiasm and Eliza smiled back. She couldn't remember when she'd felt this euphoric despite all the responsibility. Maybe she had missed living in the country.

'When Dulcie comes back from Armidale tomorrow, you'll be able to reassure her so she'll rest more easily.'

Eliza looked at Jack standing there with a grin on his face, as if he didn't have the weight of the town on his shoulders. He was oblivious of the fact that not many doctors would be concerned enough about a patient and her pets to give up a little of the precious free time he had to settle someone in to look after them.

Lately she'd wondered if the town took Jack just a little for granted. 'I know you've put this on me and in the end I'm the one carting water, but it is nice you care, Jack. You're not a bad man.'

He raised his eyebrows mockingly. 'As far as men go, eh?'

Eliza inclined her head. 'As you say.'

'Well, as you said, you'll be the one carrying water. I think you're a champ to take them on.' He glanced around. 'Are you happy with the isolation? I'd forgotten how quiet it is out here. You're not worried about the fires, are you? It's a very clean farm, and the grass in the paddocks is short up to the house.'

Eliza glanced at the mountain behind her and the lushness of the forest that came down to the back boundary in front of the creek. The front paddock had been recently slashed and there was no debris around the house to be a fire hazard. She shrugged. 'It's wonderful. I'm fine. Dad's farm was much more remote.'

Jack nodded. The tension between them slowly built, which was a shame as it had been so easy earlier. Please, don't say anything, Eliza mentally implored Jack as she willed him to go.

'I'll see you tomorrow, then.' Jack paused and looked at her for a moment as if he were going to say something else.

Finally he waved. 'Goodnight, Eliza.'

'Goodnight Jack.' She sighed with relief as she watched him drive away, and she couldn't think of a negative thing about him. 'You'd better watch your heart, Eliza May, or you'll be crying in your soup in another month or two.'

She turned to the animals—ten pairs of eyes staring at her with expectation.

'We are going to have fun, people.'

CHAPTER FIVE

WEDNESDAY morning, Eliza was running late. She'd slept on a cloud with Dulcie's feather bed and had woken after six. Then it had taken twice as long to feed everyone because the donkey had stubbornly refused to move away from the gate so that she'd had to keep climbing over the fence with the three buckets of water.

'Typical domineering male,' Eliza muttered as she poured water in the final trough.

On the way back to the house she remembered the eggs, and by the time she'd watered the hens and collected the eggs it was after seven o'clock.

'I'm sorry I'm late,' she said to Rhonda and Vivian as she hurried in.

Rhonda just smiled. 'Dr Jack rang and said you might be.'

'Oh he did, did he?' Smart Alec.

'Only a little, he said, honest.' Rhonda played down Jack's disloyalty.

Eliza took pity on the night sister's horror that she'd

caused a problem for Jack. 'I'll start the animals earlier tomorrow.' She glanced around. 'So how is everybody?'

As Rhonda finished handover report and left, Jack arrived.

Eliza looked happy and relaxed and he shelved his disquiet that he'd bulldozed her into minding Dulcie's animals. Matching Dulcie's need and Eliza's experience on her father's farm and her soft heart—the idea had been too good not to act on. But he'd worried she might be upset by the remoteness.

'Good morning, Eliza. Good morning, Vivian.'

Eliza smiled at him and he could feel the vibration right down to his toes. Hell's bells. She'd always had this effect on him but lately it felt as though he was building up a lethal level of exposure to her.

She was smiling cheekily at him and the sun came out. 'Good morning, Doctor. You're early. Were you hoping to beat me here?'

He felt the width of his own smile and control was harder than he wished. This was way outside his comfort zone and he wondered when his awareness of her had crept up to this level. 'So how did it go with your new extended family?'

He'd tossed and turned most of the night because he'd worried she'd be a little nervous. And then there'd been the feather-bed fantasies.

Eliza was waxing lyrical about her new residence. 'I love it out there. Though I've learnt the meaning of 'as stubborn as a donkey', but apart from Poco, everything went well.'

Their eyes met and the warmth in hers, even though it originated from a donkey and not from him, was a lovely way for him to start the day. But start the day he must. And drag himself away he'd better.

'What time do you think Dulcie will be transferred back?' Eliza queried as she picked up the patient notes.

Eliza had asked him a question—he really needed to concentrate. 'Some time before lunch, I imagine.' He couldn't remember being this scatterbrained when he'd first met Lydia, who was the only yardstick he had. Though, of course, these feelings were nothing like those when he'd fallen for Lydia.

'Well, Vivian and I will finish the rest of our work before she arrives.'

The two of them walked down to see Keith, while Vivian sped off to ensure the seniors were up for break-fast, and Jack remembered the first time he'd strode down the corridor with Eliza. Had it only been a couple of weeks ago?

Jack shrugged off his strangely obsessive behaviour and turned to look at Keith. The old man appeared much more himself and Eliza pulled the curtains.

Jack cleared his throat as if to start his day afresh. 'So you're almost ready for home, too, Keith?'

He could feel Eliza's surprise beside him but she followed his lead.

'If I take the dressing down now, you can see how much the wound has improved,' she said.

Jack nodded and Keith slid down his pillows to let Eliza at the tape.

Keith couldn't believe his luck. 'Are we talking soon, Doc? My dog will have forgotten what I look like.'

'No way Ben could do that.' He peered at the now exposed wound. 'That looks great, Keith. If you'll come in and see me in two days at the surgery, I reckon you can go home today, too. You're to come back here if the fires come close to home. And you can bring your dog. I'm sure we can find somewhere to tie Ben up if we need to.'

The old man's face creased with delight. 'You beauty.'

Jack smiled. 'Your old truck has been waiting in the hospital car park for a few weeks now. I hope it starts.'

Keith swung his legs out of the bed. 'A little thing like that won't stop me.'

As they walked back to the desk, Eliza beamed beside him. She genuinely cared about his patients. 'It's a pleasure to see how keen Keith is to go home. I didn't expect he'd be allowed to go—nor did he.'

Jack's face was serious. 'I've been out to see Mary's husband, Mick. He seems to think we're in for a bad run with the fires over the next few days. I thought it better that Keith got home to see things were right before it was too late.'

Eliza felt the dread in her stomach. 'What about Dulcie's farm?'

'I asked about that and Mick said the main risk is going the other way. The creek is a good break for Dulcie's too, but Mick will keep it under surveillance.' He glanced around at the quiet hallway. 'I think you're going to need all your hospital beds before we're through.'

'What about Mary's pregnancy? She only has ten days to go.'

At least Eliza understood. He was having an uphill battle getting through to Mary. 'That's the reason I was out at the McGuiness farm.' He ran his fingers through his hair. 'I want her in Armidale, at least until after the baby is born. I'm not that sure of her due date because she wouldn't go for a scan. Has some aversion to ultrasounds. So I hope this baby is fine. But if things get worse she's better here than home alone. We'll just have to keep her sitting down as a triage nurse or something.'

'I'll watch her.'

'I know you will.' He glanced at his watch. Eliza was good in the common-sense department and a couple of other departments he wished he had more time for. 'I'll scoot off and start surgery. I might even have my secretary double up the appointments so I can finish early. I'm not usually superstitious but I have a bad feeling about today.'

Dulcie Gardner arrived at eleven and settled into the ward smoothly. She could stand upright with help but had difficulty walking without assistance and her words were slightly slurred. She was improving so rapidly there was every chance she would return to full health as long as she gave her body the time it needed to recuperate.

'So you're the new matron who's minding my family?' Dulcie's medical records may have said she was fifty-four years old but she looked forty-four, with her wavy blond hair and pale blue eyes. Her smile was dragged down at one side but still quite lovely, and Eliza warmed to her at once.

'Hello, Dulcie. Yes, I'm Eliza and all your family are delightfully well and waiting for you to get better.'

'How was the bed? Did you find the sheets?'

Eliza smiled as she began to pack Dulcie's things away in the drawers. 'Your guest room has a much better bed than the one in the Bellbrook Inn.' Eliza put away powder and soap and combs and a hair drier and even found a little travel clock to put on the locker.

'You seem to have everything, considering you were whisked away in the ambulance.'

'Dr Jack packed for me. I swear that man is an angel.'

He is a good man, Eliza agreed silently. 'He was certainly worried about your animals.'

Dulcie bit her lip. 'Because I said I wasn't going if he didn't find someone to move in with them until I come home.'

Eliza smiled at the thought of Jack at a stalemate with this lovely lady. 'I'd like to have seen that.'

'Perhaps I was a little ungrateful to give him such a hard time, but I can be stubborn.' Dulcie looked apologetically at Eliza and Eliza squeezed her hand.

'Your donkey was stubborn this morning and wouldn't move from the gate. He must have got it from you, or perhaps you got it from him? I had to climb over the fence to fill the water troughs because he wouldn't move.'

Dulcie hiccoughed with laughter. 'I forgot to tell Dr Jack you have to give him an apple to move.'

They shared a smile. 'Well, no more worry about that. You did what you needed to keep your family safe.' She lowered her voice conspiratorially. 'It would do Dr Jack good not to get his way all the time. I fear he's a little spoiled by the adoration that goes on here.'

'I beg your pardon' Jack's voice held a thread of amusement so Eliza was saved from embarrassment. He didn't look at Eliza as he crossed to his patient.

'Hello, Dulcie. You look better already since the last time I saw you.'

'I am, Dr Jack. They looked after me well but it is good to be home. And I approve of our new matron.'

'She's a bit of a tyrant, though,' Jack said, as if Eliza wasn't there. 'I saw the ambulance pull up and thought I'd duck my head in to see how you travelled. You make sure she looks after you.'

'You don't need to worry. We girls have it all under control,' Dulcie said with the utmost confidence.

By lunchtime the smoke was strong enough in the distance to seep into the hospital and Eliza could feel the old dread return to her stomach.

Mary was ensconced as triage nurse and seemed content to do paperwork and initial observations and otherwise keep her weight off her feet.

Any outpatients who came in brought the smoky smell in their clothes and hair. The sun had disappeared behind the haze in the pitiless sky.

The seniors were busily assembling sandwiches again and the volunteers were filling flasks with water and juice and gallons of tea. The radio was informing listeners where backburning operations were taking place and the quarter-hourly updates had everyone's attention.

At one o'clock, the sound of a truck heralded the arrival of two new helpers and one blue cattle dog.

When Eliza looked up she knew things were getting worse. 'That must be the shortest discharge in history, Keith.'

'Joe was in a spot of bother and I thought we should come back.'

Later Eliza found out that Keith had driven over to Joe's farm and had found his young friend trapped back against the wall of his shed. Joe had been trying to hose back the flames of a grass fire caused by floating embers.

Joe's nephew had gone home to help his mother fight their own fire, and though Joe had never intended to become involved in firefighting he hadn't been able to stop himself.

When Keith had arrived they'd saved the shed but decided to block the gutters and fill them with water and then leave for town before the road was cut.

Keith's farm was safe and Ben was in the back of the truck.

'We've come to help. Reckon Doc would be spittin' if we both got sick again.'

'I think he might be at that,' Eliza grinned and pointed them towards the day-room where the sandwich factory was still going.

She watched them go and they passed Jack bearing a tray of sandwiches for the staff.

'It seems you may not get much of a break today,' he said, and Eliza felt the jolt right through her at the warmth in his expression. She finally acknowledged how much they enjoyed each other's company, how often they smiled and looked at each other and how dangerous it had all become. Why hadn't she seen this earlier?

She was a fool. 'Let's not waste time chatting, then,' she said, to hide her sudden self-consciousness, and Jack frowned.

Eliza admitted to herself it had been a less-than-gracious thing to say—but it was his fault for getting personal. He'd said she'd just stay a Nice Safe Female Friend but this wasn't the way you looked at friends. She didn't want warm looks on a day that hit one hundred degrees Fahrenheit—she didn't want them ever!

Eliza needed a minute to herself because for some reason she felt like crying. 'Perhaps you should go and see Mary. If she's fine, I'm ready to go through these admissions with you,' Eliza said in a neutral voice.

'Bossy.'

'That's why I make a good boss.' She used his rationale for Mary against him and he went.

Mary looked up as he approached and Jack thought her shoulders drooped more than normal. 'You're tired, Mary. Have a sandwich and then go and lie down.'

'You sound like Eliza.'

'Heaven forbid.' He smiled with genuine amusement and Mary had to smile back, albeit tiredly. 'OK, so maybe I am a little sore. My back aches and I'm frustrated by not being able to help.'

'You are helping. But you won't help by getting sick or going into labour and not telling me. How long has your back ached for?'

'Most of the pregnancy. Just more noticeable the more weight I'm carrying.'

Jack wasn't convinced. 'Make sure that's all it is. If you go into labour here, I want you out of Bellbrook if I have to carry you myself.'

He jammed his hands into his pockets to keep them from waving around because what he wanted to do was pick Mary up and put her in a car. He'd already lost one woman and his precious baby and he couldn't bear to lose another. Not that anything was going to happen to Mary, he assured himself, but he'd tell Eliza to watch her like a hawk.

'I'm going to ring Mick and get him to come and get you.'

Mary shook her head. 'Mick can't leave the fire control centre. I'll ring Mick's cousin to come over from Armidale as soon as I think I'm going into labour, I promise. I've another ten days to go, and that's if I don't go overdue, which most women do.'

She sounded so reasonable but… 'I don't like it, Mary. I can't force you to go home but I would like you to go as soon as Mick can get away.'

'All right, Jack. Stop worrying about me and go and

help Eliza. She has a list of patients to see and will need the beds before you get through the backlog.'

'Two bossy women, and to think, this used to be such a peaceful place.'

As he turned back through the doors he heard Mary say, 'You were in rut anyway.'

'I liked my rut,' he muttered, and went back to Eliza.

By the end of the day Eliza was feeling both the weight of the hospital and the weight of her growing feelings for Jack on her shoulders. Jack had been called out again. On the plus side, the fires were almost under control for the moment, and the gush of outpatients had slowed down.

She'd sent Mary home with her husband at three o'clock and by six Eliza was watching for Jack. She had responsibilities now and had to get home and feed the animals before dark.

They had three inpatients besides the seniors, Dulcie with her stroke; Connie, a young asthmatic child who was almost but not quite well enough to go home; and a new postnatal mum and baby, Cynthia and Liam.

Liam was Cynthia's third child and she'd only planned to stay overnight for a rest before the fires started. Because she was going home to an isolated farm with no transport, Jack wanted Cynthia to stay until the danger settled.

Jack breezed in about ten past six and had finished the round by half past. Rhonda came in early and Eliza was able to get away not long after Jack. Her shoulders ached and she smelt of smoke and charcoal from all the firefighters she'd ministered to that day.

The animals greeted her enthusiastically and helped her mood a little as she went around and shared the feed. After her shower she couldn't settle, though. She was overtired and agitated and decided a late night from a few nights ago had probably caught up with her—that and her growing unease about her feelings for Jack.

She'd been at Bellbrook over two weeks and it felt like she'd been here for months. It felt like she'd known Jack for ever.

'Well, don't forget you are leaving,' she reminded herself out loud, and wondered why she should feel even more depressed.

The fires, too, brought many painful memories and she could feel the tension creeping up her shoulders and into her heart.

Since moving to Sydney she'd avoided dwelling on bushfires, changing channels if covered on the TV or the subject when discussed by others.

But here bushfire news was all around her and she couldn't shut it out. Maybe it was time to at least learn to accept that natural disasters were a fact of life.

When the sound of Jack's vehicle penetrated her misery she wasn't sure if she was glad or sorry—she just knew that it would have been better if he hadn't come.

'Hello, Eliza.' He stood tall and a little unsure of his welcome, and she waited for whatever excuse he'd thought up for being here.

'No excuses—I'm here to see you.' He shrugged and

she shivered at the thought of how easily he could read her mind and how most of her response leant towards being glad he was there.

'Come in.' She turned away because she didn't want him to read anything else, especially stuff she hadn't even told herself, but she felt the heat in her cheeks as he followed her inside.

He didn't pretend so why was she? Because she wasn't that brave—she wanted to imagine she was immune to Jack.

She sat down in the tiny lounge room and he sat in the chair opposite. No words had passed between them as he'd followed and the silence lengthened as each waited for the other to start.

Eliza couldn't stand the tension any longer. She spread her fingers stiffly across the arm of the chair as if to stop her fists from clenching. 'Why are you here, Jack?'

He looked at Eliza sitting there, her chin lifted as she looked at him with those big, green, fairy eyes of hers, daring him to give a reason for her to throw him out.

He liked her even more for that attitude, but it threw him. What was it he wanted? Why was he here when he'd spent the whole trip out telling himself he was a fool for going near her out of hospital hours?

'I knew you were worried about the fires and I thought I'd just come out and see that you were OK.'

'I'm fine. Thank you. It was kind of you to think of me.'

'I think of you a lot.'

She sighed. 'It's a problem we both seem to have.'

'I guess you're feeling it, too, then,' he said quietly.

He watched her close her eyes briefly as she took a deep breath, and then she was back to her assertive self.

'It doesn't matter what I feel, Jack. I'm leaving soon. I've been attracted to the wrong man too many times to listen to you about feelings.' Her eyes skittered away and then back again, and he considered that tell-tale sign of her discomfort. There might be some hope.

'At least you admit you're as attracted to me as I am to you.'

'That's not what I said.'

'I just want to find out what there is between us. Maybe there's nothing at all. You said we could be friends.'

Her shoulders rose and then fell. 'I was wrong.'

'I never took you for a coward, Eliza.' He kept his eyes on her and she didn't flinch.

'That's the second time you've called me a coward. I'm not—and I'm not a fool. I wish you hadn't come and I think you'd better leave.'

'No country hospitality?'

'No.'

Maybe there was distress in her eyes, he wasn't sure, but he didn't like the feeling it gave him that he had caused her pain. Maybe he shouldn't have come. 'OK, Eliza. Perhaps you're right. I'll see myself out and you tomorrow.'

Driving home, Jack was in no better state of mind. He liked Eliza, he really did. And he admired her work and her kindness and he even vaguely understood her crazy mixed-up psyche a little. But it was that look in her eyes that drove him to question his real feelings.

From somewhere, all sorts of protective urges were surfacing and a few of them concerned wrapping her safely in his arms. Maybe it was time he moved on from celibacy. That was all his feelings for Eliza were—biology. His lip curled. There was that but it wasn't a fraction of the whole picture.

He wanted all of her and he was terrified. The last time he'd felt this way he'd been the recipient of more pain than he could stand. He'd reached a point where it had been better to lock Jack the man away and just concentrate on the outside world.

The long hours at the hospital and being out on call had been a blessing and the responsibility for the health of a town had stopped him from dwelling on any thoughts of a new life. Then Eliza had arrived and pointed her wand at the neat brick wall around his heart and turned it into vapour.

And she was nothing like he'd imagined he'd ever be drawn to. She was bossy, determined, very efficient and probably didn't need him at all. Here he was, fantasising about a woman he'd worked with for less than three weeks. And if he pursued her, if he ever had her returning his feelings, for all he knew, he might let her down like he'd let Lydia down.

So he should give up. Shouldn't he? But those damn eyes of hers were there every time he shut his own. Peace was hard to find.

CHAPTER SIX

THE next day at the hospital was a little quieter as if people were too busy to get sick. The bushfires were closer to town and a pall of smoke lay across the horizon.

After all the soul-searching she'd done the previous night, Eliza wasn't up to discussions with Jack.

When he'd gone he'd still been everywhere in the room. She'd got up and moved into the kitchen but he'd been there, too, even though he hadn't set foot in the tiny alcove.

She'd pushed open the back door and stepped out into the yard. Roxy had bounded up and licked her knee and they'd gone for a walk in the dark. She'd needed to blow Jack Dancer out of her mind but it had been too dangerous to say it out loud, even to the dog.

Now, twenty-four hours later, she managed to get through Jack's final round by agreeing with everything he said, until she felt like one of those fake nodding dogs in a car rear window.

Eliza stared out the window as Jack finished the baby check on Liam. 'So you agree with that, too?'

Eliza turned back, smiled vacantly and nodded.

Jack's lips twitched and Eliza narrowed her eyes. She searched for any memory of his words but couldn't find any.

'What did I just agree with?'

'That you haven't listened to a word I've said for the last half an hour and I bore you silly.'

Eliza's eyes glinted. 'Yep. I agree with that.' Jack just smiled and handed her the pin for Liam's nappy.

'I'll leave Liam for you to finish dressing then, and head home for my tea.'

Jack out of her hair at last. Eliza nodded. 'Sounds perfect.'

On Eliza's drive home the hazy afternoon sun grew dark in patches. There had been extensive backburning and some areas still smouldered. Eliza switched on her headlights to improve vision as she crawled along the side of the hill. She saw more wildlife than she had the previous evening. Smoke swirled unexpectedly every few hundred yards, a bit like thoughts of Jack in her head, she thought grimly.

Five minutes later Eliza edged her vehicle over for an approaching car and as she squinted to reduce the glare from the other car's headlights, a large marsupial shape bounded out of the bush on her left. The big male kangaroo darted left and then right in fright as the two cars approached, and finally froze in the middle of the road with indecision.

Eliza slammed on her brakes and swerved between the big kangaroo and the high left bank with millimetres to spare. She heard the snap of her side mirror and she winced as it was wiped from the side of her car and branches slapped the paint on her passenger door. Luckily she managed to pull over without hitting the bank with her bumper.

When her car stopped she whooshed out her breath, turned off the engine and sank back against the seat. That had been too close to hitting the kangaroo. She wouldn't like to have been driving fast.

When she played back the scene in her mind unease crawled around the edges of her memory. Something was missing.

It was quiet as she thought about it and then she realised.

The other car had been travelling at a much greater speed and it would have been hard for the driver not to have swerved close to the drop.

Eliza looked back up the way she'd come but there was no car to be seen. She peered further down the road in the opposite direction and a patch of clear in the dusky smoke showed no car.

Eliza swung her wheel tightly and turned the Mustang in a half-circle to face the other direction and crawled slowly up the road and around the bend. She leaned out the window to look at the gravel edge and, as she drew level with where the animal had crossed, she saw the skid marks leading to the rim of the ravine.

Not good. Eliza pulled up, switched on her hazard lights to warn approaching traffic and climbed out of her car.

The tyre marks disappeared short of the low fence and then reappeared as a swathe of broken scrub before careering down the hillside.

She needed help before she attempted to find the occupants because the least helpful scenario would be for her to injure herself in a climb down the ravine, and no one knew she was there. This was not the sort of country where passing drivers noticed a broken branch or two and investigated.

She dialled the emergency number, notified the police and ambulance then went back to her car for a torch and her first-aid kit.

The kangaroo had disappeared and Eliza glared in the general direction in which the marsupial would have escaped.

'Good one, Skippy,' she muttered, and scrambled through the undergrowth at the side of the road to climb the wire fence that the car had managed to sail over.

When she was on the other side of the fence she could see the black marks disappearing down the slope where the tyres had ripped through the soft soil as the driver had tried to brake.

Her shoes were not designed for mountain trekking and she skidded when she couldn't grab bushes to slow her descent. She tightened her lips in sympathy for what must have been going through the mind of the driver in the uncontrolled descent.

Finally she picked up the car by way of a glint of metal, but lost her footing as she took her eye off the hillside to examine the wreckage. The last twenty feet she accomplished faster than she'd intended but managed to land at the bottom still on her feet.

She stopped because she bumped into the rear of what she could now see was a red sports car, and she pulled herself through the bushes at the side of the vehicle until she came to the passenger door.

She reefed the door open and the interior light came on, but the car was empty. There was blood on the steering-wheel but whoever had been in there had managed to get out in case the car blew up.

Eliza looked around and spotted the outline of a woman as she sat upright against a tree.

'Are you all right? I'm a nurse.' Eliza didn't want to frighten her.

Eliza shone the torch onto the woman's chest, careful not to blind her, but suddenly it didn't matter. The woman fainted and that was when Eliza saw she was heavily pregnant. She slid slowly sideways in an ungainly heap and Eliza scrambled across to stop her head, at least, from hitting the ground.

Eliza rolled the woman's weight slightly to one side and tried to elevate her legs onto a log to send more blood to the brain, but she didn't rouse when Eliza spoke to her.

The unconscious woman's breathing was slowing and her pulse was more difficult to palpate than Eliza had expected. She felt the coldness of dread creep over her own body.

In the distance, the sound of an ambulance could be heard, and Eliza hoped they would hurry because she had a horrible suspicion internal injuries were draining

the mother's life away. If the mother died the baby
would die, too, unless they were somewhere they could
perform a miracle.

The next fifteen minutes seemed to last for hours
though they extricated the woman more easily from the
ravine than Eliza could have hoped for via a lower farm
gate. The ambulance had been able to drive along the
valley floor and back up to the road in half the time it
would have taken to carry the patient out up the slope.

Just as the ambulance drew up to the hospital the cardiac monitor suddenly squealed in protest. The woman's
heart had stopped.

'Cardiac arrest.' Eliza felt dread in her stomach and
connected the bag to the tube the paramedic had inserted
when they'd first arrived. Eliza and the paramedic began CPR but both knew that even the best resuscitation
wouldn't be enough for the baby, or the mother, if they
didn't stop the internal bleeding.

Jack met them as they opened the doors and took the
situation in at a glance. He was relieved and grateful to
see they had positioned a wedge under the patient's side
and had an intravenous line in.

Jack listened as Eliza reeled off what she knew as
they pushed the ambulance trolley into the mini-theatre and transferred the woman onto the emergency bed
with barely a break in the cardiac massage.

After two shocks and a dose of cardiac stimulants
there was no discernible improvement in the woman's
cardiac output. Jack shook his head.

'If you guys continue the CPR,' Jack spoke to the ambulancemen, 'Eliza and I will do the section.'

'Caesarean section? What? Here?' The ambulance officers were astounded but Eliza had heard of this before to save pregnant trauma victims.

Jack knew what had to be done. 'We'll worry about infection if she survives. If we don't get that baby out, Mum has no chance, and without a live mother the baby will die as well.'

Jack turned his focus back to the woman and Eliza drew a deep breath. So be it. She knew it was true. 'Even if it's too late for the baby, we could save her doing this. We'll lose her anyway if we don't try. What do you need, Jack?'

'Everything, but we'll waste time getting it. We both need gloves for our own safety and I'll make a vertical incision. I'll need a scalpel, some antiseptic and a blanket for the baby. If she survives, we'll worry about antibiotics and sewing up later.'

'Should I listen for foetal heartbeats?'

Jack looked at Eliza. 'We don't have time. This is the best chance both of them have.'

During the next three minutes Eliza felt as if she were looking down at the scene from a distance somewhere up on the ceiling, although her body responded as she told it to.

'No anaesthetic—get her belly exposed,' Jack was firing orders. Eliza grabbed a packet of gloves and spoke over her shoulder.

'Rhonda, get the gear ready for the baby. It feels

about full-term size and I'll help you when we have her or him.'

Jack knew he had to get the baby out fast. He'd read all the literature and agonised over the might-have-beens with regard to his own personal tragedy. The amazing thing was, there was a very slim chance he could still save this woman's life if he could deliver the baby and get the sequestered blood from her uterus and legs back into her bloodstream by unsquashing the bulky weight of her uterus from the large blood vessels below.

There wasn't much hope, he knew that too, but the woman had none if they didn't try. If any one knew about this scenario, Jack did. If Lydia had been sectioned as soon as she'd arrested, they might have saved her and his son. Or maybe not. He'd never know. But this woman would have every chance he could give her.

'She can sue me later for the scar,' Jack muttered to himself as Eliza poured the contents of a bottle of antiseptic over the pale stomach that seemed so huge on such a tiny woman.

The scalpel swooped and a thin red line appeared beneath the woman's breasts down to the top of her pubis. This wasn't the time for a bikini cut.

Jack slashed again, deeper this time, and he saw Eliza wince as she held open the wound with a large pad. There was very little bleeding as the woman's uterus appeared beneath the slack abdominal muscles and Jack continued doggedly until a gush of amniotic fluid heralded their entrance into the baby's space.

Jack captured the baby's head and then eased the rest of the baby's limp body out of the cavity. Eliza clamped and cut the cord, suctioned and then took the little girl from him. The baby was white and limp and Eliza hurried over to the bench where Rhonda waited with a warm towel and the resuscitation equipment.

Eliza rubbed the little girl briskly as soon as she'd laid her down, and then tilted the baby's head slightly. Rhonda looked terrified.

Eliza talked her through it. 'For newborns you always start with five slow, bigger breaths with the baby-sized ventilaton bag to force out any fluid from the baby's lungs. This allows better inflation if she starts to breathe for herself. If you don't expel that first fluid, it prevents severely depressed infants from being success-fully resuscitated.'

'The baby looks dead,' Rhonda whispered. She'd had very little experience with babies. 'Shouldn't we listen for a heartbeat?'

'You don't have to. Just feel the umbilical cord for any pulsation, but the breaths are the important thing in the first few seconds.' Eliza watched the little chest rise and fall as she squeezed the bag. 'Air entry looks good. There's no heart rate I can pick up so you start cardiac compression. Circle the chest with your hands and use your thumbs over the sternum just under the nipple line. Compress like this for about a third of the depth of the chest.' She showed Rhonda quickly. 'We should have about ninety heartbeats and thirty breaths in one minute.'

They settled into the three compressions of the tiny

chest to one smaller breath from the oxygen bag, which was needed for circulation.

The baby twitched and Eliza felt the first flicker of incredulous hope in her own chest. 'Come on, baby. If you're going to do it, it has to be in the next minute or two.' Eliza prayed this baby was as resilient as she knew most babies were. 'Babies want to live,' she said to Rhonda, but she was really talking to herself. 'They are designed for sometimes rocky starts.'

The baby gave a tiny gasp and then another, and Eliza paused in her bagging to check for a heart rate. She could feel the tiny pulsations and the beat speed was climbing fast.

'You can stop compressions, Rhonda, we only need to concentrate on the oxygen now.'

When the baby gave a weak cry, Eliza felt the tears prickle behind her eyes, but there was no time for emotion. Rhonda straightened in shock and Eliza disconnected the bag from the oxygen tubing and held it near the baby's mouth. The feeble cries grew louder until there was no doubt that she would survive.

The baby settled into a more consistent breathing pattern and after another thirty seconds Eliza glanced across at Jack. 'You go, girl,' she said, and then looked across at Rhonda.

Rhonda was unashamedly crying. 'I can't believe we just did that.'

'I need you here,' Jack called over his shoulder and Eliza nodded to the nurse beside her. 'Keep her warm and keep the oxygen blowing about an inch above her mouth.'

She moved back to Jack, and he nodded congratulations at her success. 'The placenta is out and I've packed the uterus. We can take the wedge out from under her now that the weight of her uterus has gone.'

The ambulance officer stuttered in shock. 'W-we've got the b-beginnings of a heart rate here, if we can keep it going.'

Eliza couldn't believe it. She'd never expected to save both the mother and baby. 'Could she make it, too?' she asked Jack, and he nodded.

'She'd better. We've just given her the best chance we can.'

Jack was grimly determined now there was hope. He mightn't have been able to save his own family but their lives hadn't been wasted if he saved others from what he'd learnt. He wasn't going to let this patient slip away from him.

With a steady heart rate they could run in the needed fluids and the litres of O-positive blood that were arriving from the Red Cross fridge. The woman's heart rate on the monitor was settling down and, although she was still deeply unconscious, her oxygen saturations were creeping up.

'We'd better get some suture material here and repair this wound so they can airlift her out to a city hospital.'

The next hour saw the arrival of the adult retrieval team in the emergency helicopter and Jack's shoulders sagged as his patient's care was transferred to the new crew.

'Amazing job,' the intensive care doctor congratulated the Bellbrook team, and Eliza and Jack smiled tiredly.

After the police had been, Jack drove Eliza to her car and the silence stretched between them.

Finally Jack spoke. 'This is when I hate being the only doctor in town. I couldn't have done it without you.'

'You were incredible—so focussed on what needed to be done. I still can't believe the mother and baby survived, but I never want to do that again.'

'Tell me about it. She only looked about thirty and we still don't know her name.' They'd pulled up beside Eliza's car.

The sky lit up with a flash of sheet lightning and the slow rumble of thunder followed soon after. Rain would help put out the fires and the break from the heat would be good.

Jack looked mentally and physically exhausted and Eliza didn't feel much better. But she didn't want him to leave her.

'Follow me back to Dulcie's, Jack. Just for a while. I don't want to be alone just now and I don't think you should be either.'

He didn't take his eyes off the steering-wheel as he waited for her to get out, then he nodded, and she heard him sigh.

'It's a strange old world,' he said.

A short time later they both turned off their engines and Roxy greeted them at the gate.

'Yes, I know I'm late,' Eliza said, as Roxy proceeded to cover her in wet doggy kisses. 'And don't lick me.'

Jack smiled faintly at that and Eliza thought it almost worth the dampness to see his spirits lift. 'Come inside,' she said. 'I'll check the animals with a torch later. I filled all the troughs this morning and they'll last until I get to them.'

'I think if I went to sleep I'd never wake up.' Jack followed her into the house and fell into the armchair in the lounge room. His arms hung limply over the sides and she watched him for a moment. His hair was tousled and his skin was paler than usual. 'I'll make us a cup of tea,' she said quietly.

A sudden weight on his chest roused Jack and he realised Dulcie's cat had jumped up. He pushed the cat down onto his lap and stroked it absently.

Life was strange.

If the woman today had been Lydia, if he could have saved his wife and their baby, would their marriage have been different? His son would be three years old now and he didn't suppose that grief would ever go.

But had he really been at fault for the breakdown of their marriage and ultimately Lydia's and his son's deaths?

It was time to let go. He really had loved his wife in the beginning. But she'd been harder to love when she'd become bitter. He'd wanted his baby, ultimately more than Lydia had, but he hadn't known pregnancy would ruin their marriage. He'd actually thought it a wonderful surprise when Lydia had told him.

He'd tried to be there for her. Not work such long hours. But she'd really only been happy when she'd been in Sydney. Goodness knew what sort of mother she'd have been. Perhaps he'd be going through a messy divorce, child access problems. He'd never know.

But Lydia's death, and his son's death, had not been in vain. Because of them he'd known what had to be done today, and another woman and her baby would live.

He and Eliza had done a good job. So had Rhonda and the ambulance officers. They had all achieved an amazing feat.

He could hear the kettle whistle in the kitchen. Eliza was in there. He wished Eliza was here. Now. In his lap instead of the cat.

'Sorry, cat!' He grinned at the purring animal and gently pushed her off so he could stand up.

He followed the kettle's whistle into the tiny kitchen.

Eliza didn't turn as he came into the kitchen. He trapped her against the sink as she put cups on a tray. 'The kitchen's too small for two, Jack. I'll bring the tea out.'

'There's more room if we stand like this.' He took the cups from her hands and pulled her around and into his arms until her nose was buried in his chest.

Her body felt soft and luscious beneath his hands and his fingers tightened on her wrists as he closed his eyes. He dropped his chin down onto the top of her head. Her hair smelt like smoky citrus and he sighed as he relaxed. She felt so good in his arms.

Eliza frowned. 'Right,' she said, and pulled her head back with a touch of impatience. Her mind was full of what she could whip up for dinner and she missed the change in Jack's focus.

When she tried to step back she realised he still had hold of her wrist. 'What are you doing, Jack?' Then she looked up and saw the expression in his deep brown eyes and unexpected heat hit her low in the stomach like a kick from the donkey.

He just held her, and held her, for several minutes, and it *was* wonderful to rest her head against him and draw comfort from his arms. Then his mouth came down in slow motion and when his lips grazed hers she couldn't help but sigh into him. She needed this and by the feel of Jack against her, he needed her, too.

What started as a gentle comfort kiss slowly deepened into something much more. Strong, slow strokes from his tongue, mirrored by his hands on her body and her hands on his, ignition of flames that had been simmering below the surface for both of them. Suddenly there was no 'both', no 'two people', there was only mutual hunger and a raging desire to oust their shared demons.

When Jack's pager went off, it took a few seconds for him to realise what the sound was. It took Eliza even longer and he had to hold her away until she opened her eyes.

They stared at each other and neither could believe the state of undress they'd achieved in so short a time.

Eliza brushed her hand over her mouth and took a deep breath. 'You'd better answer the page.' Then she turned back to the sink and leant over the cold metal to breathe the fresh air coming through the window.

Jack stared at the back of her neck. Her skin was still pink from where his hand had cupped her, and her white lace bra hung loosely open at the back. He shook his head and picked his shirt up from the floor then went into the other room to phone the hospital.

He'd never behaved like that in his life before. It was as if someone else had shifted into his body and demanded he kiss Eliza, and once he'd started he hadn't been able to stop. She was his oasis in the madness of today but he'd almost created a bigger madness with his lack of control.

His fingers shook slightly as he dialled the number on his phone.

When he came back all traces of the lover had gone and his face was expressionless. 'One of the firefighters, a cousin of mine, is badly injured an hour from town. They don't think he'll make it if they move him so I'm going up to stabilise him before the chopper comes in.'

She nodded and even had the presence of mind to thrust two bananas and a carton of juice into his hand. 'You have to eat something.' He headed for the door but then he stopped again and turned around.

'Eliza.' He shook his head as if unable to find the words, and she made it easy for him.

'Later, or not at all. It's been a big day, Jack, and yours will be even bigger. Good luck.'

Eliza watched him go and she stood looking out of the door as his car receded into the distance. What the heck was she doing? They'd been practically naked in the kitchen and she could guess what would have happened next. Unless he'd pulled a condom out of his pocket in a stellar example of self-control, she could have been pregnant and regretting this day for ever.

Or would she have? Did circumstances cause situations like this or were they just excuses? If she hadn't cared about Jack, deep down, would she have been in this position?

She was way too close to the edge of falling for Jack and she needed to get a grip or leave town, now. Leave Jack before she found herself loving another man who needed healing. But she was trapped until Mary had her baby.

The soft, easily suckered side of Eliza whispered that maybe if he admitted to loving her she could think of them together with a glimmer of hope. But she was scared. Rightly so. She'd thought she'd been in love before—although she'd never experienced the intensity or reckless abandon she'd felt in the last few minutes. But that had probably just been exacerbated by the horrific drama of the day.

She'd just have to see what the next day brought but the glow remained.

CHAPTER SEVEN

'I THINK it would be better if we didn't mention that I called out to see you at Dulcie's,' Jack said. 'Just for a while.'

She froze and the morning round shattered into reality. Another 'secret' relationship.

Her face felt stiff as she struggled to keep it bland and fight down the sudden nausea that gripped her.

'Why is that, Jack?'

He leant on the desk as he looked at her and he frowned. 'Just don't, OK?'

Eliza stared at this stranger she'd probably given her heart to. Was he going to give her a reason or tell her he wasn't regretting last night? But, of course, he didn't. She couldn't believe how much of a fool she'd been. Again.

She'd seen this one coming. She'd opened herself to this risk and look where it had left her. Next-morning regrets from a man who should have grown out of them.

Not that she'd planned to shout their attraction from the rooftops but a look or a touch of his hand on hers at work, celebrating a new closeness, would have been good to her. Second thoughts and secret relationships were something she'd vowed never to settle for again.

Regrettably, she couldn't leave today. She'd ring Julie, though, and get the agency moving on looking for a replacement. It could take weeks to get away but she could be strong for that long.

Jack behaved as if nothing had happened, and Eliza supposed she had actually given him the opportunity to do exactly that when she'd said to him 'Later, or not at all,' in Dulcie's kitchen. But she hadn't thought he'd take her up on it.

Eliza would have to be thankful that she'd woken up to Jack before she'd done something irretrievable.

She needed to immerse herself in work. Twenty-four seven.

'I'd like to take Dulcie out on Saturday for the morning, back to her place to see her animals. Are you happy to give her leave?'

Jack thought about it and then tilted his head in agreement. 'Of course. If you think she can manage it. It will be a good indication of her progress. I'll bring her out if you like.'

Eliza's hand tightened on the folder she carried and the paper actually creaked until she made herself loosen her grip. Jack at Dulcie's again was the last thing she wanted, but there was nothing she could do to stop him.

'If you think you should.' The words only just escaped her clenched teeth but he didn't notice. 'We'll finalise the time during the week.'

Jack seemed satisfied with that and finally he left the

ward. Eliza walked away, turned into one of the empty rooms, leant back against the wall and closed her eyes. She was a fool, fool, fool!

Jack was confused and shaken by his response to Eliza last night and he was glad she wasn't making an issue out of a moment. The trouble was, he wasn't sure it had just been a moment. He didn't want to destroy something fragile by rushing something that they both weren't ready for. He'd done that with Lydia and had lived to regret it.

He certainly didn't want half the town, most of them relatives, breathing down his neck if he courted Eliza, but he wasn't certain Eliza understood that.

He hoped he hadn't hurt her. He'd apologise if he had the next time he saw her, but a part of him was relieved that, on the surface at least, she wasn't making a meal of last night. They'd sort it out. But he'd panicked when he'd pictured the buzz on the grapevine.

She didn't realise what this town was like, the power of the gossip, the accidental destruction that could happen. Though it seemed he'd done some destroying of his own.

He had full intentions of pursuing Eliza, if she'd have him after the way he'd put it so badly.

But he was beginning to realise that nothing was worth the price of losing Eliza.

During the rest of the week Jack found out just how elusive Eliza could be, but it only made him more determined to break down her reserve. He'd never had a hard time apologising to a woman before. Especially now that he accepted he was falling more in love with her every day.

Eliza's face kept him awake in the brief times he had to sleep or appeared in his mind when he opened his eyes in the morning. The memories of her skin against his, her breast beneath his hand and the connection he'd felt when he'd kissed her all taunted him.

As each day finished with Eliza more distant than before, he began to hope the visit with Dulcie would clear the air because it would give them both some time away from work. It had better. He was beginning to feel obsessed with Eliza May and he didn't do obsession well.

On Friday night Eliza dusted and oiled furniture, although the smooth feel of the old timber made her think of Jack and the time she'd run her hands over his chest, solid and warm beneath her fingers. She had it bad. She scrubbed the kitchen, especially the table, but the memories wouldn't clear from the room.

She spread fresh flowers in vases around the little cottage and threw the sparkling windows wide because she could still imagine Jack beside her and she wanted the rooms fresh and untainted.

She wanted Dulcie to get as much joy out of her visit as possible—somebody should—and Eliza wanted to stay busy so she couldn't think of Jack back in this house again.

Saturday morning Eliza mowed the lawn and swept the verandas, and the activity almost kept her mind off the thought of Jack bringing Dulcie.

The weather turned on a sunny day and Eliza put extra chairs on the veranda in case Dulcie wanted to look out over the lawn.

She slipped into the shower an hour before they were due, and she dressed for Dulcie, not for Jack, but she needed to feel at her best for her self-esteem.

At ten o'clock Jack's car pulled up and Eliza met them at the gate.

Dulcie's eyes filled with tears. 'Eliza! It looks so wonderful.' Roxy barked and circled excitedly when she saw her mistress.

Jack, dressed in dark jeans and an open-necked shirt, looked so dear to her that Eliza's heart sank. It was too late. She did love him. How on earth was she going to get through this day?

He walked across with a white paper bag balanced on his hand and a wicked smile on his face. 'I've brought a teacake.' He handed it ceremoniously to Eliza before he opened Dulcie's door and helped the older woman out of the car.

'Down, Roxy.' Dulcie laughed. 'Yes, I know you want to lick me. That's enough. Yucky.'

Eliza carried the cake and smiled at the dog's excitement, all the time feeling as though she were looking through thick glass at the scene. Jack looked across at her strangely a few times but she just stared blandly back.

When Roxy had calmed down, Jack followed Dulcie up the path to the veranda. Although the older woman managed the path without strain, the steps were not so easy.

'Take your time,' Eliza said quietly, and with Jack's help Dulcie finally reached her door.

Dulcie stared around with tears in her eyes. 'It all looks so wonderful. How can I ever thank you, Eliza?'

'You have—by letting me stay here. Besides, your feather bed is much better than the Bellbrook Inn.'

She ushered Dulcie in. 'I bought biscuits because I'm a terrible cook, but now we have Jack's cake we'll put the kettle on and have a party.' She glanced at Dulcie's flushed face. 'How are you feeling?'

'I'm not doing too bad with my walking, but getting onto the veranda was more difficult than I'd bargained for.'

Jack stepped in. 'The occupational therapist will concentrate on steps this week and that should help. Don't rush—you're planning for the long term.'

'Sit down and I'll get the tea.' Eliza pulled out a firm chair from the table.

Dulcie smiled. 'Can I get it? I know I'm being impatient, but I'd like to see how I manage in the kitchen.'

Eliza winced at thought of being left with Jack. 'Fine, as long as Dr Jack carries the heavy teapot.'

Eliza and Jack stood in the centre of the room together and Eliza tried not to look into the kitchen where they had almost made love. When she glanced at him, Eliza found he was watching her.

'The cottage looks great, Eliza.' Those were his words but the expression in his eyes said, I remember you here.

Eliza felt the heat in her cheeks and looked away. She'd tried not to think about that day but obviously Jack had no such compunction.

She swallowed the lump in her throat and tried to keep her voice even. 'The cottage is easy to keep clean.'

Jack glanced towards the kitchen where Dulcie was still clattering dishes. 'I'd like to come back this evening. We need to talk, Eliza.'

Eliza shook her head vehemently. 'I'd prefer that you didn't!' She lowered her voice. 'There's nothing to talk about.'

Obviously Jack wasn't used to people saying no to him. Well, he'd just have to learn, Eliza thought.

'You can't ignore what happened between us, Eliza.'

'I thought we both agreed nothing did happen. If it had, I could certainly ignore it.'

Dulcie's voice floated through. 'Can you carry the tray, Eliza, please?'

'I'll get it and come back for the pot,' Jack said, but he was watching Eliza as he stood up. Then he was gone but she could feel his look like a dose of sunburn.

This was too much. He'd discovered she was weak around him and he was relying on that weakness to break her resistance. What she couldn't figure was why he'd suddenly decided she was worth the effort.

Dulcie walked carefully back into the room and her face showed her obvious delight with her first kitchen enterprise. 'It wasn't too bad. To carry things is a problem, but I could buy myself a cake trolley until I get steadier.'

'Another couple of weeks will make a huge difference,' Jack said as he followed her with a large pink enamel teapot. 'Love the spout on this, Dulcie.'

'It was my mother-in-law's. She gave it to me before she died.'

Eliza tilted her head. 'I didn't know you were married.' Anything to take her mind away from Jack.

'Happily widowed,' she said, and Eliza had to smile.

'So who would be your next of kin? Do you have any children?' As soon as she said it Eliza remembered Jack had said Dulcie had a daughter she was estranged from. It was too late now to take the questions back.

Dulcie's eyes clouded. 'One—but we haven't seen each other for ten years. We're stubborn women, the Gardners, and it took my pregnancy before I made up with my own mother.'

'Maybe that's when I'll see mine, too,' Eliza said, and then wondered what had possessed her to blurt that out. She wasn't planning to get married, let alone the next step of having a baby, and she certainly had never thought of forgiving her mother enough to seek her out. Or maybe lately she had?

Many things seemed to be changing since she'd come to Bellbrook. She was more accepting of bushfires, was getting used to being the object of a town's conversation, could almost consider living in the country again, and now she was even contemplating finding her mother.

Dulcie reached across and patted Eliza's knee. 'And you've never heard from her in all that time?'

'She sends me birthday and Christmas cards but I've never answered.' It didn't actually sound very mature when she heard herself say it out loud. 'We haven't spoken since my father died.'

Dulcie shook her head. 'If she's still writing them she must be waiting for the day you answer.'

Jack lightened the moment. 'Well, if my mother were alive I would be speaking to her. But, then, men are much easier to get along with than women.'

'Yeah, right,' Eliza was glad to change the subject. 'Cut your cake and make a wish.'

Dulcie laughed and said, 'If you touch the plate with the knife, you have to kiss the nearest girl.'

Eliza felt a sense of *déjà vu*. Now, why on earth would she remember her mother had said that all those years ago? It was probably the only pleasant memory Eliza had of her, and she began to wonder if maybe she had only remembered the bad things.

'Oh, goody. I can rig this one.' Jack grinned and the devil glinted in his eyes as he raised the knife.

Eliza panicked. 'Well, that would be you, Dulcie. I'm off to wash up.' Eliza pushed back her chair but she wasn't quick enough.

Jack sliced into the cake, scraped noisily against the plate underneath and swooped to drop a kiss on her cheek as she leant forward to rise. The kiss was warm and sweet and very quick, but Eliza felt the aftershocks of his lips on her skin and knew that she had to get out of there.

'And one for my other nearest girl.' Jack laughed and proceeded to peck Dulcie's cheek as well.

'Don't you hate a show-off?' Dulcie laughed but her cheeks were pink with pleasure.

The morning passed swiftly and before Dulcie began to tire they finished with a walk around the animals so Dulcie could say goodbye. Jack helped her back into his car.

'Thank you both so much. I've had a lovely morning.' Dulcie struggled with her seat belt but finally managed to do the clasp without help. 'I'll see you on Monday, Eliza.'

'You did beautifully, Dulcie.'

Jack walked round to the driver's side of his vehicle and paused before getting in. He looked at Eliza across the roof. 'I'll see you this evening.'

Eliza didn't flinch. She'd go out straight after she'd cleaned up. 'Not here, you won't.'

Before Eliza had a chance to get away, she heard the sound of Jack's car coming up the road and she gritted her teeth. He'd said evening. She dashed across, locked the front door and then scooted through to the kitchen to slip out the back.

Roxy appeared beside her but seemed torn between the sound of Jack's approaching car and walking with Eliza.

'Come with me.' Eliza urged the dog to follow her round the corner of the house and out into the shelter of the trees. If she stayed on the fence line, she should be protected from view. She stamped down the thought that she was being melodramatic.

'Eliza?' Jack's voice floated across the paddock and Roxy barked.

Eliza winced. 'For goodness' sake, Roxy. Either be quiet or go and see him, but don't come back to me.' Of course Roxy went to see Jack and showed him the way to Eliza.

Eliza resigned herself to looking foolish if she didn't find a good reason for lurking in the bushes and she glanced around frantically for one.

A vibrant patch of purple everlastings would have to do as a reason for her position. She began to break off the thick stems and had collected a sizable bunch before Jack appeared.

Jack tried not to smile at Eliza pretending to pick flowers. He'd seen her dash across the yard and had had a fair idea where she was even before Roxy had telegraphed to the world that her temporary mistress was hiding in the trees. 'Gone bush?'

Eliza tucked her hair behind her ear, but it promptly slipped out again. 'I asked you not to come.'

Asking was putting it kindly, Jack thought. 'Actually, it was more of an order not to visit.' Of course, that had made him want to come more.

She glared at him briefly and if she'd had any kind of fairy magic he would have keeled over from that look. Then she went back to picking those ugly flowers, which he couldn't see why anyone would want.

'You're not very good at following orders,' Eliza muttered.

He shrugged. 'Never have been—but I could learn.'

'I doubt it.' She wasn't meeting his eyes and that was frustrating in itself. This new wall she'd erected between them was currently impervious.

'What is it you want from me, Jack?' Now she was

staring at him and the fire in her eyes made him wonder what he'd done to ignite this white rage. 'Are you looking for a free feed, a shoulder to cry on or just sex?'

He opened his mouth to dispute them all but she wouldn't let him talk.

'You don't want commitment, you've told me nothing about your past and you don't want your safe little world disturbed to risk your heart. Now you want a fling on the side as long as we keep it secret. What's in it for me, Jack?' She spread her arms wide and talked to the treetops. 'I'll tell you what's in it for me. Nothing.' She glared back at him. 'Now I'll tell you what I'm willing to risk! Also nothing! So there you go. We're the perfect pair to stay apart. Now, will you leave?'

'OK, Eliza. Maybe I haven't been fair to you at times but I'm trying now. I think we've been through too much together to act like we're strangers and pretend there's nothing between us.'

Eliza was implacable. 'There *is* nothing between us, Jack.'

'I'd like to take your word for that but I'm not so sure any more.'

Jack paused for a moment and looked around at the trees and the paddocks stretching away from this little woman who was growing so large in his life. He wasn't sure what he wanted but he knew they couldn't just be friends any more.

'You're being hard on me, Eliza. Without getting in too deep, you could let me show you the other side of me. Despite how I tried to bury it, there's more to me than being Bellbrook's only doctor.'

'Heaven forbid we get in too deep, Jack. I'm not sure there *is* more to Jack than the doctor.'

'Give me a chance. Come to my house.' He tilted his head and raised his eyebrows, like a kid asking for a treat.

'What if someone sees me, Jack? I thought you wanted to keep our non-relationship a secret?'

'I'm sorry I said that.' At least he now had the chance to say it. 'I have been sorry for a week but you've never let me near you. What we have, if it is a relationship or the beginning of one, is very young, and brittle, and easily damaged. I just didn't think you needed the well-intentioned interest of my many friends and relatives. I know I didn't.' He went on, persuasively, 'I'll make you dinner, so you can't say I just want a free feed. I've done my crying so I won't need your shoulder. And the sex is something we could discuss later.'

Her eyes widened in disbelief and he laughed. 'I was just baiting you. We don't have to discuss sex at all.'

They didn't need to discuss it. Just the mention of the word and the air became charged between them. Desire lay there between them like a big, soft, bouncy feather bed and both of them knew it. The searing memories had been there ever since that explosion of emotion and heat in Dulcie's tiny kitchen.

He hurried on. 'You could see my house. You must have wondered where and how I lived. What I do in my free time?'

'Never thought of it.' This time he knew she'd lied

because she looked away and then back at him with reluctance.

'Really?' He said mockingly. Caught you there, he thought, with the first glimmer of hope that this visit wouldn't be a complete failure.

Eliza tapped her knee for Roxy to come back to her and prepared to turn back to the house. 'You really do have tickets on yourself.'

She was running away and Jack couldn't let her. 'Well somebody has to vote for me when you obviously don't think I'm anything special.'

Eliza snorted. 'This whole town thinks the sun shines out of your...armpit. You don't need me to join them.'

She was waiting for the dog and then she was going to walk away from him. He needed to have the last word and get out of here with the upper hand. 'I'm not going to bicker with you, Eliza. You are invited to tea tomorrow night. I will expect you at eight.' He hoped she couldn't tell it was more bravado than expectation, but he had to try.

Eliza scoffed. 'Don't eat lunch as you might have two meals left over from your tea.'

She'd said 'might'. That was promising, he thought as he watched her walk away.

Sunday saw Eliza driving to Armidale with the top down and the wind blowing her troubles away. Except it didn't work. She'd hoped if she left the valley she'd get away from the memories of Jack.

Of course, she took him with her. Every bend in the

road, every mountain she passed, every cloud in the sky made her think of the ups and downs of her relationship with Jack.

By the end of the day, when she turned back into Dulcie's driveway, she still didn't know what to do.

At seven-thirty Eliza stood indecisively in front of the mirror. So much had happened in the last few weeks, so many poignant events, emotion and heartache, and to-night could spell more drama. Should she give Jack one more chance to show promise for a future together or should she shield herself from the chance of more hurt?

The trouble was, the last thing she wanted to do was look back in years to come and regret not listening to him, just once.

If she went to dinner she wasn't committing herself to Jack for life. She doubted they could ever be just friends. It didn't feel like that. She felt finely balanced on the edge of something she wasn't sure she wanted and certainly didn't trust could be long-lasting. She wasn't quite back to the point of hoping something good could come of this.

The clock ticked and she wavered.

CHAPTER EIGHT

WHEN Jack opened the door, Eliza knew she was late
but she was glad she'd taken the extra time to iron her
favourite dress. It was emerald green and rustled when
she walked, and she chose to wear it when she was feeling in need of extra strength. Eliza had never needed
strength as much as she needed it tonight.

Jack's eyes widened appreciatively and he had a hidden smile, as if he'd found something especially pleasing.

'Come in, Eliza. You look beautiful and I'm so glad you
came.' He showed her through the black-and-white-tiled
entry into a book filled room that was a time warp of country life. Tapestry floral chairs, dark wood walls and rose-
coloured carpets on the polished wooden floor all reflected
from the huge wooden-framed mirror above the fireplace.

Jack's glance brushed over her again and she had no
doubt of her welcome. 'I have a small present for you.
I was going to give you this later but in view of your attire, I can't wait,' he said.

She'd never seen him like this—playful, at ease in his
surroundings, the country gentleman.

He crossed to an old-fashioned dresser and lifted a cloth-wrapped pouch about the size of a small pineapple, which looked quite heavy. 'When I saw this, I knew I had to buy it for you.'

When she pulled the ribbon, the cloth fell away from a glass snowball sitting on top of a beautifully wrought wooden carving. The fairy inside the snowball was dressed in a billowing green frock very similar to Eliza's dress and she had bright green eyes, red hair and delicate silver wings.

Eliza laughed and shook the snow in the ball. The fairy seemed to smile at her. 'Thank you. I've always loved these ornaments.'

'I'm glad.' He looked enormously pleased that she liked it. 'I think of you as the Queen of the Fairies.'

Eliza raised her eyebrows. 'And who are you?'

'Me?' He touched his chest. 'I'm hoping to be the handsome prince but something tells me you've picked me for an ogre.'

'Spare me. Please, not the martyr.' She looked away from him. 'So show me your home.'

Jack shrugged but there was pride in his glance around. 'As you can see, it hasn't changed much since my mother was alive. I'm not really into modern furniture and I have a fetish for polishing old wood. I find it soothing.'

He looked a little embarrassed at the admission and Eliza couldn't help teasing him.

'You make a very handsome housewife.' Eliza said, impressed despite herself. 'Are you sure you don't have a cleaning lady?'

He shook his head. 'Would you like to see my ironing basket? Ironing doesn't turn me on at all.'

She knew what turned him on. My word, she did. Simple, irrelevant choice of words, but the connotations vibrated around the room so that Eliza could almost hear the clanging of danger signals.

They walked through to a glassed-in summer-room that overlooked the river and in the distance the Bellbrook Inn. An old-fashioned swing seat was positioned to capture the best of the rural view over the paddocks, the little sheds on the hills, dotted animals and the winding river.

This room was less formal but still bore the marks of an organised person. Eliza could tell this was his favourite part of the house. He gestured to the seat and she sat primly as far away from him as she could.

Conversation would be a good start, Eliza thought, shifting nervously. 'So, what do you do when you're not saving lives, Dr Dancer?'

'I play at farming but admit one of my cousins does the real farm maintenance. I like to fish, I eat my way around my relatives as a social butterfly, and I sit here and watch the world go by from the safety of my seat. Or I did before you came along.'

He began to swing gently and she wanted him to stop so she could concentrate on the situation. Why did men immediately have to start swinging as if they wanted to take off—couldn't they just ease into a slow glide? She dragged her feet to slow him down and he shot her a wicked glance and slowed to barely rocking.

'Going too fast for you, Eliza?'

'Hmm,' she said wryly, aware of his double meaning and not happy he could bait her so easily.

Eliza forced her shoulders to relax and looked out over the bluff at the view. She would prefer it if he didn't know just how nervous she felt, but couldn't hope he'd miss it. 'So this is how you saw Carla and I swimming that day.'

'And where I saw the fellow get stung the day before.'

She sniffed. 'So you say. I'm not sure that really happened.' She looked at him from under her brows. 'I think you just wanted to evict us from your river.'

'Nobody owns the river—or other people. You don't have to be afraid of me, Eliza.'

That was the problem, Eliza thought. She was the one with unrealistic yearnings. 'It's not you I'm afraid of.'

The silence lengthened as he caught her gaze and held it.

Then he smiled and it was the sweetest smile she'd ever seen. It tore a gentle hole in the fear around her heart like a feather through a spider web.

He leant across and touched her lips gently with his finger and then stood up. The spell broke and she blinked to reorientate herself. How could a smile make her forget everything she'd promised herself? It was as if he'd kissed her!

'I'll just get the entrées and the champagne,' he said, as if nothing had happened.

Eliza fanned the heat in her face with her fingers but she didn't have as much time as she'd hoped to un-scramble her brain.

A drinks trolley preceded him through the doorway. It was laden with tiny dishes of prawns and olives, and toothpicks with chicken and satay, and a big silver ice bucket with champagne and two glasses.

Eliza felt like an extra in the seduction scene. She didn't want to be the star. She tried to lighten the atmosphere. 'Your mother taught you well.'

'I like to have everything to hand. I hope you don't mind eating here instead of at the table?'

She shook her head. The view was incredible and Jack had brought napkins and side plates.

They sat on the swing and nibbled on juicy prawns and tangy chicken and he encouraged her to at least sip the champagne.

But she still knew so little of his past.

'So tell me about the young Jack. What happened to your parents?'

He traced her shoulder with his fingertip and the sensation ran through her as he talked. She wasn't even sure he knew he was doing it. 'Mum and Dad died five years ago. They had a lot of trouble having kids—apparently it's genetic on my mother's side, but only passed down through daughters. She miscarried frequently and I can remember thinking that she should stop trying to have babies and just concentrate on me. She pretty well did except for those times when she was so incredibly sad at losing another child.

'Christmases with Mum started with church in the morning, presents when we came home and then she would cook and cook until the table would groan with the weight of turkeys and hams and rumballs and white Christmas cake and every vegetable, every fruit, punch bowls of fabulous non-alcoholic punch. We'd have ten or twenty for Christmas lunch, all relatives or friends so that Mum would feel there were enough people to share with.'

She squeezed his hand to hear more and he went on.

'My father was a simple man, incredibly intelligent but secure with his farm and his family and amazing with animals and their illnesses. When I grew older I realised he'd trained himself to be a vet just by reading books and connecting with the animals.

'When I was at uni I'd bring home my medical books and we'd sit and try to figure out something I couldn't understand. He'd read it once and be able to explain it to me so that I understood.

'I'd say to him that he could have been anything and he'd say what more could he want to be?'

'They sound amazing.' Eliza compared Jack's wonderful home with her own and vowed her children would look back on their childhood like Jack could.

'I was very fortunate.'

Eliza squeezed his hand. 'What happened?'

'Dad was older than mum, he was eighty-two when he died. I found him leaning up against the bench in the work shed. He'd just slumped there and died when his heart gave out.'

'And your mother?'

Jack sighed. 'She'd had a lump in her breast that she'd told no one about, least of all her son, the doctor. Not long after Dad passed away she became sick and it was too late.'

'A year later I met my wife towards the end of uni and we married quickly, but that wasn't so good. I imagine Mary has told you what happened.'

Eliza nodded. 'One day you could tell me more but not now.'

He nodded. 'Mary is the sister I never had and Mick is my best friend.'

'Now there's you.' His voice was gentle as if he knew she considered flight. 'We connected from the first moment—didn't we, Eliza?'

She didn't answer for a moment because the simple question was loaded with extra weight—deep undercurrents that had appeared from nowhere. He didn't hurry her but she knew he was waiting for her answer.

She sighed. So this was it. Which way should she go? Keep fighting or let him in a little? But how would she stop? She couldn't lie. 'Yes, we did.'

'Was it the suddenness that shocked you, too?' he said quietly.

Eliza remembered her first sight of Jack and how she'd denied the chance of attraction so fiercely to herself. Eliza nodded but inside that huge bubble of fear and trepidation and disbelief was being melted by the warmth of his shoulder rubbing warmly against her and it felt so right. What she felt couldn't be a mistake.

Now the touch of even his shirtsleeve seemed to have a life of its own by creating a field of energy between them.

Jack took her hand and drew it over into his lap and her fingers felt as if they glowed when he held them like that. She could see so many promises in his face but maybe that was just wishful thinking on her part. She felt incredibly aware of him as the silence lengthened and she had no control as the feeling built up.

This was all about touch and connection and without conscious thought her finger lifted and outlined his black brows and strong cheekbones.

He caught her fingers and kissed her palm, all the while not taking his eyes off her face, and she shuddered.

'This is what I am afraid of,' she said quietly. 'What if I let all this out and we connect like this and then you run away?'

'I would never do that—could never do that—once I gave you my heart.'

'Have you, Jack? Have you given me your heart?' Eliza ran her hand across his shoulder and down his arm. Just to touch him. In reassurance that he was really there and this was really happening.

'Yes.' His voice was very deep and she felt the goose-bumps rise on her arms.

It was too sudden. Too confusing. 'How long have you felt like this?' She needed to understand how this could happen.

He was watched her face as if willing her to believe him. 'It began on that first day. You had my heart as soon as you stared at me with those amazing eyes of yours. I thought you glowed like an angry fairy and when I looked into your eyes I couldn't breathe.'

Eliza shook her head. 'You were brusque.'

'I was in denial.'

She smiled. 'I know that feeling and I've been fighting it.'

'What about the way you responded to my kiss at Dulcie's?'

She blushed and he smiled at her confusion. 'That surprised us both, I think.'

'I don't know where that came from,' Eliza said.

His eyes darkened. 'Somewhere elemental, I should think. I've never experienced that loss of control before, like being sucked into a vortex.' His eyes caught hers. 'I think about that day a lot.'

She, calm and steady Eliza, was way out of her comfort zone. 'What are you doing to me, Jack? I can't believe how I'm feeling at the moment. It's too big to imagine you as the other half of me. How could we work together for these weeks and not have felt like this the whole time?'

He grimaced. 'We had walls up for protection, and past hurts, and other people needing us more than we could spare to give to ourselves.' He shrugged. 'Baggage. Fear our feelings wouldn't be returned.' He dragged her across so she was sitting in his lap, and the swing chair made protesting noises at the unevenness of the weight.

They both laughed and the naturalness was such a wonder to Eliza she felt as if Jack had placed a spell on her—and she was supposed to be the magical one.

'Do you feel strange?' she asked him quietly.

He grinned back at her. 'Like Christmas morning as a kid, or waking up on your birthday, or your best friend has come to play and you've been waiting all morning and finally they are here and just as excited?'

'Yes.' Eliza thought about it. 'All of those.'

'Well, you should be excited because we have the most amazing future ahead of us.' Eliza fought down the fear that she couldn't quite let go of. It wouldn't be like before, he meant what he said, and the feel of him against her could only be honest.

It was the warmth that surrounded them that fascinated Eliza. Here with Jack she felt safe and relaxed and amazingly at home with a man half an hour ago she hadn't been sure she should even be visiting. How the heck had that happened?

So this was what it was like to really connect with someone.

She'd never felt anything like this towards either of the men she'd been going to marry. How frightening to think she could have settled for the wrong man and missed this total connection.

'Stop thinking!' Jack's voice intruded and she turned to face him. 'Don't think of anything but us at this moment because people wait their whole lives for a minute of this feeling—let's dissect it later.'

Eliza nodded and she put her hands around his neck and stared into his eyes. 'You're right. Sometimes I think too much. Sitting here feels wonderful.'

'It's going to get better.'

'Show-off.'

When Jack kissed Eliza for only the second time it was a homecoming. His lips on hers, the gentle fan of his breath on her face and the rub of his cheek against hers created more magic. When he pulled away to smile and then kiss her again, she laughed with the joy of it. The wonder of his hands cradling her face as he tried to convey how much he treasured her was the moment that splintered the last of the ice around Eliza's heart and she felt the tears sting her eyes.

'I'm terrified. What if something happens to take this away? I've waited my whole life to believe in love.'

'Shh. Let me kiss you.'

They kissed until the sun went down and then he took her hand and drew her into his bedroom, austere and practical with dark heavy furniture, but Eliza didn't notice.

The green dress fell to the floor, along with his shirt and trousers, and soon they were naked. He took her hand and led her to the old-fashioned bed where she lay like a pagan princess as he turned away briefly to protect her from pregnancy.

In a way she was glad of this moment to breathe and ground herself in what had become such a storm of emotion. A tiny flicker of doubt almost broke through but then Jack was back and they touched with heated skin on heated skin. They lay still for a moment just feeling the velvet between them until Jack raised one hand and stroked her breast.

'So beautiful. So lush and yet you are so tiny. I'm afraid I'll break you.'

Eliza ran her hand over the solid curves of his chest, 'Gorgeous,' she said. 'I'm not afraid at all.' And kissed his throat.

Then they meshed, sliding, hands caressing and mouths seeking. A wondrous blur of sensations with joy and discovery that had no place in time. No haste, but not too slowly, until Eliza cried out and Jack hugged her close with his own damp eyes.

She'd never dreamed it could be like this, so much a moment of togetherness and bonding. She lay snuggled in his arms and accepted that with Jack she'd found her place.

Before dawn, Eliza slipped out of bed and showered. Jack made her a coffee and then kissed her again, and the next time she looked at the clock she knew that by the time she'd driven home, fed the animals and dressed for work, she would be late.

'I have to go now, Jack. I'll be late.'

'I know,' he said, grinning, and then his phone rang. It was a callout and he'd have to go as well.

Eliza drove home and the dawn had never seemed so beautiful.

Eliza was in the shower when the phone rang.

'Eliza? It's Mary. My waters have broken, the ambulance is up in the bush somewhere with Jack and Mick, and the pains are coming every three minutes. I don't think I can drive.'

'You'll be fine, Mary. Have your bag ready and...' she did a quick calculation of the five minutes into town and then the ten out to Mary's '...I'll be there in about fifteen minutes.' That only left her time to throw on a pair of trousers, a T-shirt and her running shoes.

* * *

When Eliza pulled up in a cloud of gravel in front of the McGuinnesses place the lights were still on all over the house and Mary was waiting on a chair beside the door.

She didn't get up when Eliza climbed out of her car and by the time she'd made it to her side, Eliza could see she was in strong labour.

'Well, I guess you'll have your baby at Bellbrook. Seems only natural.'

Mary tried to smile but beads of sweat stood out on her forehead. 'I honestly thought I would have time to get to Armidale.'

'Let's concentrate on getting you somewhere achievable, like my car. I'll even let you sit on my white seats.'

Mary swallowed a bubble of hysterical laughter and took a deep breath. 'I don't know if I can walk.'

Eliza hadn't worked in labour wards for nothing. 'Of course you can walk! Up you get.' She slid her hand under Mary's armpit and heaved her out of the seat.

'You're quite strong for a little woman, aren't you?' Mary gasped, and Eliza chuckled.

'You have no idea.'

They made it to the car before the next pain, and Mary smiled weakly when she saw that Eliza had covered her seats with a pile of towels. 'Hopefully I won't soak through those.'

Eliza shut the door on her and sprinted round to the driver's side. 'Least of my worries at the moment. Let's get you into town.'

Eliza passed Mary her mobile phone. 'Get Rhonda

to prepare for the birth and to try and get a message through to Mick and Jack. I'd really like those two to be here for you when the time comes.'

'Me, too, but I don't like their chances.' Mary moaned.

Eliza shot her a look as she accelerated around a corner. 'Hang on, Mary. It's much nicer if you can do this near a bed.'

They arrived at the hospital with a squeal of brakes and Rhonda was at the door with a wheelchair. It took three of them to get Mary out of the car and about sixty seconds to get her into a spare room that Rhonda had set up as an emergency labour room.

Eliza was privately glad they weren't going back into the emergency room they'd had the drama in earlier.

'Thanks, Rhonda,' she said, and Rhonda nodded. Eliza had another thought. 'Do we keep Syntocinon or Pitocin here for after birth?'

'It's drawn up and on the bedside cabinet.'

'You're an angel because we're going to need it soon.'

To Mary she said, 'Let's get you into a gown and onto the bed, Mary. I'd love to have a feel of your tummy and a listen to your baby's heart rate, if that's OK.'

As soon as Mary was settled, Eliza quickly palpated Mary's large belly and established that baby was lying head first, and on his mother's right side. Then she used the old-fashioned trumpet-shaped foetal stethoscope, one end of the metal tube resting against Mary's tummy and the other against Eliza's ear. She glanced at her watch and counted the galloping heart rate that trembled in her ear.

'One hundred and fifty. Perfectly normal despite the fact that someone pulled the plug out of his or her bath and they're sliding towards the exit sign.'

'Only a midwife would say that,' Mary gasped, as the next pain surged over her. 'I feel like pushing.'

Murphy's law, Eliza thought, and prepared for the birth.

Out loud she said, 'That's fine, Mary. Just listen to your body and do what it tells you to do.'

'It's telling me to push.' Mary sucked the air into her lungs and proceeded to do just that.

'Well I didn't have to worry about getting your dilatation wrong because I can see a little patch of brown hair—your cervix is certainly out of the way.'

Another screech of brakes outside heralded the arrival of Mick and Jack, and the door burst open to admit the dishevelled men.

Mick was wild-eyed and black with soot from head to foot. 'Oh, my God, Mary, my love, I'm so sorry I wasn't here for you.'

Mary just grasped her husband's hand and pushed again.

Jack took one look at the progress Mary had made already and rushed to the basin to wash his black hands.

He spoke over his shoulder to Eliza. 'Have you got oxytocics for after the birth?'

'Yes. Rhonda has it all prepared. If you're not ready soon, I'll have to catch this nephew or niece of yours so get your gloves on, Dr Dancer.'

Jack grinned at Eliza and briefly a flash of warmth flared between them before he pulled his gloves on hurriedly. Once he was gloved, Eliza stepped back and picked up the camera from Mary's bag.

Within two minutes Mary and Mick's new daughter was lying on her mother's stomach gazing up at her mother like a possum. Eliza took a quick series of photos and everybody sighed with relief, although Eliza wasn't happy with the new baby's colour. She shifted the tiny oxygen tubing nearer the newborn's face.

Mary stretched down and kissed her daughter on the forehead. 'I want to call her Amelia.'

'She looks blue.' Mick's voice was strangled by the overload of emotion from the last few minutes.

She did. Eliza placed her hand on his arm. 'So would you if you'd come through the tunnel that fast. Give her a couple of seconds to catch her breath and we'll check her out.'

Eliza glanced at Jack as she reconnected the oxygen bag and mask onto the tubing and gave a few clearing inflations as she held it over Amelia's face. The baby girl was still pale and although blue-tinged hands and feet were normal with newborns, Amelia's tummy was as blue as her lips. Her central cyanosis was deepening.

Jack was distracted by extra bleeding that suddenly gushed at the business end of the bed with the imminent delivery of the placenta, and Eliza prayed that Amelia would be fine. She'd seen something similar a few years previously and that ending hadn't been good. Amelia didn't look fine.

'I need you up here, Jack,' she said quietly, and her

words sliced into his concentration. He blinked and focussed on the baby. 'I think you should listen to her heart,' Eliza said.

CHAPTER NINE

MICK looked from Eliza to Jack and then at his daughter. Even as a layman he could tell something was deeply wrong.

He went to speak but Mary laid her hand on his arm and gripped him. 'Wait,' she said, and there was a deep resignation in her voice that frightened him more.

'What's going on?' His voice had risen and Mary squeezed his arm sharply.

'They don't know! Give them time to find out, love.'

He subsided but the tears formed in his eyes as he looked at his daughter. She was deeply blue and her respiration rate had risen despite the oxygen that Eliza held to her face. Now Eliza was assisting the respirations with squeezes of the bag, but Amelia's blueness continued to deepen.

'Her heart sounds are all over the place. Apart from the patent ductus, she has back-flow into every chamber. Probably stiff lungs as well, as the ventilations aren't working well.'

Urgently Eliza assisted Jack to insert an endotracheal tube—to ensure the most efficient oxygenation to Amelia—but it didn't help.

'Get MIRA on the phone.' Jack shot the order at Eliza, and she nodded and sped over to the emergency phone number list and grabbed the hand phone.

'My poor baby,' Mary said, and her eyes filled with tears. Mick looked from Jack, to Mary, and then to Eliza—as if one of them at least would give him hope. All the faces said the same and it was unthinkable.

'What's that? What's going on? Do something, Jack,' Mick cried.

'MIRA is the mobile infant retrieval team in Sydney, Mick, to see if there is anything else we can do.' He kept his eyes on the new father—Mary knew all this too well.

'They are our only hope. I think Amelia has serious congenital heart and lung problems that make it incredibly hard for her to live outside the uterus. Inside the uterus, she was fine while Mary was supplying the oxygenated blood via the placenta. The blood didn't need to go through the parts of Amelia's heart and lungs that aren't functioning. Now she has been born she can't get enough oxygen to her brain and other organs because her heart and lungs aren't working anywhere near properly.'

Eliza handed the phone to Jack. 'It's Dr Hunter Morgan from MIRA, Jack.'

Jack closed his eyes for a second to clear his brain and then spoke into the phone to explain Amelia's problem.

All they could do was listen to Jack's end of the conversation. 'We've done that. And that. Yes. No. No improvement. All of that, too.' He looked at them all and the pain in his eyes was mirrored in theirs.

Jack's voice had risen slightly. 'Isn't there any thing else we can try?' There was a long pause. Jack's voice dropped and the final words were a whisper. 'I see. Thank you,' Jack said. 'We may as well take it out, then.' Jack looked at Eliza and mimed removing the ET tube.

'Goodbye.' He put the phone down.

Eliza closed her eyes and then opened them to do what was asked. It was the little things like this that broke you up. Amelia's little face returned to normality without the plastic tube distorting her features. It was good the tube was gone for her last few minutes.

Mary nodded and she bit her lip so hard a drop of blood appeared at the corner. She gathered her daughter closer to her heart and held on for dear life. Her daughter's life.

Jack turned to the parents. 'I'm sorry, Mick, Mary. There's nothing I can do.'

Mick shook his head. 'You're sorry? What do you mean, you're sorry? Get a chopper. Get them to fly her somewhere she can get help.'

Mary stroked her husband's arm. 'It's too late, darling. Even the best hospital in the world couldn't save her. She stayed alive to meet us but now she has to go.'

Mick looked at his wife as if she were mad. 'Go? Go where? You can't just let her die.'

Rhonda fled from the room. Jack watched her go and wished he could go, too. He couldn't take any more from this day. This was too horrific—but Mary and

Mick needed him. He looked across at Eliza and thanked God she was here to at least share the burden.

She looked quite composed, in fact. He found that irked him. Of course she was composed. She'd even looked composed when she'd woken in his arms that morning. We're all just ships in the night for her. But this was tearing his guts out and Mary was looking at him as if he'd tell her she was wrong and her daughter would be alive this time tomorrow.

'Amelia's going to die, Mary,' he said in a strangled voice, and before he knew it he was kneeling beside the bed and weeping as if his heart were broken. Weeping for Mary and Mick and Amelia, and for himself and baby he lost three years ago. The three of them formed a hand-holding circle around Mary's baby as she turned darker and darker and her breaths turned to gasps.

Eliza looked on, excluded by their closeness and crying inside for all of them. But someone had to steer the ship and she quietly went about the business of preparing for the worst.

She cleared the room of the debris from the birth, gathered fresh clothes for Mary and made tea and coffee for Jack and Mick.

Eliza was the one who dressed Amelia in beautiful clothes so she could lie with her mother. She gently suggested Mary have more photos and handprints taken to treasure in the future, which she then proceeded to take.

She arranged for the minister to come and baptise Amelia and talk with the parents and greet the relatives that began to trickle in with the news. And the sun brought the heat of a new day.

Mary and Mick were lying together on the bed with their hands around their cooling baby daughter, and Jack left the room like a zombie and shuffled his way to his car.

He couldn't believe this had just happened. What should have been a joyous event was a tragedy he didn't feel he would ever get over. Good people like Mary and Mick shouldn't have to endure this. Nobody should have to endure this loss.

The events of this morning brought back all of the pain of losing his wife and son, and the combination had meant he'd lost it in there. He'd promised himself three years ago he wouldn't cry. In front of everyone! In front of Eliza who had been the professional one!

'You can't drive home, Jack.' Eliza spoke quietly beside him and he turned towards her with stricken eyes. He tried to speak but couldn't and Eliza moved to wrap her arms around him, but he stepped back.

Eliza felt as though he'd slapped her. 'I know you are devastated, Jack. We all are.'

Finally he found the words and all the anger at the repeated unfairness of fate spilled from his lips in a torrent of grief aimed directly at Eliza. 'You don't know anything. You were as cool as a cucumber in there. You're all on the surface, Eliza. You're like Lydia, no depth. I can see that now. Stay away from me.'

Eliza felt the air whoosh from her lungs as if she'd

been stabbed in the solar plexus. 'You don't mean that, Jack. I care for Mary a lot…and I care for you.'

'You care for Eliza, full stop. You can handle anything—so handle this. I'm not coming in today and maybe not tomorrow either, and I'm taking the weekend off as well.' And with that he wrenched open his car door and climbed awkwardly into the seat. He didn't look back and Eliza watched in disbelief and horror as he drove away from her with his harsh words indelibly printed in her brain.

Eliza wanted to run. And hide. Hide like her father had and like she always did from situations that were too painful.

Jack had the power to hurt her because she'd fallen in love with the wrong man—again. Only this time it was a hundred times worse than before.

If Jack thought she was unaffected by Amelia's death then he hadn't ever really seen her. He was just another man who had leant on her and not been interested in the real Eliza.

Eliza's neck drooped as the weight of Jack's outburst hung over her. She lifted her eyes and stared at the glint of sunlight that was his car in the distance.

Jack was wrong about her, but that was his problem. And she couldn't run. Normally, working for the agency allowed her to leave but this time she wouldn't go. Mary needed her and the hurtful, harmful things Jack had said didn't change that.

He might think they were true, and the old Eliza might have thought she had been rejected again because she was worthless, but this time she'd stay as long as Mary needed her.

Jack might look at her with horror and say she didn't cry, but inside she'd been weeping rivers of tears for two beautiful people and their baby daughter who'd had the shortest time together. But they had had time together— Amelia had waited to meet her parents before she'd left, and Mary and Mick would learn to treasure those few owlish looks from their daughter before she'd closed her eyes for ever.

Eliza turned and entered the hospital. Rhonda would finish her shift in an hour and Eliza had just enough time to go home, shower and feed the animals before she needed to come back for the day.

On the drive home she passed the spot where the un-known woman had driven off the edge of the ravine, and she wondered how they both were. How tragically ironic that those two had survived such a horrific accident and yet Mary's baby had died from a natural birth. Eliza wondered what God's grand plan had in store for that other baby girl.

It must be something amazing to spare her against such odds. And what special mission had Amelia ac-complished during her few minutes of life?

Now the tears started to fall and Eliza pulled in un-der the moon gate and parked her car in front of Dulcie's house. Her head fell down on the edge of the steering-wheel and great racking sobs tore from her chest and she sobbed as if she would never stop.

After a few minutes she raised her head and realised

that Roxy was howling outside the car door. Eliza drew a deep breath and turned the handle to let her in. The dog stood up on her hind legs and buried her wet nose under Eliza's armpit.

'Yes, you can lick me,' Eliza said, and then she climbed out of the car and hugged the warm body of the dog. She stood up and the sun shone in her eyes and Poco the donkey brayed for attention.

One of the roosters crowed and Eliza headed for the pens. She may as well do all this in these clothes, at least it would be easier to climb the fence with her trousers on.

By seven a.m. Eliza was back at the hospital and a shattered Rhonda went home.

Eliza carried the breakfast tray into Mary's room and to her surprise she found Mick was gone.

Mary looked up, saw Eliza and held open her arms.

'Thank you for everything, you wonderful, wonderful woman,' she said in a broken voice. Eliza almost dropped the tray in her hurry to return the hug.

'I'm so sorry, Mary. Amelia is so perfect and beautiful but here so short a time. We're all devastated.'

'I know. I thank God every minute that she was born here, with my friends around me, and not somewhere cold and distant where I didn't know the staff and where they might have whisked her away to die away from me. I'm just sorry you had to carry the burden on your own, Eliza. I know you have.

'Poor Jack is distraught—it must be like losing my sister and his son all over again. But maybe part of Amelia's gift will be the healing of Jack now that he has allowed himself to grieve for his own child along with mine.'

She shrugged painfully and closed her eyes as the grief overwhelmed her again.

Eliza couldn't believe that Mary could still think of others through her own pain. She wasn't sure that Jack was worth it, the way he'd just treated her. She brushed her own tears away and raised her chin. 'Where's Mick?'

'He's gone home to shower and have breakfast. He's angry at fate and he's angry at me because he says I was too accepting, but that's a man's way. They hit out when they see our strength because they know they are no-where near as strong. Strong women frighten them.'

Eliza saw the wisdom in Mary's quiet words and it was as if a light shone brightly out of the darkness. Now was not the time to sort this out, but later things would change. That concept would explain so many things in her life.

'You are right, Mary,' she said resolutely, and there was something in Eliza's voice that made Mary look at her. Strength passed between them and then they both looked at the tiny cot in the corner. Without a word Eliza brought Mary's daughter to her for a kiss.

'I'll go home this afternoon,' Mary said. 'The visitors can come here instead of home and before dark we'll say goodbye to Amelia and leave her with you.'

Eliza nodded and the day started.

Mary showered and pushed her breakfast around her plate, and all the time Amelia stayed in the room with her mother.

'These are sad days for the hospital, Eliza. First that terrible accident and now Matron's baby.' Dulcie Gardner's blue eyes were even paler with tears.

'Yes, Dulcie. But comfort is found in strange places. Like me minding your house for you. I went home so upset this morning I cried, and do you know who gave me comfort? Your dog, Roxy. She was so wonderful and I realised how lucky I was to be in that place at that time.'

'I'm glad, my dear.' And indeed she did look brighter to think that her dog had helped.

'How do I stop her licking me, though?' Eliza asked as she helped Dulcie put on her shoes.

Dulcie nodded. 'She does have a busy tongue. Just say, "Yucky," and she'll step back.'

When they both smiled, they stopped and looked at each other, and Eliza thought of the strength of women. A man would think they were callous but they were carrying the pain of loss yet moving on.

'Did they ever find out who that poor young woman was?' Dulcie asked.

'Not yet. Or who she was visiting. She's not off the critical list, yet but the baby is doing well.' Eliza finished tidying the room.

Eliza heard Dulcie talking to herself as she left. 'That's a blessing, then. Poor little mite.'

True to his word Jack didn't come in, even to see Mary before she left, though he phoned her.

Donna came in for the night shift an hour early and shooed Eliza home.

'You've done a mammoth job, and everyone knows it. The hospital thanks you, Eliza.'

'Donna! Thank you. Rhonda was wonderful, too. And thank you for coming in early. I must admit I'm shattered and will be glad when Friday comes and I can have days off. This has been the week from hell.'

Donna nodded vehement agreement. 'Jack's feeling it too. I've never known him to take more than a day off before.'

Eliza did not want to talk about Jack. 'More fool him, then. Goodnight, Donna.'

At home, Eliza watered the animals and then wandered down to the creek, where the steady trickle of water splashed over pink and yellow pebbles in the creek bed.

No other sounds intruded except birds, cracking twigs from Roxy hunting in the undergrowth and the evening wind in the tops of the trees. The sun was still red-ringed with smoke. It hung low in the sky, but the heat from the day was still in the air. There was a deeper swimming hole at a bend in the creek where if she stripped off her clothes she'd be able to sit or lie in the water and get cool.

Eliza glanced around and, of course, there was no one in sight. She shrugged out of her clothes. Soon she was lying on her elbows with the cold water swirling around her, draining the tension from her body and washing away the hurtful things that Jack had said.

Mary's words came back to her and Eliza wondered if she truly had such strength, maybe that was why men in her past had come for healing and then left. It made sense.

Perhaps even her mother leaving her father, because she had been strong enough to do so, made sense. And her own father, leaning on her, retreating from society because he didn't need them while he had Eliza, using her strength because he couldn't go on without it. She felt the weight of failure she'd carried with her drifting away down the creek.

Her mother leaving hadn't been Eliza's fault. The fact that her mother had been able to walk away from her daughter showed enormous strength, and maybe one day Eliza would find her and ask why.

Eliza stood up from the water and waded back to the bank. She might be strong but she was bone tired and needed to sleep.

The next morning Eliza took an apple down to the gate and Poco obligingly moved away. She'd been too tired to remember that yesterday. Eliza grinned at the grey-nosed donkey. 'I've got your secret now, haven't I, old son?'

On the drive into the hospital the day promised to be a little cooler. In fact, Eliza wondered if there were rain-clouds gathering on the horizon again.

Considering the past week, the day was uneventful and again Jack didn't show up. Eliza had a few minor outpatients, which she managed on her own, and any-one she was worried about she consulted Armidale's outpatient clinic before sending them home.

After work she drove out to Mary and Mick's house and spent half an hour with them. She left a cooked chicken and bread rolls from the shop in case Mary didn't feel like cooking, but refused Mary's offer to join them. She judged them best visited in short bursts.

The rest of the week followed the same pattern and Eliza didn't try to vary it. She was too thankful for the brief window of relief from Jack.

On Friday night, Eliza arrived home and it was still light. What should she do? It seemed like for ever since she'd had two days off work and she didn't know how to fill the time.

She could go to see Jack but more than likely such a visit would open her up for more pain.

A visit to Jack might help him, not herself, and it was time she nurtured herself without saving others.

She deserved it.

She was worth it.

'I'm worth it.' It felt good just to say that out loud.

She would stay home with the animals and potter. She would lie in the sun with a book and doze in the afternoon and renew her spirit. Her soul needed it and from now on she would look after herself.

Eliza waited for Jack to do his morning round on Monday and she remembered the first day she'd waited for him.

It felt so long ago. Since then she'd seen so many sides of him.

He had a caring side with all his patients, like Dulcie, waiting with the sick woman and worrying about her pets.

She'd seen the strong and efficient side, with the unknown woman and her emergency Caesarean. Not many doctors would have handled that situation so calmly.

Then there was his humorous side, his puns and sense of the ridiculous that could make her laugh.

But his tortured side was too deep. too hurtful, and he made her cry. She didn't need that.

Regardless of how much her emotions were involved, she wasn't going to sacrifice herself on the altar of Jack's needs.

The tiny flicker of hope that had whispered he might someday come to her as a whole man was gone. It had disappeared into the sunrise with his car last Monday.

Now she could hear his voice rise to greet someone outside and then his footsteps echoed down the corridor. Eliza waited at the nurses' station with a neutral expression on her face.

Jack had no idea where the last week had gone. He'd been to see Mary and Mick at least once each day but otherwise his phone hadn't rung and he hadn't left his house.

It was time to put all the grief behind him and move on—which meant he had to return to work!

And face Eliza.

This would be the hardest part.

He knew that he'd been unfair to her. And not just because he'd left the whole responsibility of the hospital with her. He'd been cruel and unjustified in his lashing out. Although he couldn't remember exactly what he'd said on the morning of Amelia's birth, he knew he'd dumped his grief and pain and uselessness on the one person he shouldn't have. Why were people always hardest on the ones they loved?

The incredible night he'd spent with Eliza in his arms felt like a distant dream, and he'd failed her when he'd known how fragile she was with giving her heart. He just hoped she'd forgive him.

Jack rounded the corner. There she was! Five feet nothing and terrifyingly efficient. In fact—plain terrifying. She made him feel things he'd vowed never to feel again and unlike Lydia she didn't need him to look after her. He probably had nothing to offer her that she couldn't get for herself. If she ever forgave him.

Her hair swung around her cheekbones as she glanced away and then back at him, and he couldn't tell if she was still angry because she didn't meet his eyes.

CHAPTER TEN

'HELLO, Eliza,' Jack said.

Jack looked older and drawn, and Eliza fought the impulse to pull his head down on her chest and tell him it would be all right.

He didn't want her and even if he did, he'd be another millstone around her neck because he couldn't free himself from his past. He'd have to wake up to himself without her.

She'd been there. Loving emotionally scarred men who couldn't return unconditional love, and the cost was too high. She wasn't going back.

'Good morning, Doctor.' She didn't give him time to comment on her formality. 'Dulcie is coming along well. She managed to dress herself completely this morning, though we still need to work on her step-climbing.'

'Excellent. How are you coping with the animals?'

'Fine.' She picked up her pace and smiled at her patient as she rounded the corner into Dulcie's room. Jack could do nothing but follow.

'Matron tells me you are improving every day, Dulcie,' he said.

'I think so. What I want to know is how well am I going to get, Dr Jack? I'm eager to get home and I did well on my first visit. I'm too young for this invalid stuff.'

Jack nodded in sympathy. 'I'll speak to the occupational therapist today and see if there are any improvements we could make in your house to make it safer. I know she thinks you're progressing well.'

Dulcie had questions that she'd had time to think about. 'Am I at risk of having another stroke or will the blood-thinning medication I'm on now stop that?'

'The tablets you're on will certainly cut down the risk, and in a way you were lucky to have a mild stroke and warn us that you were in danger of a major stroke, which would be a lot harder to recover from.'

Jack hesitated. 'I'm hoping you'll return to almost full strength in your right side within the next month and you should be home in less than a week if we get everything right.'

Dulcie smiled with relief. 'I can wait if the news is going to be that good. For a while there I thought I was gone. There are a few things I need to straighten up before I die.'

'Well I'm hoping you'll live a long and productive life, Dulcie, so don't talk about dying yet.'

They left Dulcie and did a quick check with the seniors and all the time Jack tried to start a personal conversation. Eliza was having none of it.

'Well that's it, thank you, Doctor. Have a good day.' Eliza spun on her heel and walked back towards Dulcie.

She could feel his eyes on her as she went, but it was better this way.

'Eliza. Stop!'

His voice was quiet but there was a note of command in it she'd never heard before. Despite herself, Eliza stopped.

'Please, look at me.'

She stared at the corridor in front of her for a moment and then her shoulders stiffened as she turned. She would not allow him to hurt her again.

'Yes?'

He took three steps and then he was right beside her and she could feel the heat coming from his body because he was close. Too close.

'I need to apologise for the things I said after Amelia died.' He looked down into her face and his dark eyes were shadowed with remembered grief.

He was still thinking about himself, not her—or them. *He needed* to apologise for his own sake, not for hers or for what they had between them. 'If that's what you need to do, then go ahead.'

He winced and Eliza sighed. It would be better to get this over quickly instead of being confrontational. 'Forget I said that. I'm listening.'

He stared at her for a moment as if to judge how receptive she was, and then gave a tiny shrug.

'I was overwrought and to attack you was unforgivable. In my defence, the last few days had been especially emotional—not just with the present but with a lot of issues I should have dealt with years ago. You have helped me with those too, Eliza, and I had no right to take my pain out on you. I am deeply sorry.' He even looked the part. As apologies went, it was fairly impressive.

Eliza could feel the tears prickling behind her eyes but she had too much at stake herself!

'All right, Jack. I know what sort of week you'd had—because I had it, too. You hurt me but you woke me up as well. The big discovery is I *am* passing through here and we'd both do well to remember that.'

Jack shook his head in denial. 'There is more than that between us, but I guess we can start there.' He held out his hand. 'Friends?'

Eliza shook her head. 'No. I'm not interested. There is no start to any relationship between us. Julie is looking for my replacement now.'

That night Jack tried to speak to Eliza at her house but she refused to open the door. She turned off the outside light and turned the television up so he couldn't even talk to her through the wood.

On Tuesday he called again and left a teacake and flowers on her step.

When he called around on Wednesday night the flowers were dry and wilted and a dog dish sat where he'd rested the cake.

On Thursday morning news came through that the police had identified the young woman from the crash.

Two policemen from Armidale appeared at the hospital and asked for Dulcie Gardner.

Eliza tried to contact Jack but he was on a call and out of range. She could only hold Dulcie's hand as the news was broken to her and they both sat, stunned. The driver had been identified as Bronte Gardner, Dulcie's daughter, and she was still in serious condition in a Sydney hospital.

When the policemen left, Dulcie looked up at Eliza, pain and confusion and guilt dark in her eyes.

Her voice cracked. 'How could I not know my daughter was fighting for her life?' She clutched at Eliza's hand. 'Go and see your mother, Eliza, before you end up with regrets it will be too late to do anything about.'

Eliza nodded, because it was the only comfort she could give. 'We'll arrange for you to see Bronte as soon as possible, Dulcie.'

'I know.' She bit her lip. 'I feel so helpless and useless. I think I'd like to be by myself. I know I can call you if I need you.'

Eliza hugged her and slipped out of the room and closed the door.

Eliza leaned back against the corridor wall and closed her eyes. She saw the woman she now knew as Bronte Gardner in her memory, and the events that had followed were something she would never forget. Perhaps Bronte and her baby would come back here for a while to spend time with Dulcie.

It was almost too much to grasp. When Eliza opened her eyes, Jack was there.

Jack had picked up Eliza's missed call on his mobile, and had called in at the hospital on his way back to the surgery. He suspected there would be no light reason for Eliza to call him after the way she'd been with him all week, but he hadn't expected her to look as lost and vulnerable as she'd looked, leaning against the wall with her eyes closed.

His step quickened and he moved up beside her. 'Eliza? Are you all right?'

'No. I don't think I am.' It was a moment of weakness he didn't expect as she stepped forward and leant her head on his chest. Automatically Jack put his arms around her. She was soft and forlorn against him and he tilted her chin up with his finger and searched her face. Her eyes were huge damp pools of green and he felt that jolt he'd suffered the first day he'd seen her. He searched for something to keep himself from crushing her to him.

'Since when do you admit to human frailty?'

She buried her chin into his chest again and mumbled into his shirt. 'The woman from the car is Dulcie's daughter.'

Jack nodded his head. 'Ah. Poor Dulcie. I was afraid she would be. After we talked the other day I passed my suspicions on to the police and they were going to follow it up.' He felt Eliza stiffen beneath his hand as she stepped back. He seemed to have found another way to alienate her.

She lifted her chin and sniffed. 'Of course, you didn't think to warn me?' Those damn eyes had changed again and he deeply regretted she'd pushed him away because the possibilities had been good. He was beginning to feel that the only way he was going to pierce Eliza's shell was to get her into his arms and kiss her.

'It was only a suspicion and I hoped my hunch was wrong.' He glanced towards Dulcie's closed door. 'How is she?'

'Devastated and guilty she didn't try harder to contact her daughter in the past. You go in and see her. I'll make her a cup of tea. Would you like one?' He shook his head and she watched him knock and enter the room.

When Jack left, Eliza went back in to Dulcie. The older woman's eyes were red-rimmed and Eliza sat on the arm of her chair and put her arm around her shoulder.

'I'm so lucky it's not too late to say all the things I should have said. She was a lovely little girl, you know—but we clashed so badly when she became a teenager, and I was young, too. My husband used to say we were too much alike.'

Eliza didn't say anything. She just listened.

Dulcie stared out the window as if she could see all the way to Sydney. 'Dr Jack says there doesn't seem to be a father in the wings, so the baby is being looked after by the hospital until Bronte is well enough to look after her. Dr Jack is going to ring her doctors and find out what he can for me. She will get better, won't she?'

Eliza nodded. 'The hospital she's in is a major centre with a wonderful reputation. I'm sure she will. She must be a fighter to have done so well.'

Dulcie looked up at Eliza and her voice was stronger. 'I could help. I've been given another chance to right the wrongs with my daughter. I just hope she'll come to me when she can. It seems she'd already decided to come once, hopefully she will again.'

'I'm sure she will, and I know you will be a wonderful mother and grandmother.'

Dulcie shook her head in distress. 'How will I manage? When should I try to manage? I want to do the right thing.'

Eliza squeezed her hand. 'Take things slowly and we'll arrange help when they arrive and until you all get settled. You could even have a day or two here to get used to each other and caring for the baby. You're still young, Dulcie. You'll be fine.'

'But I'm so out of practice with babies.'

Eliza patted her shoulder. 'And I haven't had any. I'm only good with new babies.'

Eliza couldn't become tangled up in Dulcie's plans. She needed to be free to escape from Jack as soon as Julie could find a replacement. 'I'll be there in the beginning, but if you get stuck you can ask Jack. He won't know either but he's great at finding people to help you.'

When Jack turned up that evening for his round, Eliza was busy and this time she didn't stop what she was doing. The situation between them was deteriorating and he needed to do something drastic.

Eliza had stayed in with a new mum to discuss settling techniques for her baby and after pausing, patiently waiting with them for a few minutes, Jack went on the round without her.

Later, Jack arrived at Eliza's house and she refused

to open the door again. But this time he wasn't going to give up, or he wasn't going to before his pager went off and he was called away. When he finally made it back her lights were out.

Jack knew he'd blown it but this was ridiculous. She wouldn't escape him over the weekend, even if he had to break down the door.

CHAPTER ELEVEN

ELIZA'S friendship with Mary saved both of them from despair and Eliza dropped into a routine of visiting every evening after work for an hour or so.

They didn't discuss Jack because Eliza refused to, but Mary enjoyed hearing about the changes and admissions at the hospital. Eliza began to hope Mary might take up some part-time work to get her out of the house.

Nearly three weeks after the night with Jack, Eliza broached the subject. 'So, when do you want to return to work, Mary? Julie thinks she's found someone who is interested in part-time work here. I'll have been here eight weeks this time next week. That was my initial contract. You know I can finish up whenever you're ready to return to work.'

'I don't want you to go, Eliza. I admit I do think of going back to fill the horrible emptiness here, but then in the mornings I just can't seem to get myself motivated to even come in for a few hours.'

'Perhaps that's how we should start.' Eliza needed to leave despite the heartache of going. She'd wanted to go weeks ago but hadn't wanted to push Mary. She knew it was vital to make a fresh start with her own life and this time it would be different.

Mary saw that Eliza had drifted off into her own thoughts. Her eyes showed concern for her friend. 'How about you and Jack?'

Eliza glanced at Mary and then away again. 'What about Jack and I?'

Mary settled herself on the lounge beside Eliza and sighed for her friend's pain. 'Jack is alive for the first time in three years, though he seems a bit manic at the moment.'

Eliza shrugged. 'Jack and I don't have a relationship. I'm not going to be an emotional crutch for any man again.'

Eliza grimaced at Mary. 'The first time I had bad luck, the second started a pattern, and then there was Jack.' She shook her head vehemently. 'I don't think so, Mary.'

Mary tilted her head. 'But you and Jack are so well suited and could have a wonderful life together.'

Eliza avoided her eyes. 'I'm not staying around for the final episode.' She stared out the window at the mountains beyond the dam. 'The next man who asks me to marry him had better be damned sure I'm what he wants and have the church ready.' She grimaced at herself.

She drew a deep breath. 'That's why I think it's time for me to leave.' She looked across at her friend. 'But I will stay until Julie has found a relief for you.'

'Do you love Jack, Eliza?'

'No,' she lied. 'I can't afford to.' She tried to avoid the memories that filled her mind when she thought of Jack. 'If I didn't have such a poor history I might conceivably risk my heart again, but this time I have to think of myself first. I'm worthy of a full man, one who wants to shout our love from the treetops and thinks of more than himself. I value myself now and I have you and Bellbrook to thank for that. It's because I'm strong I can walk away. I won't stay and hope he won't let me down.'

Mary nodded. 'I appreciate that, Eliza, and I understand your reluctance to be the rock again in a relationship. I just hope you both work it out. I promise I'll think of easing back to work.'

They went for a walk in the garden and when they returned Mary drew a deep breath. 'Could you stay and do the mornings for next week to see how I go? What if I started at lunch and finished when the night staff come in? That would be six hours each.'

Eliza nodded. Just the mornings. She'd miss Jack's evening rounds, Eliza thought as she forced a smile in Mary's direction. 'That sounds perfect, if it's not too much for you.'

On Friday night after work, unknown to Jack, Eliza had offered to drive an almost fully recovered Dulcie to Sydney to spend some time with her daughter, who was off the critical list.

The two women left early Saturday morning for the weekend, and Eliza dropped Dulcie off at the large city hospital where she had relative's accommodation for the night.

The sub-lease on Eliza's flat had ended and she needed to unpack her belongings again. And she'd decided it was time to face her mother.

Eliza pulled the crumpled business card out from the back of her father's photograph frame. She'd never been able to throw it away, although she'd almost forgotten where she'd hidden it. Eliza's mother had given it to her twelve years before at her father's graveside.

Mays of Mosman, Interior Decorator. Not the sort of profession there would have been a call for from the isolation of her father's farm.

Eliza stared over the distance of time and instead of closing her mind she allowed the images from that day to wash through her memory. Surprisingly there was very little pain.

She could see her mother, elegant, dressed in a charcoal silk suit, stern-faced and determined to ensure Eliza didn't isolate herself from the world any longer.

Eliza remembered her own anger that her mother hadn't shed a tear and had accused her after the service of never having cared for her father.

Gwendolyn hadn't disputed Eliza's assumption. She had even said that leaving the valley had been the best thing she'd ever done, and that Eliza should leave, too.

Eliza had wanted to run and hide in the hills just as her father had done for the last ten years, but her mother had thwarted that from afar by selling the farm. Apart from the money Eliza had needed to start nursing and live on campus, Gwendolyn had placed the money in trust for Eliza for her twenty-first birthday.

Eliza squeezed the business card between her fingers for a moment and then sighed. She could have a look, anyway.

When she pulled up outside her mother's shop she could see it was a prosperous business.

The understated chic and price tag on a tall, thin vase in the window confirmed Eliza would never have shopped there.

Eliza pushed open the door and browsed her way around the room past matching dinner sets and fine glassware, while the only customer completed her purchase.

'Hello, Eliza.' Her mother's voice was calm but the green eyes so much like Eliza's were startled.

'I wondered if you'd recognise me,' Eliza said, and moved up to the counter.

'What brings you here?' Gwendolyn asked, and Eliza wondered the same thing. Just what had she been hoping for or expecting from this woman she barely knew?

Gwendolyn glanced at the door as another customer entered and then looked back at Eliza.

'Please, don't go away. Stay and have lunch with me in a few minutes. I close the shop at lunchtime on Saturdays.'

It was almost as if she was glad she had come. Eliza nodded and stepped back to resume browsing while Gwendolyn attended to her customer.

Her mother looked older, which was extremely reasonable when she considered they hadn't seen each other for twelve years, but it was something Eliza hadn't factored in when she'd envisaged this meeting.

Eliza remembered when she'd visited Julie's mother with Julie once. The rapport between the two blond women, more like sisters than mother and daughter, had made Eliza realise the magnitude of her own loss.

As she surreptitiously watched Gwendolyn smile at her customer, Eliza wondered if her mother felt she'd missed out, too. There was a certain sadness under the professional exterior and immaculate make-up. Eliza experienced the first thoughts of regret that she hadn't accepted her mother's overtures earlier.

As soon as the customer left, Gwendolyn turned the swinging plaque on the door to CLOSED. 'Where would you like to go?'

'It's your town.' Half of Eliza wanted to leave and the other didn't know what she wanted.

Gwendolyn knew what *she* wanted. 'Somewhere we can talk because I may not get to see you for another twelve years.'

'Are you saying that's my fault?' Eliza was beginning to think perhaps it might have been.

'I'd say the blame lies somewhere in the middle, but I'm glad you're here. I think of you a lot.'

Six words, but they changed many things. Her mother did think of her.

Eliza sighed. 'I guess I needed to grow up. At least you sent Christmas and birthday cards. I've never sent anything.'

Her mother smiled ruefully and closed the door behind them. 'You never cash the cheques.'

Eliza felt her own lips tug. She'd never have imagined they could talk like this. 'I've a pile of them somewhere.'

'My accountant hates you.' Gwendolyn gestured to a low slung sports car. Eliza nodded and climbed in with her mother. The conversation stalled until they were seated in a secluded corner of a leafy restaurant.

'Why keep sending money?' She may not have cashed the cheques but Eliza had never been able to tear them up either.

'Because I have it and you'd have a return address if you ever wanted to find me. Because I hoped one day you'd forgive me for leaving you, because I never forgave myself.'

This was the crux of everything. This was what she had come for. 'Why did you leave and why did you leave me?'

'For a hundred reasons, but mostly because I didn't love your father. I left you with him because he was a better parent than I was and you adored him.'

Her voice was steady but Gwendolyn had a shine in her eyes that Eliza suspected was tears. 'I didn't want you to learn bad choices from me. I met and fell in lust with your father and should never have married him.'

She shrugged unhappily. 'I tried to make it right when you were born but as each year passed I became more bitter and frustrated by the closed lifestyle. When I realised I was going out more to stop myself going insane and the gossip started to circulate, I knew it was time to leave. I never regret leaving your father but I have always regretted leaving you.'

Not a good enough reason. 'I could never leave a child of mine.'

Gwendolyn looked across sardonically. 'Did you want to come with me?'

She had a point. 'No. I loved the farm and the animals and Dad. I still love the country, but I seem to have acquired the skill of choosing men who lean on me to heal their emotional problems and then go on their way.'

'It's genetic,' her mother said dryly, and they both smiled.

This wasn't too bad. Eliza began to realise she should have made this move years ago. 'Why didn't you take me with you after the funeral?'

'You were eighteen. Legally a grown woman. I gave you my card and said come any time. I didn't think it would take twelve years.'

'That's not very maternal.'

'You told me you never wanted to hear from me again.'

Eliza remembered that.

Gwendolyn stretched her hand out and patted Eliza's fingers. 'How about we just start from here and see where we go? At least keep up with Christmas and birthdays and who knows? We may even come to enjoy each other's company.'

They smiled at each other and suddenly it didn't seem too far-fetched to have her mother somewhere in her life.

* * *

Sunday afternoon arrived and it was time to drive home. Except it wasn't home—it was where Jack belonged and she didn't.

Eliza collected Dulcie from her daughter's hospital and drove back to Bellbrook with a heavy heart. In the car she answered questions about the visit with her mother and Dulcie complacently congratulated herself on being responsible for their reunion.

Dulcie's daughter continued to improve and that visit had also been a success.

Monday saw the start of the shared week with Mary and Eliza began to pack her things.

As arranged, Eliza started work at seven and finished at one and Mary started at one and finished at seven.

By Wednesday Mary had settled back into the hospital and Eliza knew she was free to leave.

Eliza had stayed on at Dulcie's while the older woman settled into home life again. Now Dulcie could manage the cottage and the animals well. It was rewarding for Eliza to see her settled. She felt she'd achieved some good things during her time at Bellbrook.

Dulcie's daughter and granddaughter would come for an extended stay in two weeks time.

The sooner she could put Bellbrook behind her the better, but there was still Thursday and Friday to get through.

Jack was at a loss and beginning to panic that Eliza would leave and he'd lose her for ever. She wouldn't talk to him, or stay in the same room with him for longer than a few minutes. He'd written her two letters but both envelopes had been returned unopened. Finally he turned to Mary for help.

Mary stared at the frame on the dresser. The picture showed Amelia right after she was born, eyes wide open and inquisitive, and an emotional Mick in the background.

She shook her head at the tragedy. 'I don't know what I would have done without Eliza. I wouldn't have the beautiful photos and memories I have of Amelia, I know that. We were all so devastated and would never have arranged everything so well.'

Jack had trouble talking about Amelia's birth. Even though he'd known, and later tests had confirmed, that Amelia's heart and lungs had been incompatible with life, he'd felt there must have been something he could have done. Eliza's iron control and strength on that dreadful day still frightened him. 'She had enough distance to be able to do what those closer to you would have found difficult.'

Mary shook her head. 'That's not it at all, Jack. Do you believe that Eliza was distanced?' She shook her head and he got the feeling she was disappointed in him. 'You weren't there when I panicked at home, you didn't see the way she managed to get me to the hospital and into that bed and to the point, right at the end, when you and Mick arrived.

'She was the one who remembered to take photos that I'd sell my house to get back if I lost.'

Mary huffed at him in despair. 'Eliza didn't do all

those things because she was safely distanced. She did them because she cared and she's strong and she's my friend.'

Mary stood up. 'Eliza is a very special woman. If you love her and let some stupid misunderstanding or fear of yours stand in the way, you will regret losing her for the rest of your life!'

Jack shook his head. 'I do regret it and I think I have lost her. I found something in Eliza that is beautiful and strong and I want that back. I thought she loved me the way I love her, but now there is a wall between us that I can't break.'

'Can't or won't, Jack.' Mary snorted. 'I heard that Eliza was seen leaving your house the night before Amelia was born.'

She stared mercilessly at him. 'Why was Eliza sneaking around? Why hadn't you taken her out to the most public restaurant and shown her off? Why isn't she wearing the biggest diamond you can buy? Eliza can't settle for half-measures or maybes. She's been let down too many times.' She shook her head. 'You know that!'

Jack spread his hands. 'I know.'

Mary wasn't going to go easy on him. 'Too many men have promised and not delivered, and now you've joined them. I don't know what happened between you two but you'd better sort it out as fast as you can.'

Jack didn't answer but Mary's words had him thinking. It hadn't just been a night, it had been a trial by fire and everything he'd dreamed that it could have been had come about that night. But the next day he'd blown it.

Behaved as if what they'd shared had been nothing. Thrown her offer of comfort back in her face—as if she had been a stranger who couldn't help.

No wonder she'd changed. Frozen. And he couldn't get to her. She'd refused to talk to him, and had even threatened to leave the hospital immediately if he continued to harass her.

So he had left her alone, because if he waited he'd always got what he wanted, but Mary was right. He had to make plans or she would be gone. He had to believe she still loved him and that she was only scared he would let her down.

A glimmer of hope lightened his thoughts. There was only one way to prove his love to her but it would take a few days to organise. But he had plenty of helpers.

It started on Thursday. After days of Jack hounding Eliza to forgive him, she'd been driven to threaten she'd walk out. He'd finally left her alone but then something strange had started the next afternoon.

As she drove down the main street of town after work, people came out and waved at her. Some older men on the corner clapped their hands and even the sour old lady from the tumble-down house next to the post office had waved and smiled.

Eliza couldn't figure it out unless they'd heard she was leaving and were saying goodbye.

She went to the post office for stamps for Dulcie, and when she entered, Mrs Green came around the counter and hugged her. 'I'm so pleased for you, dear. We all couldn't be happier.'

Eliza smiled and thanked her and wondered why they would be pleased she was leaving. It wasn't quite the sentiment she'd expected but, then, Bellbrook had bestowed a few of those moments on her during her time here.

When she'd gone to fill her car with fuel the garage proprietor had grinned from ear to ear and said he was 'right pleased you came here, we all are. You're a good girl'.

'Thank you.' Eliza paid for her fuel, smiled and left with a puzzled look on her face. What was going on here?

Joe came out of the rural produce store, all smiles at seeing her, and hailed her from across the road. 'Great news, Matron,' he called and gave her the thumbs-up. Eliza smiled and waved back and swallowed the lump in her throat. She felt like leaving town now.

Then she ran into Carla of the first swimming incident. Carla held out her hand. 'I'm really happy for both of you.'

Eliza blinked. 'Both of who?'

'Why, you and Dr Jack getting married, of course.'

Eliza stared and backed away. She held her hands out in front of her. 'It's not true. Who told you that?'

'Everyone knows.'

'It's not true.'

Clearly Carla didn't believe her. 'Sure. But that's what I heard.'

Eliza fumbled with her key in the ignition and nearly stalled the car as she did a three-point turn to get back to the hospital. She couldn't ask Jack, but Mary would surely know how this had all started.

As soon as Mary saw Eliza she swooped and hugged her.

'Congratulations. I'm so happy for you both.'

Eliza shook her head wildly and held up her hands again. 'You've heard it, too. It's not true.'

'It must be. Jack told me.'

'He can't do that. He can't just tell everyone we're getting married and expect me to fall in with his plans.'

'The church is booked for ten a.m. on Saturday.'

'What?' Eliza's voice carried shrilly down the hallway and she clapped her hand over her mouth at the echo. Eliza looked around but there wasn't anyone else in the corridor. Her head was spinning.

'I'm sorry, but this is ridiculous.'

'He's invited your mother.'

'What?' Her voice was quieter but still shrill.

Eliza looked wildly from side to side. 'I have to find Jack. Where is he?'

'He had to go to Armidale to see the administrators at the hospital. He's arranging time off for your honeymoon.'

'I'm not having a honeymoon. I'm not having a wedding. Does he expect me to meekly turn up at the right time? How can a man who didn't want me to tell anyone do this?'

'I guess it depends how desperate he is.' Mary's words hung in the air and Eliza started to believe Jack really had created this fiasco. She'd kill him.

Eliza turned around slowly, and as Mary watched her sympathetically, she walked away. Was Jack that desperate to marry her?

CHAPTER TWELVE

JACK rang the doorbell at Dulcie's early that evening. 'Mary said you wanted to see me.' Jack was dressed in black trousers and a white shirt open at the neck, and he carried a yellow rose. Eliza had never seen him look so handsome. The pain sliced through her at what might have been, but she couldn't trust him.

She should have left days ago. It was too cruel.

'Let's walk in the garden.' Eliza couldn't meet his eyes and she hurried past him on the steps to get ahead. He caught up to her and there was a strange expression in his eyes that didn't fit any of the scenarios she'd dreamed up in her mind. She felt more confused than ever.

Eliza stopped and faced him. 'I'm not marrying you!' she said baldly. 'You can't just get married. You have to have a licence and banns read in church and invitations and things.'

He shrugged but that soft smile stayed on his lips. 'You met all those criteria before and you didn't get married. This time you will marry but without the banns. The application for a licence you need to sign tonight.'

Eliza shook her head. 'I'm not signing anything!'

Here was his angry fairy from the first time he'd seen her. Her green eyes were flashing and she stood with her hands on her hips and glared at him, although there was a shadow of pain at the backs of her eyes. He'd caused that and he felt his heart squeeze in regret. She came up to his shoulder and he loved her so much it hurt to breathe—just like the first time he'd seen her.

There had to be a way to get through to her. His voice softened. Where had she been at her weakest? 'What about if I kissed you? Would you marry me then?'

Jack took Eliza's hand and she shuddered at the feeling of his fingers around hers. He stared down into her eyes. 'I know you didn't believe me when I said I fell in love with you, Eliza. But it's true.

'I want to change your mind. I ask you to give me one more chance at winning the woman I will love for ever. Be my bride, here, on Saturday, in front of the whole town and all your friends. They all think we belong together, as I do, and I've asked them to help me sway you. Will you let it happen? Marry me, Eliza, please.'

She shook her head and her eyes filled with tears.

Jack went on ignoring her denial. 'We could start the rest of out lives together with no more misunderstandings between us and no more delay.'

Eliza could taste the tears and her head was so confused and unsure and terrified that she turned her back on him to get away to think about this, but he still had hold of her hand. Her arms stretched but he didn't let go and she turned back to face him.

He opened her palm and pressed a little ring with an enormous emerald into her palm. 'Will you wear my ring?'

It was all too much to grasp. How could this happen? She shook her head and before she could make any sense he took her chin in his other hand and settled his lips on hers.

Slowly, as if seeing through mist, floating like a piece of driftwood in Dulcie's creek, she finally glimpsed the sunlight shining on paradise. Eliza began to wonder if she'd been wrong.

Jack against her, his mouth and his breath entwined with hers, murmuring he loved her. When the kiss deepened she sank against him. The feel, the taste, the scent and the strength of him surrounded her, and his arms around her kept her safe. He felt so strong and sure and Jack-like, so sure for both of them, she could feel her resistance dissipate.

When he stepped back she stared at him and took a deep breath.

This risked everything. 'Maybe you should have kissed me earlier.' She smiled whimsically. 'I love you, too, but if you hurt me, I don't think I will survive.'

He hugged her. 'Neither would I. I'm sorry I took so long to kiss you. When I realised how stupid I'd been on our first morning together I could have kicked myself, but it wasn't because I wasn't proud and honoured to have you in my heart. I had ghosts to lay, and I'm sorry I hurt you.'

He tilted her chin up towards him with his finger. 'You haven't said yes yet.'

'Yes,' she said faintly, and at the wonder in her face he kissed her again.

'It's OK. Now I have you. I can be a simple man, too, when I have all I want. Are you sure you can live at Bellbrook for ever?'

'I could live in Antarctica for ever if I was with you but, yes, I've grown to love Bellbrook and I have good friends here, too.'

'I'm not asking you to be isolated. We'll do dashes to Sydney and paint the town red before coming back to our home. I've learnt I'm not irreplaceable and we need to get away even if just to appreciate how great it is here.'

'I think you're irreplaceable but that sounds wonderful.'

They left Dulcie's and drove to his house where they spent hours talking and making love. Late in the evening Jack rose and brought back a platter of food which they devoured sitting up in bed.

'We are going to have the most beautiful wedding in the world but now we need to drive to town to see the minister. I've run out of excuses and he's a little suspicious of my fiancée's consent.'

'As he should be! Imagine everyone in town knowing I was getting married this Saturday except me. They applauded me on street corners and I thought they were glad I was going.'

Jack laughed, which was very unsporting of him. 'Forgive me.'

'Maybe.' She pretended to glare again and he couldn't help kissing her.

Later, after they'd satisfied the minister that they were truly in love, and deserved to be married, they left the tiny church. Jack took her home again to his house on the hill and they sat on the swing seat and held hands and watched the stars.

'There is so much to do.' Suddenly Eliza felt swamped with the enormity of an imminent wedding.

Jack smiled and kissed her. 'Tomorrow your mother is coming and she's ordered a truckful of bridal gowns for you to choose from. She mentioned beauticians and a hairstylist so I doubt you'll have much time for me after tonight. From my conversations with her, she's dying to do something for you and I doubt you'll need to lift a finger. Between Gwendolyn and the ladies of Bellbrook, everything will be perfect.'

Everything was happening too fast but Eliza wasn't complaining this time. She'd sit back and enjoy the ride. 'How many conversations have you had with my mother?'

'Enough to know she will be a part of our lives in the future—as she should be.' He leant across and kissed her to change the subject. 'Did I tell you I love you?'

Three days later the most beautiful wedding in the world began.

The wedding march thundered out of the huge old organ that took up most of one wall of the tiny church. The music was enthusiastically rendered by one of the ladies from the hospital auxiliary in an equally loud hat.

Magnificent floral arrangements had been assembled from gardens all over the valley by the members of the Country Women's Association and the air was heavy with floral scent and a few satiated bees.

The minister, who had christened Jack and his family for decades, had prepared a resounding homily on the evils of gossip and the strength of love.

All heads turned as Eliza entered the church with her hand resting in the crook of Keith's arm. The old farmer wore his Sunday suit and his wrinkled face beamed with pride at the beautiful young woman beside him.

Eliza floated down the aisle towards her husband-to-be who waited with his hand outstretched. On his lapel he wore a tiny pair of crystal wings.

A ripple of satisfaction flowed around the church as friends and family saw the look of adoration on Jack's face and the bride's mother unobtrusively dabbed her damp eyes.

When the bride and groom stood together in front of the altar and repeated their vows, the solemn words were so clear and firm that they carried easily to the furthest pew.

Here were no second thoughts, no doubt that they would love each other always, no hesitation in uniting in holy matrimony.

Afterwards, to an even louder swell of triumphant music, Dr and Mrs Jack Dancer greeted their family and friends—and there were so many of them!

Later that night, finally alone in a luxurious mountain retreat near Byron Bay, Jack held his fairy queen tight against his heart. The spell around them shimmered in the moonlight and he silently thanked his family and friends for bringing his heart to him.

'I love you,' he murmured to Eliza as she slept beside him. In her sleep, her hand crept into his, and he held her close all through the night.